The Silas Stories

W.P. KINSELLA

The Silas Stories

THE FENCEPOST CHRONICLES

THE MISS HOBBEMA PAGEANT

BROTHER FRANK'S GOSPEL HOUR

 HarperPerennial
HarperCollins*Publishers*Ltd

HarperCollins books may be purchased for educational, business, or sales
promotional use. For information please write: Special Markets
Department, HarperCollins Canada, 55 Avenue Road, Suite 2900,
Toronto, Ontario M5R 3L2

The Fencepost Chronicles was first published by Collins Publishers in 1986.
The first HarperPerennial paperback edition
was published in 1995.

The Miss Hobbema Pageant was first published by HarperCollins
Publishers in 1989. The first HarperPerennial paperback edition
was published in 1995.

Brother Frank's Gospel Hour was first published by HarperCollins
Publishers in 1994. The first HarperPerennial paperback edition
was published in 1995.

These three books were first published together
in this omnibus edition in 1998.

Canadian Cataloguing in Publication Data

Kinsella, W. P.
The Silas stories

Contents: The Fencepost chronicles—The Miss Hobbema pageant—
Brother Frank's gospel hour.
ISBN 0-00-648195-7

I. Title

PS8571.I57S54 1998   C813'.54   C98-930819-7
PR9199.3.K443S54 1998

98 99 00 01 02 03 04 WEB 10 9 8 7 6 5 4 3 2 1
Printed and bound in Canada by Webcom Limited

The Silas Stories

The Fencepost Chronicles

ACKNOWLEDGMENTS

The following stories have previously appeared in magazines:
"Truth" in *North Dakota Review* and *Alberta on Ice*;
"The Truck" in *Matrix*; "To Look at the Queen" in *Wascana Review*;
"The Practical Education of Constable B.B. Bobowski" in *Event*;
"The Indian Nation Cultural Exchange Program" in *Canadian Forum*;
"The Bear Went Over the Mountain" in *Vancouver Magazine*;
"Dancing" in *West Coast Review*; "Real Indians" in *Waves*;
"The Fog" in *NeWest Review*; and "Indian Joe" in *Prism International*.

To my grandson Jason

Contents

Truth 1

The Truck 15

Beef 31

The Managers 49

The Practical Education of Constable B.B. Bobowski 77

To Look at the Queen 93

The Indian Nation Cultural Exchange Program 115

The Performance 137

The Bear Went Over the Mountain 151

Dancing 169

Real Indians 183

The Fog 197

Indian Joe 213

The Fencepost Chronicles

Truth

No matter what they say it wasn't us that started the riot at St. Edouard Hockey Arena. The story made quite a few newspapers and even got on the Edmonton television, the camera showing how chairs been ripped out of the stands and thrown onto the ice. There was also a worried-looking RCMP saying something about public safety, and how they had to take some of the 25 arrested people all the way to St. Paul to store them in jail. Then the station manager read an editorial about violence in amateur hockey. None of them come right out and say us Indians was to blame for the riot; they just present what they think are the facts and leave people to make their own minds up. How many do you think decide the white men was at fault?

There was also a rumor that the town of St. Edouard was going to sue the town of Hobbema for the damages to the arena. But nothing ever come of that.

Another story have that the trouble come about because my friend Frank Fencepost own a dog named Guy Lafleur. Not true either. Frank do own a dog named Guy Lafleur, a yellow and white mostly-collie with a question mark for a tail. And Guy Lafleur the dog *was* sitting on a seat right behind our team players' box. That dog he bark whenever our team, the Hobbema Wagonburners, get the puck. And every time he bark Frank would shout the same thing, "Shut up, Guy Lafleur you son of a bitch." A lot of heads would turn every time he said it, because, as you maybe guessed, St. Edouard was a French Canadian town. But it was something else that started the riot.

We never would of been there anyway if Frank hadn't learned to read and write. Someday, I'm going to write a story about the time Frank go to an adult literacy class. Now, just to show off, he read everything in the *Wetaskiwin Times* every week, even the ads. One day he seen a notice about a small town hockey tournament that offer a $1000 first prize.

"I think we should enter a team, Silas," he say to me.

"What do we know about hockey?" I say back. Neither me nor Frank skate. I played a little shinney when I was a kid, but I don't much like ice and snow up my nose, or for that matter, hockey sticks.

"Let's go see Jasper Deer," say Frank, "there's a $200 entry fee to be raised."

Jasper is employed by Sports Canada. All the strings on Sports Canada are pulled from Ottawa. Jasper he have an office with a gray desk big as a whale, in the Consolidated School building. About fifteen years ago Jasper was a good hockey player. I'm not sure what Sports Canada is, but I know they figure if they give all us Indians enough hockey sticks, basketballs and volleyballs, we forget our land claims, quit drinking too much, get good jobs so we can have the weekends off to play games.

Jasper is glad to have anybody come to see him. He was Chief Tom's friend, was how he come to get this cushy job, though he would rather be trapping, or cutting brush than sit in an office. He is already blearyeyed at ten o'clock in the morning.

"You want to enter a team in a tournament, eh?" he say to us, pushing his desk drawer shut with his knee, the bottles rattling.

Hobbema has a team in the Western Canada Junior Hockey League, so once guys turn 21 and don't get signed by any NHL team, they got no place to play.

"It'll be easy to get some good players together," Frank say, "and playing hockey keep us young people sober, honest and religious."

By the time we leave Jasper is anxious to put his head down have a little sleep on his desk, but he agree to pay for uniforms, loan us equipment, and rent us a school bus to travel in. I write down all those promises and get him to sign them.

Trouble is, even though a thousand dollars sound like a lot of money to me and Frank, the guys we approach to play for us point out it don't even come to $100 each for a decent sized team. So the players we end up with is the guys who sit in the Alice Hotel bar bragging how they turned down NHL contracts ten years ago, plus a few of our friends who can stand up on skates, and a goalie who just got new glasses last week.

The uniforms are white as bathroom tile, with a bright red burning wagon on the front, with HOBBEMA in red letters on the back. Some people complain the team name is bad for our Indian image, but they just ain't got no sense of humor.

Frank is team manager. I am his assistant. Mad Etta, our 400 lb. medicine lady, is doctor and trainer, and Guy Lafleur is our mascot.

St. Edouard is way up in north-east Alberta, a place most of us never been before. Gorman Carry-the-kettle drive the bus for us. We have a pretty rowdy trip once we get Etta all attended to. She squeeze sideways down the aisle and sit on the whole back seat.

"I'm surprised the bus didn't tip up with its front wheels about three feet off the ground," say Gorman.

"Don't worry, you'll balance things out," we tell Gorman. He is about 280 lbs. himself, wear a red cap with a yellow unicorn horn growing out of the crown.

We stop for lunch in a town called Elk Point, actually we stop at the bar, and since most of the team is serious drinkers, it is 3:00 p.m. before we get on the road again. I have to drive because Gorman is a little worse for wear. When we get to St. Edouard, a town that have only about ten houses and a little frame hotel gathered around a wine-colored elevator as if they was bowing down to it, we find we already an hour late for our first game. They was just about to forfeit us.

The game played in a hoop-roofed building what is a combination curling rink and hockey arena. It sit like a huge haystack out in a field half a mile from town. Being February it is already dark. All I can see in any direction is snow drifts, a little stubble, and lines of scratchy-looking trees wherever there's a road allowance. The countryside is not too different from Hobbema.

Soon as our team start to warm up, everybody, except maybe Frank, can see we is outclassed. We playing the St. Edouard Bashers. Their players all look as if they drove down on their combines. And they each look like they could lift a combine out of a ditch if it was to get stuck. Most of our players are hung over. And though most of them used to be hockey players, it easy to tell they ain't been on skates for years.

The St. Edouard Bashers is young, fast and tough. Someone mention that they ain't lost a tournament game in two years. There must be 4,000 people in the arena, and they all go "Booooo," when our team show itself.

"I wonder where they all come from," says Frank. "There can't be more than fifty people in the town; sure must be some big families on these here farms."

They sing the national anthem in French, and after they done with that they sing the French national anthem. Then about a half a dozen priests, and what must be a bishop; he got a white robe and an embroidered quilt over his shoulder, come to center ice where they bless a box of pucks. The priests shake holy water in each goal crease. The players all cross themselves.

"We should of brought a thunder dancer with us," says Frank. "Make a note of that, Silas. We do it next time."

I don't bother to write it down. I'm already guessing there won't be a next time.

Right after the puck is dropped St. Edouard take hold of it, carry it right in on our goal. They shoot. Our goalie don't have any idea where the puck is; by pure luck it hit him on the chest and fall to the ice. The goalie, Ferd Tailfeathers, lose his balance fall forward on the puck.

About that time a half-ton St. Edouard defenceman land with a knee on Ferd's head, smash his mask, his face and his glasses about an inch deep into the ice.

Guy Lafleur stand up on his seat and bark like a fire alarm.

"Shut up Guy Lafleur you son of a bitch," says Frank.

Then looking out at the rink where Ferd lay still as if he been dead for a week or so, he say, "That fat sucker probably broke his knee on Ferd's head."

But the St. Edouard defenceman already skating around like he scored a goal, his stick raised up in the air, his skates making slashing sounds.

It is Ferd Tailfeathers get carried from the ice.

"Who's buying the next round?" he ask the referee, as we haul him over the boards.

"They take their hockey pretty seriously up here, eh?" says Frank to a long-faced man sit next to Guy Lafleur. That man wear a Montreal Canadiens toque and sweater, and he have only four teeth in front, two top, two bottom, all stained yellow, and none quite matching. I notice now that almost everybody in the arena, from old people, like the guy next to Guy Lafleur, to tiny babies in arms, wear Montreal Canadiens sweaters. Somewhere there must be a store sell nothing but Montreal uniforms.

"You think this is serious," the old man say, "you ought to see a wedding in St. Edouard. The aisle of the Catholic Church is covered in artificial ice, at least in the summer, in winter it freeze up of its own accord. The priest wear goal pads and the groom is the defenceman," he go on in a heavy French accent.

"I didn't see no church," says Frank, "only big building I seen was the elevator."

"You seen the church," say the old man, "elevator got torn down years ago. You guys should stick around, there supposed to be a wedding tomorrow. The bride and bridesmaids stickhandle down the aisle, careful not to be off-side at the blue line; they get three shots on goal to score on the priest. If they don't the wedding get put off for a week."

Another old man in a felt hat and cigarette-yellowed mustache speak up, "We had one priest was such a good goaltender there were no weddings in St. Edouard for over two years. Some of the waiting couples had two, three kids already—so the bishop come down from Edmonton and perform a group ceremony."

Knocking Ferd out of the game was a real unlucky thing for them to do. I'm sure they would of scored ten goals each period if they'd just been patient. In the dressing room we strip off Ferd's pads, look for somebody to take his place.

Frank tell first one and then another player to put on the equipment.

"Put them on yourself," they say to Frank, only not in such polite language.

"You're gonna have to go in goal," Frank say to me.

"Not me," I say. "I got some regard for my life."

"Put your goddamned dog in the goal," say the caretaker of the dressing room. We can hear the fans getting restless. They are chanting something sound like "Alley, alley, les Bashers," and stomping their feet until the whole building shake.

"You guys should go home now," the old caretaker say. "They just looking for a bad team to beat up on. The way you guys skate it will be like tossing raw meat to hungry dogs."

"I think he's right," I say. "Let's sneak out. We can fend off the fans with hockey sticks if we have to."

We are just about to do that when Frank get his idea.

"It's why I'm manager and you're not," Frank say modestly to me that night when we driving back toward Hobbema.

We hold up the game for another fifteen minutes while we try to find skates big enough to fit Mad Etta.

Etta been sitting in the corner of the dressing room having a beer. Her and Frank do some fast bargaining. End up Frank have to promise her $900 of the thousand dollar prize money before she'll agree to play. Frank he plunk a mask on Etta's face right then and there.

"Not bad," say Etta, stare into a mirror. The mask is mean looking, with a red diamond drawed around each eye and red shark teeth where the mouth should be.

When we ask the Bashers to loan us a pair of BIG skates, they tell us to get lost.

"We've got to default the game then," we tell them, "guess you'll have to refund all those fans their money."

That make them nicer to know.

"Yeah, we didn't bring them all the way up here not to get in a few good licks."

"Besides the fans are in a mean mood. They want to see some blood. We're going to get even for what happened to Custer," say their biggest defenceman, who is about the size of a jeep and almost as smart. He give us his extra skates for Etta, then say, "We'll score four or five goals, then we'll trash you guys for a full hour. Get ready to bleed a lot."

We set Etta on a bench with her back to the wall. Me and Frank get one on each side of her and we push like we was trying to put a skate on a ten pound sack of sugar.

"I'm too old for this," puffs Etta. "What is it I'm supposed to do again anyway?"

"Just think how you'll spend the $900," says Frank, tie her laces in a big knot, "and everything else will take care of itself."

Three of us have to walk beside, behind, and in front, in order to steer Etta from the bench to the goal. The fans are all going "Oooh," and "Ahhhh."

I get to walk behind.

"If she falls back I'm a goner," I say.

"So keep her on her feet," huffs Frank. "I figure you value your life more than most, that's why I put you back there."

"That's one big mother of a goaltender," say one of the Bashers.

"More than you know," says Etta, but in Cree.

"Alley, alley, les Bashers," go the audience.

Once we get Etta to the net she grab onto the iron rail and stomp the ice, send chips flying in all directions, kick and kick until she get right down to the floorboards. Once she got footing she stand with an arm on each goal post, glare fierce from behind that mean mask what painted like a punk rock album cover.

Soon as the game start again the Bashers get the puck, pass it about three ways from Sunday, while our players busy falling down, skate right in on Mad Etta and shoot . . . and shoot . . . and shoot. Don't matter where they poke the puck, or how often, there is always some part of Mad Etta blocking the goal.

After maybe ten shots, a little player zoom in like a mosquito, fire point blank; the puck hit Etta's shoulder and go up in the crowd.

"That hurt," shout Etta, slap with her goal stick, knock that little player head over heels as he buzz by the net. She get a penalty for that. Goalies can't serve penalties, but someone else have to. The Bashers take about twenty more shots in the next two minutes.

"You're doin' great," Frank yell from the bench.

"How come our team never shoot the biscuit at their goal?" Etta call back.

"We're workin' on it," says Frank, "trust your manager."

Things don't improve though, so Etta just turn her back on the game, lean on the net and let the Bashers shoot at her backside. There is more Etta than there is goal; even some shots that miss the goal hit Etta. I think it is a law of physics that you can't add to something that is already full.

There is no score at the end of the first period. Trouble is Etta assume the game is only one period long.

"I got to stay out there how long?" she yell at Frank. "I already earn more than $900. That little black biscuit hurt like hell," she go on. "And how come none of you guys know how to play this game but me?"

The players is all glassy-eyed, gasp for air, nurse their bruises, cuts, and hangovers.

As we guide Etta out for the second period, Guy Lafleur go to barking like a fire siren again. He always hated Mad Etta ever since one day he nipped at her heels while she huffing up the hill from Hobbema General Store, and Etta punted him about forty yards deep into the mud and bullrushes of the slough at the foot of the hill.

When she hear the dog Etta spin around knock a couple of us to the ice, make Frank afraid for his life, and go "Bow-wow-wow," at Guy Lafleur, sound so much like a real dog that he jump off his seat and don't show his nose again until after the riot.

The way we dressed Etta for the game was to put the shoulder pads on, then her five-flour-sack dress, then tape one sweater to her chest and another to her back.

Soon as she get to the goal she have to guard for the second period, she don't even stomp the ice, just fumble in the pocket of her dress, take out a baggie with some greenish-looking sandy stuff in it, sprinkle that green stuff all across the goal line. Frank rush off the bench, fall twice on the way 'cause he wearing slippery-soled cowboy boots.

"What are you doin'?" he yell at Etta, who is waddling real slow, force each skate about an inch into the ice every step, and is heading for the face-off circle to the left of her goal.

"If I stay in front of that little closet I'm gonna be so bruised I'll look polka-dotted. I've had enough of this foolishness."

"But the goal," cries Frank.

"Hey, you manage the team. I'll do what I do best," and Etta give Frank a shove propel him on his belly all the way to the players' gate by our bench.

As the referee call the players to center ice, Etta sit down cross-legged in that face-off circle, light up a cigarette, blow smoke at the fan who stomping their feet.

The St. Edouard team steal the puck on the face-off, sweep right over the defence and fire at the empty goal. But the puck just zap off to the corner as if there was a real good goalie there. After about ten shots like that the Bashers get pretty mad and the fans even more so. It is like Etta bricked up the front of the goal with invisible bricks.

The St. Edouard Bashers gather around the referee and scream at him in both of Canada's official languages, and all of Canada's swear words.

The referee skate to the net, test with his hand, but there is nothing to block it. He stick one skate into the net. He throw the puck into the net. Then he borrow a stick from one of the Bashers and shoot the puck in, several times.

"Stop your bitchin' and play hockey," he say to the St. Edouard players.

"I bet I could sell that stuff to Peter Pocklington and the Edmonton Oilers for a million dollars an ounce," Frank hiss into my ear. "You're her assistant, Silas. What do you think the chances are of getting hold of a bag of that stuff?"

"It would only work when Etta stare at it the right way," I say.

"Hey, Edmonton Oilers could afford to buy Etta too. She's more valuable than Wayne Gretzky. And we'd be her agents . . ."

"Forget it," I say. "You can't buy medicine."

Les Bashers keep shooting at our goal all through the second period and into the third, with no better luck.

It a fact of hockey that no matter how bad a team you got you going to score a goal sooner or later. At about fifteen minutes into the third period, Rufus Firstrider, who skate mainly on his ankles, carry the puck over the St. Edouard blue line, try to pass to Gorman Carry-the-kettle, who been wheezing down the right wing.

The goalie see the pass coming up and move across the goal mouth to cover it, and there's a Mack truck of a defenceman ready to cream Gorman if the puck even gets close to him. But Rufus miss the pass entirely, fall down and accidentally hit the puck toward the net and score. That is all the goals there is: Hobbema Wagonburners 1, St. Edouard Bashers 0.

It was them and their fans what started the riot. We all headed for the dressing room, except for Frank, who jump into the stands looking for Guy Lafleur, and suffer a certain amount of damage as a result.

After the RCMP cooled everyone off and escorted us to our bus, Frank show up with a black eye and blood on his shirt, while Guy Lafleur have a notch out of one ear but a big mouthful of Basher hockey sweater to make up for it.

They got carpenters screwing the seats back in place and men busy resurfacing the ice. The Bashers decide to start the tournament over the next day, playing against teams they can beat. They agree to pay us $2500 to go home and never enter their tournament again.

And that's the truth.

The Truck

"How old does a truck have to be before it's antique?" Frank ask me. We is sitting in the Alice Hotel Bar with our girlfriends: Sadie One-wound is mine, Connie Bigcharles is his.

"Ain't sure," I say. "Antiques is usually cracked, dusty, and scarce."

"You figure Louis' truck would be an antique?"

"It's cracked and dirty," says Connie, "and I ain't ever seen a truck that old that's still running."

"What year is it?" asks Sadie.

"Nobody's sure. I think it started out as a 1947 Ford, but I'm sure every part on it been replaced at least once, and not always with 1947 Ford parts. It had at least five engines that I know of, and we had to change the registration numbers a couple of times to keep the finance companies from carrying it off."

I remember once Louis' truck got stopped at a road block in Edmonton and a constable look over all the papers I hand out the window to him.

"The serial number and registration show this vehicle to be a 1976 Cadillac Coupe de Ville," say the constable, scratch his head, breathe licorice into the truck as he shine his flashlight in the eyes of the eight or so people who jammed in the cab.

"Shhhhh," says Frank, "we done that as a surprise gift for Louis, and we haven't told him yet. Louis always wanted to own a Cadillac, but this was the only way he could ever afford one."

"You must have to pay a lot larger insurance premium," say the constable, stare again at our pink insurance card.

"Well sure," says Frank, "Cadillacs is a lot more expensive to insure."

When we explain that Louis who own the truck is blind, that constable's eyes get big.

"Don't worry, he hardly drives at all anymore since he turned eighty," we tell the constable.

"They're right," says Louis, who we even forgot was with us: my sister Delores sitting on his knee in her chicken dancer costume, pretty well cover him up. "Used to be I could tell the make of a car by the smell of it," Louis go on, "but last week I smelled a Fargo and it turned out to be a Jeep."

"But it had a Fargo bumper," says Frank.

"Still no excuse," said Louis. "I'm just getting old."

Even the constable have to smile at that, and since the truck appear to have insurance, and I got a driver's license, he let us go.

"How come you're all of a sudden interested in antiques?" Connie ask Frank.

"Well, I hear on the radio that Smilin' Al's Toyota Truck Center and Amalgamated Recreational Vehicle Showplace, just off 104 St. on the Calgary Trail, in Edmonton, the Oil Capital of Canada, going to give away a brand new Toyota truck; going to give 100% trade-in to the owner of an antique vehicle of some kind . . . but I didn't get the rest of the details."

"There has to be some kind of catch," I say. "If there's one thing we've learned it's that businesses never give away anything for free unless they profit ten times over from it. Also, Indians never likely to get any of the free stuff."

"Let's check it out anyway," says Frank, and the girls agree.

We drive up to Smilin' Al's place the very next morning, about fifteen or so of us in Louis' truck. Mr. and Mrs. Blind Louis is in the cab with us, Mad Etta our medicine lady sit like a queen on her tree-trunk chair in the truck box. We all feel kind of like we know Smilin' Al Nesterenko 'cause we seen him on the TV so many times. Smilin' Al have thin blond hair on a big, square head. He wear shiny blue suits with the jackets open so his belly can escape. He come on the TV grinning out of the side of his face and carrying a sledgehammer. He always standing beside an old car or truck.

"Friends," he say, "Smilin' Al Nesterenko is going to break down prices again," and then he swing the sledgehammer, bash in the windows and lights of that car or truck.

At one time Smilin' Al played tackle for the Edmonton Eskimos football team.

"Some people will say I blocked one too many field goals with my head," Smilin' Al will say into the camera, "and that I'm about eight bricks short of a load. But if my prices are too low who's gonna benefit, me or you?" Then he whack that car some more, sometimes even throw bricks through the windshield.

They say Smilin' Al comes to work in a green-and-gold painted limousine, drove by a guy in a football uniform. I don't think he's near as dumb as he pretend to be.

I notice as I park that there's a bunch of what are called Classic cars and trucks on Smilin' Al's lot. Most them are real old vehicles, but they been restored until they look better than new. Their bright colors and shiny paint always make my mouth water. I sure hope that someday I get to own one of them.

"We come to win the new truck," Frank announce to the salesman who asked if he can help us.

"Good luck," say the salesman, "so did all these other people. What kind of car did you bring?"

"We brought our truck," we say. "It a genuine 1947 Ford," and we point it out at the curb, where it sort of droop like a frost-bit cabbage leaf. Our poor old truck sure look sad beside all these Classic cars.

"Here's a card with all the rules," says the salesman. "You'll have to get in line clear around the block there, if you want a chance to win."

I read the card out loud to everybody. The whole thing is pretty complicated. In the showroom window is a bingo machine, and inside the machine the little ping-pong balls, instead of having bingo numbers printed on them, have the make and year of a car or truck range from 1920 to 1963. Every hour from 10 a.m. to 10 p.m. three of these old vehicles get to line up in front of the showroom window, and if the machine cough up the right make and model why the winner get to trade for a brand new Toyota King-cab truck, got automatic transmission, and every other extra known to white man and Indian. The card say that truck worth over $16,000.

One catch is, they write down your license number and you can only go through the line-up three times, ever. It don't look to me like the odds of winning are very good. It take us all that day, and after we park in the line-up overnight, half the next before we get to the front.

While we waiting we dream a lot about winning.

"It be kind of sad to part with this old truck," says Sadie.

"How many babies you reckon got their start in here?" says Frank.

We all think about that for a while, and we all talk up some memories, especially about times we been to the Golden Grain Drive-In Theater up near Millet. Drive-In theater known as Foreskin Park. Bet half the babies on Hobbema Reserve got their start there.

"Let's see," Louis Coyote say to his wife, get a nice smile on his old face, "I think we started off Jimmy, and Muriel, and Boniface, and Champagne . . . right here on the front seat. Maybe even a couple of others . . . who knows?"

"We haven't got a kid named Champagne," says Mrs. Blind Louis. Her and him can never agree, not even on how many kids there are in Louis' family.

"Sure we have," says Louis. "She's the second youngest. I seen her around someplace today," and he turn his milky eyes over the car lot.

"That's Charlene," says Mrs. Blind Louis, real cross.

"Close enough," says Louis. "She should be called Champagne; she's light and bouncy, taste sweet, and make an old man feel good."

"Oh, you knew my name all along, didn't you, Daddy?" say the little girl Charlene, scramble over two or three people, sit on Louis' knee and hug his neck.

When we get to the front of the line we feel kind of out of place, all of us jammed in our old rickety truck while beside us is two restored and rebuilt cars, a 1950 Ford and a 1956 Lincoln. Both shine like stars on water, even their owners shine, wear silky jackets, like expensive ski clothes.

Frank and me go into the showroom to see how the numbers get picked.

There is a real pretty girl there: second runner-up for Miss Edmonton Eskimo, somebody say. She wear a bathing suit and a banner say MISS AMALGAMATED RECREATIONAL VEHICLE. She take the ping-pong balls out of the back of the machine.

"Just like a chicken laying an egg," says Frank.

She hand them to the sales manager who hand them to Smilin' Al, who announce the year and make.

When Frank try to push behind the machine, Miss Amalgamated Recreational Vehicle say "Where do you think you're going?"

Frank grin in that way he have that usually charm white ladies pretty good. But Miss ARV give him a push, stomp his moccasin with the back end of her high-heel shoe.

"Don't worry, I still love you," Frank say as he limp away.

We don't win. Not then or the next time we go through the line-up. We all go home disappointed. After we think about it we decide to plan a little before we come back.

"We need an edge of some kind," says Frank.

We ain't in much of a hurry to try again 'cause we heard somebody say it liable to be months before a winning number come up. Even then Smilin' Al ain't gonna lose much. Most of those restored cars worth up to $10,000 dollars or more.

I can see where Smilin' Al might not want us to win. I also figured Frank would be that *edge* he was talking about, only trouble is

Miss Amalgamated Recreational Vehicle don't like him. But we got one more chance, there's a guy on the reserve name of Phil Carry-the-kettle, that I don't think ever been turned down by a woman.

I think I understand how Frank attracts girls, even though he ain't good-looking, dressed fancy, or drive a big car. He does unexpected things; he have more nerve than any other five guys put together; girls go for men like that.

Phil Carry-the-kettle, I can only describe as dangerous-looking—he is tall and dress like a cowboy: tight denim clothes, leather boots, vest, belt and hat. He always look as if he might go wild at any time—and it is that sense of danger attracts girls.

Some guys is surprised when women chase after them, but Phil ain't. I asked him one time how he managed it, and this is what he said: "Women are easy to handle as dogs, just look 'em in the eye and let 'em know you like 'em. Find out what they want from you: every one of them wants something, maybe it's just to be treated nice, to have a door opened or have you light her cigarette, or she might want to hear 'I love you,' or that you're interested in staying around permanent, or some girls just want a stud. It don't take long to find out. Then you give 'em what they want. And as soon as they get comfortable you take it away from them—that make them appreciate you more." Phil laugh and smile his lopsided smile at me.

"I should teach in a college, huh? That's how you handle women, Silas. I don't mind givin' away my secret. You can even write it down if you want. Real men are *born* knowin' how. If you have to ask, doesn't matter what you hear it won't do you any good. Most men are too chicken to carry out the last step; they're the ones end up married with a trailer-house full of kids and a finance company breathin' on them."

I'm not sure Phil is all that happy; he have lots and lots of women, but . . . . Anyway we figure if any guy we know can get close to Miss Amalgamated Recreational Vehicle, it be Phil Carry-the-kettle.

In order to get Phil to even come up to Smilin' Al's Toyota Truck Center, we have to promise him a hand-tooled saddle he seen in the window of Western Outfitter's Store in Camrose.

"Hey," we tell him, "soon as we win the new truck we'll sell the spare tire, the radio and the tape-deck and give you the money to buy the saddle."

"I don't work for promises," Phil says. So we have to pay him in advance. He is the kind of guy who might not keep his end of the bargain and we couldn't do a thing about it. Even Frank been known to leave the room when Phil Carry-the-kettle get riled up.

It probably best if I don't tell about how we got the saddle. Frank have to have a certain number of stitches taken at the hospital in Red Deer after he do the acquiring. And we all look nervous for the next week or two every time we see an RCMP car.

Phil drive up to Edmonton in his red sports car, ride alone, while all the rest of us cram in Louis' truck. But just like we figure, he hit it right off with Miss ARV. He take her home the very first night, and every night for the next two weeks.

"About the second night I was there her boyfriend came by, looked like a model for men's sissy clothing. I knocked him down two flights of stairs and he ain't been back," Phil tell us.

Phil also make us buy gas for his car, loan him meal money, and dancing and drinking money.

"Goddamn," says Frank, "if she decide to go on the pill we gonna have to pay the prescription."

I don't argue that it ain't true. But a few days ago Phil come

up to me smiling and picking his teeth with a flavored toothpick.

"The whole thing is rigged," Phil tells me. "You know that
machine that spin all the balls, well it sorts them all too." He go
on to say that Miss Amalgamated, her real name is Debbie-June,
goes behind the machine before every drawing, and as Smilin' Al
looks out the window and announces what cars are competing,
she takes out the balls for each one. Smilin' Al figures to let the
contest go on for two years before he let someone win, and then it
will be a friend or a relative or someone with a classic car worth
almost as much as the new truck. He also told Debbie-June the
contest has increased his business 50% already and he's getting
more popular every day.

"Which kind is Debbie-June?" I ask Phil.

"What?"

"What does she want from you?"

"Oh," and Phil smile as the light dawns, shows his big white
teeth. "She want it all. She like to be treated nice, told 'I love
you,' and that I'm her permanent man. She need a stud service
too, real bad," and he laugh some more.

"You think you can get her to help us?"

"Do birds have feathers? Listen, I'm gonna disappear for a couple
of days. The day I get back she'll set herself on fire if I was to ask."

Phil sure know what he's talking about. He make himself
scarce, and as soon as he do Debbie-June start looking pale and
acting nervous as a mink. About every ten minutes she ask one of
us if we know what's become of Phil and when he coming back.

"He's probably gone rodeoing," we say, "maybe to Arizona,"
and as we watch Debbie-June get an expression on her face like
she just sunk a fish-hook in her finger.

"What are you guys hanging around here all the time for?" one of the salesmen ask us. "When are you gonna put your truck through the line-up again?"

"We got our medicine woman working on it," we say. And we have. Just to keep Smilin' Al and his friends busy, we had Etta set up shop in the parking lot. She build a real campfire on the pavement, boil up roots, and leaves and stuff in a saucepan we bought her. We tell Etta she is just a decoy, but she say it won't do no harm to cook up a real spell. Etta really like the orange-plastic truck-box cover that go with the pickup; with it she won't have to ride out in the open air no more. Some TV station even take pictures of Etta casting a spell so her friends can win a new truck, and her photo appear on the front page of the *Edmonton Sun*.

Three days later Phil come swaggering into the showroom. As I watch Debbie-June it look like her blood expand, because she get pinker, prettier, and taller, all in about one minute, not to mention happier.

"I'll just tell her unless she does what I ask her, I'll be goin' away again tomorrow," Phil whisper to me. "Better go get your truck in line."

Frank and Mr. and Mrs. Blind Louis spend the night in the truck in the line-up. It is about noon the next day before they get to the front.

Sure enough Smilin' Al stare out the window and announce: "In five minutes we'll have the next drawing. The vehicles eligible are a 1956 Lincoln Continental, a 1932 Chevrolet Coupe, and a . . . 1947 Ford Pickup truck."

While he was making the announcement Debbie-June was nowhere in sight. Then Al grab a handle on the machine and it spit out three ping-pong balls. Debbie-June appear, pick up the balls and hand them to Smilin' Al, who put them in the side pocket of his suit coat.

He take the balls out one at a time and read them.

"1939 Terraplane," he say. "1955 Chev Bel-Air. 1947 Ford Pickup truck."

There is a very long pause and then all hell break loose.

Smilin' Al ain't smilin' anymore. He fire Debbie-June right on the spot, then look around to see who else he can make suffer.

But the sales manager get him by the arm and pull him off to one side, all the time pointing at the radio man who doing a remote broadcast from the showroom, and talking a mile a minute.

Smilin' Al finally calm down. Frank and Mr. and Mrs. Blind Louis come inside and he shake their hands, while we all clap and cheer some.

"This ain't a Classic car; this is a classic piece of junk," Smilin' Al growl when he examine Louis' pickup.

"It still won the contest," we say.

"I admit we won't be able to resell it," says the sales manager, "we'll just haul it directly to the junkyard."

"I'm gonna put it on TV and smash it all to rat shit," says Smilin' Al.

"Still, it's good publicity," says the sales manager. "Here, get a picture of the old man and his driver," he say to a salesman who carrying a flash camera. "When you stop to think about it we couldn't have a better winner than a blind 83-year-old Indian. We killed off three minorities all at once, so to speak."

"Face the camera, Mr. Ki-o-tee," say the man with the camera.

"You think that thing can steal my soul?" Louis ask nobody in particular.

"You already sold yours when you bought your Skidoo," says Mrs. Blind Louis.

Boy, the new truck sure is fancy. It is a King-cab, have little seats behind the regular ones that pop down. "Bet we be able to cram over ten people in here," says Frank.

"And that's just in the front seat," says Connie.

There is soft, fuzzy seat covers of a purple color and them seats lean back far enough to almost make a bed. Late one evening last week, Frank and Connie sneaked out there and tried them out for comfort.

Smilin' Al sign the new truck over to Louis, and Louis make his X to give the old truck to Smilin' Al.

"We sure gonna miss Louis' old truck," I say. "We all growed up with it around. It was kind of like a grandfather to us."

"You want to trade back?" says Smilin' Al. "Even up."

We thank him a lot but don't take up his offer.

We get lots of pictures taken with us standing beside the truck, and a newspaper lady write down all our names, even Mad Etta's, who tell her real name: Mrs. Margueretta Black Horses.

Frank seat himself behind the wheel.

"I want to *drive*," he says.

"You got to wait for us," I'm saying, but Frank ain't listening very good. He revving up the engine and I can tell he want to do a wheelie.

I think what happen is Frank's foot slip off the brake at the same time he revving the engine, 'cause I get just a flash of the surprised look on his face as the truck take off like a rocket, shoot across the parking lot, the service road, and right onto Highway 2, the main road between Edmonton and Calgary. There is a big screech of brakes, a clash of metal, and a dull bang like a far off explosion, then a lot of rattling, pinging, and popping as pieces of metal scatter across the highway.

We all run out to the highway, and there is our brand new truck crushed right under the back wheels of an eighteen-wheeler. Our truck been drug about a hundred yards and has suffered a certain amount of damage. Bet the driver of the eighteen-wheeler sure wonder where Frank came from.

On the other side of all the mess Frank is sitting on the road, he has lost his cowboy hat, one boot is off, and he got a look on his face as if someone just asked him a question that was too hard for him.

Mad Etta feel him up and down but he ain't neither bleeding or broken.

"Put this here blanket around him and sit him in the tr . . ."

We all realize together that our new truck is nothing but scrap and the old one belong to Smilin' Al . . . for the time being.

"For winners we sure ain't got much to show for it," says Etta.

For once in his life Frank don't have nothin' smart to say. Connie kiss his face a few times and walk with one arm around his waist. The foot without the boot gettin' pretty wet on the slushy pavement.

Beef

S ometimes being cheated ain't as bad as it made out to be. Back over a hundred years ago when the Government take the prairies away from the Indians and give us back these little reservations, our Chief Three Eagles make his mark to an agreement that, to help us Indians become farmers, the Government going to give every family two to four cows depend on its size.

But Three Eagles wouldn't accept the gift. I seen picture of Three Eagles wearing a breastplate, decked out in buckskin, feathers, and beaded wampum. He have the proud face of a hunter and warrior, and he wasn't about to be a farmer.

"I am not a tree," is what Three Eagles said. "My people do not root themselves to the land; we are traveling people. Indians soar like the birds. Just as the white man is a pale ghost of the Indian, so cattle are weak ghosts of buffalo. Farms are prisons. You do not put an eagle in a square cage."

It lucky Three Eagles died young.

We didn't know any of this history until I read in a magazine about how some Blackfoot Indians down south of Calgary, just last year hit up the Government for the cattle they was supposed to have got in 1877. They got a priest to do the research that prove their Chief Crowfoot refused the cattle, but that the Indians was still entitled.

Biggest surprise though was that it being an election year, the Government coughed up, not cattle but money.

The magazine explain it this way. "Both sides agreed early on that it would be foolish for the government to drive that big a herd onto the reserve: sorting, distributing, branding and fencing would have been virtually impossible."

Instead, every person on the reserve got $25 in cash money, and another 1.6 million dollars went to the tribe's bank account.

I showed the article to Bedelia Coyote.

"If it happened to the Blackfoot, I bet it happen to us Cree, too," I say. "I sure wouldn't mind that $25."

"You think small," says Bedelia. "You should be looking at the 1.6 million. Oh, what I could do with that . . ."

Bedelia is one of a group of young people has started a Back to the Land Movement. They think they can go back in the hills, hunt, trap, and live off the land like the old time Indians did.

Myself, I'm kind of fond of electricity, cars and televisions. But if that's what they want to do . . .

Bedelia take the case to a priest of our own, Fr. Alphonse up at Blue Quills School. He head right off to Edmonton to check over papers at the Parliament building and Provincial Museum. Guess he's happy to have something to make him feel useful. He don't have much success turning Indians into Christians, and spend most of his time read books in his office and say mass for two or three old women in babushkas.

To shorten up the story, it turn out we got the same claim as the Blackfoot, only there more people on Hobbema Reserve, so we have more cattle and money due us.

I lose interest after a while, but Bedelia and Father Alphonse push right on, even get the story and their pictures in *Alberta Report* magazine one time.

It take two years but the Government offer up something called Treaty 11, which offer the Ermineskin Reserve 4,000 cows and 40 bulls.

"What about the money?" say Bedelia.

"That's just another part of the process," say Fr. Alphonse. "We formally refuse the cattle and ask for money instead. We have to put it all in writing and it will take another year or two to resolve. We'll ask for the value of the cattle, plus compound interest for the last hundred years . . ."

"I'd rather have the cattle," says my friend Frank Fencepost. "If the tribe got a million dollars, you figure Chief Tom and his friends gonna let us get our hands on any of it?"

Frank and his girlfriend Connie Bigcharles has joined this here Back to the Land Movement though I'm not sure why. Only tool Frank really capable with is a bottle opener. As for Connie, she like tight sweaters, white lipstick and her "Pow-wow Blaster" radio, that all silver, big as a suitcase and can shake leaves off trees when the volume is up. Connie ain't never farmed in her life. She don't even grow houseplants.

I never thought I'd say this, but I think maybe it was a mistake for Frank Fencepost to learn to read and write. Ever since he done that, it open up to him about a hundred more ways to get into trouble.

Frank has learned to read upside down, so just by standing across Fr. Alphonse's desk he can read the name and address of the bureaucrat in Ottawa that the Ermineskin Nation Back to the Land Movement deals with.

Frank he grin like a Japanese general while he write to the Government say we happy to accept their offer of cattle and could they ship 400 a month until we get all of them. And he sign the letter Fr. Alphonse Fencepost, Instrument of God. "Fr. could stand for Frank, couldn't it," say Frank. I suggest he send it to the Department of Graft, Patronage and Corruption, but Frank copy out the real return address from the envelope.

"Don't mess with your spiritual adviser," he tell me.

The Government write direct to Frank agree to send us the stock 400 at a time. And it coming in the name of the Ermineskin Nation Back to the Land Movement, Ms. Bedelia Coyote Executive Director. So there's no way Chief Tom can get his greedy hands on the cattle or the money they going to make for us.

"No problems," say Frank. "We just put the cattle to graze in the hills. The bulls make the cows pregnant. Our herd grows. We sell off the calves and yearlings—invest the money in real estate . . ."

"What about back to the land?"

"Hey, land is land. I'm gonna build my ranchhouse in Wetaski-win; it have a three storey, twelve-suite apartment block attached to it."

But first we have to do a lot of work. We build a corral between Ben Stonebreaker's store and our row of cabins on the hill. We will put the first 400 cattle there, herd them in little groups to the pasture land. When we get the first 400 settled, we order 400 more.

The Bank of Montreal in Wetaskiwin after we show them the letter actually loan us some money to buy fence posts and log poles to make a corral. Out of that money Frank he buy himself a silk western shirt, cowboy boots, a ten-gallon white hat and a string tie.

"Just call me J. 'Tex' Fencepost," he says, and walk around with his chest pushed out, supervise the rest of us as we dig post holes and nail the poles into place with 6" blue spikes.

Fr. Alphonse sure is surprised when he get a letter from the Department of Indian Affairs say they can't honor his refusal of the cattle because they is already on their way to us, and we should try to get our records in order.

Fr. Alphonse and Bedelia do a little investigating and discover what Frank has done.

"How could you do something so stupid?" roar Bedelia.

Me and Rufus Firstrider is working on the corral. Frank laying down in the shade, his cowboy hat pulled down until his face don't show at all.

"Show a little respect for your ranch foreman," say Frank. "Besides, what's stupid? We got 400 cattle arriving, and they gonna come 400 a month almost forever. We get to keep the money we make. We all gonna be rich ranchers. Gonna call my spread the Ponderosa."

"We were going to do something positive," say Bedelia with less anger than I expected. "You'll be sorry," she predict before she stomp off.

As usual, Bedelia turn out to be right.

We actually get the corral finished the day before the first cattle due to arrive. I read somewhere about this here guy named Murphy who has a law about *Whatever can go wrong will go wrong.* I bet Murphy was an Ermineskin Indian.

Boy, we sure is excited when that first cattle transport turn off the highway and onto the main street of Hobbema. Little kids and old people are all along the street waving pennants left over from when the Edmonton Oilers won the Stanley Cup for hockey. People toot their car horns and wave.

The truck back up to the corral, let down its end gate and the first Herefords, with wine-colored bodies and square white faces, step down onto the reserve. Eathen Firstrider, Ducky Cardinal, Gerard Many Hands High, and a couple of other guys who worked the rodeo circuit are there on their ponies to guide the cattle into the corral.

The second truck waiting to unload when the first one is empty. Then another one, and another, and another. Each truck hold about 35–40 cattle, and after a while it seem to me there is close to 400 cows in the corral. But when I look toward the highway there are cattle transports lined all the way down the hill and about four deep all along main street.

It seem some clerk in the Government in Ottawa add an extra zero to our order. And there is 4,000 cattle arriving instead of 400.

"It ain't our problem," the truck drivers say. "Our orders are to deliver these cattle to Hobbema. This here is Hobbema. If you ain't got a corral, we'll just drop them in the street."

And they do.

By the end of that day there is more white-faced cattle on the Hobbema Reserve than there is Indians. The corral get so full it start to bulge at the seams. Then come a couple of trucks say they carrying the bulls.

"Can't turn these dudes loose," a truck driver say. "They're mean mothers if I ever seen some."

We have to chase a few hundred cattle out onto the street so the bulls can go into the corral.

"They must weigh 5,000 lbs. each," says Frank, watching the wide, squat Hereford bulls wobble into the corral on their square, piano-legs. Each one got a bronze ring in his flat pink nose.

"Lookit the equipment on them suckers," says Frank. "I bet that's what I was in a former life."

"In the present one," says Connie, and Frank grin big.

The trucks just keep unloading. I guess word must work back to the end of the line that we ain't got no more corral space. Some of the trucks way out by the highway drop their loads and sneak away. Soon all the trucks are doing that. The main street of Hobbema look like a movie I seen once of a cattle drive somewhere in the Wild West of about a hundred years ago.

The cattle fill up the school grounds and is munching grass among tombstones in the graveyard behind the Catholic church. One step up on the porch of Ben Stonebreaker's Hobbema General Store bite into a gunnysack of chicken feed and scatter it all about. Four or five more climb onto the porch and one get about halfway into the store before Ben's granddaughter Caroline beat it across the nose with a yard stick and make it back up.

My girlfriend's brother David One-wound have himself a still in a poplar grove a few hundred yards back of town. RCMP can't sniff out his business, but it only take the cattle a few minutes to find it.

"They could work for the RCMP, use them as tracking cattle," says Frank. "And they'd be close to being as smart," he say.

The cattle like the sugar in the throwed out mash, and some of them get as close to mean as these docile kind of cattle can.

Ben Stonebreaker has five cattle prods in his hardware department, and he sell them out in about five minutes. Mad Etta our medicine lady was herding three or four half-drunk cows out of her yard when Ephrem Crookedneck, who decide to put as many cows as he can into his garden, what only fenced with chicken wire, and call them his own, either accidentally, or by mistake jab Mad Etta with his new electric cattle prod.

"Honest to God, I thought she was one of them. You seen her from behind. It was an honest mistake," he say, after the doctor taped up his cracked ribs and put his dislocated arm in a sling.

The cattle push up against the pumps at Fred Crier's Hobbema Texaco Garage, and before long one of the pumps leaning at a 45 degree angle. Old Peter Left Hand's chicken coop kind of sigh and fold up like a paper cut out, ruffled hens running everywhere, some squawking from inside the flattened building.

Traffic on Highway 2A is tied up, and somebody in a pickup truck hit a cow right in front of the Hobbema Pool Hall. Some young guys built a fire in a rusty oil drum and they barbecue the dead cow. Other guys is stripping down the pickup truck while the driver trying to call the RCMP.

"*We* is the law here," Rufus Firstrider tell the truck owner.

Constable Chrétien and Constable Bobowski, the lady RCMP, come by, but there is some situations even too big for the RCMP. Constable Bobowski jump out of the patrol car, get shit on her boots, jump back in, then back out to wipe her feet on the grass. They stare through the windshield at the thousands of cattle milling around—some of them cattle bump pretty hard into the patrol car. Finally, they ease away a few feet at a time. I'm told they put detour signs on the highway a mile above and a mile before Hobbema.

It ain't near as much fun as we thought it would be to have 4,000 cattle. Turns out nobody like our cattle very much. Cattle is dumb, and determined. They go just about anywhere they want to. They eat grass and gardens and leaves, knock down buildings, and some get in Melvin Dodginghorse's wheatfield, tramp down his crop. Six or seven of them eat until they die. Then they smell up the air on the whole reserve.

White farmers and even some Indians claim they going to sue the Ermineskin Nation Back to the Land Movement. The main street, and the gravel road to the highway, and even the walking paths is covered in cow shit. Seem like everyplace you can name is downwind of our herd.

It is also pretty hard to keep 40 bulls in a corral when there is close to 4,000 cows outside the corral.

"Do something," everybody say to Bedelia Coyote and Fr. Alphonse. But there is a point where people get overwhelmed by a situation and Bedelia and Fr. Alphonse is in that position.

People try to get Chief Tom in on the act, but he stay in his apartment in Wetaskiwin with his girlfriend, Samantha Yellowknees, and after they put pressure on him, decide he have serious government business in California for the next month. Chief Tom don't like the smell of cattle no better than the rest of us.

Everybody grumble. But we got what we said we wanted. It pretty hard to complain about that.

Everybody now eat good anyway. Old hunters like William Irons and Dolphus Frying Pan, have a couple of cows skinned and quartered before you can say, "hunting season," and everybody got steak to fry and liver to cook. William and Dolphus have blood up to their elbows and they ain't smiled so broad since they got too old to go big game hunting.

Next morning a tall cowboy arrive with a cattle transport offer to buy up cows at $400 each. He put down the ramp at the rear of his truck and pay cash money to whoever load an animal up. He load up 40 cows and promise to come back as soon as he can.

"If he's paying $400, these here animals must be worth a lot more," says Frank.

All the time the truck was being loaded, Bedelia was yelling for them to stop, shouting about our heritage and don't sell the future for pocket money. But nobody pays any attention and somebody even shove her out of the way, hard.

Frank get Louis Coyote's pickup truck and using the same ramp we use to load Mad Etta when we want to take her someplace, we get three cows into the truckbox rope them in pretty tight.

Frank he head for Weiller and Williams Stockyard in Edmonton.

Most of us don't really have any idea how much a cow is worth. But after Frank make that first trip to Edmonton he report, "They is paying 80¢ a pound and these cows weigh around 1,000 to 1,200 pounds." The three he crammed in Louis' pickup truck bring $2,640 cash money.

When people find that out everybody want to get in on the act.

When the cattle transport come back, David One-wound announce we going to "nationalize" it and the driver just barely get away with his empty truck and ten guys yipping on his heels.

A couple of people load cows into their wagon boxes and start their teams out for the long trip to Edmonton.

Some of the young cowboys like Eathen Firstrider, Robert Coyote and Ducky Cardinal decide to do a real cattle drive and start about fifteen cows in the direction of Edmonton.

Some other people tie a rope to the neck of the tamest cow and lead her, walking in front of her, in the direction of Edmonton.

Bedelia is still yelling at people to stop and is still getting ignored. Fr. Alphonse gone back to his office at the Reserve

School, wishing, I bet, that he'd never found out about us being cheated.

It is kind of sad to see all the crazy goings on. If we could just get organized we could make a lot of money for years and years to come. But people ain't ready to listen to Bedelia; they just go on their own way selling cattle here, there, and everywhere. Local white farmers stop people as they walk up the ditches offer less than half what the animal would bring in Edmonton. But people is too greedy to say no. Ogden Coyote trade a cow for a 10-speed bicycle, have bright pink tassels on the handlebars.

I remember reading in, I think it was *Time* magazine about how in Africa, when some little country that been a colony for a thousand years get its independence, the people don't know how to act. They spend foolishly, act like fools and their country end up in a terrible mess.

I wish I was a leader. I can see what should be done, but I don't know how to go about it. I'm a watcher.

"*You* could stop this foolishness," I say to Mad Etta. "People would listen to you. Why don't you do something?"

"Hey, they *are* doing what they want. Water rise to its own level. You put food in front of hungry people they going to eat good before they think about planting seeds for next year. Same with money. I know what should be done, but the people ain't ready for it yet. Maybe, Silas, when you're an old man . . ." and she stop and stare wistful off into the woods behind her cabin. "But in the meantime, I got a bull and six cows tethered in the pines down the hill. How soon you figure we can use Louis' truck to take them to Edmonton?"

The next morning Frank come bounding into my cabin, smiling like he just got it on with a movie star.

"Hey, Silas, our troubles are over," he yell. "I had me a dream last night and these here cattle going to make us rich."

"How are they gonna do that?"

"All we need is some old sheets and some paint."

"For what?"

"Hey, we gonna sell advertising space on our cattle." Frank is grinning so wide I'm afraid he's gonna dislocate his ears.

"That's crazy."

"No it's not," and Frank jump up on a kitchen chair, then jump off quick, run to my bed and pull a sheet off with one hard yank, leave the rest of the blankets and Sadie right where they were. He set two chairs about four feet apart and drape the sheet over the chair backs.

"Pretend that's a cow. We tie a sheet over her, then . . ." and he pull from his pocket a huge magic marker about the size of a shock absorber, and paint on the sheet HOBBEMA TEXACO GARAGE. "We do that on each side of the cow, then we put them to grazing along the highway. They'll be just like billboards."

No matter what I say to Frank, whether I laugh or make fun of his idea, he stick to his guns.

"There's only one thing to do," I say, "let's go make some sales calls."

In Wetaskiwin we get a parking place in front of Mr. Larry's Men's Wear, COUTURIER TO THE DISCRIMINATING GENTLEMAN.

We troop inside.

"We're here to see Mr. Larry," I say to a tall man dressed so fancy he could lay right down in a coffin and feel at home.

"I am Lawrence Oberholtzer, the proprietor."

"I'm Frank Fencepost, ace advertising salesman. How do you like me so far?" and Frank stick out his hand grab one of Mr. Larry's long pale hands that was by his side, and shake hearty.

"I would just as soon not answer that," he say, his voice able to freeze water or shrivel plants.

"I'm gonna show you how to become the richest businessman in Wetaskiwin."

"I already *am* the richest man in Wetaskiwin," say Mr. Larry. "Now please get to the point."

"How would you like to have 4,000 cattle with your name on them?"

"Don't tell me; you're cattle rustlers."

Frank explain his idea.

"You can even advertise on more than one cow. Show him, Silas. This is my assistant Silas Running-up-the-riverbank."

Mr. Larry nod at me.

"Picture your cows grazing in a row beside the highway, Mr. Larry."

I take out four sheets I been carrying, unfold them, drape them over racks of suits. When I finished they read like this:

THIS HERE STORE
IS A FANCY PLACE
SHIRTS & SUITS
FOR EVERY RACE
CHINK OR JAP
CHRISTIAN OR JEW
MR. LARRY'S
IS THE STORE FOR YOU.

Frank he look so self-satisfied he just know it is impossible for Mr. Larry to turn him down.

Out on the street we gather up the sheets from where Mr. Larry threw them and decide to call on Union Tractor Company.

Six businesses later, we put the sheets in the truck and head for the Alice Hotel to have a beer.

"They'll be sorry," says Frank. "I can't help it if I fifty years ahead of my time."

The cattle problem solve itself, sort of like flood water recede slow until you never know the water been high at all.

Everybody on the reserve eat good for a few weeks. The old hunters is happy as pigs in a barnyard. A lot of us carry cattle off to sell in Edmonton. Louis Coyote buy twin Skidoos for him and Mrs. Blind Louis.

I buy me a new typewriter but it ain't no smarter than my old one, so it get pushed to the back of the kitchen table and my little sister Delores, who claim she going to tell stories just like me, pound on it once in a while.

Frank buy a video recorder and him and Connie pick out about a hundred movies. Frank is working on tapping into the power line to the UGG Elevator so's they can watch movies soon as they get a TV, which Frank is working on too.

Mad Etta was about the only smart one, she corral two of them Hereford bulls, and got them in separate pens behind her cabin We drive her around to local farms and she sell their services.

"Etta ain't going to go hungry for awhile," she says, rocking back and forth on her tree-trunk chair. "It sure nice to be supported by somebody who enjoy their work," she say and laugh and laugh.

"It's back to the drawing board for us," say Bedelia and Fr. Alphonse. "We got a lot of work to do yet," they say. According to them, the Cattle Treaty was only one of 23 claims outstanding. They going after money for land of ours been given away, used for highways, irrigation canals, and Government Experimental Farms.

"Anytime you need help negotiating," says Frank, "the great Fencepost is available, free of charge."

Frank never quite understand why they don't answer him back.

The Managers

For Jim Jamieson

This time the trouble start when a black limousine with blue-tinted windows turn off the highway and pull up to the Hobbema General Store. The passenger window purr down and a tough-looking dude with more scars on his face than a nine-year-old's knees call me over with a beefy finger.

"We're here to pay a call on the chief," he says.

"Yeah, well this is just the reserve, you won't find no chief here."

"Well, where will I find him?"

"Depend on what you looking for him for."

"What do you mean?"

"Well, he might be someplace if you was wanting to pay him money, while he might be someplace else altogether if you want to collect money from him."

"I understand *that*," say the guy, who wear a woolly-lamb of a hat that make him look like a Russian secret agent. "We have a business deal to discuss, guaranteed to make lots of money for your tribe."

"If this deal's so good," say my friend Frank Fencepost, who's wandered over, along with Eathen Firstrider, "how come rich white guys like you want to share it with us poor Indians?"

"A matter of capitalization," he say, "you understand capitalization, Tonto?" And the guy curl up one lip to show a lot of white teeth.

It is a bad mistake to get on the wrong side of Frank Fencepost. Mad Etta is the only person it is worse to have for an enemy.

"I just learned to read and write," says Frank. "I put a capitalization at the beginning of each sentence, use one for names, places, proper nouns. Like if I say to you, 'Hey, Dirt Bag,' all three words would get capitalization." And Frank put one of his big hands on the window frame, stare in without blinking at the scarfaced man.

"Hey, no offence," says the guy, make a weak smile. "I could make it worth your while to find the chief."

"Chief lives up the hill there where there's no roads, but we could walk you up easy."

The guy lean across and talk to the driver who we ain't had a good look at yet. They both turn their necks around and we guess there must be somebody in the back of the car, too.

Nobody say anything but the three doors of the Cadillac open quiet as if they had no locks and three guys step out. They all wear dark topcoats. All three is short and broad, two have slick black sideburns, while the guy in the back have hair the color of white marble. All three look to be tan although it is barely June.

The three guys are named Gino, Rocco, and Mario.

"We're Hughie, Dewey, and Louie," says Frank, who got a box with about 5000 comics on the back porch of his cabin.

"Nice to meetcha," says Rocco, who is the one with the woolly-lamb hat.

Just before we walk these here parties up to the cabins, Frank stick his head in the door of the pool hall and whistle up the David One-wound Auto Parts Co., who is my girlfriend's kid brother, and his friends Michael Bonneyville and Wilfred Robe. On days when there is nothing to do on the reserve, which is most of the time, they practice stripping down cars and putting them back together.

"Joy to watch," is how Ben Stonebreaker, of Hobbema General Store, describe what they do. "There should be an Olympic event for them to enter, 'cause I bet they is the best in the world."

The hill is steep, and the road greasy and muddy, and these dudes skid around pretty good in their slippery city shoes.

We take them to Mad Etta's cabin. Rufus run ahead so Etta is expecting us. Rufus let us in and he have the guys take off their hats and coats. Rufus set the men on two old kitchen chairs and a nail keg. We can hear Etta moving around behind the blanket partition, make puffing sounds, and other noises sound like she doing something rude to a piece of venison.

"I thought you said these Indians were rich?" say Gino, who is the older one.

Rocco just look uncomfortable and don't say nothing.

Etta waddle out from behind her sheet; she wear her five-flour-sack dress, got squirrel tails pinned down the sleeves and sides, got more elk teeth glued to her than you find in a medicine man's bottom drawer. The teeth shine like ivory in the lamplight.

Etta perch herself up on her tree-trunk chair where she look down on the three visitors.

"That will be $25 each, please," she say in a deep voice.

"What the hell for?" say Rocco.

"Old Indian custom," I say.

"Sort of a gesture of friendship," say Frank.

"You get it back if the deal go through," add Rufus.

Gino snap his fingers and Rocco dig in his inside pocket, take out a big, expensive leather wallet, and hand me $75, which I pass on to Etta.

"Now what is it you want?"

"Well, sir, we represent certain parties who have a very lucrative financial . . ."

"No. No. What's the matter with you?"

"The matter?"

"What sickness do you suffer from?"

"We ain't sick. We came to . . ."

"Don't waste your medicine man's time . . ."

"Aren't you the chief?"

"Chief!" I say in a surprised voice. "We thought you wanted the medicine man."

"We said chief," Rocco say real loud. "Where's the chief?"

"Oh, he live in Wetaskiwin. We take you right there. We sure sorry for the misunderstanding."

Rufus already handing them their coats and hats.

"How about our money?" says Rocco.

"Did the deal go through?" says Frank.

"Well, no, but . . ."

"No deal, no money, let's move right along," and we all file outside, leaving Etta, sitting in her chair, smiling up her sleeve where the $75 is sleeping.

When we get back down the hill, that big limousine suffered a certain amount of remodeling. It sitting on its rims with the hood and trunk both up and all the doors open. The radio and stereo and air conditioning is gone, along with the spare wheel, the front bumper and grill, and any engine parts that unscrew quickly.

"What's happened here?" say Rocco.

"Your car's been stripped. You never seen a stripped-down car?" says Frank, and grins big.

Rocco fumble in his inside pocket again, come out with a mean-looking gun so big it's a wonder it don't tip him over.

"You gonna put the car out of its misery?" say Frank.

"No, I'm gonna shove this up your nose and keep it there until the car is back together again." And he move toward Frank.

Frank duck around a kerosene barrel on the porch of the store. "Hey, it's a matter of capitalization, Rocco. You should understand that . . ."

Before Rocco can go on, Gino snaps his fingers again.

"It's a City car, for chrissakes," he say, "forget it. We want to see your chief and we'll pay you $25 each to take us there," he say to us.

"Why didn't you say so in the first place?" we say, and I run across the street start up Louis Coyote's pickup truck. Rufus take his $25, decide to use it to buy groceries. Gino sit in front with us, while we put Rocco and Mario in the truck box.

Everybody I know from our reserve is either real poor, plain poor, or just getting by. But that don't mean there ain't quite a bit of money around. Money that pass through the hands of us Indians, not me and my friends, but the bigshot Indians like Chief Tom and his cronies. "Pass through the hands," is how Indian Affairs people talk, when they speak to the newspaper or TV about a business venture that gone bad. And we had plenty of those.

Militant Indians yelp like hungry dogs but not much else. The ones who go along with the Establishment are the ones able to get their hands deepest into the government pockets. They first make the government people feel guilty about how us Indians been treated, then they propose a business deal; a landscaping company, a furniture-making company, a fish-packing plant, and the government put up half the money while the other half come from oil royalties held in trust for our tribe. That money come from the government, pass through Indian hands, and end up in white pockets.

Indians like Chief Tom and his friends fancy themselves businessmen, but as Mad Etta say, "It like dressing a coyote up in a suit and tie. Underneath his suit, he still a coyote. Only talent they have is for making white people feel guilty. They don't know nothing about managing money, not that they should, but they too proud to get smart businessmen to help them. Instead they take help from the first white people who offer it, which is the same people been selling Indians bad liquor, cheap clothes, junk food, and cars with bad transmissions for the last hundred years or so."

The landscaping business lost $300,000, and the furniture-making company turned out to be making furniture that was twenty years out of style: $500,000 lost. There ain't anywhere this side of British Columbia can produce enough fish to keep a fish-packing plant running, and even then the fish cost twice their worth to truck in: $1,000,000 down the drain.

Some smiling guys from Hollywood with about a million dollars worth of gold chains around their neck, sweet talk nine million dollars to make a movie about an Indian. They got a famous white actor to play the Indian, and the movie showed for about three days at theaters in Edmonton and then disappear into wherever those kind of movies go. I heard they were going to show it on TV in Italy. I guess they like Indians in Italy.

Chief Tom wearing more expensive suits these days and his girlfriend Samantha Yellowknees driving a white Porsche. Her and Chief Tom flew to Hollywood for thirty days to sign the movie contract.

Chief Tom live in a fancy apartment in Wetaskiwin, got a squawk box at the front door, a sauna bath and a swimming pool in the basement.

Samantha Yellowknees answers the door, and she, like always, wear a lemon-colored dress, make her look cool as a glass of Kool-aid. She have her hair up in a bun, and carry a clipboard.

Gino introduce himself, bow a tiny bit and kiss her hand.

"These here is Rocco and Mario," Frank say. "They're flunkies. Rocco's hobby is manslaughter," and Frank grin.

"My assistants," Gino say in a resonant voice like a priest.

Chief Tom is wearing a blue velvet smoking jacket. Their apartment got more furniture in it than a second hand store, and it even closer together. I think the Chief and Samantha must of gone through the Marv Hayden Furniture Store in Wetaskiwin and said, "We'll take one of each."

Rocco and Mario look a little worse for wear, there ain't much in the way of springs in Louis' truck and we didn't spare the bumps on the way to town.

"They're bouncing like rubber balls back there," Frank say at one point on the trip into town.

"It's good for them to be put in touch with their roots occasionally," said Gino, and he smiled by moving his upper lip up.

"Here's the deal, your highness," Gino say to Chief Tom, after
we all get settled in the living room. When he hear those words
the chief expand about an inch in all directions, and his mouth
form a self-satisfied little smile, though it try not to.

"We are, ah, brothers representing a certain city in Montana.
The city owns a baseball team, the Montana Magic of the Universal Baseball Association. The team has recently become available, and since your tribe is known to be interested in lucrative
investment opportunities, we thought we'd take the liberty of
making an approach, and since you yourself have a reputation as a
shrewd businessman, we thought we'd come directly to you."

"If he butters him up anymore Chief Tom will squirt right
across the room," whispers Frank.

If there's one thing Chief Tom understand it is flattery. I guess
that because he's a politician. I remember Mad Etta saying, "To be
a politician you got to know how to flatter and lie."

"The Montana Magic was purchased by the city in question
about a year ago. The operation has been very successful, but the
city doesn't feel it should be involved in private enterprise of this
nature . . ."

Pretty soon Chief Tom get out a bottle of brandy and little pot-
bellied glasses for everybody, even me and Frank.

At first Chief Tom try to get rid of us.

"Thank you, Simon," he say to me, "for delivering these gen-
tlemen. You can run along now."

Frank already plopped down on the sofa and got his boots on a
glass-topped coffee table.

"We'd sure like to stay, Chief Tom. We're studying this here
business management course at the Tech School, and we'd like to
see how a real professional businessman like you do things."

"Well," say Chief Tom, pointing at us but talking to Gino and his friends, "I always like to try to do everything possible to stimulate the intellects of our young people like Frank and Simon."

"By the way, my name's Silas."

"Whatever," say Chief Tom.

Gino go on to explain that there's a baseball park and land go with the team. "Very profitable," is how he describe the operation, again and again.

"What we had planned to do was drive you down to see a baseball game tomorrow night, but we had an unfortunate problem with our car out at the reserve . . ."

"Wasn't us," say Frank.

"Just send the bill to the Ermineskin Tribal Council," say Chief Tom.

"Very kind of you," say Gino. "But I think I have an even better idea. I'll charter an aircraft and fly you down tomorrow. At my expense, of course. How would you like that?"

Chief Tom expand about another inch and accept.

"And you young men are cordially invited," say Gino. "It will be a good lesson in business for you."

Boy, I never been in one of these private planes before. It seat eight people, got eight velvet seats and a bar and everything. There is Gino, me and Frank, Chief Tom and Samantha, and the pilot. Rocco and Mario get to stay behind and wait for the car to get fixed. I bet Chief Tom sure be surprised when the bill come to six thousand dollars or more for missing parts on that limousine.

"See, there it is, right down there," say Gino after he have the pilot fly right over the stadium.

That baseball park ain't exactly what we expected. It ain't in the city, but is a full two miles out of town, off a gravel road, sitting like a button on the prairies, what are wide and green for as far as one care to look.

The second time we ever seen the baseball field we was riding in the back of another limousine, and it dark, the way only the prairie can be at night. Gino stop that car, pull off the road a half mile or so from the ballpark, and we step out of the car. The air is dew-damp, and the only sound is a few insects ticking and purring. We're too far away to hear any sound from the stadium. The ballpark look like a splash of molten gold. My blood speed up, and every one of us breathe deep of the night air, what have a bite to it, even in June.

"I bet that's what the end of the rainbow look like," whisper Frank, who ain't one to be in awe of very many things.

Behind a green board fence is a small grandstand. Only way it is different from the seating along first and third base is that the bleacher is closed up so you can't toss garbage or see down to the ground. There is a tiny trailer behind the main grandstand that open up to be a concession. And there two trailers outside the outfield fence, one used as a dressing room, the other as an office and home for the managers of the team. Eight tall, silver light standards gleam down onto the field.

And boy when we get up close we see that baseball stadium, what have a name, Magic Field, is about as full of people as it can get. Gino has been saying it hold 4,000 people. "Of course," he say, "you won't expect it to be full tonight, after all this is only a Tuesday, the crowds don't really come until the weekend."

But it is full, and there three lines of people back half a block from the concession, and kids with baskets sell hot dogs, beer, peanuts, and ice cream all through the stands.

Samantha look at the ticket prices, ask again how many

people the place hold, make a bunch of chicken scratchings on her clipboard.

"Fifteen thousand dollars," she whisper to Chief Tom.

"How many games do they play a season?" ask Samantha.

"Fifty games at home, fifty on the road," answer Gino.

"How do you get more people in here on the weekend?" ask the chief. "Looks to me to be full up tonight."

"Oh, well, we cheat a little," says Gino. "We sell Standing Room tickets and people stand along the foul lines, even sit against the outfield fence."

"Three quarters of a million dollars, not counting the concessions," Samantha say toward Chief Tom's ear, and the gold of the floodlights reflect in both their eyes.

The Montana Magic baseball team get beat pretty bad. In fact, except for about three players they look like some of the teams our Hobbema Buffaloes baseball team play against in the summer. I bet our pitcher Gorman Carry-the-kettle could of done as good as the guy who pitch for the Magic.

"People come here to watch baseball," says Gino. "It doesn't matter whether the team wins or loses, although winning is better," and he smile real friendly. "But it's the game that counts, the thrill of competition. After all, this *is* America."

The Magic have orange and black uniforms, just like Hallowe'en costumes, and they play against a team from Carson City, Nevada, which I think is a long way away.

Gino get us all rooms at the Holiday Inn, tell us to charge our meals. Frank he get a date with one of the girls who sell hot dogs, keep her overnight with him. The next morning the three of us look around downtown while Gino take the chief and Samantha to "look over the financial end of the operation."

"Don't worry," Frank tell the girl who is named Cindy, or Cathy, or Candy, and is still wearing her orange and black concession uniform, "me and my friend here going to buy the team and we'll be here all summer to manage it." Then he phone room service and order up six cheeseburgers to go, in case we get hungry on the plane.

Gino see us right back to Chief Tom's apartment. He kiss Samantha's hand again, and shake hands all around. "We'll be waiting at the Travelodge for your decision," he say.

"That sound like an interesting business proposition," the chief say to Samantha, as soon as Gino is gone. "The financial incentives look propitious. I think we should recommend accepting this financial equity, when the Band Council meets tomorrow."

Samantha just go, "Ummm," and scribble madly on her clipboard.

"Chief Tom," I say, "what I wonder is, if that team doing as good as they say, why do they come looking for investors? If it's so good, there should be a lineup of people waiting to invest."

But the chief he spout some more double talk and don't even come close to answering my question. I can tell by look at the set of his mouth that the Ermineskin Indians going to own themselves a baseball team.

That's when I start to think on what Frank told that girl as a "lover's lie." Soon as we're outside I say to Frank, "Hey, if the band buy that baseball team, they *are* going to need somebody to manage it."

"You figure you could do it?"

"Both of us," I say. "One of the things I've always wanted is to get my hands on some money to spend, even if it's other people's. Remember Willard Dodginghorse? He never had a pot to piss in

or a window to throw it out of until he got to be manager of that
fish-packing plant. Inside of three months he was driving a Buick,
moved his family into a new house, and bought three Skidoos."

"Yeah," says Frank. "And that packing plant been broke for
close to three years and Willard ain't even had to look for work.
They say he put everybody in his family on the payroll, even little
Belinda who was only four months old, was drawing $200 a week
as a fish-scaler."

"We *could* manage a baseball team," I say.

"We know how to play baseball," says Frank.

"And I saved up $430 once . . ."

"Before I talk you into going someplace we never been before
and spending it all," and Frank laugh.

Lucky we was only five minutes late for the meeting next
night, otherwise it would of been over before we got there. Chief
Tom been head honcho for so long he got all his friends on the
council.

"If Chief Tom says 'Shit!' they all fill their drawers," says
Bedelia Coyote. Bedelia like to call herself a watchdog, try to
keep the chief from wasting too much money. One time we
ganged up with her and stopped him, but the chief can call more
meetings than we have the gumption to go to.

"All in favor?" the chief is saying as we come through the door.

"Wait just a minute," yell Bedelia. "I haven't finished discussing the motion. Did you have an accountant study their
books? Did you get a lawyer to check on the contract? Did you get
a real estate agent to appraise . . ." and, boy, Bedelia ramble on
about five minutes, say all the things I thought about yesterday
and a few more besides.

Chief Tom give one of his political answers which take fifteen

minutes or so and don't say one single thing. "I trust this clears up
any apprehension you might have about this investment opportunity," he finish up.

"You didn't answer my . . ."

"Shhh!" I tell Bedelia. "For once in his life Chief Tom is right.
Let him be."

Me and Bedelia generally work on the same side, so she eye me
up and down from under the blue polka-dot bandana tied around
her forehead.

"Trust us," say Frank, smiling. Frank could grin the bark off a
tree.

"Well, okay," say Bedelia and sit down.

Chief Tom stare at me and Frank, and if his face was electric
we'd be warm as toast.

Soon as the vote pass we sidle up to Chief Tom.

"I know a lot about baseball," I say, "and I study for three years
at the Tech School in Wetaskiwin . . ."

"And I can read and write," says Frank.

"And we'd like to manage this here baseball team," I say.

Bedelia curse under her breath and kick over a folding chair.

"Well, young people, I appreciate the offer, but I hardly think
you have the financial acumen . . ."

"We'll work cheap," we tell the chief.

"And it keep us off the streets."

"And if we away from home we don't get any more reserve girls
pregnant," say Frank.

"That one move might solve our birth control problems," say
Chief Tom, one eye smile just a little bit. That is the closest I ever
knew him to make a joke.

"Then you'll hire us?"

"No."

"No?"

"You young people don't understand the workings of the business world," say Chief Tom. "While we do indeed need management personnel for this baseball team, which, incidentally, will henceforth be known as the Montana Indians, there is certain protocol to be followed . . ."

"What you mean is, the jobs go to your friends."

"There are certain favors to be repaid," say the chief.

"But we got Bedelia off your back tonight. You owe us something."

"Perhaps at a future time . . ."

"What if we was to promise not to tell Samantha what you was doing last week when we seen you up in Edmonton?"

"But I wasn't doing anything. I had a business meeting at the Four Seasons Hotel."

"You know that, and we know that, but what if we told Samantha we seen you with Mary Big Drum, from the Indian Federation office. She's a pretty woman, single. Bet she'd like to get her hands on a handsome chief . . ."

"And I bet Samantha's awful hard to live with when she's mad," I say.

"On the other hand," say the chief, "I think you young men have learned one of the secrets of success in business—always have something to hold over your competitors' heads, real or imagined." He puff up his chest and call across the room. "Samantha, dear, I've decided to hire Simon and Frank to manage our new enterprise."

The first inkling I get that things ain't as they should be is from Frank.

"You know, Silas," he say, "that girl in Montana tell me that was the first night she ever work at the ballpark. She say it was the first night any of the food-selling people work there."

My stomach make a little dropping motion, like I was in an elevator.

The second sign I get that maybe we ain't heard the whole story is when an article appear in the *Calgary Herald* the week after us Ermineskin Indians buy that baseball team.

INDIANS RESCUE INDIANS

Edmonton (CP). The financially troubled Montana Magic of the Universal Baseball Association were rescued Friday by the Ermineskin Band of Hobbema, Alberta, and immediately renamed the Montana Indians. Chief Tom Crow-eye of the Ermineskins announced his band had purchased 100% of the stock of the financially troubled team. The Indians, the baseball club that is, lost over $300,000 so far this season.

The Montana Indians players have not been paid for three weeks, and player representative Stanley "Bad News" Ballantine, former major leaguer, says the team will not play until all overdue salaries are paid.

And there is another thing. It seem when we get to Montana that me and Frank ain't replacing anybody. Some lady clerk in the City Light and Power Department been managing the team.

I thought I was the only one never heard of the Universal Baseball Association, but it seem like nobody else ever hear of it too. In the sports section of the daily newspaper it show there are teams in Williston, North Dakota; Casper, Wyoming; Provo, Utah; Carson City, Nevada; and Rapid City, South Dakota—all places that ain't very big, or interesting, or close together.

I don't think most of us, including Chief Tom who think he's so smart, ever heard of the word *affiliation*. That's what the Montana Magic had lost about a month before we bought them.

We find out real quick that the other five teams in the league have what are called *major league affiliations*, and which is why last year the team was called the Montana Cubs. The long and short is that a major league baseball team sponsor the Universal Baseball Association clubs, supply young players, rent a baseball park, supply money for wages, traveling, baseball, uniforms, groundskeepers, and a few dozen other things that we never even thought of.

Without an affiliation we are an independent team and have to pay all our own expenses. It don't take us long to find out there is no way for an independent team to break even. The big league teams *expect* to lose money in places like Montana. The Universal Baseball Association clubs are called farm teams.

"I never seen a farm could slurp up money like this here business," says Frank, after we been there for a week or two. Every mail be full of bills.

And there is never any money coming in.

Lucky for us the team was on the road for the first week we was there, 'cause on the first night they were at home, after we bought up about a ton of food and hired in all the concession people from before, only nine people pay to get into the game.

By asking a lot of questions the next day, I find out that, since the city want to sell the team real bad, Mr. Gino get them to promise a day off with pay to *all* city employees if they go to the baseball game and take their family and friends the night we was brought to the park.

I put in a call to Chief Tom and suggest this here baseball team is like flushing money down the toilet, and we should maybe hire back Mr. Gino and his friends to sell it for us quick.

Chief Tom yell at me for being wasteful. "The statement I have in front of me indicates the club to be a sound financial operation. If you don't keep it that way you'll have to be replaced."

"To start with we need another $100,000 over and above what you give us already just to pay the bills," I say.

"You have a ten-game home stand," say the chief, "use the gate receipts."

I explain about nobody coming to the park.

"Nonsense," say the chief, "perhaps it was just a cold night?" Then he pause for awhile before he say, "Oh, alright, I'll send you $50,000, but then you have to manage with what you take in. It's called the *profit motif*. You have to take in more money than you spend . . ."

I just about drop the phone on the floor when I hear he going to send me that money. I guess what Bedelia Coyote and other people been telling me is true.

"You guys are so dumb," Bedelia has said to me and my friends more than once. "There's millions of dollars floating around. Chief Tom and the Tribal Council are just dying to spend money. In fact they *have* to spend money. If they don't invest the royalties and Government money, the Government take it back at the end of the year and use it for the Alberta and Saskatchewan Navy."

"Ain't no Navy in Alberta," I say. "Ain't no ocean."

"Don't matter to the Government. There's a Navy in Edmonton. Ship is called HMCS Nonsuch. Only they don't have a ship. Guys just dress up in Navy uniforms and march around in circles on a concrete lot."

"But they won't usually give us $50 when we ask for it."

"If you'd let me handle it we'd have lots of money. First you have to incorporate a society, draw up a constitution, elect officers, set up a project, get Government approval . . ."

"It's easier to steal . . ." says Frank, and I have to agree.

With the money Chief Tom send us, me and Frank rent an apartment in town, got two bedrooms, carpet all through, and a squawk box on the door. We bring our girls down from Canada and it is just like a big holiday. Frank want to buy furniture but I say no we should wait for two months see if this baseball team stay in business.

The day that baseball team get back in town two players come in, one ducking his head about a foot to get through the door of the trailer. Frank gone into town; he went to order a little sign to go on each desk in the office, one to say SILAS ERMINESKIN, the other to read J. FRANK FENCEPOST, GENERAL MANAGER.

"I'm Bad News Ballantine," the tall ballplayer say to me, and by his tone of voice I think he expect me to know who he is. I don't hardly follow sport at all, except to read headlines in the *Edmonton Journal*, and *Calgary Herald*, once in awhile.

"And this here's Benny Santiago," and he point to the stocky, dark man who follow him in. "He used to play for the Braves."

I don't have any idea what to say to these guys. I sure wish Frank was here.

"Either of you guys know Wayne Gretzky?" I say, and smile kind of foolish.

"What the hell did he say?" the tall man ask the short man. Mr. Bad News is about six-and-a-half feet tall, thin as a pole, have high cheekbones, red hair, and looks as if maybe he got a baseball stuck inside one of his cheeks.

"I'm Silas," I say. I was going to say Mr. Ermineskin, but I just couldn't bring myself to. "What can I do for you?"

He stare at me out of pale blue eyes, and I'm sure he didn't understand a word I said.

"Money," he say, "Moola, dinero, wampum."

"How much and for what?" I say real slow, and clear as I'm able.

"Our paychecks are two weeks overdue, and none of us pick up a bat until we get paid," he say, and the dark man with him nod his head up and down.

"My boss says you was paid up until tomorrow. That's what the salesman who sold us the team, Mr. Gino . . ."

"Our last checks bounced higher'n an infield pop-up," says Mr. Bad News.

I take our brand new checkbook out of the desk drawer and try and look like a manager should.

"How much do we owe you, Mr. Bad News?"

"Don't you know?" he say look at me kind of strange.

"Well, the lady who got the records still promising to deliver them . . ."

He shake his head and glare at me and then name a figure.

"That your salary for the whole year, or maybe two?" It is more money than I ever made in my whole life, even counting five-finger bargains, and all the things Frank creatively borrows.

I guess he can tell I don't believe him, 'cause he whip a sheaf of papers out of his back pocket, toss them down on the desk, turn and spit tobacco juice on the floor of the trailer.

"You just read that, Sonny. That's my contract with the Montana Magic, and you bought it when you bought the team."

I pretend to read all the *whereas* and *heretofore* words, but I can't understand any of it.

"How many players did you say was on this here team?" I ask.

He slap a hand to his forehead. "Why wasn't I happy when I was in the Bigs?" he say. Then to me, "Eighteen. Don't you know nothin'?"

"Do they all make as much money as you?"

"Naw. Me and Santiago here are the stars. The other guys are just scuffles and frauds, and club players."

"That's good," I say, open up the checkbook and write out their checks with my hand hardly shaking at all as I add the three zeroes after the numbers on the check for Mr. Bad News.

Our Indians play six games that week, lose them all, and the most people to come to a game is on Saturday when sixty-five show up.

The bill for the lights come in and it is also two months overdue and is for more than it take me to live on for a year.

Mr. Bad News Ballantine show up in my office after the last home game, say to me "Where's the bus?"

"What bus?"

"How the hell do you expect us to get to Williston, and then to Rapid City?"

I sure hate to look dumb. But I never thought of how the team traveled.

"Do you think you could call up a bus for me? You been here a while and . . ."

"You got to book the sonofabitch a week in advance."

"Oh."

"And you got to hire a driver."

"Oh. I figured one of you guys drove."

"We play baseball. Speaking of which, you should have our meal money ready."

"Meal money . . . ?" It turn out that they get $20 a day, each, in cash. And things just keep piling up like that. I have to admit I don't know anything about managing anything, and it ain't near as much fun as I thought to have a sign on my desk with my name in raised-up letters.

We finally rent a yellow school bus, have BROTHER DAVE'S GOSPEL CRUSADE written in blue letters on the side.

"Brother Dave went bankrupt," the rental man say to me.

I have to drive the bus 'cause we can't scare up a driver on short notice. Frank come along for the ride—we tell Connie and Sadie to sit in the office and that it's okay to sign our names to checks if there is bills to pay, or if they need anything for themselves.

Boy, baseball players is about as close to animals as they should be allowed to get and not be kept in cages. About all they do as we creep across the prairies in that oily-smelling school bus, is drink beer, fart, sing dirty songs, and have food fights whenever we stop for meals. They bring about two dozen hamburgers on the bus once, and Bad News Ballantine stand at the back with a bat while a pitcher name of Lumpy throw the burgers and he hit them. One time a half a bun covered in ketchup hit the glass right by my face, slide slow down the windshield, go plop right on the fuel gauge. Frank punch some guy for getting mustard in his hair. And I didn't know I was supposed to make hotel reservations for the team.

When I try to find us a place to stay, I learn that baseball players is about as welcome as Indians at big hotels. In Williston, Mr. Bad News finally direct me to the Gravel Pit Motel, where we settle everybody in for the night in rooms with linoleum floors, and beds with mattresses that sag like hammocks in the middle.

Baseball players also have a hard time getting used to working for Indians.

"Where do you Indians get all of your money?" ask that pitcher named Lumpy.

"We don't really know," I tell him, being honest. "Oil men pay the Government. Government hold our money, check how we going to spend it before they give it to us."

"They can't check very good or you wouldn't own this team," say Bad News. "Whole franchise is about as valuable as a bucket of cold piss."

"Think I could pass for an Indian?" ask Santiago. "I'd like to get my hands on some of your money."

"I used to think that too . . ." I say.

"We been poor all our life," say Frank. "When I was a kid I was so poor if I didn't wake up in the morning with a hard-on, I didn't have nothing to play with."

On the next road trip I rent us a better bus, but we run out of money on the way back from Nevada.

I try to phone the girls but a telephone lady come on the line to say that our number is no longer in service. I think the telephone bill is one of many I been pushing to the back of my desk. It take all the money we been sent just to pay off the players.

"We don't have any money to buy gas," I tell the players, as we stopped at a truck stop somewhere in Utah.

"Don't look at us," say Bad News Ballantine, after we ask if maybe they'd cough up some of their meal money for gas. They do buy me a meal, and Frank too, though they take a vote on Frank and he only win by a score of 9–8, with one player too passed out to vote.

The players say if they buy gas, they going to head the bus for California, as that the direction most of them live.

I phone the reserve, and over the Tribal Council's phone come Chief Tom's voice, but it be a recorded announcement: "This is Chief Tom Crow-eye speaking, myself and my executive assistant Ms. Yellowknees will be in Europe for the next six weeks where we will be drumming up support for Indian land claims, among potentates of the Scandinavian nations. Please leave a message after the tone."

I managed to squeeze in the word, "Help," before the operator tell me I can't leave no message 'cause nobody is there to accept the charges.

Frank then go for a walk into that Utah town, accompanied by his jackknife. He come back with a four-foot piece of garden hose and while we all drink coffee in the truck stop, Frank he become what Bad News Ballantine call our "designated siphoner."

It don't seem like much use to bring the players back to Montana, but I hate to be responsible for losing them on the road.

Frank finally siphon us all the way back to our ballpark. The first thing the girls say to us is, "They turned off the lights."

That was one bill I really mean to pay, but if I didn't pay wages, there wouldn't of been any players. So what good would the lights have been?

When the players show up for that night's game and find no lights, they corner me and Frank in our office. "Listen,

Baitbucket," is how Bad News Ballantine start his conversation with me, and I afraid for a minute that they might do us a certain amount of harm.

"Can't get no blood out of a turnip," Frank tell them, when they complain that their contracts guarantee them travel money to their hometown.

"Yeah, but I bet we could get blood out of an Indian," say Bad News, shake a baseball bat under Frank's nose.

That afternoon we sent Sadie and Connie back to Alberta with Louis' truck.

"How about if you was to help yourself to whatever is loose around here?" I say to the players. And before I even get the words out of my mouth, Bad News Ballantine got the electric typewriter off my desk hugged to him like it was his lost baby. Somebody else get the adding machine, the stapler, and a tall lamp that sit in the corner. Inside of ten minutes the trailer is empty and the players scattered like dandelion fluff. They also carried away their uniforms, balls, bats, even the bases. Seems odd to me but somebody even unscrewed and carried off the toilet seat from the dressing room trailer.

Next day, me and Frank try to salvage whatever we can.

We sell the little concession trailer for $200, and a used lumber dealer take the bleachers and fence off our hands. He come in with a couple of flat-deck trucks and a crew of men and in eight hours everything is gone, even the backstop and the scoreboard.

Early next morning we get waked up by somebody pounding on the door of the trailer. There is two tow trucks outside and a man with a sheaf of legal papers.

He is repossessing the trailer for some bills we owe. I don't bother to ask which ones. We just barely get our clothes on, and take a little food out of the refrigerator. They plant wheels under the trailers, hook on to them, and in only a few minutes there is nothing but a little dust drift a foot or two above the road and ditch.

Everything is real quiet. The sun is bright in the east, sow thistle are golden in the ditches. All that's left is me and Frank, the eight tall silver light poles, and a sky big and empty, where a couple of hawks cruise, so high they look like coat-hangers in the glare.

The Practical Education of Constable B.B. Bobowski

M e and my friend Frank Fencepost have this way of getting into trouble, no matter how hard we try to stay out of it.

I mean we try to avoid making and selling home-brew and moonshine. We figure if people want to do that it is their business. But when the RCMP come around they don't care who they make trouble for, and they *always* coming around, sometimes even with their police dog, Sergeant Cujo. That name ain't a joke, much as we'd like it to be. RCMP really call their tracking dog Sergeant Cujo, and my guess is he really get paid like a sergeant. He is one of these here German Shepherds, mean as three hangovers, drool a lot and show off his big teeth. Constable Chrétien, the dumbest RCMP in all Canada, travel with Sergeant Cujo, and the dog sit right up on the front seat of the cruiser, actually have a more intelligent look on his face than Constable Chrétien. The dog wear a little brown blanket made of the same stuff as RCMP uniforms and have little sergeant's stripes on his shoulders.

It taken us three years, but we almost got Constable Chrétien trained so that he only enforce serious laws, like big thefts, and murders where the dead person didn't deserve to get killed. Constable Greer, the old RCMP who sit all day in his office and smoke his pipe, say "If left alone things will find their own level, and the less we do to disturb the natural level the better."

All RCMPs should be like Constable Greer, especially the new human assistant Constable Chrétien have these days. The new constable is a woman, and her being around ain't a pleasure for either us or Constable Chrétien. She sign her citations B.B. Bobowski. Don't know if she have names or not. She is right out of RCMP school in Regina, and it said she graduate first in her class because she memorized every law Canada ever had, have, or likely to have, and she feel it her personal duty to enforce every one.

She also got a big mouth; she not only going to clean up all the crime within fifty miles on all sides of Wetaskiwin, she gonna "make women aware of their place in society." Some of the women she mess with is our girlfriends.

"B.B. Bobowski's so damned liberated she rolls her own tampons and kick-starts her vibrator," is what Frank says of her. We sometimes call her Ba Ba Bobowski, and make sheep sounds when we see her coming down the street. Sometimes we put the words together to make *Baba*, which mean grandmother in Ukrainian and I think some other languages too.

Constable Bobowski don't know a thing about water finding its own level. "She gonna drain the lakes and divert the rivers," says Frank.

"She has a five-year career plan," Constable Greer told us, smile real slow, blow pipe smoke at the ceiling; he got sad pouches under his eyes like a dog. "You young people are just going to have to be very patient with her; she's very ambitious."

"We all gonna get to be patient in Drumheller Penitentiary," we say. "She got to learn she can't mind the business of the whole reserve."

Constable B.B. Bobowski make it her personal project to stamp out home-brew on the reserve. She sniff around out in the dark once and stumble on Maurice Red Crow's still. She run back to Wetaskiwin for reinforcements, but Constable Greer and Constable Chrétien both tell her to wait for some serious crime. She go right over their heads to Edmonton, and about forty RCMPs raid the reserve at 4:00 a.m. the next day.

Lucky someone seen Constable Bobowski snooping around. We had time to move the still and also tear the culvert out of the road up to our cabins. We covered the hole in the road with a tarpaulin we borrow off an 18-wheeler was parked at a truck-stop on the highway.

The way we found out about the raid was when Constable Bobowski's car go nose first into the culvert hole, and the car behind ram into her, do themselves about $3,000 damage.

For all the rest of that night Constable Bobowski try to find out who to charge for taking the culvert out of the road. She even get the fingerprint man from Wetaskiwin out of bed, have him come and put white powder on that culvert, which is over four feet across and 25 feet long, try to find out whose hands have been on it. Somebody finally point out that since the culvert is on Indian land, moving it don't come under the Highway Traffic Act. Seem that there's no law against us moving our own culvert if and when we want.

"It was moved to prevent a flood," Frank told her.

"This land doesn't flood."

" 'Cause we prevent it by moving the culvert."

Constable Bobowski slap her citation book closed, sound like a gun shot. I bet at that point she wished she'd studied to become a librarian or a welder and not an RCMP.

"I doubt if she's going to be superintendent quite as soon as she plans," said Constable Greer the next day. "But you fellows had better watch out. She's mad as a wet hen."

Constable Bobowski don't give up easy. She take Sergeant Cujo away from Constable Chrétien and spend a couple of weeks brushing up that dog on how to sniff out alcohol, especially home-brew. Then she bring him to the reserve, where he go sniff-sniffing up the road between the cabins, pull hard on his leash. First thing he do is sniff out a half bottle of stale beer that been left behind a curtain on Mad Etta's window. Then he jump up and go "Bow-wow-wow," right in the face of old Esau Tailfeathers who, folks say, has been drunk since about 1947.

"Smart dog," said Frank. "He found out where we hide the home-brew."

Constable Bobowski, who could be pretty if she was to smile once in a while, stare at Frank like he was a slug leaving a gooey trail on the sidewalk. She has blond hair, cut short and watered on the sides and back to a duck-ass cut, blue eyes, and a flat little nose like a baby.

"You know, Constable Bobowski," Frank say real polite, "I mean what I'm gonna say very respectful. I bet when you take off your uniform you're a real pretty woman."

She squint up one eye and look harsh at Frank again. "When I take off my uniform I'm still a cop. And when you take off your clothes you're still a criminal. And the two don't mix. So don't try to soft-soap me, Fencepost."

"That's cruel," says Frank. "I was just trying to be nice."

"I've heard all about you," say Constable Bobowski.

"Wouldn't you like to find out if it's true or not?"

The constable just look stern and go on with her investigation. That damn dog sniff out Jarvis Lafrenierre's still, and Jarvis end up going for six months to the crowbar hotel in Fort Saskatchewan.

The other people who got stills move them deeper into the woods.

Bunch of us have a meeting at Blue Quills Hall one afternoon, try to figure what to do about Constable Bobowski and Sergeant Cujo.

"We got to stop both the dog and the woman," says Frank.

"You're being too hard on her," says Bedelia Coyote. This is what we expect from Bedelia, 'cause she is about as liberated as the constable. "She sees what a problem alcohol is on the reserve and she wants to stamp it out."

A few people go "Boo."

Bedelia is in a tough spot. She is one of us but she is also a tough woman, and since Constable Bobowski been in Wetaskiwin she helped set up a Rape Crisis Line, and she almost convinced City Council to cough up money for a half-way house for battered women, most of who would come from the reserve.

"I bet Bedelia ratted on Jarvis Lafrenierre," say somebody.

At this point I have to jump in to defend Bedelia, 'cause we know, even if she really mad with us, she wouldn't turn nobody in. No real person would ever do that.

"Can't you explain the facts of life to her?" we say to Bedelia.

"I've tried, but she says the law is the law."

If Constable Bobowski could only understand, trying to stop Indians from cooking up a little home-brew would be about as easy as arresting all the trees on the reserve, handcuffing them, fitting them all into a patrol car and driving them to jail in Wetaskiwin. I imagine Constable Greer must have told her all this, but she apparently ain't gonna let the impossible stop her from trying.

"We got to have a plan," says Maurice Red Crow.

"Which one you figure is smarter, the dog or the lady constable?" asks Frank.

"The dog," everyone shout.

That ain't the answer he was looking for, but it start Frank to thinking.

Frank decide to become friends with Sergeant Cujo. The sergeant live in a big dog house behind 12-foot chain link fencing, at the rear of RCMP headquarters in Wetaskiwin. Sometimes Sergeant Cujo is on a heavy chain so he can't get to the fence, other times he is free in the yard. When people come by he bark like crazy and run to the end of his chain, or else right up to the fence, stand on his hind legs, snarl and bellow.

Frank spend the first hour just talking soft to the dog. Pretty soon, the dog stop bellowing, stand still with his lips curled back, growl soft in his throat.

"See, he's tame already," and Frank move his hand toward the fence; the sound of Sergeant Cujo's teeth clamping together is like a bear-trap shutting.

"Well, pretty tame," says Frank, as he take a baby bottle from his jacket pocket.

Frank then rub a little hamburger on the nipple, push the nose of the bottle slowly through the fence. Sergeant Cujo sniff the nipple, then lick it good. Frank spend about two hours learning Sergeant Cujo to drink from the bottle what Frank stole from his sister Rebecca's cabin. I bet one of his little nieces is drinking from a cup today.

The bottle is full of home-brew.

After about a week, as soon as Frank come around the corner of the police building, Sergeant Cujo give a friendly "Woof!" and come bounding to the fence. He has developed a real taste for home-brew.

"I bet you got some Cree in you," Frank tell the dog.

Every day now Frank have to refill the bottle about four times from a jug he keep under the seat of Louis' truck. After four drinks Sergeant Cujo chase his tail a lot, act just as if he was a puppy again.

A few days ago, Constable Greer tell us that Sergeant Cujo bit Constable Bobowski when she come on shift at five o'clock. "We can't understand it," the constable say, "that dog is really irritable these days. We even took him to the vet but he just suggests exercising him more."

We head on downtown, smiling like we just won a lottery.

Frank also don't visit Sergeant Cujo for two days; the two days before Constable Bobowski due to bring him on her weekly patrol of the reserve.

Boy, when she arrive, Sergeant Cujo is skittish as a deer, and he snarl and snuffle like a trail bike as he strain on the leash Constable Bobowski is holding. As they go by Frank's cabin, Sergeant Cujo sniff up about a pound of dirt and jump like he been electric-shocked. He charge the door of Frank's cabin, and when Frank's little sister Cindy Fencepost open the door the dog knock her down and make footprints the length of her. He break loose from Constable Bobowski, knock over the Fenceposts' kitchen table and dive under the bed in the corner where Frank put about

40 ounces of home-brew in one of his mother's baking bowls, and then trailed a few drops out to the road.

While Constable Bobowski search the cabin and try to drag the dog out from under the bed, Frank he pour an ounce or so of home-brew on the seat of the cruiser.

By the time the constable drag the sergeant from under the bed he drank up the evidence. The dog is actually smiling; he stand on his hind legs and hug Frank like a brother.

"What you got here is a dirty old booze-sucking hound," Frank tell the constable as they walk outside.

Sergeant Cujo discover a couple of cases of empty Lethbridge Pale Ale bottles by the side of the cabin, and he lift each bottle up by the neck, drain out the last few drops.

"Sad," says Frank. "Just like a dog who suck eggs. He's gonna have to go to that big RCMP detachment in the sky."

"Maybe you could teach him to smell out stupidity," yell Frank's mother from the doorway of her cabin. "You and him could be lifelong companions."

Soon as Constable Bobowski let the dog into the cruiser, he go "Woof!" and take a big bite right out of the middle of the front seat. He grin at everybody, kind of woozy-eyed, while upholstery and foam rubber hang from his mouth.

Constable Greer tell us the next day that Sergeant Cujo been transferred to Regina for retraining, or maybe retirement.

"If a dog can get into the RCMP shouldn't be no trouble for him to get into AA," says Frank. Constable Greer crinkle up his face.

"Life will be a lot more relaxed with Sergeant Cujo reassigned," he says. And we agree with him.

But the loss of the dog don't stop Constable Bobowski from popping out from behind trees all over the reserve.

"Remember how dumb she looked the time we pulled out the culvert?" says Maurice Red Crow. "I think the way to get her is to keep feeding her phony information."

In order to do that we got to have an informant. Somebody got to continually rat to the RCMP.

"Can't be just anybody," we say, "got to be somebody who look and act the way the RCMP think a snitch should."

We consider quite a few of our own people, but none of them could ever pretend good enough. There is nobody as low as a snitch. Most people wouldn't even want to pretend they was one, even if the cause was good.

Then somebody think of Peter Lougheed Crow-eye, the Chief's son.

"He was born lookin' like a snitch," says Frank. And that's true. P.L., as we call him now, is about fifteen, fat and round as if he been filled by the air-hose at Hobbema Texaco Garage.

His father, Chief Tom, left the reserve a few years ago, have an apartment in Wetaskiwin where he live with his girlfriend, Samantha Yellowknees. P.L. always been a sissy, wear suits even when he don't have to. P.L. spend some weekends with Chief Tom, who send him to ballroom dancing lessons at Mme. Ludmilla's Dance Studio in Wetaskiwin. The Chief gave P.L. a copy of *The Rules of Parliamentary Procedure* for his tenth birthday.

Being the kind of guy he is, we were sure surprised a month or so ago when P.L. come into the Hobbema Pool Hall one night. He wearing jeans and a buckskin jacket, both of them new.

He buy three bags of Frito chips, a deck of cigarettes, ask if he can join in on our pool game. We all snicker behind our hands, but we let him, and he turn out to be almost an alright guy.

"My old man the windbag," is how he refer to Chief Tom, and he use some pretty large four-letter words to describe Samantha.

He's still too much of a suck for us to really like him, but as Frank say at the end of the evening, "He got a 50% chance of turning out human."

Now we go to P.L. Crow-eye and ask if he want to do some dangerous work for us. He curl up his lip and say "Sure." But we can tell he's scared as hell.

Next weekend when he go to Wetaskiwin, he wear his suit and dress shoes, and he get his hair cut as usual, though he'd planned to start growing his hair long like us. Still smelling of barber shop powder, he go over his lines with us at the Gold Nugget Café, then head to the RCMP office to see Constable Bobowski.

"I'm Chief Tom Crow-eye's son, Peter Lougheed Crow-eye, and I want to report a crime," he going to say to Constable Bobowski. Then he going to tell her how much he hate to see liquor on the reserve, praise her for scaring the still owners off the reserve, and tell her how he overheard that a shipment of home-brew coming to Hobbema on the southbound six o'clock train from Edmonton.

The day before, me and Frank visited Constable Greer and Constable Chrétien; they even offer us coffee. Funny, three years ago Constable Chrétien wouldn't have done nothing but stick the barrel of his gun up our noses.

"We can't tell you what's going on, but we hear rumors. We suspect Constable Bobowski going to get pretty excited about something tomorrow afternoon," we say.

"And maybe we should let her call in the troops from Edmonton," say Constable Chrétien, who been getting smarter every year he study with us.

Peter Lougheed Crow-eye, the snitch, do his job real good and that evening about 25 RCMPs, both plainclothes and uniforms, raid the south-going train when it stop at Hobbema. They search all the freight cars and make all the passengers get off. All they find is three passengers with illegally open liquor on their persons. They write out citations and go away mad. We reckon Constable Bobowski now have two strikes against her.

I heard once, maybe even read it in a book, that if you want to hide something, best place is to put it out in plain sight, only in a spot where people never expect it to be.

Right on the big wooden deck of the railroad station, has been sitting for the last month or two, a tall metal barrel, say KEROSENE in bright red letters on the side. Old Gertie Big Owl been selling kerosene, either from the station or from Hobbema General Store, for years and years. One night we hired George Longvisitor, who own a portable welding rig attached to his truck, to do certain alterations to Gertie's barrel. Now there are two hoses and two sections to the barrel and people who know can buy either kerosene or home-brew.

"If they was to have a taste-test the kerosene would win," says Frank.

But that idea I read in the book really work. If you ain't looking for something, you don't see it. One day Constable Bobowski lean right on the barrel and visit with old Gertie for about half an hour, while Gertie's filling orders for both kinds of kerosene.

My experience is that hardly anybody, anywhere, know what they're doing. The important thing is that they look the part. People listen to suits and uniforms no matter how stupid the advice. That is why Constable Bobowski believe Peter Lougheed Crow-eye when he feed her more bad information: he have that oily, well-fed, shifty-eyed look RCMPs expect from an informant.

P.L. assure Constable Bobowski that Maurice Red Crow, David One-wound, Ovide Powder, and at least two other guys not only going to ship moonshine to Hobbema, but they traveling with the shipment themselves.

She call straight to Edmonton for assistance again, and by an hour before train time there are more RCMPs than stray dogs on the reserve. Some are carrying rifles, one is even crouched behind the barrel on the station platform, and another is on the roof of the station house.

"They must have watched all the old Jesse James movies just like we did," says Frank.

We was going to sneak some water barrels onto the train when it stop a few miles up the line at Millet, just to give them a thrill. But if there is one thing we learned years ago it is that RCMPs have no sense of humor.

This time a couple of big cheese RCMPs come down in a chauffeured black car; they sit fifty yards down the street, watch as the train get surrounded from both sides as it pull to a stop.

Later, when everything has quieted down and after the RCMP didn't find a thing, Constable Bobowski get called over to that long, black car. As she walk past the station, Frank and Rufus and a few other guys lean against the station wall going "Ba, ba, ba."

I sure wish I could of heard what was said in that car. The man in the front seat was sort of barking at Constable Bobowski; I bet he ain't gonna lick her face like Sergeant Cujo would of. I guess you can't get demoted down from constable, at least and stay in the force.

After the train, the limousine, and all the other RCMPs have left, I watch as Bedelia Coyote go over to Constable Bobowski's patrol car. I been listening to Bedelia rehearse what she going to say for most of the afternoon.

"You can arrest me if you like," she going to say. "I knew there was no moonshine on that train and so did everybody else on the reserve. You been had. And you gonna keep on being had until you smarten up. You got to learn that if people ain't ready to change laws don't matter a damn.

"You know I ain't got no use for those mealy-mouths from the church, but there's a poster up in Fr. Alphonse's office at the school that say something about changing things that can be changed and accepting things that can't. Well, that poster's a hell of a lot smarter than you . . ."

Then Bedelia's gonna try to talk her into putting her energy into things she's good at. She even gonna hint the moonshine makers might contribute to the Crisis Line and projects like that.

Bedelia could end up in jail. It hard to figure if Constable Bobowski had enough schooling from us yet or not.

To Look at the Queen

I been keeping a secret for over a year now. It was one of the conditions that they let us out of jail.

"You must not tell anyone about this for at least a year," a gray-faced Englishman say to us. "There has been quite enough embarrassment of late."

He was a detective with Scotland Yard. I never was able to understand why the English police force was called Scotland Yard. It was in a big stone building, not a yard, and I'm pretty sure it was in London and not Scotland. Though maybe it is like Edmonton being in both Alberta, Canada, and North America.

How me and my friend Frank Fencepost come to get to London, England, is a story itself. I ain't very political. Me and my friends try to keep Chief Tom Crow-eye from ripping us off too badly, and we tangle with the Government over the silly rules they expect us Indians to follow. But I never been involved in this business of aboriginal rights and land claims and all that stuff, and neither have my friends. I don't understand the issues. And I'm pretty sure most of the guys involved, especially the ones who yell the loudest, don't either.

I think the charter flight to London, England, had to do with both land claims and the new Canadian Constitution. The Constitution is something else I don't understand and don't want to.

Near as I can see a bunch of smart Indians got some Government grants so they could fight the Government. And, as part of the fight, they all decide to go to England, talk to the Parliament there, maybe even get to see the Queen.

Martin Red Dog, from a reserve over near Regina, say to us in the Alice Hotel bar one night, "This trip ain't gonna change anything, but we sure gonna have a hell of a party. And how else is a whole planeful of poor Indians going to get to see England unless the Government pays for it?" And he laugh, show a gold tooth in his long bronze face.

They charter a plane to leave from Vancouver, stop in Calgary, Regina, Winnipeg, and Toronto, before going over the ocean. Going to be 180 Indians from all over Canada, Martin Red Dog tell us.

Chief Tom, though he don't even care about local rights, let alone national or aboriginal, would have liked to go, but him and his girlfriend Samantha Yellowknees already going to Hawaii for a holiday he call a research trip, at Ermineskin Band expense.

Chief Tom name the people from Ermineskin Reserve who get to go on the trip, and he pick his friends Thomas Fire-in-the-draw, Baptiste and Cynthia Wind.

"None of them could tell the Constitution from a trash can," say Bedelia Coyote when she hear. "Their only qualifications is they vote whatever way Chief Tom tell them to."

"That's the way politics work," says Frank Fencepost. "When I get to be dictator I make you a Queen, Silas here a King, and Blind Louis Coyote Prime Minister. Say, which is higher, King or Dictator?"

"Whichever you decide," I say.

The chief couldn't have picked more shifty guys than Thomas Fire-in-the-draw and Baptiste Wind. And Cynthia Wind, I think, is a cousin of Chief Tom. Thomas and Baptiste both wear old suits from the Salvation Army, hang around the reserve do odd jobs for Chief Tom, who slip them Government money some way, but even then they is still mooches, bum cigarettes, food, rides, and booze, even though they supposed to be Christian and belong to the AA.

"You hear about how Baptiste phoned up the AA one night?" says Frank.

I just smile at him knowing he don't need my answer in order to go on.

"'Do you guys take cara drunksh?' he ask. 'Why yes, we do,' say the AA person. 'Do you want to join?' 'No, I want to reshign,' say Baptiste."

"I wonder if they really going to see the Queen?" say Bedelia.

The Queen, I think, is a nice lady, and I wouldn't want to be her. Having people stare at you all day every day, must be worse than having a regular job. The Queen, considering she's white and over 50, ain't near as ugly as she could be. I do wonder though why she lets people dress her the way they do. She always look like pictures of missionaries come to convert us Indians back around 1900.

We seen Prince Philip, right up close so we could tell he was a real person, when he visit the reserve one time. He seem like a regular guy, and even show he got a sense of humor. When we tell him the buffalo we was going to ride down and kill, keeled over and died of natural causes, he say, "Well, there are some who get awfully nervous about meeting Royalty."

And later on, the Prince say to Chief Tom, "I've heard that the idea for daylight-saving time came from the Indian Nation."

"Oh, yes," says the Chief, act like he know what's going on, "we Indians are responsible for much of the progress in Canada . . ." and he talk on for three or four minutes.

The Prince wait for Chief Tom to stop, then say without a trace of a smile, "An old Indian chief set the example by cutting off one end of his blanket and sewing it on the other, to make it longer."

Me and Frank and Bedelia Coyote laugh like crazy when the Prince say that.

Chief Tom is smart enough to realize he been caught in a joke, but he don't know how to handle it. In spite of being red already he blush so much it shows, stutter and look around wishing Samantha Yellowknees was there to rescue him.

"I bet the Queen is more fun than she looks," says Frank. "She probably wears satin underwear and a black garter belt."

Later that night at Mad Etta's it is Frank who suggest we go to England.

"How'd you like to go for a ride in a plane?" he say to Etta.

"Whales don't fly," say Etta.

"How come if I said that you'd knock me through a wall?" I ask Etta, but she just grin and take a swig from her bottle of Lethbridge Pale Ale.

"I'm serious," say Frank. "I know just how to do it. If there's one thing a mooch can't pass up it's free booze."

"You should know," I say.

"Trust me," says Frank. "We can go to England for about $40 worth of liquor."

Every time Frank says "Trust me," I usually end up in jail somewhere.

But everything go just like Frank expect. The three Ermineskin delegates spend the night before the plane trip at the Palliser Hotel in Calgary. We meet them in the lobby about six o'clock, and Frank flash a 26-ounce bottle of vodka and say the magic words, "Let's go up to your room and have a drink."

By two in the morning all three of them has gone from happy drunk to roaring drunk to sleepy drunk. Me and Frank been drinking from a rye bottle full of cold tea. We stagger the three of them down to our truck and make sure they is sleeping comfortable before we find a city police officer near the hotel.

"Excuse me, my good man," Frank say to a tall police officer, peering around the rims of the big, bug-eyed, black-rimmed glasses that he wearing. "I have a very sad duty to perform," Frank go on. "There are three of my people outside in a disturbingly disreputable truck, and they are, how should I say, somewhat worse for wear from the effects of alcohol. Being a law-abiding citizen, I feel it my duty to see they don't drive and endanger innocent lives."

The constable look Frank up and down, but boy, in a suit, with his hair combed, and his lips closed over the place where he got teeth missing, Frank look like a banker or a teacher or a minister. In fact, he is clutching the Bible he stole out of Cynthia and Baptiste's hotel room.

"Thank you, we'll look into it," say the constable.

"God bless you, officer. I'm the Reverend Frank, and this is my assistant, Standing-knee-deep-in-running-water, a recent convert to the Lord's work."

"Ummm, yes," say the constable.

"The rehabilitation of our people is one of the most pressing problems facing the Indian Nation these days, don't you agree?"

I move in and tug at Frank's sleeve. I think he is laying it on too thick even if the guy is a policeman.

"Well," says the constable.

"You will be kind to them officer, for they know not what they do."

"We have to catch our plane, Rev. Frank."

"Don't interrupt your evangelist, Standing-hip-deep-in-muddy-water. You don't suppose you could spare a coupla bucks for the Lord's work, do you, officer?"

We is at the airport bright and early, tugging Etta out of the back of a taxi. I'm Thomas Fire-in-the-draw. Etta and Frank is Cynthia and Baptiste Wind. Cynthia's passport don't look anything like Etta, but we count on all Indians looking alike to the customs people.

"I see you have the same last name," a man in a blue uniform say to Frank and Etta. "What relation are you?"

"Wife," says Frank.

"Son," says Etta.

"This is your wife?" say the customs man.

"Any law against liking big ladies?" says Frank.

"You ever had to sleep in an unheated cabin in winter, you'd appreciate me," says Etta. "But my son here is a joker, aren't you, Sonny Boy?" and she crush Frank up against her until I can hear his bones crack.

"Don't be rough, mummy," says Frank through gritted teeth.

Since there's nobody else on the plane from Hobbema, we use our own names. Only other time we have to lie is at the hotel when we claim our friends' reservations.

Martin Red Dog has made contact with lots of politicians and next day we get invited to "an informal reception" at a snooty private club.

I don't know why it should of surprised us, but it did; politicians in England is just the same as in Canada. They dress fancy, have that overstuffed look about them, and is only interested in "What's in it for them."

The people who form the government, even though they is Conservatives, just like Premier Lougheed in Alberta, don't want to see us.

"We can't do them any good," says Martin Red Dog with a sigh. "You ever notice how it's always the party *out* of power who have a big interest in Indians?"

"We don't have any oppressed ethnic minorities here," a red-faced fellow with a thicker accent than ours begin.

"We used to have Druids," say a hefty, white-haired fellow in the corner, sitting deep on his neck in a leather chair, "but we murdered them all. Frightfully easier than dealing with land claims, and all that folderol."

I think he was joking, but these Englishmen keep such straight faces it hard to tell.

". . . but we do have coal miners," the first fellow go on. He wheeze considerably, like he just walked up a flight of stairs. "They are victimized and downtrodden by the industrialists. We thought perhaps you'd care to join one of our demonstrations. We're going to march on 10 Downing Street, Saturday fortnight."

"What did he say?" Frank whisper to me.

"I think he said the miners are going to demonstrate in front of the fort on Saturday night."

We thank the politician for the offer but say we ain't up to demonstrating after our long trip.

That night a couple of guys with their coat collars turned up are leaning in a doorway when me and Frank come out of the hotel to look for a restaurant.

They have sharp, musical accents and it take us a two block walk and through most of dinner before we start to understand their language.

They're from Ireland. All I know about Ireland is that they always bombing each other because they don't like the English. That make as much sense as Canadian politics, so guess things aren't any sillier over here, just a different silliness.

These fellows want us to put in a word for *their* land claim. They explain their problem to us for a couple of hours; we don't understand a word but we sympathize anyway.

"Do ye want to receive some military training?" ask a fellow whose name sound like Shamus, "we could putcha in touch with the Libyans."

"Would that be the Women's Libyans?" ask Frank. "We got trouble with them in Canada, too."

"As far as I can see, being in the military service would be worse than being in jail. I sure wouldn't want to march around wearing a uniform, having some big mean white man telling me what to do," I say.

"Just substitute Indian Affairs Department for Army, and you got our lives now," says Frank.

Shamus don't understand that we making jokes, and he

explain Libyans ain't women, but A-rabs who train guerrillas to fight, and make bombs, and hand grenades.

"I didn't know gorillas was that smart," says Frank, and even I ain't sure if he's joking or not.

"Our politicians are so dumb it would be unfair to blow them up," we tell them. "It would be kind of like killing a turkey just because it's stupid."

"And politicians ain't even good to eat," say Frank.

"All fat," I say.

These two Irish guys sure can eat, though, and drink. They put away two meals each and introduce us to dark ale, which taste a little like 10–40 motor oil, and I think cost more.

They leave us with the bill too.

"Forty-one pounds," the waiter tell us.

"Of what?"

"Currency, old sport."

"You sell money by the pound? I collected five pounds of pennies once . . ."

Together we got $20 Canadian. The waiter ain't looking for kitchen helpers. He call the police even though I try to tell him we got diplomatic impunity, which is something I read about in a newspaper. And Frank say he going to put a curse on the whole restaurant. Frank rub butter on his face, ruffle his hair, paint mustard on his cheeks and dance around the foyer of the restaurant and then down the aisles between the tables.

The police wear blue uniforms, coal-scuttle hats, and are so polite they ain't the least bit of fun. After they take us to jail, one of them phone the hotel and Martin Red Dog come down and get us after he stopped at the restaurant and paid our bill. We borrow all the money Martin Red Dog will loan us, tell him to bill the Ermineskin Band Council, and he promise he will.

We visit some night clubs after that. Frank he collect himself a girl with a bright pink Iroquois haircut.

"We are blood brothers," he tell her while he is trying to take her clothes off in the back of a taxi.

He have to tell the taxi driver about five times that we want to go to the Chomondley Hotel. Finally, the girl break in to say, "The Chumly, luv," and the driver take right off.

"You know the reason I like to ride in taxis?" says Frank. "It's the only time I get to tell a white man where to go."

That pink-headed girl have a friend, but her name is Cecily and she wearing a tweed skirt, high heels, have mousey-colored hair and is going to school to be a librarian. After I tell her I write books and she tell me she reads books, we don't have nothing to say to each other. There must be a law of nature of some kind that an outgoing person—either man or woman—have a friend who is just the opposite, that they drag everywhere, the shy person digging in their heels.

Cecily gets all nervous about going to our hotel, so halfway there we have the taxi driver change directions and go to their apartment, a flat they call it, though it ain't no flatter than any other apartment I ever been to.

Frank and his girl hop right into bed, which is behind a screen have a picture of Japanese soldiers on it. Me and Cecily play dominoes and drink tea at the kitchen table.

From behind the screen the pink-haired girl say something to Frank about birth control.

"Hey, in Canada we got a new contraceptive for men. I use it all the time; it's a pill. I just put it in my shoe. When I walk on it, it makes me limp."

The girls don't want us to stay all night.

"Use my body and then tell me to get lost, you women are all alike," say Frank. His girl don't mind making a date for the next night. Me and Cecily are glad to see the last of each other.

There ain't no taxis around and it is after two in the morning when we get outside.

"Let's walk to the hotel," I say, taking a deep breath of the sweet, foggy air.

"Hey, I know what that is," I say as we walk along, our boots clicking on the stone streets, "that's Buckingham Palace, the place where the Queen lives."

"I bet I could leap right over that fence," says Frank, point at the tall, wrought-iron fence, that is black, about fifteen feet high and have spear points on top of each bar of the fence.

"Not a chance," I say.

"Let me show you," say Frank and look all around. The streets is deserted and scarves of fog are rubbing around our ankles as we walk. "See all I do is take a run, a jump, grip with my hands and swing myself over into that there hedge."

"No way," I say. But me saying something has never stopped Frank before.

He back clear across the street, pump his feet up and down in one spot for a few seconds, run full speed at that high, black fence. He jump, but not very high, grab on to a bar and swing his body up. He don't rise but halfway up the fence and his body hit parallel to where he gripped and bang hard against the bars. What I see then is that Frank grabbed on to the edge of a hidden gate, and the weight of his body swing a section of fence back into the tall hedge. It make an opening about a foot wide for us to squeeze through.

"That was what I had in mind all along," says Frank. "I got the eyes of an eagle. I seen this here gate all the time."

The Queen's yard is like the biggest park I ever been in. There is lawn enough for a golf course, flower beds galore, and thousands of trees and shrubs. We stroll around for awhile.

"Look!" say Frank, as the palace loom up in front of us, dark gray, against a pale sky that already thinking about morning.

We walk past a place where there is about a hundred wide steps going up to somewhere. Just past those stairs is a little door, like one to a basement. Frank step down into the doorwell and try the handle. The door open.

"Come on," say Frank.

"I don't think we ought to be here," I say.

The palace is dark and quiet and our boots sound like we walking inside an empty oil drum.

The floors is either marble or carpet thick as muskeg, and the whole place smell of velvet, just like a theater. There are tiny lights high up on the walls, which are all twenty feet or more high, covered in wallpaper, tapestry, or stuff look like carpet. There are pictures all over the place, most of dark scenes of men in riding clothes, or men wearing white wigs. There are little tables in the hall have vases or glass ornaments on them.

We climb up a few floors, then down, then up. I wonder if we'll ever find our way out.

Frank he peek into a room now and then, flip on the light, then flip it off.

"This here must be a hotel, Silas," he says and I have to agree. Once I walk through the Empress Hotel in Victoria and this is about the same except the furniture is more expensive and there's more of it.

"Maybe it's the hotel part of the palace, or maybe this is what palaces is like."

Frank push open a door have a crest shaped like the Queen's hat glued to it, and turn on the light.

"Wow, look at that!" say Frank. What he is staring at is a light fixture I bet is made of real diamonds. They dazzle up my eyes and make bug-like shadows of brightness on the walls.

"Shhh," I say, and point to the bed, what covered in a silky blue spread. "Those bedcovers got a lump under them."

But I'm too late. The lump move, sit up, and even though I flick off the overhead light, must of seen us, cause I seen her. I feel like the first time I ever get arrested, like my blood is squishing along real fast and like there's ants on the back of my neck.

"Excuse me," a very English voice say out of the darkness.

"We was just on our way out," say Frank, trip over something, make a loud stumble.

There is a little click and a bedside lamp come on. I am standing by the door, my hand still on the light switch, Frank has fallen over a coffee table, is just getting up, holding at least one of his ankles.

"Whatever are you doing here?" say the Queen; she got her hair in plastic rollers, just like a real person, and I guess what I notice most is that she is small, maybe only 5'2" or so. I always thought of her as being about seven feet tall. She got her nightgown pulled together at her neck with one hand.

"You don't have to be afraid of us, Mrs. Queen. We was just passing by and thought we'd drop in," I say.

"Yes, well, you. . . ah . . . needn't be afraid of me either. In fact, you could call me . . . or . . . do you have names?"

"Sure. You can call me Chief Frank," says Frank. "And this

here is my friend Silas Ermineskin. Silas has had a book printed up."

"Four books," I say.

"How interesting," say the Queen.

"Yeah, I'm one of the better known chiefs in Canada," say Frank. "A real big wheel. Like if they was to have a King among Indians . . ."

"He's exaggerating just a little," I say.

"You're not terrorists then . . ." and the Queen let out a big breath of air.

"Constable Greer of the RCMP call me a holy terror one time," say Frank.

"We flew over here from Canada to see about the Constitution. Our leaders was hoping to see you . . ."

"I don't think this is the time or the place . . ."

"We just find our way in here by accident. We was sightseeing. We is really sorry to disturb you . . ."

"I think perhaps you'd better be going . . ."

"It must be really fun to be Queen, eh? Being able to do anything you want and all . . ." say Frank sitting down on the end of the Queen's bed.

"It's not exactly all that it's cracked up to be," the Queen say in a wistful voice.

"But you're rich. I seen you riding in cars big as house trailers . . . and they put down carpet for you . . . and you travel."

"Believe me, ah, Frank, Chief Frank, there are disadvantages . . ."

"I'd trade places with you."

"I wonder for how long?" and even in the bad light from the bedside lamp I can see the Queen make a sad little smile. "Where have you and your friend been today, Frank?"

Frank pause for a minute try to gather together his thoughts.

"All over. I can't remember all the places, but we walked about twenty miles, I bet. Seen parks and old buildings, and ships in the harbor, and we ate lunch at a restaurant where they wrap my food in a newspaper. Just tonight we been to three nightclubs, for supper we ate grapes at the Hare Krishna's house, and they wanted us to shave our heads . . ."

"You know, Frank, if you were King, you wouldn't be able to do any of those things . . . at least not without thousands of people and reporters and television crews following you around."

"I was on the TV once; I liked it."

"I wonder if you'd like to be on the telly every day of your life, and have the whole world waiting for you to make a mistake, spill your food, say something embarrassing . . ."

"Hey, I do all those things every day, right, Silas?"

"That's true," I say.

"I'm sure you do. But you couldn't anymore, if you were King. People expect their leaders to be perfect. If you stumble and spill, and say foolish things, if you show emotion, if you get cross, or angry or impatient, people lose respect for you . . ."

Frank, he light up a cigarette.

"Would you mind?" the Queen say, nod toward the package Frank about to return to his shirt pocket.

"You smoke?"

The Queen's eyes flash across Frank's surprised face.

"Are you shocked?"

"Well, no," say Frank, hold out his package to the Queen, then light a cigarette for her. "It just that you're the Queen."

"I don't smoke in public, but this *is* my home."

"Why don't you smoke in public?"

"People don't expect us to be human."

"But most ordinary people smoke."

"That doesn't make any difference."

I know what she means, but I can't explain it. People who come to interview me or talk about my books are surprised to find I'm just an ordinary Indian. I don't know if they expect me to have wings or feathers, but they want me to be different.

I remember once me and my littlest sister Delores was in the Safeway grocery store in Wetaskiwin when we meet Miss McNeil, Delores' grade-one teacher. Miss McNeil have a basketful of groceries.

"Oh, Miss McNeil," Delores say, "do you eat?"

"Where's Prince Philip?" ask Frank. "He off traveling somewhere?"

"No. His room is several doors down the hall."

"Do the public expect you not to have sex either, just because you is Queen? Boy, you'd never get me to be King if that's true . . ."

"Well, if we have sex, we certainly must never mention it. But Philip and I just find it more comfortable to have separate bedrooms."

"I'm glad we didn't open up Prince Philip's door by accident," say Frank. "I bet he would have punched us out. Maybe he even sleep with a sword under his pillow."

"We met Prince Philip once," I say. "Bet he'd even remember us. He come right to Hobbema Reserve and we stage a buffalo hunt for him only our buffalo sort of died of old age . . ."

"Oh, yes," say the Queen, and she laugh right out loud. She got a real pretty laugh. "The prince regales everyone with that story. I wish I'd been there. You have no idea how boring most social occasions are, everyone tip-toeing around, whispering, afraid everything won't go smoothly. The Prince and I have very pleasant memories of our visits to Canada."

"It gets so cold in Canada the politicians walk around with their hands in their own pockets," says Frank.

"That's another thing you couldn't do if you were King, Frank, is express your opinion. We of the royalty have to remain neutral, that way everyone is able to fantasize that we're on their side, no matter what the disagreement or argument may be about."

We visit for a while longer, until Frank notice the Queen yawn. Then he say, "Well, I guess we should get moving. We're keeping you up and all. And I've decided I won't be King of Canada even when they ask me to."

"Yes, I suppose you have other things to do, and I do have a rather busy day tomorrow. But . . . just one other thing. The Prince mentioned a . . . how shall I put this delicately? A rather enormous . . ."

"Mad Etta," we say.

"Yes, the Prince was very impressed by her . . ."

"She's here with us," I say. "Etta's traveling incogmento, but you might reach her at the Chomondley Hotel, if you was to ask for Cynthia Wind."

The Queen has got out of bed and put on flowered slippers and a Chinese-looking robe. She walk across the room and open a door that among her shelf of books, and there is a little bar. She take down three small, pot-bellied glasses what was hanging upside down like bats on a wooden rack, and she splash liquor in all three. I can tell by the smell it is brandy.

"Good luck," say the Queen, raise her glass to us.

"To the Queen," say Frank, and we all three touch glasses, making the sound like the first notes of a bell chiming.

"You should make sure you keep the doors closed at night," says Frank. "Otherwise just anybody could walk in here."

"I'll remember that," say the Queen.

"Nice talking with you," I say.

"My pleasure," say the Queen. She smile at us, and I think she mean it.

We close her door real quiet.

We would've got out without disturbing anybody, I think, if Frank hadn't decided to take home a souvenir. He pick up a long-necked vase the color of winter smoke, and as he go to put it under his jacket, it slip right through his fingers, crash in a thousand pieces on the stone floor. Guess the sound wake up whoever was supposed to be guarding the palace.

Boy, in less than half a minute, I bet we is surrounded by a whole army of policemen. We sort of get carried along just like we was in a big crowd that was going someplace.

"I feel like I been rode hard and put away wet," says Frank.

We get asked questions for hours and hours, when all we'd like to do is get some sleep.

Turn out some of them men from Scotland Yard been following us and they seen us having dinner with those Irish guys and figure sure we was there to hurt the Queen.

Neither of us say we talked with the Queen, we think they might execute us or something if they found that out. Besides, the way these men talk, the Queen might get into trouble for visiting with us.

Our pictures is all over the newspaper the next day:

INDIANS ARRESTED
INSIDE
BUCKINGHAM PALACE

Full Investigation Of Palace
Security Under Way

Canadian Indians, Thomas Fire-in-the-
draw and Baptiste Wind, were arrested at
3:30 a.m. inside Buckingham . . .

By the end of the day that information work its way back to
Canada where the real Thomas Fire-in-the-draw and Baptiste
Wind, who I guess by now is over their hangovers, show up on
TV saying they ain't never set foot out of Alberta in their lives.

The next morning, the police take us to a big room where,
along with all the pink-faced Englishmen, are three or four small
dark men. These men speak to me and Frank in languages, sound
as if they spitting out tacks and paper clips. The Englishmen talk
among themselves as if we didn't understand English. They are
trying to decide if we are Libyan, Iranian or Iraqi terrorists. Then
to make matters worse, the Palestinian Liberation Organization
claim credit for us, say we was there to blow up the Queen.

"We is just poor Indians from Canada, got lost on our way back
to our hotel."

"Can you prove it?"

"Mad Etta," we both say. They bring in Etta, but she ain't who
she says she is either, so they just put her in a cell next to ours.

I finally remember fingerprints. "We all been arrested in
Canada, plenty of times," I say. "If you was to send our fingerprints to the Alberta RCMP. . ."

"Or B.C. or Saskatchewan," say Frank, "or North Dakota or Utah."

"That will be quite enough, thank you," say the English
detective.

I never thought being arrested by the RCMP would turn out to
be a good thing. But our fingerprints prove out who we is.

Just as they about to let us go, Frank breaks the news to them that him and me had a drink and a smoke with the Queen. They don't believe us.

But after we describe the inside of the Queen's bedroom for them, they just kind of slump down in their chairs. I guess they can see themselves losing their jobs.

That's when the head of palace security say to us that if he "cuts the red tape," and send us home to Canada right away, we got to promise not to mention seeing the Queen for at least a year.

I bet we home in Alberta for a month before Etta tell us that the morning after me and Frank arrested, the Queen invite her for tea, all by herself. The rest of the chiefs and the big wheels in their blue suits get to stay at the hotel. "A guy who look like an undertaker deliver the invite in a cream-colored envelope as thick as cardboard," say Etta. They even send to the hotel, instead of a limousine, a van, where the whole side roll open and Etta able to waddle right inside without all the hassle of pushing and pulling.

She was at the palace for over two hours.

"What did you talk about?" we all ask.

Etta smile in that secretive way she have when she know something the rest of us don't.

"You wouldn't be interested," say Etta. "Just women talk. Us women in positions of power have unusual kinds of problems."

The Indian Nation Cultural Exchange Program

E very once in a while the Government tries to do something nice for us Indians. Usually it is just before an election when that *something nice* is announced. Whether it ever come about or not is another matter. Sometimes they announce a new program, then after the newspapers get tired of writing about it, they file it away, hope no Indian will ever apply.

That is the way it was with the the Indian Nation Cultural Exchange Program.

OTTAWA TO SPEND
TEN MILLION
ON WESTERN INDIANS

was how the *Edmonton Journal* headline the story, and right up until the election, whenever some sneaky looking politician from Ottawa speak within 50 miles of any Indian Reserve west of Ontario, he mention the program and the amount but be pretty vague about the details. He know that after the election that program get filed deep in a Government vault somewhere.

That would have happened to the Indian Nation Cultural Exchange Program if it weren't for Bedelia Coyote. Bedelia is famous for causing the Government grief. Not that they don't deserve it. One time the Government send 52 John Deere manure spreaders to our reserve. Nobody asked for them, and hardly anybody farm enough to want or need one. Some of my friends try to strip them down as if they were cars, but nobody want to buy the loose parts. Eventually a few of them disappear, the way a cattle herd get smaller if it ain't tended. All that happen maybe eight years ago and there are still eight or ten manure spreaders rusting in the slough below our cabins.

"They should have sent us 52 politicians," say Bedelia. "They're all born knowing how to spread manure. It keep them busy and they be doing something useful for the first time in their lives."

"Even crime wouldn't pay if the Government ran it," say our medicine lady, Mad Etta.

It is Bedelia who go to the Wetaskiwin office of our Federal Member of Parliament, a Mr. J. William Oberholtzer.

"The Conservative Party could run a dog here in Alberta and win by 10,000 votes," I say.

"J. William is about two points smarter than most dogs," says Bedelia. "I seen him tie his own shoes one day. Most politicians don't have that much coordination."

Bedelia have to go back to Mr. Oberholtzer's office every day for about three months, and she have to fill out a whole sheaf of forms, but finally they have to give her the details of the Indian Nation Cultural Exchange Program. Turn out that three people, under 25 years old, from each reserve in Western Canada, can visit another reserve at least 250 miles away to learn the other tribe's culture and teach them about their culture.

"I'll teach them how to drink," says my friend Frank Fencepost. "That's part of our culture, ain't it?"

"Unfortunately," say Bedelia.

"I don't know," says Frank, screw up his face. "I can't drink like I used to. Used to be I could really put it away. But now fifteen or twenty beers and I'm right out of it," and he laugh deep in his chest, sound like someone pounding on a drum. "Maybe I teach them how to have sex appeal instead."

"And I'll demonstrate brain surgery," says Bedelia.

"Yeah, you're right," says Frank. "Can't teach other people to be sexy—you either got it or you ain't."

"Bedelia is a little like the wind," our medicine lady, Mad Etta, say, "she slow but steady—wind wear down even mountains eventually."

Bedelia fill out another ton of forms and finally all the papers arrive for people from our reserve to apply to go somewhere else. We get out a map of Canada and try to decide where it is we'd like to go.

"How about California?" says Frank. "I hear they got good weather and pretty girls down there."

"California ain't in Canada," we say.

"Then we'll go down there and talk them into joining up with us."

We argue for a long time about different places, but we know we going to where Bedelia decide, because she done all the work so far.

"You guys ever been to the Land of the Midnight Sun?" Bedelia ask.

"We been to Las Vegas," says Frank.

Bedelia's look is so cold it could freeze us both solid.

"I'm talking about the Arctic. There's a place on the map called Pandemonium Bay, only 300 miles from the North Pole. There's an Indian Reserve there and I think that's where we ought to go."

Like Frank, I'd a lot rather go where it's hot. But I smile at Bedelia and say, "We're with you." I mean, how many times does the Government do favors for poor Indians?

I remember another time the Government decide to do us Indians a favor. Someone in Ottawa get the notion that we all need new running shoes. Everyone on the reserve. Someone must of told them that Indians like running shoes, or that we all barefoot.

To save money they do the project by mail. Everyone on the reserve get a letter, a big, brown envelope that have a five-foot-long sheet of white paper about two feet wide, folded up in it. Instructions are that everyone is supposed to trace the outline of their right foot on the paper and send it to Indian Affairs Department in Ottawa. Then they supposed to send everyone their running shoes.

We have more fun laughing over the idea than the time we move Ovide Letellier's outhouse forward about ten feet, so when he go to park his brand new Buick behind it, the car fall nose first into the hole.

There are really over twenty people in Louis Coyote's family, and there is hardly enough room to get all the right feet on the paper. The kids draw around feet with pencils, pens, crayons, finger-paint, peanut butter, Roger's Golden Syrup, and 10–40 Motor oil. Some people leave their shoes on; others take them off.

Frank Fencepost draw around a foot of Louis Coyote's horse, and of his own dog, Guy Lafleur. When the running shoes come in the mail, Smokey Coyote get four short, fat shoes, and Guy Lafleur Fencepost two pairs of tiny-baby ones.

When the Government give you something, you got to take it. Mad Etta she put that length of paper on the floor to use as a doormat. The Government write her three letters, say she got to trace her foot and send it to them. Finally they send her a letter say she liable to a $500 fine and 60 days in jail if she don't do as she's told. Mad Etta sit down on a sheet of paper, trace one of her cheeks, and mail it off. A month or two later come a letter say they only make shoes up to Size 32, and her foot is a Size 57.

The kids use running shoes for footballs. We use them for fillers on the corduroy road across the slough. We tie laces together and toss them in the air until the telephone and telegraph lines along the highway decorated pretty good. For years there was faded and rotting running shoes hang from those lines like bird skeletons.

Me, Frank and Bedelia put in applications under the Indian Nation Cultural Exchange Program, to visit Pandemonium Bay Reserve, Northwest Territories.

"Pandemonium Bay has the worst climate and the worst economy in Canada," say Mr. Nichols, my teacher and counselor at the Tech School in Wetaskiwin, after I tell him where we're going.

He go on to tell me it is almost always below zero there, and in real temperature too, not this phony Celsius nobody understands. And he say it snow in July and August, which is their nicest weather of the year.

"The ground never thaws, ever," say Mr. Nichols.

"But I bet the nights is six months long," say Frank. "I don't mind that at all. In that country when you talk a girl into staying the night, she stays the night."

It is the better part of a year before the money comes through. We are the only people ever apply under the Indian Nation Cultural Exchange Program, so everybody make a big deal out of it. There is a picture in the *Wetaskiwin Times* of some suits from the Department of Indian Affairs, present Bedelia with the check. Me and Frank are there, me looking worried, my black hat pulled low, my braids touching my shoulders. Frank grin big for the camera. And of course Chief Tom is there, stick his big face in the picture. He discourage Bedelia every step of the way, but when the time come he take as much credit for what she done as he dare to.

Bedelia is serious about almost everything. She belong to so many organizations I don't know if she can keep track. There is Save the Whales, Free the Prisoners, Stop the Missiles, Help the Seals, Stop Acid Rain, and I bet ten more. If there is anything to protest within 200 miles, Bedelia is there. She is stocky built, with her hair parted down the middle; she wear jeans, boots, and lumberjack shirts, and she thinks I should write political manifestos, whatever they are, and that I should put a lot more social commentary in my stories.

"My motto is 'Piss in the ocean'," Frank tell her when she start on one of her lectures.

In a joke shop one time I found a little button that say "Nuke the Whales" and that about turn Bedelia blue with anger. But she means well even if she's pushy. And she's a good friend.

People is sure odd. Soon as everyone knows where we're going, they start to say, "Why them?" and "Aren't there a lot of people who deserve to go more?"

"If people had their way they'd send two chicken dancers and a hockey player," says Frank. "And how come none of them ever thought of applying to go?" It is true that none of the three of us dance, sing, make beadwork, belong to a church, or play hockey.

To get to Pandemonium Bay we fly in a big plane to Yellowknife, then make about ten stops in a small plane, been made, I think, by glueing together old sardine cans. The plane feel like it powered by a lawn mower motor; inside it is as cold as outside, and there is cracks around the windows and doors let in the frost and snow. The pilot wear a heavy parka and boots, have a full beard make him look a lot like a bear. And he only growl when Frank ask him a lot of questions.

Pandemonium Bay is like the worst part of the prairies in winter, magnified ten times. Even though it is spring it is 30 below.

"Looks like we're on the moon," says Frank, stare at the pale white sky and endless frozen muskeg.

"Looks just like home," says Bedelia, sarcastic like, point to some burned-out cars, boarded-up houses, and dead bodies of Skidoos scattered about. There are gray and brown husky dogs with long hair, huddled in the snowbanks, puff out frosty breath at us, while a few ravens with bent feathers caw, and pick at the bright garbage scattered most everywhere.

Though the Government make a big deal out of our going, *pioneers* they call us in some of their handouts, and send about twenty pounds of propaganda to Pandemonium Bay, with copies to each of us, Chief Tom, Mr. J. William Oberholtzer, Premier

Lougheed, and goodness knows who else, there is only one person meet our plane.

But when we see who it is, it explain a whole lot of things, like why Bedelia has told us at least a hundred times that we don't have to go with her unless we really want to, and that she could get a couple of her demonstrator friends to travel with her, or even go by herself.

"There won't be much for you guys to do up there," Bedelia said, like she wished we weren't going.

"Hey, we make our own fun. I never been arrested in the Northwest Territories," said Frank.

The only person who meet the plane is Myron Oglala.

Myron, he is the only man Bedelia ever been interested in. He is a social worker and she met him at a Crush the Cruise demonstration in Edmonton a year or two ago, and bring him home with her for a few days. Bedelia never had a boyfriend before, so that sure surprise us all. "A woman needs a man like a fish needs a bicycle," is one of Bedelia's favorite sayings.

Myron is soft and wispy, have a handshake like a soft fruit, and, though he claims to be a full-blooded Indian, is going bald. If you ever notice, 99 out of 100 Indians, even real old ones, have a full head of hair. That is something we is real proud of. We call Bedelia's friend Myron the Eagle, which we lead him to believe is a compliment, though Bedelia know the truth.

She was as proud of Myron as a mother cat carrying a kitten by the back of its neck. And she explain to us when we get too nasty with our teasing, that her and Myron have an *intellectual communion* with one another.

"I bet you can't buy that kind at the Catholic Church," I say.

"Right," says Frank, "that's why you and him spend fifteen

hours a day in your bedroom with the door closed."

Bedelia just stomp away angry. "No reason you shouldn't have sex like everybody else," we say. "But with *Myron?*" And we roll around on the floor with laughter.

Bedelia did admit one day not long after that, that if she was ever to have a baby she'd name it Margaret Atwood Coyote.

We knew Myron was up north somewhere, but we didn't know where, or guess how badly Bedelia wanted to see him again.

"Well, if it ain't Myron the Eagle," says Frank. Myron stare at us through his Coke-bottle glasses, not too sure who we are. I sure hope he recognize Bedelia.

But we don't have to worry about that. Bedelia hug Myron to her, spin him around. She show more emotion than I ever seen from her, except when she's mad at someone.

Myron is expecting us. He have a Department of Indian Affairs station wagon and he drive us a few blocks to what look like a super highrise apartment.

"What's that?" we ask. That huge, semicircular building sit on the very edge of this tiny village, look like something out of a science fiction movie.

"Pandemonium Bay is an accident," say Myron. "Somebody couldn't read their compass, so they built a weather station here when it was supposed to go 600 miles up the pike. By the time somebody pointed out the mistake they'd already bulldozed out an airport, there was so much money tied up they had to leave this town where it was. Bureaucrats from Ottawa, who had never been north of Winnipeg, hired a town planner from New York to build a town for 3000 people. He designed and built this . . . ." What is in front of us is a ten-story, horseshoe-shaped apartment building.

"There was supposed to be a shopping center inside the horseshoe, the stores protected from the wind by the apartments. But there's never been more than 150 people here, ever," Myron Oglala go on.

"I guess it ain't very cold in New York, 'cause the architect installed an underground sewage disposal system, so environmentally sound it would even make Bedelia happy," and Myron smile from under his glasses. It is the first hint we have that he has a sense of humor.

"The sewer system froze and stayed frozen. Indian Affairs spent a few million thawing pipes and wrapping them in pink insulation, but they stayed frozen. The big problem is the pipes are all in the north wall where it's about 60 below all year round," and Myron laugh, and when he do so do the rest of us.

"Folks still live in the first floor apartments. They put in peat-burning stoves, cut a hole in the bathroom floor, put the toilet seat on a five-gallon oil drum, use the basement to store frozen waste."

"Native ingenuity," says Frank.

"Common sense," says Myron, "something nobody in Ottawa has."

Me and Frank get to stay in one of those apartments. The Danish furniture is beat to rat shit, but there are two beds, with about a ton of blankets on each. Four brothers with a last name sound like Ammakar, share the next-door rooms. We find them sitting on the floor in a semi-circle around their TV set. They are all dressed in parkas and mukluks.

"Don't you guys ever take off those heavy clothes?" ask Frank.

"You don't understand," say the oldest brother, whose name is George, then he talk real fast in his language to Myron.

"George says the local people have evolved over the years until they are born in Hudson Bay parkas and mukluks."

All four brothers smile, showing a lot of white teeth.

These Indians seem more like Eskimos to me. They is wide-built and not very tall with lean faces and eyes look more Japanese than Indian. They are happy to see visitors though, and they bring out a stone crock and offer us a drink.

"This stuff taste like propane gas," say Frank in a whisper, after his first slug from the bottle. The four Ammakar brothers smile, chug-a-lug a long drink from the crock, wipe their chins with the backs of their hands. They speak their language and we speak Cree, so to communicate we use a few signs and a few words of English. The drink we find out is called walrus milk. And if I understand what the Ammakars is saying, after two swigs you likely to go out and mate with a walrus.

They sit on the floor of their apartment cross-legged, even though the place is furnished. Ben Ammakar bring out a bag of bone squares and triangles, got designs carved on them. He toss them the blanket like dice. Him and his brothers play a game that is kind of a complicated dominoes. They play for money. Frank, he watch for a while then say to me in Cree, "This is easy. Boy I'll have these guys cleaned out in an hour. Which pair of their mukluks you like best? I'll win one pair for each of us." Frank draw his cash from his pocket and sign that he want in on the game. I put up a quarter twice and lose each time, though I don't understand the game the way Frank does. I decide to go back to our place. I've never liked games very much anyways. Frank has already won three or four dollars and is so excited he practically glowing. Bet his feet can feel those warm mukluks on them.

I watch television in our apartment. There is a satellite dish on the roof of the apartment and they get more channels than the Chateau Lacombe Hotel in Edmonton.

Earlier, when I mention the big, frost-colored satellite to Myron Oglala, he laugh and tell about how local people react to the television shows.

"*The Muppet Show* is the most detested show on TV," he say, "and the character everybody loathe most is Kermit the Frog. In local frog lore the frog is feared and hated. Frogs are supposed to suck blood and be able to make pacts with devil spirits."

"It really is no fun being green," says Frank.

"I bet the people who make *The Muppet Show* would sure be surprised at a reaction like that," I say.

"Up here they call the TV set *koosapachigan*, it's the word for the 'shaking tent' where medicine men conjure up spirits, living and dead. A lot of people fear the spirits of the TV are stealing their minds," says Myron.

"Just like on the prairies," says Frank.

About midnight I hear Frank at the door. He come in in a cloud of steam, take off his big boots and hand them out the door to somebody I can't see.

"I lost everything but my name," says Frank, hand my boots out the door before I can stop him.

"I only lost 50 cents," I say, feeling kind of righteous.

"Yeah, but I know how to gamble," says Frank.

To get our boots back Frank have to agree to do a day's work for Bobby Ammakar.

I don't like the idea of working. Just walking around Pandemonium Bay can be dangerous. Without no warning at all ice storms can blow up, and all of a sudden you can't see your own shoes, let alone the house you're headed to.

Bedelia and Myron spend all their time together. There ain't nothing for Frank and me to do except watch TV. This is about the worst holiday I can imagine. Also, nobody is interested in learn about our culture, and these Indians don't have much of any that I can see.

"They worship the Skidoo," says Frank. "At least everywhere you look there's a couple of guys down on their knees in front of one."

"You want to learn about our culture?" says Bobby Ammakar. "We take you guys on a caribou hunt."

And before we can say hunting ain't one of our big interests in life, the Ammakar brothers loaned us back our boots, and we is each on the back end of a Skidoo bouncing over the tundra until there ain't nothing in sight in any direction except clouds of frosty air.

Ben Ammakar is in front of me, booting the Skidoo across the ice fast as it will go, and, when I look over my shoulder, I see we lost sight of Frank and whoever driving his Skidoo. After about an hour we park in the shadow of a snowbank look like a mountain of soft ice cream. I think it is only about three in the afternoon, but it already dark, and once when the sky cleared for a minute, I seen stars. The wind sting like saplings slapping my face, and my parka is too thin for this kind of weather.

When I go to speak, Ben Ammakar shush me, point for me to look over top of the snowbank. Sure enough, when I do, out there on the tundra is a dozen or so caribou, grazing on whatever it is they eat among all the snow and rocks.

Ben take his rifle from its scabbard and smile. He take a smaller rifle from somewhere under his feet and offer it to me.

"I'd miss," I whisper.

If Frank were here he'd grab it up and say, "Fencepost has the eye of an eagle," then probably shoot himself in the foot.

Ben take aim, squeeze off two shots, and drop two caribou, the second one before he do anything more than raise up his head; he don't even take one step toward getting away. The other caribou gallop off into the purplish fog.

"You're a great shot," I say.

"You learn to shoot straight when your life depend on it," says Ben. "If you could shoot we'd have had four caribou."

"You speak more English every time I see you."

"We didn't know if you guys were real people or not. We thought maybe you were government spies." We have a good laugh about that. I tell him how back at Hobbema we been doing the same thing to strangers all our lives. "But if we'd of killed four caribou, how'd we ever carry all the meat back?" I ask.

"Where you figure the dead caribou is gonna go?" ask Ben. "And they don't spoil in this here weather."

"Polar bears?" I say.

"Not this time of year; they go where it's warm."

Ben climb on the Skidoo and turn the key, but all that come out is a lot of high-pitched whining and screeching, like a big dog been shot in the paw. At the same time one of them ice storms sweep down on us so we can't see even three feet away. The wind blow ice grains into our faces like darts. Ben take a quick glance at me to see if I'm worried and I guess he can tell I am. My insides feel tingly, like the first time an RCMP pulled my hands behind my back to handcuff me.

"Get down behind here," Ben yell, point for me to let the Ski-doo shield me from the wind. He get on his knees above the motor, push a wire here, rattle a bolt there.

"I know some mechanics," I say. "I study how to fix tractors for two years now."

I get up on my knees and look at the motor. I take off one glove, but the tips of two fingers freeze as soon as I do. I think my nose is froze too.

"I think the fuel line is froze up," I say.

I wish Mad Etta was here. It hard to be scared with a 400 lb. lady beside you. Also Etta would be like having along a portable potbellied stove. Etta like to joke that if she was on a plane crashed in the wilderness that stayed lost for six months, everyone else would be dead of starvation but she would still weigh 400 lbs. It true that Etta don't eat like the three or four people she is as big as.

The wind get stronger. The Skidoo motor ice cold now.

"Are we gonna die?" I say to Ben Ammakar.

"You can if you want to," says Ben, "but I got other ideas." I don't think he meant that to be unkind. I sure wish I never heard of Pandemonium Bay and the Indian Nation Cultural Exchange Program.

"Come on," say Ben, stand to a crouch, move around the end of the Skidoo.

"We can't walk out," I yell. "At least I can't; my clothes are too thin."

"Be quiet and follow me," says Ben. I sure wish I had his leather clothes. I didn't even bring my downfill jacket; I didn't expect to be outdoors so much.

I grab onto the tail of Ben's parka and stumble over the uneven tundra. We aren't even going in the direction we come from. The wind is so bad we have to keep our eyes mostly shut. I don't know how Ben can tell what direction we're going in, but in a couple of minutes we stumble right into the first dead caribou. Ben whip a crescent-bladed knife out from somewhere on his body, carve up that caribou like he was slicing a peach.

I don't even like to clean a partridge.

In spite of the cold air, the smell of caribou innards make my stomach lurch. Ben pull the guts out onto the tundra, heaving his arms right into the middle of the dead animal, his sealskin mitts still on. I'm sorry to be so helpless but I can't think of a single thing to do except stand around freezing, wonder how soon I'm going to die. Ben clear the last of the guts out of the caribou.

"Crawl inside," he say to me, point down at the bloody cavity.

"Huh?"

"Crawl inside. Warm. Caribou will keep you alive."

"I can't," I say, gagging, and feeling faint at the idea.

"You'll be dead in less than an hour if you don't."

"What's the good? The caribou will freeze too."

"My brothers will come for us."

"How will they know?"

"They'll know."

"How will they know where we are?"

"They'll know. Now get inside," and Ben raise up his bloody mitt to me. I think he is about to hit me if I don't do as I'm told. All I can think of as I curl up like a not born baby, is what a mess I'll be—all the blood, and the smell.

"Face in," says Ben.

"Why?"

"You want your nose to freeze off?"

I squeeze into the cavity, breathe as shallow as I know how, my stomach in my throat, I'm scared as I've ever been. Ben drape the loose hide across my back. It *is* warm in there.

"Don't move. No matter what," he says. "My brothers will come. I'm going to the other animal. Don't move."

And I hear his first few steps on the ice and rock, then nothing but the wind.

It pretty hard to guess how much time has passed when you freezing to death inside a dead caribou. I have a watch on, one of those $7.00 ones flash the time in scarlet letters when you press a button. But the watch is on my wrist, under my jacket and shirt, and I'm scared to make a move to look at it. I try thinking about some of the stories I still want to write, about my girl, Sadie One-wound, about some of the things I should of done in my life that I didn't. Still, time pass awful slow.

I'd guess maybe three hours. The more time go by, the more I know Ben has saved my life, even if it is temporary. Out in the open I'd be dead, and maybe Ben too, tough as he is.

Then from a long way away I hear the faint put-put-put of Ski-doos. At first I'm afraid it is only the wind playing tricks, but the sound get louder, and finally a flash of light come through a crack between the ribs and the loose hide, hit the back wall of the caribou and reflect off my eye.

I try to move, but find I can't budge even an inch. I push and push. The caribou is froze stiff with me inside.

"Silas, Silas, you dead or alive or what?" I hear Frank yell.

"I'm here," I say. My voice sound to me like I'm yelling into a pillow.

There is a ripping sound as the hide pulled away from my back. Then Frank's hand shove a jug of walrus milk in front of my face, but I can't move to grab it and he can't position it so I can drink.

"Lie still." It is David Ammakar's voice. "We cut you out with a chain saw."

I hear the chain saw start. "Buzzzzz . . . rrrrr . . . zzz," go the saw. I know I ain't frozen when I can feel those blades about to cut into places all over my body. I sure hope Frank ain't operating it.

Eventually they cut the ribs away and somebody grab onto the back of my parka and pull me out onto the tundra.

Ben is there, smile his slow smile at me; his face is friendly, but his eyes is tough. We both look like we committed a mass murder.

"I told you they'd come," say Ben, slap the shoulders of his brothers with his big mitt. I tip up that jug of walrus milk, going down my throat it feel like kerosene that already been lit. But I don't mind. It great to be able to feel anything.

"Lucky they didn't leave the search up to me," says Frank. "Soon as we got home I borrowed five dollars from Andy Ammakar and was winning back my stake, when these guys, without even looking at a watch, all sit silent for a few seconds, listening, then Andy say, 'Ben ought to be back by now.' They get up, all three at the same time, right in the middle of a round, and head out to start their Skidoos."

" 'Hey,' I said. 'Let's finish the game, and the walrus milk,' but they just get real serious expressions on their faces, and nobody say another word. We drive for miles through a snowstorm thick as milk, and find your Skidoo and you, first try. I don't know how these guys do it."

That night there is a celebration because me and Ben been brought back alive. An old man in a sealskin parka play the accordion. And we get served up food that I'm afraid to even think what it might be. A couple of men sing songs, unmusical, high-pitched chants, like the wind blowing over the tundra. A couple of other men tell stories about hunting.

Then Frank stand up and say, "Listen to me. I want to tell you a story of how I brought my brothers in from the cold." He then tell how he sensed we was in trouble, and how he convinced the Ammakar brothers to stop playing dice and drinking walrus milk, and start the search. When he is finished everyone laugh and pour Frank another drink.

"Come here," Ben Ammakar say to me. He carrying a funny little instrument, look something like a dulcimer, have only one string that I'd guess was animal and not metal. Ben pull at my arm.

"Why?" I say, holding back.

"You guys are here to learn about our culture. You and me going to sing a song to those two caribou, tell them how grateful we are that they saved our lives, ask them to forgive us for killing them before their time."

"I can't sing," I say.

"What kind of Indian are you?" say Ben. "When you open your mouth the song just come out, you don't have nothing to do with it." Ben pull me to my feet and we walk to the front of the little group.

He pluck at the dulcimer and it make a "plong, plong," sound, not musical at all. Ben sing a couple of flat notes, then make sounds in his throat like he imitating the call of some sad bird.

Frank staring around bold-faced, his black cowboy hat pushed to the back of his head. There are already two or three girls got their eyes bolted to him. "The best way to learn about any culture is to make love with their women," Frank said to me on the flight up. I bet he ain't gonna have to sleep alone for the rest of our stay here.

Ben Ammakar point at me and plonk on the dulcimer.

I've a truly flat voice and a tin ear. But it look like I've found a culture where everybody else have the same problem.

I've never felt so shy in front of a group of people. But I had a lot of time to think inside that dead caribou, and there no question it *did* save my life. I open my mouth and sing; the sound that come out is more high-pitched then I would of guessed, but flat as all the prairie. "Thank you Mr. Caribou for saving my life today. Please forgive me for killing you so I could go on living." After those first lines it is easy. Almost like when people get up and give testimonials at Pastor Orkin's church back home. Ben echoes my words, so do his brothers who sit in a circle on the floor in front of us. "Thank you Mr. Caribou for giving up your life," I sing, and as I do I raise the blood-stained arms of my parka towards the ceiling.

The
Performance

T his story came about because I read books. I read a book written by an Indian. One of the stories he told went a little like this: In maybe 1900 a bunch of Indians was at a big exhibition in St. Louis, which is down in the middle of the United States somewhere. They was hired to do a ceremonial dance, but they decide to dude-up that dance some, because at that exhibition was peoples from Africa who done really fierce dances. The Indians got to be friends with an African pygmy and he joined in their ceremony. They dressed up an Indian to look like a cannibal and right in the middle of that dance the cannibal make like he biting the pygmy and as he do blood spatter all over 'cause the Indians had killed a sheep beforehand. That pygmy disappear and all that's left on stage is blood and sheepmeat. There was thousands of people watch the dance, most believe what they see, send in police to arrest the cannibal. It was then the Indians perform a reverse dance, bring the pygmy back to life, leave the police and audience scratching their heads and saying "How did they do that?" while the Indians laugh behind their hands.

One rainy afternoon at Hobbema Pool Hall I tell my friends that story. We all have a good laugh on how they "put one over" on the white man, which is kind of what life is all about.

"I wonder if white men is still that dumb?" I say.

"I wonder if Indians is still that smart?" says Robert Coyote.

"You know," say Molly Thunder, who is just the best chicken dancer in Western Canada, "we got a letter inviting us to perform at the Calgary Stampede in July."

By *us* Molly mean her and Carson Longhorn, my sister Delores, and the group of dancing students Molly teaches. The group call itself The Duck Lake Massacre, and come crashing on stage to the bang of drums and the whack of finger cymbals. Molly's dancers is always decked out in feathered costumes and animal masks, look real scary. Audiences, even here on the reserve, always like to be scared just a little.

"Maybe you could liven up your show," says my friend Frank Fencepost. "I be your cannibal," and Frank bare his teeth, raise his arms over his head, jig around try to look fearsome.

"Sounds like fun," says Carson Longhorn, "but where would we get a pygmy?"

"They're little black midgets, aren't they?" says Molly.

That stop us all for a minute. Somebody suggest using a kid, but I bet even white people could tell the difference between a child and a pygmy.

Then a light shine over the heads of four or five of us at the same time.

"Melvin Bad Buffalo," we all yell. And we smile and slap each other on the shoulders.

Melvin Bad Buffalo is a genuine Indian dwarf. He at one time wrestled professionally. Wrestlers always have good guys and bad guys, and Melvin was a bad guy. I seen him wrestle once, when I was just a kid, at the Sales Pavilion in Edmonton. Rider Stonechild took me. Melvin come to the ring wear a black ten-gallon hat, a buffalo robe, and carry a spear. I remember that he bounced on the ropes a lot and was in a tag-team match partnered up with another Indian name of Little Beaver. They fought Tom Thumb and Pancho Villa, the Mexican Jumping Bean. Melvin Bad Buffalo pull the other wrestlers' hair and gouge their eyes when the referee wasn't looking, which seem to be all the time.

After Rider brought me home, me and Frank and our friends play wrestling-match games for a month or two. But that was a lot of years ago and Melvin Bad Buffalo ain't fared so good. He is still a dwarf, got little tree-trunk legs, and a body solid as a ham. His head is normal size, tall and rectangular as a shoe-box. He ain't wrestled for a good five years I bet, and he just hang around the Alice Hotel, sweep the floor of the bar, empty ashtrays into a gallon tin what used to hold ketchup.

Melvin's real name is Crawford Piche, and he come from our reserve. Craw, as his old friends call him, have too much of a fondness for beer, and now got the start of a sad little belly, make him look like a starving kid.

He look at us like we was crazy when we ask if he like to join Molly's dance troupe.

"We gonna do a special dance at the Calgary Stampede and we need a pygmy. You figure you could act like one?"

"How much?" is all Crawford want to know. "They give us acting lessons at Wrestling School," he say with a crooked smile. "But I was made to promise I'd never tell."

"A hundred dollars every time we do the dance, and we supposed to do it three nights," say Molly Thunder. "That's more than anybody else is getting. And that's only if Mad Etta agrees to help us, and you mind your manners with the booze "

"That old walrus Etta couldn't cure somebody in perfect health," says Crawford Piche.

"A matter of opinion," I say.

"If she's so damn smart why couldn't she do nothin' for me?" he say, curl his big upper lip, take a crooked cigar out of a box in his shirt pocket and light it.

It true that Etta didn't do anything for Crawford, but it only because she didn't try, and the reason she didn't try was because he demanded a full cure and don't even say please.

"If I'm the only pygmy available I figure I should get $500 all told."

Him and Molly argue for a while, but he do have a point. Indian dwarfs is few and far apart. Molly finally give in.

Later on we tell Etta the story.

"You figure you can make that kind of magic?" I ask her.

"Do sows have tits?" says Etta. "Is Chief Tom snow-white inside?"

About the first of June the group have its first practice. That is when they find out what I always knew—that Frank Fencepost got at least three left feet, and no noticeable rhythm.

Molly Thunder is pretty smart though. It is my job to make Frank look like a cannibal. I got books out of the library and by rubbing on charcoal and then a little furniture wax, I make Frank black and shiny as a bowling ball.

To get a costume a couple of us climb up a pole at the Land of

Eden Recreational Vehicle Center, outside Camrose, and we cut down a few of them triangular plastic flags that snap and crack in the wind. Frank going to wear a loincloth made from plastic flags.

"Loincloth got to come at least to my knee or my natural endowment frighten off the audience," Frank say, grinning. "Or else all the women will be rushing the stage." He stop for a minute. "Might not be such a bad idea at that."

When she find out Frank can't dance a lick, Molly Thunder take a chalk and draw two footprints on the stage, she then teach Frank to fit his own feet over the drawings. She have him stand like a weightlifter flexing his muscles, a calf-skull rattle in each hand.

"We're going to give you a permanent so you have fuzzy hair for the performance," Molly tell him. "All you have to do is bounce on one spot on the stage just like you were on a trampoline."

It is also my job to get Melvin Bad Buffalo ready for the dance. I call him Melvin to his face, 'cause I figure he like that better than his real name. I figure it best if I'm on the good side of anybody I got to rub down with charcoal and floor wax.

Still, Melvin usually show up for rehearsals hungover, unshaved, and as Frank say "Mean as a goat with a sore dick."

But when he want to Melvin can dance like hell and the program shape up real fast.

We into the second-last week when Molly Thunder have Mad Etta come to rehearsals. By that time most everybody know their dance steps. All that is left is for Frank to attack Melvin Bad Buffalo, and for Etta to make that dwarf disappear in a splatter of blood.

Too bad Melvin Bad Buffalo is such a mean dude. First time Frank come up to him on stage, put his hands on Melvin, reach in as if he going to bite his neck, the professional wrestler in Melvin react. At least that's what Melvin said after he broke Frank's choke-hold and fling Frank over his shoulder. Frank get his wind knocked out and it about half an hour before he's ready to try again. He is about the palest-looking cannibal I ever seen.

Melvin throw Frank at least once on each of the first three days they practise together.

"We ain't gonna need no phony blood," says Frank. "We just use Melvin's. I'll bite the head off him just like he was a chicken . . ."

"You're just the geek to do it," says Melvin.

They throw real punches at each other until we pull them apart. Frank come out on the short end of that fight too.

But if we thought we had problems with Frank and Melvin, they ain't nothing compared to what happen after Mad Etta arrive on the scene.

Etta's job is to sit in the middle of the stage, on her tree-trunk chair, just like a queen, be decorated like a public Christmas tree, with furs and feathers and elk teeth. It take me and Rufus Firstrider a whole day to put super-strength casters on her chair so Etta can be wheeled around the stage. The dancers going to twirl and rattle all around her. There will be some cut-up meat hid under her costume. Frank and Melvin is to fight and while the dancers block off the audience view, Melvin Bad Buffalo going to be hid under Etta's dress, the dancers will run off stage wheeling Etta on her chair and all that will be left is Frank, all covered with blood, and a few pieces of meat people can believe used to be part of Melvin.

"We'll play it by ear after that," says Molly. "Audiences today are used to blood and guts on TV and in the movies; they may not give a care about what we done. If they don't make a fuss we don't do the second part of the dance."

Backstage on the first day Melvin say to Etta, "Listen you old elephant, let's get it straight that I'm only doing this for the money . . ."

"I thought I heard a voice," interrupt Etta, stare straight ahead over the top of Melvin's head. "Sound like that little polecat Crawford Piche. Anybody seen him around lately?"

Crawford-Melvin jump up and down to make himself seen.

"Oh, it *was* you talkin'," says Etta. "I thought maybe your mind might have growed up, even if the rest of you didn't. But I guess not. You was always dumb as a salt lick."

"You gonna get shot for a moose one day . . ."

Etta reach down and pick Melvin Bad Buffalo up by the biceps, lift him until they is face to face.

"It ain't nice to talk to your medicine lady in such a rude way. We going to work together. In fact you gonna be hid under my skirt . . ."

"If I knew that was part of the deal I never would of agreed. I'd rather be under a granary with seven skunks . . ."

"So if you want to live long and die happy," Etta go right on, "and have us use pig meat in the act instead of dead polecat, you better start being nice to know."

If Melvin's stare have heat to it, Etta would be fried golden. And though he don't talk back I bet he sure thinking rude thoughts.

We put on the show at Blue Quills Hall the last week of June, do everything but use the blood and pig meat. While Frank and Melvin act out their fight, all the dancers have their feathered bustles facing the audience, block off the view real good as Melvin get slipped under Etta's long, buckskin dress.

"Have to kill off a whole herd of moose just to cover that old woman," Melvin say, but never when Etta is within hearing.

When the dancers move aside there is Frank all alone, beat his chest like it was a drum, with Melvin nowhere in sight. The audience seem to like the dance.

So do the organizers at the Calgary Stampede who make us preview the act for them. They make everybody do that 'cause one time they got surprised by a stage act what have naked dancing in it. Seems people in Alberta aren't up to seeing anybody naked. Churches and newspapers kicked up a stink for months about that so now every act get looked at by representatives of the Stampede, a church minister, a school board member, and somebody from Alberta Culture, an organization that sometimes gives money to artists and writers as long as they promise to be unsuccessful. We don't even disappear Melvin at the Stampede preview.

"Look at the school-board lady," says Molly, "she likely to think there something nasty going on under Etta's skirts. Less these people know the better." And she's right, the school-board lady got a face like a dried apple and wear a green hat shaped like a sieve, have little wild roses growing out of it.

"Be nice to me, old woman," Melvin say to Etta before almost every practice, "I been known to play with matches," and he smile showing his bad teeth.

Melvin in his own way been sucking up to Mad Etta for the last couple of weeks, hoping I guess that she give him some medical attention. He bring her a bottle of beer a couple of times, and he give her a barrette for her hair, shaped like a butterfly. He claim he found it on the street, though my girl, Sadie, saw him buy it at the Woolco Store in Wetaskiwin. Can't say as I blame Melvin for wanting help, guess nobody likes being a dwarf. But he still act like it is something Etta owes him, just because he's there.

About two hours before we due to perform the dance for the first time, on the big outdoor stage at the Stampede, in front of 20,000 or more people, Melvin he go on strike.

"I want you to work some medicine on my body," he say to Etta, "or I ain't goin' on stage."

It hard for me to understand people like Melvin. Even though he live his life in a white world, when the chips are down, he believe in the old ways and medicine.

"First," say Etta, sitting like a bear, way up on her tree-trunk chair, "it take me a week or more to prepare, and second, I never been able to change the way people was born. I can cure most sickness if the sick person believes in me . . ."

But Melvin don't let her finish. If he was just a good judge of character everything would of been okay. I can tell Etta is weakening, and she, in another minute, especially if the word *please* squeezed itself out of Melvin's mouth, would have agreed to at least try to cure him of some of his ills.

But Melvin Bad Buffalo don't see any of that. All he sees is a big, old woman tower over top of him, and he jump around like a kid who don't get his own way, call Etta every nasty name there is, plus two or three he invented himself.

When he finished swearing at Etta, Melvin decide to leave. But me and Frank and ten or so other people won't let him. He put up a certain amount of struggle, but we lock him in a box, big as a garbage dumpster, what used to hold everybody's costumes.

The time for the dance arrive. Rufus push Etta's chair on stage, while Etta hold Melvin by the shoulder, steer him along. Melvin look mean as any pygmy ever did.

The P.A. system announce the Duck Lake Massacre from Ermineskin Reserve, Hobbema, Alberta, and all the dancers rush on stage in a wave of color and a screech of sound. And the Mystical Dance of the Ermineskin Warrior Society be underway.

The drums throb loud and the dancers clatter around the stage, whirl, whirl, spin and swirl. Frank leap out, look so fierce he even scare me a little. Even Melvin Bad Buffalo dance like his pants was on fire.

The part of the circle at the front of the stage break open, now look a little like a horseshoe; Melvin and Frank circle each other, while above them, on her chair, Etta sit like a stone statue of a god.

Frank leap in and bite Melvin's neck; blood spurt ten feet in the air from the sausage skin Etta filled with something red and hid under Melvin's collar. The dancers stop running and rattling; they tiptoe around in their moccasins. The audience gasp when the blood splash, and the whole place get quiet.

Frank and Melvin finally lock together, Melvin scream a couple of times, and somebody in the audience answer him. The dancers close in around them, bustles toward the audience, rattles crackling like lightning.

I wheel Etta's chair off stage, pulling it straight back from where I been hid behind it. The dancers part again and there is Frank covered in more blood than most people care to see, chewing on a dripping piece of meat, that people might assume was part of Melvin Bad Buffalo, who, I hope, is comfortable and behaving himself under Etta's skirt.

The dancing stops. All the dancers including Frank take a bow.

But it is plain to see the audience don't know whether to applaud or not.

"Half of them are in shock," says Etta, peering through a crack in the curtain.

One of the Stampede people who previewed our dance, has already arrived back stage, and is saying to anyone at all "What are you people trying to pull?"

The dancers all race off stage.

"I think we better do the second half of the dance," says Molly. "They fell for it."

The stage manager is tearing his hair. "You tricked us!" he yell at Molly. "There's no second half to your act."

"There is now," she says.

Suddenly there are about six blue-suited policemen back stage.

"We want to question the cannibal," says one of them.

Frank has put a blanket over his head and all that showing is his shiny black feet.

"Where's the little guy?" says another cop.

"We're going to bring him back to life right before your very eyes," says Molly. "Let's roll, guys," she yells, and the dancers all start quivering their rattles and thrumming their finger-cymbals.

The dancers charge onto the stage, all but running down the stage manager. I push Etta out.

"Where's the little squirt?" says Etta.

"I thought you had him," I say.

"Said he was going to the bathroom."

"Oh, oh," I say.

Frank dancing on his spot, waving pig meat in the air. He is supposed to slip the meat under Etta's chair, pull out Melvin Bad Buffalo. The dancers dance. They close up the circle. I push myself straight back until I'm off the stage. A policeman is soaking up blood with his handkerchief.

Melvin ain't nowhere to be seen. One of the cops has his gun drawn.

When Frank reach under Etta's skirt, he sure surprised to find nothing under there but Etta. The cops round us up, take us all to jail, tell us we stay there until they find Melvin alive and *in one piece*. Ever wonder how long it take to track down a dwarf in Calgary during Stampede Week?

The Bear Went Over the Mountain

"It ain't right that you get to prepare your stories in advance, Silas," my friend Frank Fencepost say to me. "I have to make mine up right there in the Welfare office."

Actually, my friends make more money from the Welfare each month than I make from all the books I had printed up, but having books printed up make me ineligible for Welfare. Somehow it don't seem fair. Only good thing is, I sometimes get invited to travel someplace to read my stories to an audience.

Just this week I got an invite to read at a college in Vancouver. They sent a letter say somebody called the Canada Council in Ottawa will pay me $200 and my air fare. All the reserves I know of have Tribal Councils, so I figure this Canada Council must be run by Indians. And probably rich Indians at that.

Boy, I never even guessed how much it cost to fly me from Edmonton to Vancouver and back. I went to two travel agencies in Wetaskiwin, two more in Edmonton, and then right to Air Canada itself, but they all want the same amount of money;

exactly the same amount the college say they going to get the Canada Council to advance me.

"How much you figure it cost to drive to Vancouver and back?" I ask Frank.

"Fred Muskrat drove there once and he said it took three tanks of gas each way. We'll take a little moose meat, and a .22 to hunt rabbits; we can make it a pretty cheap trip."

I already told Frank the college promise to put me up in a hotel and buy me food while I'm there.

"We'll take our girlfriends and make it a really good party," says Frank.

I kind of frown up my face.

"Hey, colleges is rich," says Frank. "They won't mind if you bring your friends along."

I figure that's true. But we really was just going to take our girl-friends: Sadie and Connie. But when we tell Mad Etta our medicine lady where we's off to, she stare at us real wistful and say, "You know, Silas, I always wanted just once to see the ocean before I die."

None of us ever seen the ocean. Me and Frank was to Las Vegas once; we seen Utah, Montana, and a couple of other states, but no ocean.

It pretty hard to turn down Mad Etta, not just 'cause she weigh 400 lbs. and might throw me through the screen door of her cabin if I make her cross, but because she look soulful when she ask.

Pretty soon me and Frank is loading Etta's tree-trunk chair in the back of Louis' pickup truck, and rigging up a canvas to keep the wind off her as we driving over the mountains. Etta's all decked up in a bear-skin coat make her look pretty large. "If we was to plant a few trees on her, a whole troop of boy scouts could go hiking," whisper Frank.

When they learn about the trip, lots of our friends, and especially my littlest sister Delores, want to come with us. But we say no to everybody.

The money from the Canada Council arrive, just like the man in Vancouver, a Professor George Something-or-other from Simon Fraser University, say it would. Professor George say he writes books, too, but I never heard of him. We got a guy called Simon Fraser live right here on the Ermineskin Reserve; he sure is surprised to learn he got a university named for him. We can't very well say no when *he* ask to come along, and if we taking our girlfriends, no reason why he shouldn't take his.

Simon Fraser is short and wide, wear a 10-gallon black-felt hat, and a wide belt with a turquoise buckle. His girl is Lucy Three Hand. Lucy ride the rodeo circuit and is one of the best lady cowboys on all the Prairies. She is pretty, too; slim, with skin the color of floor wax, and always wear a scarlet bandana tied in her hair. She is a champion calf-roper and carry along her coil of rope.

Then Mr. and Mrs. Blind Louis Coyote decide to come, too. Louis he own the truck, and he ain't never seen the ocean neither. Mrs. Blind Louis figure if she was to duck Louis' head in the ocean water it might bring back his eyesight. They dress up in their mackinaws and climb under Etta's canvas, even though we offered to let them ride in the cab.

The first part of the trip through Calgary and Banff ain't so bad, but then the mountains get higher and even in low gear Louis' old truck groan and puff something awful getting up them long hills. But it roll down the other side pretty easy. The brakes ain't working so good, but the truck's always stopped before. Although it ain't always had Mad Etta in the back on a downhill grade.

Near this town called Revelstoke there is a hill about 10 miles long. About halfway down, when I touch the brake my foot go straight to the floor. At about the same time Frank point out that behind us is an RCMP car got his flasher turning.

As we traveled we was singing that old song about the bear went over the mountain, you probably heard it:

> *The bear went over the mountain*
> *The bear went over the mountain*
> *The bear went over the mountain*
> *To see what he could see*
>
> *But all that he could see*
> *Was the other side of the mountain*
> *The other side of the mountain*
> *The other side of the mountain*
> *Was all that he could see.*

Instead of slowing down we picking up speed, and I swear the flashing light on the RCMP car look mad. The girls is still singing but in pretty small voices, 'cause they holding on real tight.

We go faster and faster. As we come around a curve I can see the town down in the valley, look as if I'm seeing it from an airplane. Somebody in the back is slapping on the roof of the cab. I see a sign say "Runaway Truck Exit One-Quarter Mile." It make me glad I can read.

Only trouble is that between me and that exit road is a flat-bed truck got a Caterpillar riding on it, go only about 40 mph. There is a whole string of traffic coming *up* the hill toward us. If I was one of them Dukes of Hazzard I'd jump my truck right over the flat-bed, or drive under it, but real life ain't like that. I head into the oncoming traffic and hope they is smart enough to pull over.

We skin around the truck, even lose the RCMP what been driving like he was glued to our bumper. A sports car coming toward us miss us by about a foot, make a buzzing sound as it pass, like a bumblebee going by my ear.

But our troubles ain't over yet. Sometime while we was passing the flat-bed we miss the runaway-truck exit.

"Pastor Orkin, where are you now that we need you?" yells Frank.

We going 85 mph and picking up speed. I guess the only thing that save us is Louis' truck so old it can't go no faster. Even though we go around a corner on two wheels, and I see Etta's tarpaulin come loose and it flap like a parachute above us, I manage to keep the truck right side up until I see a service station at the bottom of the hill. The entrance is on an upgrade, but not enough . . .

We shoot through the air for about 40 feet, land with a crash and head for a gravel pit, that I can see is full of water. At the last second I cut the wheels and we swing in a wide arc, spray gravel all across the front of the service station, break the window like it was machine-gunned.

I look at Sadie, Connie and Frank. We is all pretty pale.

"Were you scared?" I say to Sadie, who still clinging to my arm.

"Only thing I worry about," says Frank, "is I heard once you could turn white from fear."

The RCMP is sitting right on my bumper. I get out of the truck, my knees wobbly as a day-old calf. I see my littlest sister Delores was in the truck-box after all. I guess she hid behind Etta's chair, or just behind Etta.

"That was fun, Silas," she says with a big, missing-toothed smile. "Let's do it again."

"You're under arrest," say the RCMP.

"We sure do want to thank you for guiding us down the hills there," says Frank real innocent. "Ain't every officer who would be able to see we was in trouble . . ."

That constable look around to be sure it is him Frank is talking to. Frank heard a line on the TV one night: "You never get a second chance to make a first impression," and he been practising it every chance he get.

The constable has pink cheeks and a fuzzy brown mustache, look like it made of weatherstripping. After he check and find we really had no brakes, he decide to let us go. "I'm gonna call the Game Warden, though," he say. "I don't think you're allowed to carry a bear in the truck-box without a muzzle."

"Tame bear," says Frank.

"My little sister's pet," I say. "Smarter than the average bear, too."

"This here's Simon Fraser," says Frank. "Got a university named for him."

"Grrrrr," says Etta from under the tarpaulin.

It take most of our money to get the brakes fixed, but the rest of the trip go pretty smooth.

First place we go in Vancouver is the hotel where the university supposed to have bought me a room. I seen a hotel like that in Las Vegas one time: mirrors all over the place—people who live in hotels sure must like to look at themselves—carpets soft as muskeg and snooty people everywhere, with oiled hair and frozen smiles.

"Snotty Towers," says Frank.

Turn out we is three days early for my reservation, which is only for one night anyway.

"How about if we stay tonight?" I say. "We worry about three days from now when it get here."

The lady desk clerk have on a pink jacket, her hair is blond, and she could be pasted right to a magazine cover she look so pretty.

"Who is *we*?" she ask, giving me a fishy eye. "The reservation is for a Mr. Silas Ermineskin. One person, one single room."

"Right," I say. "I'll just send my family here down to skid row, soon as I let them have a look at the room."

"I don't think that will be possible, Mr. Ermineskin."

And I guess that she is about to call in reinforcements, when Frank push himself up close to the counter.

"Boy, I bet there's some roses someplace fistfighting to see if they can smell as good as you," Frank say, and stare right into the eyes of that girl in the pink jacket.

I expect her to tell Frank not to be so smart, but she don't. Instead she stare him back fish-eyed for half a minute or more before she break into a big smile.

"Thanks," she say. "I bet there are two garbage cans someplace fighting to see which one can smell most like you," but even though she tries she can't say that in a nasty way.

"What time do you get off work?" ask Frank. And that girl tell him.

"You just drop up to my friend's room. If I ain't in make yourself at home. It'll be worth the wait."

Behind us Frank's girl, Connie, got her hands on her hips. "How you figure I'll look with that blond wig on my belt?" she ask.

"I don't think that's a wig," I say.

"Not yet," say Connie.

Frank turn around to her and whisper. "Hey, I'm just doin' a good deed. I'm gonna sacrifice my body so we all have a place to stay." And he put a finger to Connie's pouting lip.

"If I catch you together you both gonna have dimes on your eyes," say Connie.

About this time Mad Etta come waddling through the double doors.

"I'm growing moss on my north side from being out there in the rain," she says. "What's takin' you so long?"

The pink lady give me the key.

Boy, do we have a nice time. I learned how to use this here room service when me and Frank was in Las Vegas. We have them send up drinks, and then we all go to the dining room for supper. Delores have a red-colored drink called a Shirley Temple, which I guess must be named for a church of some kind, and all the chocolate sundaes she can eat; they bring the sundaes to her on a silver dish so tall she have to kneel on her chair just to get at it.

Frank borrow $20 from the girl on the desk, give it to Connie so she can go shopping. And while the rest of us eat, Frank rests in my room with the blond-haired girl.

In the morning the desk clerk, who by now is a man, but smell just as good as the lady, is worried about all the charges we made. When Frank discover he could make long-distance phone calls, he spend a certain amount of money trying to reach Morgan Fairchild. He knows if he could just talk to Morgan Fairchild he could get a date. "I just describe to her how I come to be named Fencepost and she send me a ticket for the next plane to California."

"Don't worry," I tell the clerk. "This is all paid for by Simon Fraser University. And this guy over here *is* Simon Fraser." Simon take off his black hat and bow to the clerk.

Out on the street it is warm but pouring rain. We head to the Indian part of town, but we forgot it was Sunday and there ain't no bars open so we got no place to meet any friends. Seem to me Vancouver ain't much different than Edmonton or Calgary. Somehow I thought people wouldn't be so poor where the weather was nice. And that people would feel better about themselves where the country was warm and beautiful. But there's more winos and street people than I ever seen anywhere.

"I want to walk in the ocean," says Mad Etta. And so does Delores. Mrs. Blind Louis still want to dip Louis' head in the salt water.

"Where's there a good beach?" we ask an Indian man lean on a parking meter on East Hastings Street.

"What you want is Wreck Beach," he say after a long pause. "Hear tell they got nude bathers down there."

"I'm all for that," says Frank, jump up and down some.

"I show you where it is if I can come along for the ride," says the fellow, who take about a full minute just to say that sentence.

"You stuck on 33 rpm or what?" says Frank.

The fellow just smile; he do that slow, too, and tell us his name is Bobby Billy, and he come from a place sound like Sasquash.

"So how do you Flat-face Indians like Vancouver?" Frank ask Bobby Billy as we drive along.

"We don't like being called Flat-face Indians," say Bobby Billy. "I'm a Squamish Indian, come from up in the mountains there," wave toward the big peaks look down on the city.

"Hey, I don't mean no offence," says Frank. "It okay if you want to call us Big-tall-handsome Indians. We don't mind."

Bobby Billy's face break into another slow smile and I see we going to be friends. He have me drive through the grounds of "The University," which I guess to be Simon Fraser. We drive a road that goes right through the middle of a golf course, and then we park where we can see the ocean for a long ways, just like it was prairie.

We get out and Bobby Billy stare at our licence plates for a long time before he say real slow, "I hear the government here in B.C. give all the bum drivers yellow licence plates," and he try to keep his face serious.

Some people are already making their way down a winding trail to the beach.

"If you go down there, how are we gonna get you back up?" Frank ask Etta.

"You let Etta worry about that," she say. "I'm not gonna get this close and not dip myself in the ocean."

"Raise the water level by five feet," says Frank, but quietly.

The sun has come out and the ocean waves look like they full of sequins. There is lots of people on the beach and in the water, and just like Bobby Billy said, off at one end is a section where people have no clothes on. We are the only people there who ain't white.

"First Indians should have had stricter immigration laws," says Bobby Billy.

Frank go clomping right over to the nude section of the beach, although he wearing lumberjack boots, jeans, a couple of shirts, a mackinaw, and a cowboy hat with a green feather stick up over the top.

"Smells like bad fish," says Blind Louis, facing into the breeze, his nostrils spread wide as he take in the air.

"We gonna dip your head in the water, find out if it make you see again or not," says Mrs. Blind Louis.

Mad Etta has waddled over to the naked side of the beach, carrying her tree-trunk chair; she set the chair down and it look from where I am as if she taking off her five-flour-sack dress.

"I don't know what everybody so excited about," says Connie. "Everybody is always naked under their clothes."

Then she draw in her breath. "Look at that!" she say, point at a man who is even more natural than everybody else. "Wow! Paint it silver and you got yourself a hell of a flashlight," says Connie.

Lucy Three Hand, the lady cowboy, has brought her rope and is practising throw lassos over Simon Fraser.

"I wish I could go in the water," says Delores, "but I don't have a bathing suit."

"You could go down to the far end of the beach there, where people have no clothes on," I say. But Delores look at me like I just broke her favorite doll, sniff up her nose just like she was a Christian, let me know in language I didn't even know she knew, that she is "grossed out" by naked people.

Frank run down the beach like he was an animal of some kind, let Lucy Three Hand rope him. Quite a crowd gather around to watch. The water has worked its way up to Mad Etta, and she sitting down on the sand, let the water splash over her big brown toes.

Sadie and me walk back up the path, holding hands. For quite a while we walk around the university, look at the big buildings, try to guess which one I might do my reading in. Me and Sadie enjoy the sunshine and soft grass, kiss each other some. I think I agree with Bobby Billy, who say on the way out here, "Weather in Vancouver's so good, only way the old-timers could start a graveyard was to kill somebody."

But when we get back halfway down the hill where we can see the beach, it look as if a riot taking place. All the Indians is gathered in a circle and surrounded by white people.

"That sure ain't the way it's done in the movies," I say to Sadie as we pick our way down the trail. Some dudes in their altogether is holding Frank in the air. Everyone is yelling.

"Keep your filthy hands off our women," one of the men say.

"I got *invited* to touch," Frank is saying while he kick the air.

Mad Etta is wet all over, her hair slicked down like it been oiled. She is pointing her fist at a group of men in green shirts, who are trying to say something to her—apologizing, I think—but she ain't listening very closely.

Bobby Billy and Simon Fraser stand off to one side, Bobby smile kind of secret as if he know something we don't.

Lucy Three Hand twirl her rope in a circle, while the yelling just keep getting louder and louder.

It is then that a policeman come along. At least he wear a uniform and carry a gun. I can't figure if he's RCMP, a Park Warden, or only one of them Commissionaires, who are mostly old army guys who like to have a job where they can push people around.

The policeman sure don't have any trouble making up his mind about who is wrong.

"You're under arrest," he say to Frank.

"Like hell," yells Connie. "He wasn't doin' nothin'."

"You too, sister," says the cop.

At this time Mad Etta pick up one of the green-shirted men and toss him into the ocean.

"What's happened?" I say to Bobby Billy.

Bobby take about 30 seconds before he answer me and another 30 seconds to speak his sentence: "Those men are from the

Greenpeace Ship, spend all their time saving whales. They took poles and try to roll yonder big lady into the ocean."

At least I understand why Etta is angry.

"See how you like it," Etta is saying.

"Assault Causing Bodily Harm," says the uniform, point at Etta. "I'm taking you into custody, sir."

Etta pick up another greenshirt and heave him at the cop, who just manage to duck. I bump the constable's arm and his gun fire into the air.

All of a sudden that uniform got his gun pointed right at my nose.

"Disturbing the Peace, Assaulting a Police Officer," he say at me.

I can smell the hot barrel of the gun. Then it ain't there anymore, 'cause Lucy Three Hand roped the constable, and his hands is tight to his sides as if he standing in a broom closet.

"Back off!" Frank yell at the white people. "Boo!" And they back up a step or two. The green-shirted men all run off carrying their poles. Sadie collect Mr. and Mrs. Blind Louis from where they been in the ocean.

"Just because I'm blind don't mean my eyes can't feel," Louis is saying.

"If it don't hurt, it don't do you no good. You'll probably be able to see tomorrow," say Mrs. Blind Louis.

Lucy got the constable trussed up like a pig, and someone else taken his gun and tossed it in the ocean. But I notice he talking into the walkie-talkie in his shirt pocket, more screaming than talking.

We all head up the trail to the cliff-top, three or four of us pushing on Etta's back. Turn out when Etta is angry she can climb hills pretty good.

It is while we loading up the truck that about 10 cars surround us: RCMP, Park Wardens, University Security, and a truck from Customs and Immigration.

We all get arrested, but me, Frank, and Mad Etta more than anybody else.

"At least we don't have to worry about how we going to pay for a hotel," says Mad Etta, wring salt water out of the skirt of her five-flour-sack dress, in the back of the police van.

In court the next afternoon, the police, some lawyers and a judge have a meeting for about 10 minutes at the front of the courtroom.

The judge stare over at Etta a couple of times. "They really thought she was beached?" I hear him say. The judge tell us if we promise to head right back to Alberta he dismiss all charges.

We promise.

"I'm sorry I keep such bad company, your honor," say Bobby Billy. "I never hang around with Alberta Indians again. From now on I just associate with regular murderers and thieves."

"See that you do," says the judge.

It take us the rest of that day and part of the next to find Delores, who because she was a kid, was kind of repossessed by some social workers. They took her to Victoria for some reason and we had to wait around while they found her and flew her back.

"I got to eat in a restaurant, and ride on a ferry, and fly in an airplane that land on the water, and they bought me a doll . . ." Delores say in a rush when she first see us. Delores, I guess, wasn't half as worried about us as we was about her.

After we get Delores back I realize I'm a day or two late for the reading I was supposed to do. We first go to the wrong university;

I never even thought there could be two universities in the same city. It take us a couple of hours just to find Simon Fraser University, and even then I have to park the truck on a lawn because all the parking lots is full.

"You were supposed to be here last night," that Professor George yell at me, when I finally find his office.

"I can read today; it don't make no difference to me."

"There were 180 people here last night and you didn't show up."

I don't think Professor George would want to know the real reasons, so I just tell him I'm late because I still think in Indian time. "I don't know what you're so upset about," I say. "I got here within a couple of days of when I was supposed to," and I smile real innocent.

"You won't get paid unless you do a reading; not that you deserve to," says Professor George, "but I'll arrange for you to read in the Faculty Lounge at noon."

I read a story to 20 or so professors, shabby-looking men with piercing eyes. Most of them could pass for winos at a Salvation Army meeting. I heard once that a story writer got to be dead before they find out who you are at a university. Guess that's true, 'cause these guys don't laugh where they supposed to, and is more interested in staring at Mad Etta and Lucy Three Hand than in hearing me.

On the way home Mad Etta pull a soggy $50 bill from her moccasin so we don't have to play gas-and-run at a service station. We buy some Cheezies and Fritos and ice-cream bars and somebody start singing "The Bear Went Over the Mountain."

"Smart bear would of stayed home," says Etta. And I have to agree.

Dancing

P astor Orkin from the Three Seeds of the Spirit, Predestinarian, Bittern Lake Baptist Church, sure been getting himself and his church a lot of publicity lately. Come Saturday night there going to be a big burning at the church grounds: records, books, newspapers, magazines, tapes, even some clothes that the church don't agree with.

On the front page of this week's *Wetaskiwin Times* is a picture of Pastor Orkin all dressed up in his white church dress, his arms raised up over his head, with a big fire burning behind him. The picture was from a wiener roast the church held a year or two ago, but it go pretty good with the headline which read: LOCAL CHURCH TO BURN ACCOUTREMENTS OF EVIL.

Me and my friend Frank Fencepost and our girlfriends was at that wiener roast. For us Indians, what religion we is depend on who is holding the church picnic. Me and Frank and Connie and Sadie and sometimes quite a few of our friends been to every church-sponsored pot-luck supper, pancake feed, or beef barbecue within sixty miles, ever since I been old enough to drive Louis Coyote's pickup truck. In return for free food we is willing to put up with whatever these church people got to throw at us.

Pastor Orkin at first used to run something called the Wayside Fundamental Baptist Church of the Fourth Dimension. He only had about six people who followed him and they didn't even have a church but used to meet in the Sons of Sweden Community Hall over near Camrose. In those days Pastor Orkin work in the accounts payable department of the John Deere Tractor Store in Wetaskiwin. Then he hook up with a couple of little old ladies who build the Three Seeds of the Spirit Church. They build it with money their dead brother earned from bootlegging, but they never know that. At first the old ladies hold their services in the morning, while Pastor Orkin have his in the afternoon. Now, them old ladies is in a nursing home in Wetaskiwin. I guess they give their church to Pastor Orkin.

Of all the religious people we come in contact with, they mostly all make a try at converting us Indians at one time or another, these fundamentalists is the strangest. "I think we just don't know it," say Frank, "but I bet the churches get paid a bounty for every Indian they convert. Instead of our ears they send in a form to the government and collect a dollar or so. Why else would they be after us the way they are?"

A lot of the time I think Frank is right. What is strange about these fundamentalists is that they *don't* want us. "God is hate," is how Frank describe what Pastor Orkin preach. And he preach it longer and louder and wilder than any of the other churches. He hate Indians, Catholics, Jews, all foreigners, and everybody who don't believe exactly like he does.

We check to be sure there going to be good food before we go near Pastor Orkin. Funny thing is that the mean-looking little women with red hands and bony knuckles is the best cooks around.

"Would you be a better cook if we gave up sex?" ask Frank. We all laugh at that, 'cause Connie can't even burn water. One time somebody at her house won a pound of coffee. Connie'd never seen anything but instant coffee in her life, so she just put a spoon of the real coffee in a cup and poured hot water on it.

"Tasted like mud-pie coffee we used to cook up when we was little kids," says Frank.

"Which would you rather have, good biscuits or good lovin'?" ask Connie.

Frank grin. "I'll steal the biscuits; you just stay fat and sexy."

Pastor Orkin and his church really *don't* want us as members. They claim we going to hell because our skin is dark. That should make us stay away, but it don't. Pastor Orkin and his followers is kind of like little kids trying to act bad by saying dirty words. No matter what they say, it comes off sounding foolish.

And it makes us feel good when we give them trouble.

"Hey, Pastor Orkin," Frank say, "you figure people with sun tans going to hell like us Indians? I mean they got dark skin just like us."

"Of course not," says Pastor Orkin.

"But how can you tell the difference between a white man with a dark sun tan and a pale Indian? Aren't you afraid you'll make a mistake?"

"The Lord knows the difference. The Lord is all-seeing."

"Yeah, but how can *you* tell which is which? I mean if I was locked up in a church for a year or two, I might get as white as you. Then wouldn't you feel bad for not lettin' me join your church?"

Frank give Pastor Orkin a bad time every time we visit their church. Their ads in the *Wetaskiwin Times* and the *Camrose Canadian* always say *everybody welcome*. Bet they'd really like to add *No Indians*, but there may even be a law against them doing that.

"Why do you insist on turning up where you're not welcome!" Pastor Orkin yell at Frank one Sunday.

"My stomach can't tell if the strawberry shortcake is Catholic, Lutheran, or Four Square," says Frank.

Frank he figure we should start our own religion.

"We could steal a few chairs, put them in that empty storefront by the Alice Hotel. We'd put up a sign say Church of the Holy Fencepost. I'd get me a white sheet to wear, and I'd just stand around with my arms raised saying, 'Bless this here Fencepost.' Silas, you could read from the Bible, and Connie and Sadie could sing 'I Saw the Light,' and Robert Coyote and Eathen Firstrider would take up the collection and slap everybody on the side of the head who didn't give at least five dollars."

We first hear about the burning over the radio. We always listen to CFCW 'cause it play all country music; bad thing is they play too many hymns, and in the evenings there is evangelists who beller for an hour or two at a time. They also let local ministers talk late at night and that was where we heard Pastor Orkin.

"Tell us again why you're going to burn all these things, Pastor Orkin," say the announcer.

"There is enough temptation in the world without young people being exposed in such a direct manner as by listening to Rock music, or dancing. And believe me dancing is temptation. A dancing foot and a praying knee do not belong on the same leg," yell Pastor Orkin.

I've always wondered if a lot of people who go to church are deaf. If that is why most ministers yell. Or if the people is deaf because most ministers yell.

That statement about the foot and the knee is the funniest thing we heard for a long time.

"I wonder if it's alright to have a praying foot and a dancing knee," says Connie Bigcharles, and we all laugh until we got tears in our eyes. But listening to Pastor Orkin is scary too, 'cause these religious peoples is never satisfied just to follow what they believe; they want to force their ways on everyone. It strange how something can make you angry, but make you laugh at the same time.

Late Friday night, after we been in town for a movie, we drive past Pastor Orkin's church. *The Church of the Open Heart* is what the sign say across the top of the double doors. But underneath there is a padlock the size and thickness of a slice of black bread.

Outside in the yard is a round-topped signboard list the hours for services and stuff. Also behind that glass is a photograph of Pastor Orkin flashing his big, wide, store-bought teeth, and with his store-bought hair falling over his forehead. When we first knew Pastor Orkin he was almost bald and had pointy teeth with black spots on them.

"Why didn't you just pray for new hair and fat teeth, instead of spending money on them?" Frank ask him one time. Pastor Orkin sure didn't like that 'cause there were a lot of people standing around after the service.

Frank take a look at that padlock.

"Want to go inside?" he ask. "Hell, I could open this lock with my dick."

We nod our heads, and it take Frank all of ten seconds to spring the lock.

Inside, the main floor is just like most churches, a few rows of blond-wood benches, a red carpet down the middle aisle, an altar, flags, mirrors, stained glass, and crosses all over the place.

The basement is just like Blue Quills Hall on the reserve—a polished hardwood floor with basketball, volleyball, and badminton courts drawn on it. There is a stage with toys scattered all over, and some blue velvet curtains partway closed, with little kids' drawings pinned on. The place smell of varnish, running shoes and wet mittens.

It is a few minutes before we see that the stuff to be burned is behind the closed part of the curtain. It heaped up to six feet high in some spots: books, records, tapes, clothes, toys, sports equipment.

"I wonder how come these holy people own so much evil stuff?" says Frank.

On shelves at the back of the stage is the church's own collection of records and books. They also got a tape deck and an expensive stereo set.

"Let's put on a record and I'll dance," says Connie. "If Pastor Orkin is right, I'll be struck by lightning and the rest of you can convert. I'm willing to take the chance," and she sway back and forth some, wiggle the toes of her cowboy boots.

"No. This is their place," I hear myself saying. "Even if what they believe is crazy, they got rights."

Connie wrinkle her nose at me and Frank make a rude noise, but they don't turn on the record player.

"Look at this book," call out Sadie. "It's called *Birth Control Through Prayer*."

"All you got to do is hold that book between your knees and you'll never get pregnant," says Frank.

There must be over 500 record albums on shelves along the back wall, most of them hymns, sung by choirs and quartets, and lone people, all of them white, and all resembling the people who attend the church. There is one whole shelf of records that is nothing but sermons by beefy looking preachers, wear blue suits and have lots of oiled-up hair.

"Look at the people on this record jacket," says Frank, "long dresses, no make-up, all scowling . . ."

"And those are just the men," says Connie.

"Hey, Silas," yells Frank. "You know why Pastor Orkin and his friends never have sex standing up?"

"No, I don't know, and I probably don't want to," I say.

"Boy, look at all this stuff they're gonna burn," says Sadie. "Here's a Willie Nelson record, and a Merle Haggard, and a Dolly Parton . . ."

"And here's a tape by *Abba*," say Connie, "and one by *Kiss*, and here's the *Beatles* . . ."

"Here's one by Johnny Cash. I thought he was religious . . ."

"Not enough, I guess."

"Let's carry off as much as we can," says Frank. "We can sell what we don't use." But me and Sadie say no.

"It is *their* stuff," we argue. "They should be able to do what they want."

"But look at this sweater," says Connie. "I bet it cost fifty dollars. It's a real crime to burn it."

"I guess it would be okay to exchange," I say, "as long as you leave yours."

Connie and Frank have their clothes changed in about a minute. I even exchange my running shoes. I sure wonder why they was gonna burn the ones I'm wearing now.

Just as Frank's about to lock up the door, I notice one of my new shoelaces is about worn through.

"I'll be right back," I say to my friends, run into the church and down the stairs into the basement.

Come Saturday night, a truckload of us drive up to the Three Seeds of the Spirit, Predestinarian, Bittern Lake Baptist Church, to see the goings on. We ain't the only curious ones. I bet all of the church's one hundred or so members is there, and so is a TV crew from Edmonton, a lot of newspaper and radio people, and a couple of hundred folks from around Wetaskiwin, Camrose, and even Edmonton, all come to see the burning.

There is a young guy, 17 or 18, got a long, straight face like a horse, is standing by the big pile of stuff to be burned. A lady TV reporter pick up one of the record albums and stare at the cover.

"This is a Lawrence Welk album," she say to the young guy, who have his hair brushcut, and wear a white shirt, tie and jacket. "What could you possibly find offensive about Lawrence Welk?"

"Must be that he plays *champagne music*," calls out Connie.

"Well, ma'am," that young fellow say, "it's just that that kind of music is conducive to dancing, and dancing sort of reminds us of sex . . ." and he pause for a long time.

"I can never figure out why these church people got so much against sex," says Connie. "It's fun and it's free and there ain't no tax on it."

"What I can't figure is how these types ever get any kids," says Frank.

"I bet they order them up from the Sears catalogue," says Connie.

"They just phone the stork and put in an order for a religious baby," says Frank.

"One of these books is a *cookbook*," says the TV lady. "How do you explain that?"

"They use wine in some of the recipes," the boy reply, and there ain't even a flicker of a smile on his face.

Religious peoples and people who get elected to their jobs always take the world deadly serious. They never guess that by being so serious they make most people laugh at them.

"How can you deny music?" the TV lady go on. "It's like denying the birds, or the wind. Do bird songs remind you of sex?"

I bet that boy wishing Pastor Orkin would rescue him, but the pastor know when to make himself scarce.

"Yeah, how about the wind?" says Connie. "Careful or it'll blow in your ear and get you all excited."

"What are *those*?" the TV lady say, pointing to a couple of big cartons that stuffed to bursting with clothes.

"Satan's apparel," say the boy, again with a straight face.

The reporter picks up a few of the pieces. "These are just blue jeans, and sweaters, and shorts, and a bathing suit."

"They cause prurient thoughts," says the boy.

"What's that?" says Connie, sticking her face in so she's sure to be on TV.

"Unclean thoughts. Sexual thoughts."

"I thought clothes was supposed to," says Connie, smirking at the boy and wiggling her hips. Connie's jeans is so tight Frank claim he can count her pussy hairs through the denim.

The boy stare at Connie and get all red; he swallow hard, his adam's apple running up his throat like a golf ball.

A while later the fire bloom up in the night sky, the flickering flames make people's eyes flash red. Each member of the Three Seeds of the Spirit church take a turn carrying some books or records or tapes up to the fire. Some of them are farmers wearing suits too short in the sleeves and legs, or farm ladies in dull dresses or baggy pant-suits, the real ugly kind like the Queen wears. But mostly they is young people: boys who ain't used to wearing suits, and pale girls in plain, ankle-length dresses, their long hair reflecting the firelight.

These people sure wouldn't like it if anyone suggested they was dancing. But they are. Sure as they been born with rhythm in their bodies.

Pastor Orkin arrive in his church dress. He stand on the church steps and pray some, but in a voice can be heard a mile away. He only allow each person to carry one object on each trip to the fire. The pastor know that when you got a good thing going you make it last as long as possible.

"Brother Sylvester," he call to the horse-faced boy, "bring the record player out here. We will play some joyful music and sing our praises for a job well done."

There is already a record on the turntable when brother Sylvester, carrying an armful of albums, wrestle the record player into place, trailing a long orange extension cord. Pastor Orkin turn up the volume, and what they call joyful music blast out into the night. The church people walk, trot, even run up to the fire, all to the beat of that music; they feel the pulse of it, the vibration.

Pastor Orkin carry some of the last records toward the fire; he spin them into the flames like frisbees, smiling his biggest and most self-satisfied smile.

"There goes Willie Nelson," call Connie, and all of us clap our hands right along with the church people.

As they getting ready to start burning the clothes and sports equipment, Pastor Orkin change the music. He take a record out of the jacket for *Great Hymns of the Western World*. But when he set down the needle what come out is an outlaw country singer name of Johnny Paycheck singing a song called "Take this Job and Shove it!" Pastor Orkin rip the needle off the record, stare around more wild-eyed than usual, then bound up the steps like a big dog and disappear into the church.

A few seconds later, from deep in the church we can hear him howl like the devil just kicked him in the shins. On the steps, brother Sylvester is taking records from their jackets, reading the labels in the firelight and not looking happy.

Frank stare at me for a long time before his face break into a big smile, as he realize that he ain't the only one capable of playing a trick now and then.

Real Indians

I knew Hogarth Running Eagle when he was just plain Martin Johnson, who got kicked out of the Tech School in Wetaskiwin for carting off 49 slide rules and two dozen pocket calculators and selling them from a divider at the parking lot of the Wheatlands Shopping Center in Camrose.

"Hell, I figured pocket calculators was supposed to go in your pocket," and he grin wide and friendly, his eyes narrowing as if a light shining in them. "And them slide rules slid right along after me as I was leaving the building."

Martin worked on a combining crew for a month, earn over $900, buy himself two expensive suits, a blue one and a black one, some white-on-white shirts, and he let the clothing salesman pick out his ties for him.

"Back when I was ignorant, it was hard to tell the difference between quality and color. See, I would have picked bright ties—yellows, reds, greens; I had my eye on a pink one," and he smile that thousand dollar smile of his again. "See when I went to apply for a job as a car salesman, the sales manager said, 'I like the way you're dressed, understated, expensive but not garish. Most Indians would buy a $300 suit and then stick a $10 piece of plastic Indian jewelry around his neck.'

"'I'm not an ordinary Indian,' I told him."

And he wasn't either.

"I'm an entrepreneur now," say Hogarth Running Eagle.

"What? You changed tribes? You ain't a Cree no more?" say Frank.

"No. I'm a businessman, but a special kind with a whole lot of irons in the fire."

He sell cars like the word no wasn't one he knew the meaning of. It was while he was selling cars that he changed his name.

"It gave me an advantage. You got to take every advantage you can get. I mean, Martin Johnson doesn't have any class. When I told customers my name was Hogarth Running Eagle, they had new respect for me. They trusted me. I mean, if you can't trust a poor, downtrodden, native Indian to sell you a good car, who can you trust?" and he smile crooked, showing how his teeth been capped.

While he was selling cars he started managing an Indian Rock band called *Redcrow*, and they got to be well known at least at the Royal Hotel Bar in Edmonton.

Since then he's sold water softeners, roofing materials, and have a crew of guys hawking discount coupons for restaurants give two meals for the price of one.

Then somehow he get interested in the travel business.

"I just said to myself one day after I seen all those ads in the window of a travel agency for Europe, Asia, Hawaii, the Bahamas, 'I bet people from far away would be interested in seeing Indian Reserves.'"

His company is called Reservation Enterprises Ltd. "We Take Reservations to See Reservations," is his slogan.

I think maybe Hogarth Running Eagle is a bit ahead of his time. But he is super enthusiastic about what he is doing. And he got some big wheels in the travel industry interested too.

"Here is what is gonna happen," Hogarth say to about a dozen of us at Hobbema Pool Hall one afternoon. "The people who sell holidays are the travel agents—so I talked the Department of Tourism into sponsoring a tour of this reserve, not for tourists but for travel agents. The World Travel Convention is in Edmonton, and next week we going to bus down a hundred Italian travel agents to see the reserve. If they like the idea there could be thousands of tourists here next summer and then we can expand to other reserves all across Canada and the USA."

"Why would we want tourists?" ask Frank.

"One word," says Hogarth, and he smile even wider than he usually does. "Money."

"*I* can relate to that," grin Frank.

"There is going to be two classes of tour," Hogarth go on. "The regular tourists stay in the Travelodge in Wetaskiwin or if they're real rich in the Chateau Lacombe in Edmonton, and we bus them down to the reserve to look around. The more adventurous ones, they get to stay with an Indian family, sleep in your house, eat with you . . ."

"I hear Italians like spaghetti," says Frank. "They'll be happy to find out Kraft Dinner is the national dish on Indian Reserves."

"No. No. You got it all wrong. Any place where we're gonna house a tourist will get special food allotments. You'll serve venison steak for breakfast, maybe badger stew for lunch, and roast moose for supper. We'll get the places cleaned up too, send down a maid service from Wetaskiwin, and we'll loan you dishes and bedding . . ."

"In other words the tourists get to see what you want them to see?" I say.

"Of course. That's the way it is all over the world. You guys have hardly been anywhere but tourists get the idea everywhere they go that the people are happy, eat good, and dance folk dances every day. And that's what they want to think. Look, I'm in show business. Fencepost, you're an actor, a liar, a thief, you understand that."

"Thanks for the good words," says Frank. "I understand what you're doing. What I don't get is why these foreigners want to come to see us anyway. I mean nobody in Canada want to come to our reserve. Even we don't like living here very much."

"It's the romance of the unknown," say Hogarth, bite the end off a flashlight-sized cigar. "Silas, you read a lot. There must be some places you'd like to visit."

"I'd like to see these here pygmies in Africa," I say.

"You figure the pygmies would like to see you?"

"Probably not."

"Right. They don't think they're unique. They hunt and fish and just try to survive. But we think they're special, and if you had a lot of money you'd pay to go look at them and their villages, taste what they eat, see them dance."

"I hear you," I say.

"Italians, Germans, most Europeans think you're unique. They've read bad books about Indians, seen American movies, looked at romantic pictures of Indian life. They'll pay good money to *experience* Indians first hand. And I'm here to cash in on their desires and see that you guys cash in too. Now Silas, if you went all the way to Africa to see a pygmy village, you'd be disappointed as hell if you found them wearing T-shirts advertising rock-and-roll singers, watching TV, and eating fast food, wouldn't you?"

"We might be able to cooperate a little," I say.

Bedelia Coyote, who we sometimes call the Queen of the Causes, because she is in favor of so many things, get all excited about the tourists coming.

"The way to retain our culture is to share it," she say. "We demonstrate our crafts, our dances, our foods, our music, and by doing so for the public we keep the customs alive and convince young people to carry on our traditions."

Sometimes I worry about Bedelia. She is so political and socially conscious she getting to sound like a politician. I don't know how wide the line is she walking on but I'm afraid she is going to fall over and by trying to be the *best* of *us*, she going to become the *worst* of *them*.

First thing she does is sweet talk Mad Etta into being a tourist attraction.

"Just like Mt. Eisenhower," says Frank.

"Only larger," I say, looking around to be sure Etta is not within earshot.

"Etta will take visitors to the woods, show them how to gather roots, leaves, herbs. Then she'll show how to cook with herbs and how to make simple medicines," Bedelia say to Hogarth. We have brought him to Etta's cabin.

"Etta knows the recipe for Kentucky Fried Chicken," says Frank. "She can name all 11 herbs and spices."

I read somewhere that Kentucky Fried Chicken made with

black pepper, salt, and one other thing that I can't pronounce. So I guess the Colonel did have a secret recipe after all.

"Excuse me," say Hogarth staring right past Etta as if she don't exist. "Listen, Silas, I know you understand, so maybe you can explain things to the old woman over there and what's-her-name." He don't have any idea how lucky he is to have Bedelia on his side. "It's a matter of concept, see. I mean, I'm not questioning her ability. I'm sure she's good and all that, but she doesn't look like a medicine man. I mean, first of all we need a *man*, a handsome old man who *looks* wise, and knows how to wear buckskins and elk-tooth jewelry.

"You know what I mean, man. He can babble away in Cree and you or Frank or me, we can translate anything we feel like. You tell the old woman to go back to brewing her herb tea, I'm sure she'll understand."

Etta rumble deep within herself like the beginning of a rock slide.

"Oh, she'll understand alright," I say.

"Good," say Hogarth, dismissing the idea of Etta. "Now, that old blind man you showed me sitting on the porch of the General Store, Louis, wasn't it? He'd make a great medicine man. We'll dress him up and, he just has to sit and look wise. Blind draws a lot of sympathy, you know what I mean?"

"Do I get to keep the clothes?" is the first question Louis Coyote ask when I tell him what Hogarth Running Eagle wants to do.

I take it on myself to tell him, "Sure."

"Boots, too?"

"You only got one leg, Louis."

"Boots," Louis insist. "Hand-tooled, have eagles and arrows and maybe some Cree writing on them. Eustace Sixkiller made a pair like that while he was in prison. I've always wanted them."

It take two meetings between Hogarth and me before he agree to boots. "As long as they're Indian boots," he say, "maybe we can get the bootmaker to demonstrate his craft?"

I make it clear I ain't approaching Eustace Sixkiller. He is as mean a dude as I've ever known. Did time for manslaughter, and he carry an eight-inch awl, called a Saskatchewan toothpick, in each boot. He use them like tattoo needles, make somebody he don't like bleed like a fresh-water spring.

"Okay, forget the bootmaker," say Hogarth. He then spend an extra hour explain just what he want from us. "I want you to think Indian," he tell us.

"I belong to a Back to the Land group," say Bedelia. "It led by an old Chief, a man who know all the old ways. They live 80 miles back in the hills, hunt and fish for food, live in tepees, make their own clothes. You could show them off . . ."

"No. We don't want anything that primitive. Those people would be poor, maybe smell bad. What we want is a . . . a happy medium."

One thing we find is Hogarth want that happy medium to happen *now*. He should know that us Indians like to think things over for quite a while before we actually take any action.

The next time Hogarth come to the reserve he ain't near so friendly. In fact he is all business. Guess he has developed what Mr. Nichols call a *sense of urgency*, which Mr. Nichols say most of us Indians was born without, and a good thing too.

"You look like hippies," Hogarth yell at us, when he find us lounging in the sun in front of Ben Stonebreaker's Hobbema

General Store. "Jesus, look at you!" he holler at Frank, who wearing a cape he cut from some curtains he find in somebody's garbage, and a white glove with the fingers cut off. "What are you, the wagonburner's Michael Jackson? I want INDIANS! You're all dressed like cowboys, for chrissakes. I want braids, wampum, spears, bows and arrows, loincloths, buckskin, campfires, pinto ponies, hides nailed to the outside walls of your cabins, tepees, travois, trick riding. You guys never seen any Western movies? Listen," and he bang the flat of his hand against his forehead, "I got 100 ignorant Wop travel agents to impress.

"Remember what we were talking about the other day? I want to see Old Time Indians . . . REAL INDIANS . . ."

"Real Indians don't eat egg McMuffins," says Frank.

"Real Indians roll their own," say Eathen Firstrider, who able to build a cigarette with one hand while ride on a saddle horse.

"Real Indians don't wear designer jeans," says Connie Bigcharles.

"Real Indians don't stuff saskatoon berries up their noses . . ."

"Enough, enough," say Hogarth Running Eagle, and his car wheels spin out gravel as he drive away mad. I think Mr. Nichols know what he talking about when it come to that *sense of urgency*.

In spite of the way Hogarth treated Mad Etta, everything would of been okay if only he hadn't welshed on the money he promised us.

I wasn't surprised. One day I asked Mr. Nichols to explain that word "entrepreneur."

"It's just a fancy way of saying organizer," say Mr. Nichols, "but it has a mainly negative connotation or meaning in our society. Usually an entrepreneur is a hustler who has no money, often calls his business 'Something Enterprises Ltd' and you'd better get your money up front when you're dealing with one, and count the fillings in your teeth and the number of fingers on each hand after he's left."

Hogarth keep postponing the money we been promised for a show. At least he buy Louis Coyote that fancy pair of boots. When he do he pay Eustace Sixkiller cash money, and treat him with respect. Eustace got dark blue tattoos on all his arms and shoulders.

We have a hard time getting Louis to wear his new boots. "I appreciate things with my fingers," he says, his blind eyes look into the distance. His old, brown fingers feel the soft leather and tooled designs, and he hold the leather to his nose and appreciate it that way too.

Hogarth rehearse Louis for his part, again and again.

"Impart them some Indian wisdom," say Hogarth.

Louis push his mirrored glasses down on his nose, so me and a few other people can glimpse his milky eyes.

"I'm only wearing one spur," he say slowly and with dignity. Then he pause a long time. "Do you want to know how a blind man can tell he is only wearing one spur?"

"Yes," several of us say, pretending we is Italian tourists.

Louis bang the heel of the boot with the spur on the floor. The spur clank real loud. Then he bang the boot without the spur.

"My ears tell me," he say, and smile behind his glasses. "They also tell me which boot it is on."

We all go, "Ooooh" and "Aaaah."

"Maybe if we put a little curl in his hair," say Hogarth. "There's such a thing as looking too Indian."

My guess is we going to have to change most of the entertainment part of the program we lined up. At least the parts that ain't very Indian, like Matthias Two Young Men, who is all set to sing

"Arrivederci Roma." Matthias fancy himself another Julio Iglesias looking for a place to happen, so he rented a tuxedo with a frilly blue shirt from Bozniak's Formal Rentals and Party Supplies in Edmonton, oiled his hair, greased his smile, and actually put wax on his teeth, after he brushed them for about two hours.

The two big doubledecker charter buses with tinted glass windows and roofs, roll onto the reserve. It is a nice fall day, with a few yellow leaves still clinging to the trees, and a woodsmoke smell in the air. We have a troupe of chicken dancers going full tilt as the travel agents step off the buses. My sister Delores whirr like a trail bike as she point her feather bustle at the visitors and dance up a storm.

Louis Coyote sit on a stump in his front yard.

"Able to predict the weather accurately, year after year," Hogarth tell the travel agents. Hogarth could pass for a Member of Parliament; he wear an expensive royal-blue suit, and had his hair styled special, "long enough to let them know I'm Indian, but conservative enough to let them know I'm a reliable business-man," is how he describe it. Speaking of Members of Parliament, Chief Tom turned up all set to deliver a half-hour welcome speech, but the drums for the chicken dancers drown him out. Now he standing on the sidelines looking ugly, thinking I bet of going back to Wetaskiwin and feeling sorry for himself.

Louis make his weather predictions. Do some rigmarole about heavy fur growing on the north side of gophers. We all laugh behind our hands, but the travel agents eat it up. He do his bit about the spur. But then there is a long silence.

"Is that all?" say Hogarth in a stage whisper.

Chief Tom take a deep breath and I can see he getting ready to fill in the gap.

"What do you expect from an old man?" says Louis. "I have 19 children," he say to the travel agents. They all scribble notes on their clipboards.

"Eighteen," say Mrs. Blind Louis, who been standing quiet by the cabin door.

"Do not most of those who ride on the range wear two spurs, if you please?" ask a travel agent in broken English; he is short and round and covered all over in a blue-striped suit.

"Ah," sigh Louis, "if one side of the horse runs can the other be far behind?"

"Now that's what I'm paying him for," say Hogarth with great satisfaction.

"Speaking of money," I say.

"Not now," say Hogarth into my ear. "You'll get paid if I make a deal with the travel agents, and when and if I feel like it."

"I was only asking," I say. He don't even see me shake my head at somebody on the far edge of the crowd.

Hogarth parade the travel agents over to Blue Quills Hall, where he's sweet talked the Blue Quills Ladies Auxiliary into serving fried rabbit, bannock, and saskatoon pie; he has promised them they'll get paid later.

The lunch go off without a hitch, though there is about 40 pieces of fried rabbit left over because Mad Etta didn't show up for free food like she usually do. Hogarth is just about to walk the agents from Blue Quills Hall over to where Frank Fencepost, David One-wound, Eathen and Rufus Firstrider, and a few other guys is painted up to look like a raiding party, when there is a great growl like a semitrailer starting up, and the side door to Blue Quills Hall push open with a crash. That door open *out*, so you know how hard it been pushed. The long black arm of a bear hold that torn screen door in the air, then toss it halfway across the hall. The bear growl again and force most of itself through the door.

The travel agents scream, and many of them shout, "Orso," which I don't need an interpreter to tell me mean *bear* in Italian.

They bang open the double door at the front of the hall and scramble across the gravel and into their big buses, all the time pushing and shoving and yelling. There is a trail of high-heeled shoes, notepads, pens, hats, sunglasses and souvenirs, strewn all across the parking lot, look like flowers been scattered.

Chief Tom's big, black Lincoln Continental is already 100 yards down the road and picking up speed.

"It's only a joke. It's only a joke," Hogarth keep repeating as the bus motors start.

The bear ain't come out of the hall. It is helping itself to the leftover rabbit.

Hogarth turn to me with a look of panic on his face. "How the hell do you say *joke* in Italian?"

"Real Indians don't speak Italian," I tell him.

The Fog

M y littlest sister Delores come running through the doorway of our cabin puffing. "Silas, Silas, there's a phone call for you down at the store."

I can tell she has run all the way; her braids are unravelled, her cheeks pink, and she smell of the outdoors. The phone is a half mile down the hill at Ben Stonebreaker's Hobbema General Store. As we walk down, I hold onto Delores' hand, and every once in a while we skip a step or two, Delores all the time talking a mile a minute. "Hurry up!" she say, pulling on my arm. But I ain't expecting a phone call so anybody who needs to talk to me can wait until I get there.

The phone is nailed to one of the back walls of the store. It made of varnished wood, is about a yard tall, and I bet is older than I am. I'm tall enough to talk into the mouth-piece, while most everybody else have to stand on their tiptoes, yell up as if they talking to someone at the top of a hill.

"Mr. Ermineskin," say a man's deep voice, the kind that set

plates to rattling on the table if he was at your house. "My name is J. Michael Kirkpatrick and I'm Bureau Chief for Best North American News Service. I've read your books and I'm very impressed. Very impressed."

That means he's going to ask me to do some work for him: interview somebody, write a column or something. The point I have to establish quick is, is he going to pay me, and if so, how much. Lots of people figure they can pay Indians with colored beads like in the old days; others figure that just because I'm an Indian I should be willing to work cheap.

I listen to what Mr. Kirkpatrick have to say, and I go "Ummmmm," and "Uh-huh," at the proper points so he won't figure the phone has gone dead.

"As you are probably aware, the Pope is on a cross-country tour of Canada. One of his stops will be at Fort Simpson in the Northwest Territories, where he will meet with several thousand native people. We would like you to cover that event as a representative of Best North American News Service, and to write about it from a native point of view, so to speak."

"How much?" I ask. I've learned from sad experience not to be shy about taking money. Editors have kept me on the phone for an hour, or I've sat in a carpeted office listening to a long explanation of an assignment, only to find out they expect to pay me twenty dollars or less for the job.

Mr. Kirkpatrick name a figure. I ask for double. He say no way. I say goodbye. He raise his price $250. I say okay.

It is while he is telling me that I going to get to ride on a chartered airplane that I get my idea.

"How would you like to not have to pay me at all?" I say.

"What's the deal?"

"Well, if you were to send two of my friends along with me, we'd settle for expenses. Medicine lady of our tribe was saying just last night how she'd like to meet the Pope. And I got a close friend I want to bring with me."

"Girlfriend, eh?" say Mr. Kirkpatrick.

"No," I say. "It's a man."

"Oh, well, I suppose it's okay." He sound kind of embarrassed. "Somehow I never thought of you Indians being *that way*. But I suppose you *are* a writer."

Boy, when I tell Mad Etta what I arranged she get as excited as I ever seen her.

"I want to have a talk with this Pope guy," she say. "You know him and me ain't so different. People believe in what he got to hand out—I can't figure out why—but in the long run it don't matter. For me, having people believe in my cures is about 90% of the battle. Maybe I can make a trade with this Mr. Pope. I seen him on the TV the other day and I can tell by the way he holds himself that he still got pains from the time he got shot. I'll take him some cowslip roots to boil up; maybe I'll even boil it for him. If he drinks the tea his pain will go away."

"Yeah, but what can he do for you?"

"I'm not real sure. But he's a nice man. And, if you stop to think about it, he believes in the old ways, just like us. Maybe I can learn from him something about *influence*. I mean we got over 4,000 people, but only about a hundred or so believe in me. I could use the secret of attracting more followers."

Frank's biggest wish is to get Pope John Paul to bless his lottery tickets. "I'll donate 10% of my winnings to his church. And I'd really like to have him get me a part in that *Knight Rider* TV show. I want to drive that superpowered car that talks like a person."

"Those ain't the kinds of miracles the Pope usually get asked for," I say.

"Right. He must get tired of being asked to cure rheumatism and back aches. I figure he'll pay attention to an unusual request."

"But you don't believe."

"Not yet. I will as soon as that car from *Knight Rider* pull on to the reserve and say, 'Come here, Frank Fencepost. I been dying to have you drive me.'"

Though it is the fall season here in Alberta, with the days warm and the trees still covered with pumpkin-colored leaves, we take parkas and sleeping bags with us. We been to the Arctic once, Frank and me, and it was below zero there, in real temperature, even in the summer.

We sit Etta on her tree-trunk chair in the back of Louis Coyote's pickup truck and drive to the little airport in the middle of Edmonton. Like they promised, Best North American News Service have an airplane waiting. It is small, hold four passengers and a pilot, but it is new. I promised myself I'd never fly in a small plane again after I went to Pandemonium Bay in a plane with doors that wouldn't close and windows where the snow blew right in, and an engine about as powerful as a sick Skidoo. But this is another time.

The pilot wear a uniform just like he was in the air force.

"Take us to see the Pope, General," Frank say, salute the pilot. "You got champagne and movies on this here flight?"

But the pilot pay about as much attention to Frank as if he was a fly buzzing around his head; what he *is* staring at is Mad Etta.

"It's alright," I tell him. "She's a medicine lady; you'll never crash with her aboard."

Etta is decked out in a new deerskin dress. "Deer population will be down for years to come," is what Frank said when he first seen it. The dress got about 10 pounds of porcupine quills on it, including a purple circle on Etta's front the size of a garbage can lid.

"Getting her aboard is what I'm worried about," says the pilot. "That door don't expand."

He's right. The little steps up to the door are like toys, and even ordinary people have to duck and turn to get inside.

"Hey, when I want to do something I get it done," say Etta. "Silas, you go inside and pull; Frank, you push."

Moving Etta is kind of like moving furniture. I seen guys get sofas and deepfreezes up twisting stairs and through doors smaller than the things they were moving.

Etta give the directions and we do the work. A couple of times I figure Etta going to get stuck permanent. Then it look like the door-frame gonna split on us, or else Etta is. I think finally Etta just concentrate and shrink herself about four inches all around, for she pop through the door like she been greased.

During the flight Etta sit on one side of the plane, while me, Frank, and the pilot, and all our luggage sit on the other.

"The News Service has a bigger plane waiting in Yellowknife to take you on to Fort Simpson," the pilot tell us.

It is in Yellowknife where the real trouble start. There is hundreds and hundreds of reporters in the tiny airport, waiting to get any kind of aircraft to fly them to the even tinier airport in Fort Simpson. There's also several TV people from Best North American News Service, who is determined to get to Fort Simpson.

"Your friends are gonna have to stay behind," say a cameraman, who is chewing on a cigar, look like Charles Bronson when he been without sleep for two days.

"No way," I say. "I'm working for nothing so my friends can go along."

"Look, no one ever thought of the shortage of transportation. Everything's been cleared with J. Michael Kirkpatrick back in Toronto. You get paid your full fee plus a $500 bonus. Your friends get a hotel room here in Yellowknife and their meals until you get back from Fort Simpson. They're lucky not to be going. It's gonna be a madhouse there."

It don't look like I have no choice. Boy, I sure hate to explain the change to Etta. When she hear what I have to say she rumble deep inside like bad plumbing.

"When Etta get mad she usually get even," I tell the Best North American people. But not knowing Etta, they ain't impressed.

There is more trouble when I get on the plane. Frank has found a seat for himself next to a lady.

"I'm editor of this here Indian newspaper called *The Moccasin Telegraph*," he is telling her as I come down the aisle. I notice he is already touching her body. "Ah, here's my assistant now. His name is Silas Gopher; he's sort of my gofer," and Frank laugh loud and hearty. He also have a jack-handle laid across his lap and when somebody from the airline tell him to move, he suggest he will do a certain amount of damage to anybody who try to take his seat from him. The pilot and his assistant have a quick meeting and decide to leave Frank where he is; instead they let the cameraman sit in the aisle. If only Frank had thought to bring Etta with him.

You know how, when a special visitor is coming you clean up your house. You do things you would never ordinarily do, like wash in corners, clean things and places a visitor would never look. Well, that is the way it is with the whole town of Fort Simpson. The town is not very big to start with, only a thousand people they tell us. Fort Simpson is located where the Liard and Mackenzie Rivers meet, it is the trading place for all the native peoples for hundreds of miles. It seem to me every one of them people must have come to Fort Simpson to see the Pope. Boy, I really have never seen so many Indians in one place at one time.

"Where's our hotel?" is the first question Frank ask after we hit the ground.

"Ha," says the cameraman. "See that row of tents down along the riverbank. That's where we stay. There's only one small hotel in town and it's been booked up forever. Shouldn't be any problem for you guys though. Indians are used to living outdoors."

"*Some* Indians," I say.

I should have asked more questions before I took this job. I mean knowing about the outdoors don't come naturally to Indians. Me and Frank ain't aren't campers or hunters or trackers. We like hotel rooms, Kentucky Fried Chicken, video games, riding in taxis, and electric guitars. But it look like we going to have to do without those things for a few days. What *is* here is like a disorganized carnival with no main event.

It is Government money that keep Fort Simpson in business, so it is Government people who organize for the Pope's visit. People who work full time for the Government is there 'cause they ain't competent enough to work anywheres else. All around town they have really spent a lot of money to show how smart they *ain't*.

To start with some bureaucrat must have ordered a thousand gallons of whitewash. All the sad buildings in this little town, what haven't even a memory of a coat of paint, have been sloshed with whitewash. Coming down on the airplane, these buildings looked like extra big, white birds scattered across the barren land.

These same Government people also imported rolls and rolls of fake grass. It is fall and what little grass there is is brown. The town is mostly rock and mud. Now, in all kinds of unlikely places is little blazes of green.

"What harm do you suppose it would do the Pope to see the land the way it really is?" ask Frank.

"If he's got a direct connection to God, then he'll know what he's seeing is phony and it won't matter," I say.

Every rock within eyesight of Fort Simpson also been white-washed.

"Looks like Limestone City," says a reporter.

"I wonder if they bath the people as they come into town, wouldn't want the Pope to smell anything bad," says someone else.

"Didn't you hear?" says a CBC cameralady, "night before the visit they're gonna whitewash us. We'll all glow like foxfire the day of the big visit."

"I wonder what we're gonna do to kill time," I say. It is only Saturday. The Pope ain't due until Tuesday. I been at events where the reporters interview each other they get so desperate for news.

All along the riverbank for as far as we can see is square little pup tents in a long row.

"That's the Press Area," somebody tells us. "Better grab yourself a tent before they're all gone."

I'm sure glad we brought heavy clothes. There are little propane heaters and portable cookstoves in the tents, but it easy to see the first arrivals been having trouble with them, 'cause about every tenth tent been burned down.

Frank and that lady TV producer he met on the plane have decided to share a tent. That evening Frank win a fair amount of money in a card game until somebody point out which side of the deck he's dealing from.

"Indians always deal from the bottom of the deck," Frank say in a serious voice, acting as if he is the one been offended. He at least bluff his way out of any broken bones, though after that no one will play cards with him anymore.

Just as I'm afraid of, since I appear to be the only Indian reporter in town, I get interviewed by other reporters for radio, TV and newspapers. They are all disappointed that I'm not excited about being here. "I'm sure this Pope is a nice man, but as I see it the Church and smallpox have done about equal damage to the Indian people over the years," I tell them. I don't think they ever broadcast or print that. Nobody want to say anything negative about anything, especially the Pope.

The natives, or the *Dene*, as the Indians call themselves, have got things pretty well organized in spite of having the Government looking over their shoulders.

"There are over 8,000 visitors here," a Cree chief from near Yellowknife tell us. Later, I heard there was only 4,000 people all told. When that guy from the news service called me he said to expect 40,000. I notice that a lot of people who have come are really old. They come off the roads in pickup trucks as beat up as the one we drive at home, all dusty, rusty and coughing; they come down the rivers in all kinds of boats powered by stuttering outboards.

Out on the flats is a tent city, not the new canvas of the press tents, but canvas stitched and repaired and patched, sun faded to the color of the hills in late fall. Lived-in tents with smoke blackening around the tops where north winds pushed smoke down against the canvas. That field of tents look exactly like pictures and paintings of old time Indian settlements I've seen at the Glenbow Museum in Calgary.

The women have set up racks of spruce logs for the curing of moose meat, deer, caribou, whitefish and speckled trout.

In the huge tepee that been built to honor the Pope, drums been throbbing day and night, and dancers dance old-time circle dances. A few, but not many of the dancers are in costume. This is real dancing by men in denim and deerskins, women in long skirts and saggy sweaters—real people, not people dressed in plastic beads and feathers made in Korea who practise their dancing on a government grant.

The people here call the Pope *Yahtitah*; it mean priest-father, as near as I can translate.

Lots of the reporters and many of the Indians have transistor radios, listen to what happen in the outside world.

"He's taking off from Edmonton Airport any minute now," someone report on Tuesday morning, his hand holding the tiny black radio close to his ear. "He'll be here right on schedule."

Then about 10 minutes later, "Take-off's been delayed for 15 minutes."

The circle dancing continues. Smoke the same color of the sky drift in the cool, damp air of morning.

"His plane's developed engine trouble," someone say. "Departure from Edmonton is delayed by 45 minutes."

Nobody's worried yet. But I imagine I can hear Etta rumbling in her room in that hotel in Yellowknife. If she got anything to cook on I bet she boiling up mysterious stuff.

After the delay stretch to over two hours people start to get nervous.

"He's gonna change planes," a reporter cry. Everyone cheer and clap. The drums in the compound get louder, like they applauding too.

"They're switching to a back-up plane; take-off's in 20 minutes."

Frank busy taking bets on the Pope's arrival time. He sit behind a table, in front of a sign he printed himself read, Frank Bank. He offers to bet money that the Pope don't arrive at all, give 2-1 odds. Indians take him up on that and the pile of money in front of him grow.

"He's takin' off!" and a cheer rise over the settlement like slow thunder. First time I ever hear a whole town make, as Pastor Orkin back home would say, "a joyful noise."

The weather been perfect Indian Summer ever since we arrived. That morning it was foggy first thing, but, as it supposed to do, the sun burn that fog off, and it was clear with a high sky when the take-off finally announced.

Over the next few hours, as the Pope fly through the air toward us, the clouds roll in, filmy and white as smoke tendrils at first, then it is like the sky develop a low roof, won't let the campfire smoke out. Fog all of a sudden rise off the river, twist around our ankles like a cat rubbing. For a while the sun look like a red balloon, then get dull as an orange, fade to the color of a grapefruit, disappear altogether.

The drum slow down as if people's hearts beating slower.

"He's due in five minutes," someone shout. The drums stop and those thousands and thousands of people stare up into the fog. It is so thick I have to strain my eyes to see the top of that 55-foot tepee out on the flats. If I get more than a hundred yards away it look like a shadow of a tepee, the real thing hid from me by a gray blanket.

The long drone of an airplane fill the air, but it is very high and going right past us, not landing.

"Too foggy," call the people with the radios attached to their ears. "Pilot gonna try again."

A whisper pass through the crowd like a shiver. The word "pray" is whispered from a few thousand mouths. People all around me bow their heads and move their lips silently. The fog is cold and a mean breeze cut through my clothes like a razor blade.

The plane make another pass over us.

The fog doesn't budge an inch.

There is a kind of keening sound rise from the enclosure of tents. I feel sorry for the old people who come hundreds of miles down river or cross-country to see this man. I'm sorry too that these people have abandoned their own religion out of fear, for something the white man force on them. If it wasn't for guns there wouldn't be but a handful of Indian Christians.

"There's only enough fuel for one more pass," someone say.

"If there was anything to their religion don't you figure their god could move aside a few clouds?" I say to no one in particular, though I got Mad Etta in mind.

The plane make its final pass and buzz away until it is less than a mosquito sound. People are actually weeping.

"We just wanted him to touch us," say an old woman in a sky-blue parka that glazed with dirt.

"They say he's gonna land in Yellowknife instead. He might come here tomorrow if it's clear."

People who come from the Yellowknife area groan with disbelief.

"Why Yellowknife? It's not on his schedule."

"They say the Pope feel a call to stop at Yellowknife and deliver a message."

At the news that he may come to Fort Simpson tomorrow, some people give a small cheer. The drums start up again and people go back to their dancing and hoping.

"That bit about him coming tomorrow is a lie," say a producer from Best North American News Service. "They're gonna wait until late tonight to announce he's not coming. Some bureaucrat in Yellowknife is afraid of a riot."

Frank have to wait hours and hours to collect his bets. But now, people who like lost causes are putting down money that the Pope will show. It is kind of like by betting on the Pope they are showing off their faith.

"I was hoping I'd feel something," a girl about my age say to me, just after she place a five dollar bet. "The old people believed he could change things. I want to believe like them, but I just don't know . . ." and her voice fade away.

Somebody sum it up good when they say, "Same as the church always do; they promise a whole lot and deliver nothing."

Nobody seems very mad, except the press people, who put in four ugly, cold days and now have nothing to write about. Some of them scared up a legend or two, about a church that was burned down, or that a great leader would die at a place where two rivers meet. And somebody else get an old medicine man to say the animals been behaving strangely for the last few days.

But the Chief of the Slaveys state the believers' attitude the next morning when he say, "The *Dene* understand weather," and after long pause, "better than most."

During the Pope's unexpected stop in Yellowknife he record a radio message for all the people in Fort Simpson. He speak strong words about Native Rights and independence. The Yellowknife TV station was there, and early next morning their tape run on the CBC and we get to see it in Fort Simpson.

"There ain't nowhere in the world you can escape from the CBC," is what Frank says, and I guess it is true.

Just like the producer say, at 11:00 p.m. that night they announce that the Pope's visit to Fort Simpson is cancelled forever. The Pope will fly to Ottawa as planned. "Serious consideration was given to a Fort Simpson visit," they say, "but it would have ruined the Ottawa program."

"We all know they wouldn't want to ruin anything for the fat cats in Ottawa," laugh one of the reporters. "Even the Pope can't pass up the bureaucrats. I wonder how many of them came a thousand miles in a canoe down dangerous rivers to see him?"

The words of the cancellation announcement ain't cold in the air before the fog lift like it was being vacuumed, in ten minutes a butter-yellow moon and stars like tinsel light up the night.

The big surprise on the TV show from Yellowknife is that on the balcony of the hotel, where the Pope speak to about 20 microphones, right beside him, the purple circle on the front of her dress pulsing like a strobe light, was Mad Etta. Etta smiling like she know more secrets than the Pope, and, as he wave to his friends, she wave to hers.

Indian Joe

I never forget the Christmas my sister Illianna got Indian Joe as a present. Pa had left us the year before and Delores was just a baby. I remember Delores peering over Ma's shoulder as we walk down the hill from our cabin to Blue Quills Hall, where the Christmas party was.

There was a big, tall Christmas tree inside Blue Quills Hall. The place smell smokey because the stove backed up. Each of us kids was gived a candy cane and a glass of lemonade. Everyone sat around with their coats on acting shy.

Finally Santa Claus showed up. All but the littlest kids could tell it was Sven Sonnegard, a mechanic at the Husky Service Station on the highway. He still got his greasy, steel-toed work boots on below his Santa Claus suit.

There were galvanized garbage cans on the stage, each covered in green and red paper, each got a sheet of black construction paper taped to it, with BOY or GIRL and different age groups written on in chalk.

We got in a long line and when a kid got to the top of the stairs to the stage, he would sneak across toward Santa Claus, head down. If Sven Sonnegard could get the kid to tell its age, he'd reach in the right barrel for a present. If the kid wouldn't tell, Sven would guess; sometimes he'd even have to guess if it was a boy or girl. One garbage can say BABY, others 1–3, 4–6, 7–9, and so on.

My friend Frank Fencepost notice the presents get bigger as the kids get older. When it's our turn, Frank he walk right up to Santa Claus and say, "Hi, Sven, I'd like to buy a quart of home-brew."

"Shut up, Kid," Sven say out of the side of his mouth, but he also have a hard time keep from laughing. We all know Sven make his living bootlegging, mainly to Indians.

"How old are you?" Sven say to Frank.

We are supposed to be in the 7–9 group.

"Fifteen," say Frank, push out his skinny chest, look Sven right in the eye.

"You ain't a day over eight," say Sven–Santa Claus.

"He's small for his age," I say.

"That's right, he's small for eight."

"I seen Constable Greer down by the door," said Frank. "How many cases of home-brew you think he'd find in your truck if he looked?"

Sven reach in the BOY 13–15 barrel, pull out a big package.

"My twin brother is at home sick," say Frank.

Santa Claus reach out another package, a basketball, and he nearly knock Frank over he push it into his arms so hard.

"My brother's brother couldn't be here neither."

Sven load another present into Frank's arms.

The line-up behind us getting restless.

"And my cousin . . ."

"Move along," said Santa. "What a good boy you've been," and push Frank so he skid clear across the stage.

"How old are you, Sport?" he said to me.

"Thirteen," I said, swallowing hard.

"Sure you are." He reach in the BOY 7–9 barrel and give me a package turn out to be a peg-board game got half the wooden nubbins missing.

It was at this party Illianna was gived Indian Joe. Joe was a mechanical Indian, run by batteries. He was six or eight inches tall, sit on his haunches in front of a drum, with little drumsticks raised up ready to play. In Joe's lower back was a switch, and when it pressed down he play. H-H-H-Rap, Tap-Tap, go the drum. The toys we was given was all used, but Indian Joe was good as new and Illianna was real proud of him.

"He look something like Pa," Illianna say on the walk home. Her being older she remember Pa better than the rest of us. I never knew him to play the drum, or have black braids, or even a red shirt with green suspenders like Indian Joe.

After Illianna got her toy home she is kind of like a miser with her money when it come to sharing. She like him so much she take him to bed with her that first night.

All that happened about three years before Illianna go off to work in the city. By that time everybody but Illianna forgot about Indian Joe. No one even notice he is one of the things Illianna take to Calgary with her.

After she been in the city for a year or two my sister married herself to a white man name of Robert McGregor McVey. He is a big wheel in some company that loan out money. Me and my friends have caused McVey a certain amount of grief over the years. The first time I ever seen their new house, I discover that in their bedroom Illianna and Brother Bob have what's called a walk-in closet. On one of the shelves sat Indian Joe. He look smaller than I remember him, but except that one of the plastic feathers is gone from his war-bonnet, he is good as new. I remember thinking it is strange for Illianna to keep a toy like that, 'cause she been married for years and have her own little boy named Bobby.

Last week me and Frank went to Calgary for a day. We park the truck and start walking around.

"What should we do?" I ask Frank.

"Let's go in the lobby of a bank and watch people withdraw money from the machines," says Frank.

We watch the machines for a while.

Later, I seen a sign take me by surprise. In gold letters in the form of an arch, just like McDonald's, it say INTERCONTINENTAL LOAN CO. LTD., Robert M. McVey, Division Manager.

"Look at that," I say to Frank. "You figure that's Brother Bob?"

"Let's go inside and see," he says.

We walk inside, and boy, the place is just like a bank. There is secretaries everywhere, dressed fancy as models. Quiet music is playing and typewriters tick. Everywhere there is machines look like a cross between typewriters and televisions.

"Good afternoon, may I help you?" a lady say. She is tall, with long blond hair, dressed in a brown, scratchy-looking suit, remind me of a doormat.

"I'd like to borrow 20 dollars," says Frank, give her a big smile. "I pay you back tomorrow for sure. I even leave my friend here. You can sell him if I don't come back."

The girl try hard to be polite.

"I'm afraid we only make industrial loans," she say.

"How about if you loan me twenty dollars personally?" say Frank, and he look at her real sad, lift up one finger point to his cheek. As he does a tear squeeze out of his eye, roll onto his cheek and stop there. Frank seen an Indian on TV do that, that Indian was sad about white men cutting down trees or something.

"How do you do that?" the girl says.

"Come real close and I show you."

The girl does, then turn to another girl and say, "Hey, Francine, come look at this."

"Maybe you've seen me on TV?" Frank saying.

Frank wipe the tears off his cheek, start the water flowing again.

"Excuse me," I say to a gray-haired lady, "is Mr. McVey in?"

"Whom should I say is calling?" she say, look right at me as if what she's asking ain't funny.

"Tell him his brother, Silas, is here."

She scowl, and I bet she is going to say something nasty to me when she remember that Brother Bob have an Indian wife. She push her face into a tiny smile and pick up a white telephone.

A few minutes later, Brother Bob, his cheeks all shiny, wearing a striped suit and vest, smell like he just bathed in shaving lotion, come out of a door labelled EXECUTIVE OFFICES.

He try to be friendly, but he is embarrassed to see me there. Bet he wishes he could dress me up in a suit like him and cut my hair.

"Why Silas," he say, "what a surprise!"

"I seen your name on the window."

Brother Bob stare around kind of nervous. Then his eyes light on Frank's back. Frank got five or six secretaries watching him cry. I notice he is also putting a stapler in his pocket.

"You *didn't* bring that Posthole with you?" Brother Bob yell.

"He's keepin' himself busy," I say. "You never even know he's here."

"Well, Silas, how would you like a tour of our business facilities?" he ask. "We've got straight state-of-the-art technology here. Everything is done by computer. I expect you'll be buying, or how is it you put it, creatively borrowing, a word processor to facilitate your writing procedures," and he give me a little chuckle.

"I facilitate my writing procedures with a felt pen and a Royal typewriter," I say. "I'm scared of these here computers."

"It's inevitable, Silas. People in the horse-and-buggy era were afraid of the horseless carriage. Now, even *you* drive a car . . ."

It get pretty noisy across the room where Frank and the secretaries gathered around a big copier. Brother Bob and me work our way over to them.

I guess Frank ain't ever seen a copying machine up close before. One of the secretaries show him how it work, and Frank put his hand down flat, push the button, and out come a piece of paper with a big, blue-black hand on it.

"Hey, I bet this here machine could copy food," cries Frank. "Silas," he yell, "run down to a restaurant and get a sandwich. I'll copy it enough times to feed the whole reserve." The secretaries all laugh. I notice a couple of them is already touching Frank.

"He doesn't really believe that, does he?" Brother Bob ask.

"Well . . ." I say. "Mad Etta teach him pretty strong medicine. If he was to copy a sandwich it just might come out real."

Brother Bob stare me up and down, but he don't have the nerve to call me a liar. He shoo all the secretaries back to their desks. Then he take both of us through a couple of metal doors, thick as the kind they have in warehouses, and into a room with no windows.

"This is our computer center," he say, wave one of his small, pink hands at the rows and rows of blinking machines. The sounds in the room is quite a bit like an arcade, except all the humans is quiet.

"You keep the money inside those machines?" ask Frank.

"Oh, no," say Brother Bob, "no money, but all our records are in there. We can establish the status of any loan account in the nation in less than 10 seconds. Here, let me show you . . ." and he actually smile at us, looking kind of purplish under the artificial light.

As I look at Brother Bob, I wonder how Illianna feel about being married to a white man, and living in a white world. She seem to be happy, and says Bob and her have lots of friends. And she has her little boy Bobby. Still, no matter how I try, I can't "walk in her moccasins," as Mad Etta our medicine lady would say. I can't imagine not being with other Indians. It seem to me I'd get awful tired of always being on display, of answering dumb questions, of always being afraid I'd make a mistake.

Brother Bob poke away at the keys of a computer and a whole page of figures appear. "See," he says. I can tell by looking at Frank that he is just dying to touch one of these machines.

"Watch this," says Brother Bob. "This machine can speak too."

He push a button and the machine talk, sound like somebody under a foot of water with his nose plugged. But once I tune my ears to it, I can understand.

"Can you teach it to cuss?" ask Frank.

"I suppose I could, if I was so inclined," Brother Bob reply, but pretty coldly.

The steel door open and that gray-haired lady stick her head in. "Excuse me, Mr. McVey, but Zurich is on the line."

"I'll be right back," Brother Bob say to us, and trot away.

"Boy, this is just like a video arcade," yells Frank, move up to the word processor and poke a button or two. "Which one do I push to shoot down all those squiggley things?"

"I don't know if we should be touching these here machines," I say.

"Where's the coin slot?"

"Brother Bob own these machines. You don't have to pay to use them."

"Wow! Brother Bob is in heaven and I bet he don't even know it." Frank go from machine to machine, poke a button here and there.

"These ain't games . . ."

"But I bet they could be," and Frank whack a few more buttons.

"We better go," I say.

About that time, a red light, look like an ambulance flasher, high above the door, start flashing, and a bell, like a fire alarm, begin ringing.

"I think I got this one working," yells Frank.

It does look as if it's turning into a game. The red light flashes, the siren bongs, it is just like our favorite arcade in Wetaskiwin.

Just as Frank really starting to enjoy himself, Brother Bob come crashing through the door.

"Don't touch that machine anymore," he yells. "Our entire loan records are in there. If it goes down . . ."

"I'm gonna blow these little green suckers away," yells Frank, pound the buttons the way a Russian pianist I seen on TV pound his piano.

"That's enough, Frank," I'm surprised to hear myself saying. I move toward him, intending to pull him away from the machine. Sometimes it seem to me Frank don't think enough before he act.

"Don't hit that button . . ." scream Brother Bob. We both dive for Frank. The machine look like it making fireworks and is about to explode.

I hit Frank like he was carrying a football and we both roll under a table, scatter a couple of wastebaskets across the room. Brother Bob shut off the machine, wipe his forehead, stare at us with his eyes bugging out.

I'm not sure if what I've done is good or bad.

"Another five seconds and our entire financial records would have been destroyed. Some of it could never be replaced."

I don't think Brother Bob realize that I was helping him. Maybe that's just as well. He march us both out of the building as if we was under arrest.

"We sure is sorry, Brother Bob," we say, but he don't even tell us goodbye.

Outside, Frank decide to wait the hour until closing time. He arranged to meet two or more of them secretaries. I decide to visit Illianna.

"We stopped in to see Brother Bob," I tell her. "He sure is busy, might be real late getting home tonight." By the way Illianna look at me I know she don't want to hear any details.

We have coffee at her kitchen table and I play with Bobby for a while, then say I'd better get going. I bet Brother Bob still ain't in a mood to be apologized to.

"I've got a present for Ma's birthday," Illianna say, "you can take it back with you." She get up and walk to her bedroom and I follow. She walk into the big closet take a package wrapped in flowered paper off a shelf. The package was sitting right beside Indian Joe.

"You still got old Indian Joe," I say, act kind of surprised.

"I got my doll, too," Illianna says, move aside a blanket and sure enough there is her one-eyed, bald doll, what at one time had platinum-colored hair. Illianna touch Indian Joe on the top of the head. "We been through a lot," she says, smile sad at me.

Indian Joe still sit behind his drum, wear green felt suspenders down the front of his red shirt. His black braids hang straight as sticks. His arms hold up in awkward half-circles, the little wood drumsticks forever poised.

"He sure does bring back a lot of memories," I say. I flip the switch in Indian Joe's back. "H-H-H-Rap, Tap-Tap . . ." go Indian Joe, which surprise me a lot. I didn't think batteries lasted for so many years.

"H-H-H-Rap, Tap-Tap," he go again, and, as I switch him off, I look at Illianna 'cause I hear her make a funny sound. My eyes catch her face just in time to see it falling in on itself. The tears flood out of her big, brown eyes.

I hold out my arms to her. She takes one step forward and clasp onto me real hard.

"Is there anything I can do?" I ask.

"No, everything's alright, Silas. Really, everything's alright."

"I know," I tell her, though I'm not sure I do. I think I can guess what she's feeling. For Illianna I bet it's one of those times when the past seems so far away—so permanently lost. I've had the feeling myself, a terrible sense of loss, like someone important has died. But then there's the worse feeling of not being able to name the person who'd died. It's a little like looking at your own grave.

I just hold her for a while as she cries into my shoulder. I believe her when she says everything's alright.

Then I hear Bobby come pounding in the back door. "Mom! Mom!" he calls.

Illianna pulls back, take a deep breath, wipes her eyes with her hands, wipes her hands on her jeans.

"Coming, honey," she says, and squeezes my hand as she turns away and walks out of the room, leaving me and Indian Joe staring at each other.

The Miss Hobbema Pageant

ACKNOWLEDGMENTS
The following stories have previously appeared in print:
"Being Invisible" in *Western Living*, and as part of a Southam Press
series on literacy, it appeared in the *Sunday Toronto Star*, the *Vancouver
Sun* and several other newspapers; "Snitches" in *Queen's Quarterly*;
"Pizza Ria" in *Edmonton Magazine* and *Vancouver Magazine*; "The
Sundog Society" in *Wisconsin Review*; "The Election" in *Whetstone*;
"Graves" in *Canadian Forum*; "Homer" in *Matrix*; "A Hundred Dollars'
Worth of Roses" in *New Quarterly*. Both "Homer" and "A Hundred
Dollars' Worth of Roses" were published in the chapbook *FiveStories*
(Vancouver: Hoffer/TANKS, 1986).

For my daughter Shannon Leah Kinsella

Contents

Being Invisible 235

Snitches 249

Pizza Ria 265

A Lighter Load 285

The Miss Hobbema Pageant 295

Forgiveness Among Animals 311

Tricks 325

Graves 341

Coming Home to Roost 359

The Sundog Society 377

The Election 391

Homer 409

A Hundred Dollars' Worth of Roses 425

The Medicine Man's Daughter 443

The Miss Hobbema
Pageant

Being Invisible

T he only time my friend Frank Fencepost ever raise up his fist to me was four or five years ago, when I suggest that maybe he should learn to read and write.

Frank and me been friends since before either of us can remember. When we was babies my mom and his used to put us in the same apple box, tie a string to it, slide us down the long hill to Blue Quills Hall or Hobbema General Store.

"You used to look like a couple of caterpillars in your snow-suits," Ma say to me once. "Even back then Frank could cry louder than any kid on the reserve."

I been covering for Frank, all through Grade School, and at the Tech School in Wetaskiwin where we studying to be mechanics. But I don't mind 'cause I'm not much of a fighter, even though I'm bigger and taller than Frank. And Frank be ready to mix it up as soon as he make eye contact with somebody, and he's mean as a bagful of bobcats when he get riled.

People think it's odd that me and Frank are friends, because we are about as opposite as two guys can be. There ain't no place Frank is afraid to go and almost nothing he is afraid to do.

Frank he run on instinct, while I think way too much. I wish I was as outgoing as Frank and that I could speak up smart answers the way he does. I mean after there been a run in with Chief Tom and Pastor Orkin, I always think of something smart I could of said, a week or two after it happen. And I'd like to take some really crazy chances sometimes, the way Frank do, and I'd like to be able to stare a white girl in the eye until she make friends with me. Frank, though he hardly ever let on, is proud of me because of all the stories I got printed up.

I guess that's why we like each other; we each got something about him that the other one don't.

"I ain't *ever* goin' to," he say, and shake his fist under my nose.

"I just suggest it as a friend," I say. "It's not like you ain't smart. If you put half as much effort into learning to read as you do hiding the fact you can't, you'd be able to out read and out write me.

"According to a magazine I read," I go on, "there's over four million people in Canada who can't read enough to get by. So you ain't alone."

"Four million," say Frank. "That would fill up Blue Quills Hall a couple of times I bet. Maybe even as many people as came to the Duran Duran concert in Edmonton."

"At least that many," I say, glad Frank ain't thinking about punching my face anymore.

We walking down the main street of Wetaskiwin, heading towards the Alice Hotel where we supposed to meet our girl-friends, when Frank ask me to read the lettering on the side of a bright-painted van. That was how come I suggested he should learn himself to read.

"You know, Frank," I said, "there ain't nothing wrong with admitting you can't do something."

"Yeah, but I'm supposed to know how."

"Who's the toughest guy on the reserve?" I ask, look like I'm changing the subject.

"Me."

"Come on. Who would you least like to have mad at you, and know they was going to pound you good the next time they seen you?"

· "Mad Etta."

"Seriously."

"I am serious," and Frank dance backwards down the street. "Well, maybe Robert Coyote."

Robert's fists is hard as if he holding a brick in each one, and he is the meanest street-fighter for I bet a hundred miles.

"You know Robert never learned to read until the last time he was in jail. He wasn't afraid to admit he couldn't."

"Yeah, but he's so tough he could wear panties and a bra to the Alice Hotel bar and nobody would laugh at him."

"Still he admitted he couldn't read, and they taught him down at Drumheller Jail."

I remember Robert joking about it when he got back to town. First thing he did was read all the signs behind the counter at Hobbema Pool Hall: NO CREDIT, NO FOUL LANGUAGE.

Robert laugh when he read that last sign, and he blast off enough swear words to turn Pastor Orkin green.

"You going to write down stories like Silas now that you learned how?" somebody ask him.

"Nah, I ain't gonna write nothing but bad checks," and he grin wicked. "The reason I let them teach me was all the guys in the joint got dirty books in their cells. And I couldn't read them. I had to be stuck with looking at the pictures in *Hustler* and *Penthouse*. They sent this woman down from Calgary to teach us and I signed up. She started us with little kids' picture books with about one word to a page.

"About the second class I bring in one of these dirty books. 'This here's what I want to learn to read from,' is what I say. She look at the title. '*Call Girls in Bondage*,' she read out loud, and the other guys in the class all laugh. 'I think you'll have to wait three or four classes before you can read this,' she say, but she smile at me real nice and I can tell she's there for more than just teaching reading and writing. There's a lot of women who get off on being around dangerous men, and she was one of them.

"I think it was the sixth week, I stay after class with my little book again. I can read most of it by then, and I pick out a real sexy part, say I'm having trouble with the words.

"She's never supposed to be alone with one of us guys. But I ain't surprised when she close the door to her office. I was sure sorry that class only last twelve weeks, and so was she."

"That your way of telling me I got to go to jail to learn to read?" Frank asked.

"You ought to do it," Robert say. "It couldn't make you any dumber than you are now, Fencepost," and he punch Frank's arm, leave bruises for about a month. But even Robert saying it okay to learn don't convince Frank.

But it look to me like he's weakening. I keep *reading* and *writing* in the conversation at the bar and at the Gold Nugget Café afterward. At the café, Frank he study the menu with a fierce eye, then he order for all four of us. I bet I only read that menu to Frank twice, and that was years ago, but he memorized the whole thing—something I couldn't do.

"Come on, Frank, why don't you give it a try?" says his girl, Connie.

"Will you teach me, Silas?"

"I suppose I could try to teach you, but I don't know the methods, and I don't think I should."

"I ain't goin' to school with no babies."

"You won't have to. Up in Edmonton, at Grant MacEwan Community College, they have what are called Adult Literacy classes. I read about them in the newspaper."

"Seems like a funny place for them to advertise for people who can't read," says Frank.

"You know, Silas," says Connie, "one time I told Frank he wasn't gonna get any more lovin' from me until he learned to write *I Love You Connie Bigcharles*. But you know Frank . . . ," and she break into a sweet smile and hug Frank's neck.

"One hug is worth a thousand words," says Frank.

Late that night, while me and Frank are sitting at his cabin, Frank says, "You know what I'd like more than anything else? To be able to read your books. I don't know how else to say it, Silas, but when you can't read or write, it kind of like being invisible."

"I never thought of it like that."

"It's like having a bad scar in a place nobody can see, or a disease on the inside of you."

"They can cure diseases," I say, "especially ones like yours that ain't fatal. You *could* be like James Redbird who got the multiple sclerosis. Ain't nothing can be done for that."

"Yeah," says Frank. "Hey, remember that dumb job I had?"

One summer Frank he got work at the John Deere Tractor Store in Wetaskiwin. It wasn't fixing tractors like we been trained to do. He got to swamp out the garage and be a general gofer. Frank did a good job, and in a couple of weeks when the assistant in the parts department went on holidays they decided to move Frank to the order desk, where he would have had to fill out forms and read work sheets. Frank, who usually afraid of nothing, quit the job altogether, rather than admit he couldn't read.

"I remember," I say.

"I don't usually quit things. I just wasn't brave enough to let them know about my trouble."

"It isn't a question of being brave. It's just a matter of wanting a little more out of life."

"Yeah, but neither of my folks were able to read. A lot of older people get by . . ."

"Times are changing too much. There's no place you can hide any more. You can't go out on a trap line and just stay there. There's no place government forms don't get to these days."

Frank laugh. "You know down at the Tech School, they've never caught on because nobody there believes there's people who can't read and write. I told them in the office one day when they wanted me to fill out some form. 'Hey,' I said, 'I can't read this, and even if I could I can't write enough to fill it out!' 'Stop goofing off, Fencepost,' the office girl say to me. 'If you couldn't read and write you wouldn't be here.' "

"So you brought it to me and I filled it out for you."

"Right. Silas, if I go, you got to come with me."

"You're still a little afraid?"

"Hey, a Fencepost is afraid of nothing."

"It's all right to be afraid. You're going to do something totally new."

"I'm not afraid."

"I know. Here, let me show you something," and I open up one of my books. "Look at these rows and rows of squiggly black lines. You're not afraid of those are you?"

"Of course not."

"You're smarter than any row of squiggles."

"Damn right."

"Well, all you're gonna learn is how to outsmart those little alphabet letters. They got secrets they been keepin' from you. But you're gonna beat them at their own game."

"Right," says Frank. "Still . . ."

"You'd like a little company?"

"Yeah."

"Okay, you got it. But I'm just gonna sit beside you. The teacher ain't gonna want me in the class because I read and write, and because I ain't paid. When she asks what I'm doin' there, you tell her I'm your friend and that I'm mute and need looking after, okay?"

"Okay," says Frank.

The registration take place at the office for Continuing Education.

I read the catalog to Frank.

There is a beginning and an advanced course in basic English for reading-disadvantaged people.

"Hey, none of this beginning stuff for me," says Frank "I got years of experience as an illiterate. I want to go in the advanced class."

I fill out the application to put Frank in the beginning class. We take the form to the counter. The woman there look it over and then say to me, "We'll need some proof of your illiteracy, Mr. Post."

"How about if you ask me to read that sign on the wall and I'll say I can't," says Frank.

"I notice you've signed your application."

"When I was just a kid, Silas here wrote out my name and I learned to copy it down. It don't mean anything, honest."

"Well . . ."

"How many people who can read and write sneak into these literacy classes?" I ask.

The secretary give me a mean look.

But that was about the only bureaucracy we suffer.

Like Frank ask, I go with him to the first class. In the afternoon Frank he bought himself a 100-page notebook with a picture of Blondie, the rock-and-roll singer, on the cover. He also acquired, as five-finger bargains, about a dozen felt pens, the same kind I use to write my stories.

"You figure I should get two pads in case I fill this one up tonight?"

"I think one will be enough for the first class."

The group meet in an ordinary classroom at Grant MacEwan College. The room is too hot and the lights are too bright. There is about 15 people there, all sit shy and stare at their feet. There is a lady about Ma's age, who look Indian, so we sit next to her. There is also a man and woman, look to be Chinese, a dark man wear a red turban, while the rest is white, range from a guy about our age to an old man with a white moustache.

The teacher is young and pretty and introduce herself as Elizabeth

Stranger. She call out everybody's name, and as she do, people raise their hands so she can check them off her list.

"There are three more people here than I have on my list," she says. "Did someone bring a friend along for moral support? That's quite all right, you know."

Frank's hand shoot up.

"My friend here is nude. He need lookin' after."

The teacher smile nice, but puzzled.

"You can't tell by the way he looks. But he can't say a word, even if you was to pay him a dollar."

I'd have had Frank here years ago if I could talk like Miss Stranger. In half an hour she have people feeling good about themselves and so proud they make the move to come to class they can hardly wait to get started.

"I know what you've gone through," Miss Stranger say. "Every billboard, every storefront, every banner is a constant reminder that you can't read. You learn to lie, to invent reasons why you can't read aloud from a book. And you develop an elephant's memory.

"People who are illiterate have to memorize signs, sometimes whole forms or order blanks; you have to guess at the meaning of words from other clues. I remember once I went to apply for a job and I stood outside a door with the word PERSONNEL written on it, studied it for a long time trying to guess what it might be. Finally I asked someone where the Personnel Office was. They pointed at the door and said, "What's the matter, can't you read?""

That was the way she let us know she been illiterate at one time, too.

"Illiteracy has virtually nothing to do with intelligence. You've all become experts in failure, but, starting tonight, we're going to put an end to your failures."

Miss Stranger get out some cards with pictures and letters on them. The letter A got a picture of an apple, the letter B the picture of a bear, and so on.

"You still want me to stay?" I ask Frank at intermission.

Frank is walking along the walls, stopping at each poster or notice he come to, point out to me and anybody else who care to listen, which letters is A's, B's and C's.

"Maybe just to the end of this class. I hope we learn some whole words when we go back in. And, Silas," Frank grin kind of sheepish at me, like he do when he get caught in a lie, "thanks for keeping after me," and he clap my shoulder with his hand.

Second half of the class Miss Stranger ask each person to tell why he or she want to learn to read and write.

"My wife just had a baby," say the guy about my age, "and I want to be able to read bedtime stories to him, like my old man did for me."

"I want to read the Bible," say the Indian woman near us, "and to pass the word of the Lord on to my friends and relatives."

We move a couple of seats farther away so people won't think we're with her.

"I am tired of working on the assembly line," say the man with the turban. "I wish to be employed in the office."

"I want to be able to write bad checks," says Frank when his turn come.

"I see," says Miss Stranger, while most everyone laugh. "Well, Mr. Fencepost, we're an equal-opportunity literacy class. Just don't call on me as a character witness if you get arrested."

"When he gets arrested, not if . . . ," I say.

"I thought you were mute," says Miss Stranger.

"This here's Silas Ermineskin who's had about five books printed up, and I'm gonna learn to read them all," says Frank.

The teacher smile and go on with the lesson.

The first three or four weeks Frank get real frustrated that they don't teach him faster. He bug me about 12 hours a day to help him sound out words and make up alphabet letters.

But then he catch on to reading a few words together, and he learn to write short sentences. One day he come to me with "My brother is a green pig" written on a sheet of paper.

I check the spelling and that all the letters is made right.

"I never knew you could write down things that wasn't possible," Frank say. I have to puzzle over that for a while. Guess only someone who just discover the wonder of writing would think that way.

I pick Frank up when his last class is over. He come out holding a little certificate that says he has satisfactorily completed the Adult Literacy Class. He read the certificate to me about 50 times, point out his name each time. He even read the name of the printer, which is in real tiny letters in the bottom corner.

We park the truck downtown, decide to go have a drink to celebrate.

As we walk, Frank turn in circles, like a dog chasing his tail, afraid he going to miss some of the signs we pass by.

"BUS STOP. NO PARKING," read Frank. "SEASON'S GREETINGS."

He stare all around for something else to read, his head going from side to side as his eyes search.

"PLUMBING AND HEATING," he read from a neon sign

across the street. "GOLD COINS BOUGHT AND SOLD. COMPLETE LINE OF WALLPAPER, PAINT AND STAIN," he call out as we pass store windows.

"HAMBURGERS, FRENCH FRIES, APPLE PIE," he go on. "JOHN THE LOCKSMITH, KEYS CUT. TRAVEL AGENCY. ON SALE. DIAMOND RINGS. MARY LYLE'S BEAUTY SALON."

Then we come to a broad fence have a whole lot of writing on it. There is the peace sign, and below it someone has written NUKE THE WHALES. There are about two dozen four-letter words. And among them is written LOVE IS A FOUR-LETTER WORD. Someone else wrote SAVE THE SALMON, CAN AN INDIAN.

"Hey, Silas," Frank yell, "I always wanted to be able to write on a wall."

I think I know how excited he is. It must be something like the feeling I had the first time I got a letter saying one of my stories was to be printed in a magazine.

I watch as Frank take out a felt pen, study the fence for a while before he write THE GREAT FENCEPOST WAS HERE! Then he smile something fierce and go bounding off down the street.

He get at least a half a block ahead of me. The streets are quiet and there is frost on the parking meters and trolley wires.

"CRAWFORD AND KIRK, ATTORNEYS AT LAW," he is yelling. "CANADA TRUST. TOYOTA COROLLA. PASSEN-GER LOADING ZONE AT ALL TIMES . . ."

Snitches

E very once in a while my father, Paul Ermineskin, show up here on the reserve. He is long enough between visits that most everyone forget, or forgive, or just push to the back of their mind the rotten things he done the last time he was here.

"Hey, Silas," he say to me, when he come over to my table at the Alice Hotel bar in Wetaskiwin. I seen him sitting in the corner with his old friend Isaac Hide, but I just hoped he wouldn't see me, or if he did that he'd have sense enough to keep to himself. "Long time, son."

"Not long enough," is what I want to say, but instead I take the hand he stick out. His hand is dry as a sweetgrass braid. Pa don't look as bad as he sometimes does. He's had his hair cut recently and is wearing new jeans and a red-and-white checkered mackinaw.

"I see you still got the prettiest girl on the reserve," he say, more to Sadie than to me, and he hug Sadie's shoulder. "Guess likin' pretty girls runs in the family."

"Only I don't get drunk and break their ribs and black their eyes," I'd like to say, but again I stay quiet.

"Nice to see you, Mr. Ermineskin," Sadie says, and hug one arm around his waist. He sure knows how to get around people. Sadie is nice, but she ain't pretty to anyone but me.

"You're gonna pay for that compliment," I'd like to say to her. "He'll probably borrow money from you before the night's over." Instead, when I speak I speak to Pa: "What you up to?" He's still standing and I don't make any move to ask him to sit, though there's an extra chair at the table.

"Me and Isaac are goin' into business together," he say, wave his arm to where Isaac is hunched over a beer in the corner. Pa's eyes move into every corner of the room as he is talking to me. He searches out every dark spot as if he expect somebody to be hiding there with a gun.

"That's nice," I say. I hope my tone let him know I don't want to hear any of the details.

We exchange small talk for a few minutes. Pa eye the beer on our table. I don't offer and he don't have the nerve to ask. Finally he head back over to Isaac.

After he's gone Sadie stay silent, sipping at her beer. She know better than to talk to me about my dad.

When, a while later, Sadie get up to go to the washroom, I see Paul Ermineskin skulk off in that direction, peeking over his shoulder, walking kind of sideways as he's known to do.

"How much did it cost you?" I ask Sadie when she get back.

"What?"

I point across the bar to where my dad got a bill in his hand, waving to catch the waiter's attention.

"How much did he borrow?"

"I gave him two ones," she say in a small voice.

More likely she gave him a five.

"I'm gonna have to start charging for the nice things *I* say to you."

Sadie glare at me, light up a cigarette.

"You tell me I'm *sweet*," she say. "You never tell me I'm *pretty*."

I don't have an answer for that. She's right. I just don't have the nerve to lie like that, even to please someone I love. Sadie stay mad at me all that night, even sleep at her folks' place instead of with me.

Pa's friend, Isaac Hide, is a bachelor, live in a cabin a mile or so back in the bush. He get some kind of pension for being shot during the Korean War. He claim his health is bad, make a little home brew sometimes that he sell to friends. He ain't a bad man, but he is skinny, and furtive, and have an unwashed smell about him. One winter him and Pa cut Christmas trees and sold them in Wetaskiwin. But soon as they'd make a couple of sales they'd both head for the Alice Hotel bar. By the time they drank up their money, then sobered up, half the trees would have been stolen off their lot.

"I hear your old man and Isaac Hide are going into competition with the Alberta Government Liquor Stores," my friend Frank Fencepost say to me a few days later.

"What they do is no concern of mine. I don't imagine Maurice Red Crow and the guys with big stills are shaking in their shoes. Pa and Isaac will have too much of a fondness for their own product to compete with anybody."

At least they picked a good business to go into. There is always a market for cheap moonshine. A day or two later Frank come by my cabin with a beer bottle half-full of a pale liquid the color of a city snowbank.

"Taste like gopher piss and gasoline," says Frank, "but it got a kick like the time I stuck a screwdriver in an electric socket up at the Tech School."

"I wouldn't drink nothin' my pa had a hand in making," I say. "I've seen too many people go blind from drinking bad home brew."

"Gives a whole new meaning to *blind drunk*," laugh Frank.

Either Pa or Isaac must have some business sense hid deep inside them, for their moonshine business pick up real quick, and, to my surprise they ain't their own best customers. They get a bottle-capper, and from somewhere Pa bought up a few dozen blue bottles, squat and square. He give out samples to the drunks who hang around the Canadian Legion in Wetaskiwin: a lot of them guys have money, own farms and businesses. I finally get talked into tasting some at the pool hall one night; it is sweet and fruity, doesn't taste like something been drained out of a radiator and had yeast added to it. And the blue bottles with the shiny copper cap sure look better than a beer bottle with a cork, which is what the other moonshiners turn out.

Inside of a month Isaac trade off his old rattletrap of a car for a Fargo King Cab truck that only four or five years old. They hire my friend Rufus Firstrider to drive deliveries for them.

"You going to have to incorporate and sell shares," somebody suggest to Pa one evening at Hobbema Pool Hall.

Frank he jump up and start to imitate some of the commercials he seen on TV, like the fat man who sell Chrysler cars, and the man who liked the electric shaver so much he bought the company.

"Compare hangovers," Frank say, pretend he walking toward the camera holding up a bottle. "If Paul and Isaac's Moonshine don't make your head hurt twice as much as the next most pop-ular brand, if one bottle don't make you feel like you swallowed a live jackhammer, we'll give you a bottle of our competitor's moonshine free. Remember, with Paul and Isaac's Moonshine we guarantee you're gonna boogie 'til you puke!" And he point a finger at the imagined camera and wink, while everybody clap their hands.

Pa joke that he gonna hire Frank as a full-time salesman. We make a lot of jokes about that, and everybody have a good time. But I notice Pa's eyes still inspecting every corner of the room. He act nervous and sneaky even when he having a good time.

It is just a day or two later that him and Isaac get a big break. RCMPs, who haven't been bothering moonshiners for a few months, led by Constable Bobowski, the meanest lady RCMP in three provinces, swoop down on Maurice Red Crow's still, what located on a farm up by the town of Kavanagh. They don't catch Maurice, but they haul out two truckloads of equipment, carry it direct to the town dump where a bulldozer trash it good. Maurice will be out of business for quite a while.

Not even a week later Constable Bobowski and her friends hit again; this time they come right on to the reserve, carry off all of Jarvis Lafreniere's equipment, dry stock and bottled goods.

Now everyone know the RCMP can be lucky once.

"But they'd need both the Pope and Pastor Orkin of the Three Seeds of the Spirit, Predestinarian, Bittern Lake Baptist Church on their side for them to make two strikes in a row," say Frank.

"Either that or a snitch," I say. My friends at the pool hall all stop what they are doing when I use that word.

"Come on, nobody on the reserve would do that," say Rufus Firstrider.

There is an unwritten law that say no matter what been done to you, it is a personal matter. We all know that beside a snitch a snake is ten feet tall.

"But there *are* always snitches," says Frank. "If there weren't RCMP would be out of business years ago."

"That's true *off* the reserve," I say. There are guys I know in the cities who make their living as police snitches, though they are frightened all their lives and always about half an inch from being murdered. RCMP are as anxious for a snitch as an alcoholic for a drink. We been known occasionally to set them up by having someone pretend to be a snitch, then give false information.

"But there have been *two* hits," someone say. "RCMP just ain't that smart on their own."

"We'll all have to keep our eyes open," I say, and everyone agree with me.

It was three nights later I stumble on Constable Bobowski doing something strange in the dark. I was walking home from Blue Quills Hall when I seen an RCMP car parked down a side road, lights off and empty. Something must be going on I figure. I follow a path down through a pine grove to where a dry slough form a clearing. It is a cloudy night so I can't see good. But I make out two figures lean on a wire fence; one of them is smoking.

They stop talking once when I kick a root and stumble. I figure anybody who meet at midnight in a secret place is up to no good. I wonder for a minute if maybe Constable Bobowski got an Indian boyfriend, or maybe Constable Chrétien have an Indian girlfriend; that would be more likely.

"What you figure goin' on down there, Chief Tom?" I say real loud, scuff the ground with my feet.

Boy, the person who was smoking crash through that fence, set the barbed wire to zinging, pound off through the bush like a panicked moose.

Turn out that other person *is* Constable Bobowski; she is cool and businesslike.

"What are you doing here?" she ask me.

"I seen the car all locked up. Thought whoever was driving it might be in trouble."

"No. I caught something in my headlights and went to investigate, but it was just an animal. You heard it running away."

We are both pretty good at lying.

"Can I give you a ride to your house?" ask Constable Bobowski. This is the first time she has been nice to me, ever.

In the car I say to her, "You got a cigarette, Constable Bobowski?"

"Sorry," she says. "I don't smoke."

"I didn't think so." And I look a long time at the side of her face.

"There were a lot of fireflies down in the slough tonight," she says as she lets me out of the patrol car.

"Thanks for the ride," I say.

First sign of daylight I'm at the slough. What I find is what I expect to find, a triangle of red-and-white checkered material hanging from one of the barbs, where whoever was with Constable Bobowski crashed through in a hurry. When I see the place in daylight I realize it only about a third of a mile cross country from Isaac Hide's cabin.

What I don't find out until Frank come by my cabin about noon is that sometime around dawn the RCMP hit Isaac and Pa's still, carry off everything including Isaac Hide and my friend Rufus Firstrider.

"Isaac'll get six months or so at the Crowbar Hotel in Fort Saskatchewan," laugh Frank.

"What about Pa? Did they get him too?"

"He was off at his girlfriend's in Wetaskiwin. I was at the poolhall when she dropped him off about an hour ago. That was the first time he heard of the raid."

"Pa's the snitch," I say to Frank. "Pa's been gettin' paid by the RCMP to sell out both his friends and his enemies."

"You better have some proof of that, Silas. You could get your old man killed. If Maurice Red Crow or Jarvis Lafreniere ever believed that . . . ."

A few nights later, I stick my head in the door of the Travelodge cocktail lounge, about the fanciest drinking spot in Wetaskiwin, and there is Pa and Isaac and a couple of women I don't know. Isaac's woman look Indian though she's dressed in expensive clothes, the other woman have yellow hair crinkled tight as a brass kitchen brush, a wide face paved with make up, and big, fat, lipsticked lips.

Pa see me before I can duck out.

"Hey, Silas, come over and meet my friends."

I move slow across the room, until I realize I'm walkin' sideways, the way Pa does so often. I sure have to watch that. I don't want to inherit *anything* from Pa.

"How come you're not drinkin' your own product?" I say and make a weak smile.

"When you want to read a book, do you read one of your own?" says Pa.

I get introduced to the ladies, but I don't even hear their names.

"What you doing here?" I say to Isaac Hide. I knew they just held Rufus Firstrider overnight and let him go; but Isaac owned the still.

"Your pa here got me a lawyer. I'm out on bail. Lawyer says the seizure was illegal, and that they'll let me go and even have to give back our equipment. A case of the big, ugly RCMP hassling us poor, enterprising Native Canadians," and everybody have a good laugh.

"Sit down, Silas, I'll buy you a drink," says Pa. He is wearing a new buckskin jacket with porcupine quill designs, western-cut pants and new boots.

"I gotta get going."

"Hey, one drink," and he pull out a roll of bills so big it got an elastic around it.

"If you're really feelin' flush," I say, "maybe you could repay the money you stole from your little girl a year or so ago." I say that loud and clear so, if nothing else, I'll embarrass him in front of his ladyfriend.

"You know that was just a loan. I always intended to pay her back."

"Well here's your chance. He stole three hundred dollars from his little girl, money she'd earned for a dance costume," I say right to the yellow-haired lady, in case she don't know how bad a company she keeping. But when I look at her face I see her eyes are close together and there ain't a sign of intelligence in them.

"It was a loan," Pa is saying, and he start counting bills off his roll. The elastic break and zoom over a couple of tables; Pa upset a drink send ice and orange juice in a flood across our table. But he lay out a row of twenties, even add one for interest, though he should add three or four. I fold the bills and stuff them in the front pocket of my jean jacket, close the button with a snap.

"You're welcome," Pa say, and laugh a little, a sound his ladyfriend pick up and echo. I don't look around until I'm out on the street. It sure make Delores happy to get paid back, but somehow I don't feel as good as I think I should.

I get to thinking that I bet the RCMP using the wrong procedure when they raid Pa's still was all part of the deal. Isaac was right and the RCMP truck bring their brewing equipment back to the reserve before the end of the week.

I'm sure surprised when a couple of days later there is a knock at my cabin door, and when I open it there is Pa. He must have watched to be sure Ma and the other kids is out.

"What do you want?" I say. I go back and sit at the table where I been working on a story.

"Just thought I'd come by and see my favorite son."

"Don't try to butter me up. You don't like me any better than I like you. You come by to see if you could steal Delores' money back? She put it in the bank this time where you can't get at it."

"I come by because I hear you've been spreading lies about me."

"What could anyone say bad about you that would be a lie?"

"I hear you callin' me a snitch."

"You are a snitch. I seen you meet with Constable Bobowski."

"You seen me?"

"I found cloth from your jacket on the fence."

"How many guys on the reserve own red-and-white mackinaws?"

"I *know*," I say.

"What is it you do, Silas?" Pa say to me; his eyes meet mine and hold on; it is the first time in our lives we ever looked each other in the eye.

"I ain't no snitch, if that's what you mean. We take care of troublemakers in our own way. We have our own law. We never call in outsiders. And I never snitched to the horsemen in my life."

"You're pretty high and mighty," Pa say. "You and your god-damned stories and books. You're the biggest snitch ever been known on this reserve . . . ."

"Hey, wait a minute . . . ."

"You don't just snitch to the cops, you snitch to the whole world. I've had people read your stuff to me when I was in the joint, and I don't admit I'm related to you. You tell everybody's secrets, no matter how awful or how personal. And you know what the worst thing is? You ain't even successful—I made more money sellin' home brew last week than I bet you make in a year. You ain't even a successful snitch."

I have to admit he's right about the money. I'm still able to draw welfare, even though I got books printed up, and had my picture and a story in the *Edmonton Journal*.

"I only sell doctored water make people forget their troubles for a few hours," he go on. "You pick the scabs off sores."

"And you never beat my mom and us kids. And you never drank up the welfare while we was starving here at home."

"Silas, I done a lot of things I ain't proud of, but if you think I turned in those still owners, turned in my friend Isaac for money . . ." Pa standing at the end of the table looking down at me. When I don't take back my accusation he say, "Well, here," and Paul Ermineskin fumble around under his coat and come out with a sawed-off .22 rifle. He lay it on the table.

A gun like that is about the most illegal thing you can own. I wonder who he stole it off of.

I guess it tell a lot about how I feel about my father, because for half a second I was afraid he was gonna use that gun on me.

"It's for you, Silas," he go on. "If you think I'm an RCMP snitch, the lowest life in the world, if you believe for sure I done it, then you better take your revenge." He stare down at the gun where it sit on the table, the butt turned toward me.

I can already smell the oily metal, the bitter odor of gunpowder.

"Look, Silas, I'm a bad bugger. Everybody knows that, including me. I mean I even stole money from my little girl. I'm sorry for it and I'm glad you made me pay her back. But Silas, I ain't a snitch. I wonder if you really know what happens to snitches. Last time I was in the joint there was this guy—we took him into the welding shop and used a blowtorch on him. Guards rescued him before we killed him, but he'll never be the same. Do you think I'd risk *that*? You name somethin' rotten and I done it, all except snitch to the cops."

"I'll make it easy for you, Silas," he go on, and he reach down into his boot and pull out a hunting knife, one I'm pretty sure used to belong to Adolph One-wound. He grip it like he might attack me. "Pick up the gun and blow me away," he say. "You can say I showed up in an ugly, drunk mood and came for you with this knife and gun. You can claim you took the gun away from me. We even make it look like there been a fight," and he kick over a chair and with his free hand sweep the ashtray and a stack of my books onto the floor.

I'm sure he's a snitch. But not sure enough to take any action. Not that I'd kill him for it anyway.

"No, Pa, even if you done it . . ."

"Silas, I make it even easier for you. If you believe in your heart that I snitched, all you got to do is spin that gun around to face me. I'll take it out to the woods and do the job myself."

"No," I say real loud. "Take your stuff and get out," and I motion to the gun but I don't touch it.

"Don't you bad mouth me no more then. Never say you didn't have your chance." His eyes glow yellow in the lamplight. They are small and deep set but full of victory, like a fighter just scored a knock-out. He pick up the gun, shove it under his jacket, and sidle out the door.

I've had my bluff called. Damn Pa! He'd make a hell of a politician. He don't have the courage for there to have been bullets in the gun. I didn't have the courage to call his bluff. The only thing we agree on is that a snitch is the lowest form of life in this world. We both think of each other as being one. And I guess we ain't likely to change our opinions.

Pizza Ria

C athy Calling Bird is the name get chosen for her, though her real name was Ria Meloche, and she was the sixth of 14 kids raised in a slant-roofed cabin miles deep in the muskeg near the back end of Hobbema Reserve.

Ria Meloche discover when she was about 14 she could sing like a real bird. She start out at talent contests at Blue Quills Hall, imitating Loretta Lynn and Dottie West, plunking away on a $10 guitar that somebody else throwed away.

In no time at all she was singing at Saturday-night dances at the Alice Hotel bar. They say Mad Etta put up the money to buy Ria's first costume: a short red skirt with a red velvet vest over a white blouse, a white cowgirl hat and white boots.

A DJ from CFCW, the country music radio station in Camrose, heard her at the Travelodge lounge in Wetaskiwin, and soon she's singing on the radio. A talent agent in Edmonton hear her and sign her up. They decide in Edmonton Meloche don't sound Indian enough, so they change her name.

She made her first record just over a year ago. It sold real well, and she right away get invited to tour as an opening act for the Statler Brothers. I seen her last month on a TV show come direct from Nashville.

Ordinarily we'd figure we seen the last of Ria-Cathy. It sure is a surprise when a fat envelope arrive for me in the mail, have United States stamps on it and a Los Angeles, California, postmark. Inside is a letter from Ria Meloche along with 16 tickets for a Statler Brothers concert at BC Place in Vancouver.

I didn't even know that Ria ever read my books, but in her letter she say she guesses her and me are the most famous people ever to come out of Hobbema. That make me her fan for life. Usually only famous people anyone can name from Hobbema is a guy who played one game in the NHL about ten years ago, a cowboy who was All-Round at the Calgary Stampede and a man who committed a mass murder on the reserve back in the 1950s.

She tell me her tour ends in Vancouver, and then she gonna work for two weeks in a country cabaret called The Texas Star that supposed to have over an acre of dance floor.

"Sixteen people is just an average load for Louis' pickup truck," grin Frank Fencepost, my closest friend, who been reading that letter over my shoulder.

"We can only take fifteen to the concert," I say. "Mad Etta take up two seats all by herself. And we have to set a skinny person on each side of her as well."

Frank is quick to make a list of who we take along.

"I think Ria might like to see some of her family," I point out. The main memory I have of Ria Meloche is her riding bareback on her pony named Bunty, a little, shaggy-maned pinto her papa must have taken in trade for furs. In her letter she ask about her horse first and her family second. I can still see her in front of Hobbema General Store, her arms around Bunty's neck, feeding him sugar cubes she bought in a flat, white box.

Her parents is true bush Indians. Ria can't even send them a letter 'cause neither one can read or write. Her mama is a short, round lady with big eyes, who seem really shy. Her papa, Baptiste, is a thick-bodied man with big, scarred hands, who wear deerskin pants and moccasins he made himself. They both work all year on a trap line and don't speak one word of English between them. Mrs. Meloche ain't ever been off the reserve in her whole life, and we have to talk quite a while before they agree to go with us. Frank suggest we take Bunty the pony along, and for a while we even consider it.

Ain't hard to fill the truck: there is me and Frank and our girl friends; the Meloches, Mad Etta, Bedelia Coyote, Eathen Firstrider; my girl Sadie's brother David One wound is there. David carry a jack and wheel wrench in a red, silken backpack. He wins bets by stripping cars of all four wheels in under four minutes.

Nobody is quite sure how Father Alphonse from the Reserve School got to go with us. Maybe Mr. and Mrs. Blind Louis Coyote invite him. Father Alphonse is French, might have some Indian blood, might not. He been around the reserve for so long we consider him almost one of us.

"As long as you and the church kick in ten percent of the gas money, you're welcome," say Frank.

The trip out to Vancouver goes pretty smooth. While we filling up at a town called Boston Bar, David One-wound win $5 from Eathen Firstrider by stripping the wheels and the grille off a Buick station wagon that got three little kids and a dog inside it. They was waiting while their mama used a washroom. The truck box got pretty crowded with all those extra auto parts mixed in there with the people.

Blind Louis take out his slingshot, what he made from a solid Y of red willow and a band of brick-colored inner tube. Mrs. Blind Louis tell him where to shoot, and as we drive along through the Fraser Canyon, he fling lug nuts at crows.

Turn out we is a couple of weeks early for the concert, which is on the 31st, not the 13th as we thought. I drive the truck down toward East Hastings Street, where David One-wound, who known as the One-wound Auto Parts Company Limited, going to sell off those wheels and grille, maybe generate some new business so we can all afford rooms in a real hotel.

We hardly get the truck parked when we meet up with our friend Bobby Billy; we find him leaning on the same parking meter as a year ago, when I give a reading at SFU. Bobby Billy look a little worse for wear, and has on only one shoe.

"Did you lose a shoe?" asks Frank.

"No, I found one," say Bobby Billy. His face break open real slow, take about 30 seconds for his whole smile to get in place. "By golly, I heard RCMPs sealed up the border to Alberta to keep guys like you on the other side of the mountains."

Bobby Billy is a BC Indian, come from the big, rainy mountains behind Vancouver.

Bobby is not much taller than the parking meter; he got a wide, pushed-in face, and laces of black hair cover his forehead. He push that hair first to one side then the other, but it always fall back like it was before. He wear a green-and-black plaid shirt, green work pants too big for him, and his one shoe.

"I'm sure glad to see you guys. And yonder big lady, too," he say, make a little bow toward Etta. "I got a serious problem that maybe you can help me with."

"Hey, there is no problem too large for Fencepost the Great," say Frank, slap a hand on Bobby Billy's shoulder. "Pour your heart out, my son."

Etta shove Frank out of the way, and it lucky the store she shove him against was boarded up or he would of been inside.

"You're movin' in on my territory," say Etta. "I'm still the medicine woman around here. Now, what's your problem, Shorty?"

"About four blocks down the drag," and Bobby Billy point east on Hastings Street, "is a place called Guido's Pizza. That restaurant been there for about twenty five years, run by a nice old man from Italy. I been helping him out for ten years or more. I washed dishes when he was busy, even chopped mushrooms for him sometimes. At closing time, Guido would crack open a bottle of wine, him and me would sit and talk all night.

"About a month ago Guido died . . ."

"Went to that big pizzeria in the sky," say Frank, who now is standing behind Bobby Billy where Etta can't reach him.

". . . and he left the restaurant to me," say Bobby. "One morning this big lawyer in a $1,000 suit show up at my place at the Boston Rooms there on Columbia Street, say Guido had no relatives and he left the restaurant to me because I was a good friend to him."

"So why's that a problem?" ask Frank. "You get to eat and drink free forever. Personally, I always dreamed of owning my own 7-Eleven store, so I could go in and hold it up every day."

Frank dance backward along the sidewalk. "Let's not waste time. Let's get down there and open it up. Time is money."

"Time is orange juice," say Frank's girl Connie.

"Time is a moccasin," say Blind Louis.

"What do we know about running a restaurant?" I say to Frank.

"Trust your chef," say Frank.

"Only tool in a kitchen you know how to use is a bottle opener," I say.

Bobby lead us down the street until we see the sign, blue letters on a white background, say GUIDO'S PIZZA. We all press our faces against the windows and peer inside.

"What are we looking at?" ask Blind Louis.

"Is that good to eat?" Mrs. Meloche say in Cree of the line of neon the color of a cardinal that spell out PIZZA in the window.

By the time Bobby Billy, who speak each word like it was water slow-dripping out of a tap, can even start to answer, Frank has opened the door by using the can-opener blade of his jackknife.

Inside it smell spicy. Tied to the top corner of the door is a little fishing bell, which tinkle pretty each time the door open or close.

Frank stare round, then say, "This place hold about ten thousand people." He pause. "If you only let them in sixty at a time."

There is red carpet down the middle aisle from the front door to the waitress station. Three steps lead up to the kitchen. The tables is solid and covered in red-and-white checkered tablecloths. The wallpaper is velvety red, soft to the touch, with a raised, swirly pattern. There is tiny electric candles at about ten-foot intervals along all the walls. In the back corner, behind a red velvet curtain, is what Bobby Billy call the family table, where Guido and his friends used to sit out of sight of customers when business was quiet.

In the kitchen, we all stand around the big, silver, two-decker pizza oven, stare at it kind of awestruck, like it something from outer space been dropped in on us.

"Teach us your secrets, strange person," Frank say to the oven.

Turn out Mad Etta is the only one of us know anything about cooking. We read the menu and see that Guido's only sell pizza and spaghetti. Eathen Firstrider fire up the pizza oven, while several of us clean out fridges and coolers of things blue and green that I'd guess was food a month ago.

We also find a good supply of beer and wine, which Bobby invite us to share while we cleaning up the place.

"Since Guido ain't around no more, we'll change the name," say Frank. "The name Fencepost Pizza appeal to me. But being the *magnanimous* person I am, I'll settle for just an Indian name, say Pow-wow Pizza Parlor."

One of the things Frank does that drive us all crazy is, ever since he learn to read and write, he try to improve his word power. He carry a little word book in his pocket, learn a new one every day, which he try to sneak into conversation. Frank has always been about as subtle as a charging moose.

Etta brew up some bread dough and we take turns at making up pizzas on little square boards, look like flat shovels. But when we try to put the pizza in the oven, it stick to the board, and when we push it off it bunch up in a big, messy lump that stick to the oven floor like glue. We even try cooking one pizza right on the board. The board turn black and the pizza stick to *it*.

(Next day we drop in to a Pizza Patio and find out you sprinkle corn meal on the board; the little corns act like ball bearings and roll the pizza into the oven.)

Just as we get ready to leave that night we get our first customers.

We didn't lock the front door after we came in, and even though only the kitchen lights is on, four people come in, sit down and start looking at menus.

"What should we do?" we ask each other.

"Trust your waiter," say Frank, and he run toward the dining room, trip down the steps from the kitchen, stagger all the way to the table.

"Welcome to Pow-wow Pizza. I'm your waiter, Bucking-off-the-mountain. What can I get you dudes?"

The customers, two couples who probably work in a bank, and been to a book-burning, just stare at Frank with their mouths open. It could be that Frank being dressed in denim with a ten-gallon hat, one braid in front, one braid behind, surprise them a little.

"We're the new owners," say Frank. "We come from Hobbema, Alberta, Canada, where men are men and so are at least half of the women."

"Where's Guido?" someone finally ask.

"Out," say Frank.

"When will he be back?"

"Not for a while."

"How long?"

"A long time."

"How long is that?"

"A real long time," say Frank.

The women are pulling at the men's sleeves.

"I think we'll eat Greek," one man say as they get up.

"Hey, we can cook you something Greeks eat. What do Greeks eat?" say Frank as he follow them toward the door. "Grease! That's where they come from, right? I got twenty years experience cooking with grease. Sit yourselves down."

But those people is pushing at each other to be first out the door.

"The secret of success is to delegate authority," announce Frank, while we all having coffee at somebody else's café.

Frank been reading a book called *How To Be A Millionaire By Age 30*, and I guess that is one of the things he learned.

As Frank pop a set of pepper-and-salt shakers in his pocket, he say to Connie, "For instance, instead of teaching you and Sadie to be waitresses like that girl over there," and he point at a young woman in a pleated yellow miniskirt and brown jumper, have three plates balanced down each arm, "I'd hire her to do a good job waiting tables for us, *and* train you girls at the same time." Frank smile like he just invented something.

When the waitress come to our table, Frank stand up, bow a little, doff his cowboy hat and say, "Hello, beautiful lady, what's your name?"

"Don't even bother," the girl say, scowl at Frank; she is waiting on six tables, all got four or more people at them.

"That must be an Indian name," say Frank. "Allow me to introduce myself: I am Fencepost, president of the Rocky Mountain Multiple Orgasm Society. Actually, I'm looking for Hot To Trot. Have you seen her?"

"Don't pay no attention to him," say Connie Bigcharles, have a good grip on Frank's shoulder to show who he belong to. "He has problems. Last week his mother told him to take out the garbage. He took it out to dinner and then to a dance hall."

"Last night down on Granville Street he see a sign say WET PAINT, so he did," I add.

"I know his type," say the waitress, come close to smiling.

"Seriously," say Frank, "underneath I'm a different guy: shy, sensitive, caring . . ."

"Conniving," say Bedelia Coyote.

"Right. No. Listen. Under this," and he pat his chest, "is a serious person looking for another serious person." He pause. "Under that is two floors of pay parking . . ."

By the time we get to dessert, the waitress, whose name is Tina Louise Bodnarchuk, agree to at least come by Guido's and talk about working for us.

"How come you've got a priest with you?" ask Tina Louise.

"A Fencepost leaves nothing to chance," say Frank.

"I am from the tribe of fishing people," say Bobby Billy in his slow monotone speech. "In my language a priest is the stick we use to club fish to death."

"I've thought of everything," say Frank. "We got a priest to pray for us; a blind man so we can park in the handicapped zones; my friend, Standing-knee-deep-in-running-water here, write books; and they used Mad Etta over there as the model for BC Place."

Mrs. Meloche, who never been in restaurants before, order up three pieces of lemon pie all at once. She ain't caught on that you have to pay for all the food get delivered to your table.

Over the next few days it is Mad Etta who take charge of things, though it is Frank who think he do. Tina Louise does come to work for us, and she train Sadie and Connie to wait tables. The rest of us stay out of sight of the customers.

"Public ain't ready to find fifteen Indians running a pizza place," growl Mad Etta.

"It's like being guards after years of being inmates," say Frank, scratch his head in puzzlement as he sit at our family table, tired, sweaty, and so covered in flour he might pass for a white man.

The first lesson we learn about running a restaurant is to hate the public. Restaurant customers is dirty, ornery, stone-cold thieves, and every one of them splashes when they eat. What they don't spill on the tablecloth they toss on the floor, and if anything's left over they wipe it on the walls.

They steal dishes, glasses, knives and forks, salt shakers and ashtrays. If they thought they could get away with it, they would carry out the tables and chairs.

Late one night we all sitting around the family table. There is only six customers eating at a table by the front window; three sailors and their girl friends. We hear the fishing bell on the front door tinkle, but just barely. Frank put an eye to the slit in the curtains.

"Look at that!" he whisper.

Soon we all peering through that slit. Me at the top, then Frank, Etta, Connie, Sadie and Bobby Billy. What we see is one of them customers untying the bell from the door. He get it loose, peer around like a dog about to steal meat, raise his pant leg and tuck the bell into his sock.

"We gonna serve that dude as ground beef on our pizzas for the next few days," say Frank, rub his hands together. "Let's go pound him good."

But Etta get a grip on Frank's arm so he can only hop up and down on one spot.

"What are you gonna have if you fight?" say Etta.

"A good time," say Frank.

"You gonna have broke furniture and dishes, and you don't collect the check from those guys. You can buy another bell for a dollar."

"Less than that," I say, "but it's the idea."

"Give me the bill," say Etta.

She total up their pizza and drinks, then write, "One Bell, $10," and add it to the total. Etta waddle out with the coffee pot and the bill, ask if they enjoy the pizza, and they say they did.

When they come to pay, one of them notice the added item.

"What the hell's this?" he yell.

"For the bell in your sock," say Etta, smile from way down deep in her face.

"We ain't gonna pay," the sailor say.

"I could call the police," say Etta, "have them look in your sock. Or," and she raise up a heavy black skillet she brought down from the kitchen. "I could teach you guys not to steal."

She smile some more. "Or, you could pay the bill I made out and everyone go home happy."

Them sailors look at Etta, and at me, Frank, Eathen, Bobby, Mr. Meloche and Blind Louis.

"Right you are, Mama," one of them say, and cough up the $10.

The way we learn to do delivery orders was we bought a map of Vancouver, glued it to a piece of cardboard; we put one colored pin where the restaurant sat, another where the delivery supposed to go. Then somebody drive, somebody navigate, somebody keep the pizza wrapped tight in a moose-hide robe.

We also learn fast that on delivery orders we got to take a phone number and call back, because people like to place phony orders.

One night we get a call for four large pizzas; I phone the number myself and a boy's high voice confirm the order. But when we get to the address the people never ordered pizza and they have a different phone number. We go back to the shop, not knowing what to do next.

"The beat cop is a friend of mine," say Bobby Billy. "I bet he could help."

That cop, a Constable Rudd, drop in for free coffee a couple of times a night. Constable Rudd is almost as slow-spoken as Bobby Billy, and has a handlebar mustache that look like a squirrel tail been glued under his nose. He make a call to headquarters and get us the address where that telephone located.

About eight of us show up at the house, where a skinny kid of about 15 with a thin nose and about a pound of acne on his face answer the door. He is real surprised to see us.

"That'll be $45," say Frank, hand him the pizza boxes.

"I didn't order no pizza," he say in that high voice I heard over the phone.

We yell back and forth for a few minutes until the boy's father appear. He look like he could lift Mad Etta if he put his mind to it.

"Is he at it again?" he say to us. Then he pick that greasy kid up by one arm and slam him against the wall. Both the wall and the kid crack a little.

"Did you order this stuff?" the father yell. He have to threaten to slam the kid against the wall again before he admit he did.

"I hope those are big pizzas," the father growl at us. "This punk's gonna eat every crumb of every one, or die trying." Then he pay us our money.

"There's enough there to feed twenty people," say Frank. "We add anchovies to every one before we make the second trip."

We can hear the kid making gagging sounds as his father drag him away.

In a few days we doing a good business for Bobby Billy. We close up the night Ria Meloche sing with the Statler Brothers. We all howl up a storm when she come on stage, and afterwards we go backstage where she say hello to her mama and papa, thank us for bringing them, then spend five minutes asking about her horse.

"Soon as I get a permanent place to live I'm gonna send for Bunty," she say.

"Hey!" say Frank. "How about if some night after work at the cabaret you come down to our restaurant and sing for us?"

We all make agreeable sounds.

"Well, I don't know," say Ria. She look over her shoulder at the man behind her. "I don't think so."

"It appear to me that these days Ria is casting a shadow don't look anything like her," say Frank on the way back to the restaurant.

"A beautiful girl with a coyote's shadow," rumble Etta.

"If you want I could make her come to the restaurant," say Ria's mother in Cree. "We owe that little flat-faced Indian Billy for feeding us."

"We don't want her to do nothin' she don't want to," say Etta, smile at me with one side of her face. Without speaking, Etta and I agree there's not much chance Mrs. Meloche have any influence over Ria anymore.

Bobby Billy sure ain't dumb, just bashful. With Etta's help he catch on quick to running the business. We are about ready to head for home and leave Bobby Billy to become a millionaire, when the city health inspector drop in.

Oh, boy, that health inspector rip us up one side and down

another for about an hour. Guess the place hadn't been inspected for years. It ain't just a matter of cleaning and washing: the kitchen-floor tiles have to be replaced; all the walls have to be painted; an electric dishwasher have to be installed; the water heater have to be replaced because it don't heat the water enough to kill germs; the cooler ain't cold enough and the chimney need replacing. We don't even have to get estimates to know the repairs is more money than we got.

"In the Bible," Father Alphonse begin, "they had plagues and locusts . . ."

"Here they got health inspectors," finish up Frank. "He a first cousin to Mr. Clean, or what?"

The health inspector send us a registered letter, give us 14 days to shape up or close up. We all try to figure ways to make money again. All we can come up with is Cathy Calling Bird.

"If she sang for us for three nights we could make enough money to pay for the repairs. We could put ads in both newspapers, put on a $5 cover charge," say Frank.

We load up the truck and head off again to The Texas Star. But talking to Ria-Cathy mean also having to talk to her shadow. It has a name, Justin Barlow. He is a big, heavy-set guy in satin cowboy clothes. He have sideburns shaped like thick pork chops. He speak in a slow drawl, spend a lot of time pushing his $200 cowboy hat back on his head, mopping his brow with a red handkerchief, and smiling.

Ria tell us Justin Barlow is her manager; she also let us know he played steel guitar for Ray Price's band, the Cherokee Cowboys, until Ray Price retired.

"Y'all got to understand that Cathy can't just go singing any old place at any old time," Justin Barlow say to us.

"She has contracts to honor, recording dates, and I have to decide what's good for her career."

"Friendship don't count?" say Bedelia.

"Something you got to learn, little lady, is that successful people always have hangers-on tryin' to pull them down. The real successful people peel off those hangers-on just like old clothes. What it amounts to is successful people don't need friends. Ain't that right, Cathy?"

"I guess so," Cathy say, but she don't look too happy about it.

This is mid-afternoon in the empty cabaret, which is kind of like a forest at dusk. There is actually a cold breeze inside the building, and that acre of empty tables is like a barren field.

"Perhaps I could be of service?" say Father Alphonse.

We all look at him. Father Alphonse don't want anything as much as just to be useful. He been stuck out on the reserve with us Indians because he wasn't very competent.

"A bishop's kind of like a banker, and some priests with big congregations is as powerful as lawyers or accountants, but if we was to give Father Alphonse a name it would be the Dishwasher Priest," is the way Frank describe him.

"I could speak to her of compassion," say Father Alphonse. "Appeal to her better nature. Point out the God-given opportunity to help her spiritual brothers and sisters in distress."

"Give it a shot, Father," say Mad Etta.

He take Cathy off to a distant table, Father Alphonse gesturing often, wiping sweat from his narrow forehead. Cathy continually shake her head, looking over her shoulder to where Justin Barlow lurk among the musical instruments on the bandstand.

Finally, Father Alphonse give up.

"She'll do it for me," Ria's mama say, and pad over on her

moccasined feet to catch Ria before she get back to the band-stand.

I walk part way with Mrs. Meloche, thinking seriously of stopping her. I sure hate to see this little lady disappointed. Ria's a city girl now, and ain't gonna pay no attention to her mama, who's dressed shabby and smell of campfires.

But she sort of slide away from me and pull Ria down at a table, where they do about three minutes of furious Cree speaking before Ria slam her hand on the table, stand and march away real mad. She talk for a minute to Justin Barlow almost as furiously as she been talking with her mother. She stomp her foot at him and stride back to her mama. They whisper back and forth for a minute. Mrs. Meloche come back to us, say to Mad Etta, "Four nights, any time you want her. Me and Baptiste always pay our debts."

She give a small smile from her round, weather-burned face.

"Ah," say Father Alphonse to Mrs. Meloche, rubbing his skinny hands together, "a mother's touch."

Even after all his years on the reserve Father Alphonse speak only halting Cree, and he speak it with a bad accent. "I suppose you spoke to her of love and loyalty, duty to family and to God," he go on.

"Who is this guy?" Mrs. Meloche say real sharp, as she light up a roll-yer-own cigarette, spit a piece of loose tobacco past the priest's ear.

"Yeah, that's exactly what she did," I break in to tell Father Alphonse. "You wore Ria down, her mother just closed the deal." Father Alphonse smile so hard he almost radiate light.

Because I walked part way with Mrs. Meloche, I was the only one heard the conversation. Boy, I underestimate this lady live all her life in the bush. Guess when you put your life on the line in

40-below weather, have to kill for your food and clothes, you learn to state a case plain, don't worry about hurt feelings. What she said to Ria was, "If you don't help our friend who feeds us, when I get back to the reserve I'll kill your pony."

A Lighter Load

"There are people," says Mad Etta, our medicine lady, "who spend their lives creating bad situations, because the only thing they're good at is making the best of them."

"Is Rickey Westwind one of those?" I ask.

"It beginning to look that way," says Etta, swigging from her bottle of Lethbridge Pale Ale.

"Why do you suppose he come to you in the first place? He never been one to have anything to do with the old ways."

"Guilt works in funny ways. If that's what his problem really is."

That mean Etta don't think guilt is Rickey's real problem. A couple of years ago, I wouldn't have realized that right away. Maybe I am learning something by being her assistant, though she never seems to give me a chance to do much of nothing.

Rickey Westwind just been at Etta's cabin for about two hours. He been, as Frank Fencepost would say, pouring his guts out. Rickey ain't even lived on the reserve for maybe five years. I'd guess him to be 28 years old, a guy everybody predict would be successful, and so far nobody is disappointed. But they will be if he tells the world what he told Etta here tonight. Rickey worked for a bank for a few years after high school, learn to do accounting. He dress in suits and ties, smell like a bouquet of flowers all the time. He live in Wetaskiwin, marry himself a white girl; they got twin daughters, and he went to work for Department of Indian Affairs a couple of years ago, have a job to do with giving out grant money for construction projects.

It was sure a surprise when Rickey come driving up to Etta's cabin in his big wine-colored Buick. He put on khaki pants and a plaid sports shirt, guess so he figure to look more Indian, but, like all his clothes, they appear perfectly clean, like they never been worn before. Rickey is thin and sink-chested, his hands are long and bony, he have a thin mustache and black eyebrows that stand out on the yellowish skin of his forehead.

"I've done something real bad," he tell Etta.

"There are degrees of bad," says Etta. "You hit-and run somebody? Stole a steak from Safeway? Killed your wife and kids?"

"I've stolen," he said. "Well, not really. I took money to let somebody know about bids on a construction deal. Then I let them put in a lower bid."

"Who really got hurt?" ask Etta.

Rickey Westwind pause for what must be a full minute, before he say real quietly, "Me."

It turn out that some sneaky friends of Chief Tom Crow-eye was behind the trouble. Gerald Proulx and Augustus Fryingpan from the reserve, and Lucien Benoit, who is only a Metis, live in Edmonton and own a big construction company. They gave Rickey Westwind and his assistant Peter Cougar $5,000 each to fix the contracts.

"What should I do?" Rickey ask Mad Etta.

"I think you got something in mind already," says Etta. "Before you do anything consider careful about who got hurt. The original low bidder lost out, but he don't know that. Indian Affairs actually saved money by getting a lower bid. You and Peter Cougar got some extra money. What you did ain't honest, but it wasn't hurtful. If you feel real bad about it, I'd suggest you take the money and give it to a charity: Bedelia Coyote set up a shelter in Wetaskiwin to help battered women and kids. I think that would make everything even. Learn from your mistake and don't do it again."

It plain from the way Rickey Westwind was fidgeting around while Etta talking that he ain't interested in what she is saying.

Etta sigh big.

"What is it *you* want to do?"

"I'm going to the RCMP and confess everything."

"You got a real sore conscience, eh?"

"Yeah," say Rickey.

"You gonna hurt a lot of people if you do that. I hear you got a nice wife and some pretty kids. What about your assistant? Shouldn't he have a say in whether you go to the police?"

"I've gotta do it, no matter."

"Lucien Benoit and those friends of Chief Tom are big-time crooks. They might kill you to keep you from testifying."

"I gotta do it. I got to make things right."

Etta sigh again.

"Has the church got anything to do with this?" she ask. "You believe those devils the Catholics always pushing gonna burn your hide if you don't come clean?"

"Not really. I was fed that stuff as a kid. But I got to confess for myself."

"What you doing is taking a light load and turning it into a heavy one. Not the other way around. Only person who is going to get any satisfaction from you confessing, is you."

"If that's true, I'll just have to live with it."

"You'll be kind of a hero, you know. Is that what you're after?"

"A hero?"

"Sure. You'll drag down those friends of Chief Tom, maybe even the chief himself, if he ain't kept his hands snowy-clean."

"No. I don't care about anybody else. I got to square myself with the world."

"That's what I was afraid of," say Etta. "You know there are some people who are only happy when they're unhappy?"

"I'm not one of them." Rickey get up off his chair. "I'm sorry I come. I thought you'd be happy I want to be an honest man."

"Only if it done for the right reasons. When are you planning on going to the RCMP?"

"First thing in the morning."

"Have you told your wife yet?"

"No."

"Don't you think you owe it to her?"

"What difference would it make?"

"Maybe not much to you, but a lot to her. And what about your assistant? I know Peter Cougar. He ain't smart enough to do anything crooked. You got to prepare him. If you don't do it, I will."

"I'll talk to him," Rickey said reluctantly.

"No. Silas will stop by his place and bring him over here. Tonight. You go home and sleep on your idea. You don't go to the police until we talk again."

Etta indicate by a wave of her hand that his time with her is over, and Rickey Westwind let himself out the door. It easy to tell he ain't used to being waved out doors.

"Don't just sit there," say Etta to me, "get over to Peter Cougar's. If he ain't home, wait for him, and bring him back here."

Peter is a year or two older than me. He still live with his folks here on the reserve. He is barrel-chested, with a wide, flat face. He wear black suits, and black-rimmed glasses. His eyes are big and sad and he puff when he walk fast, a little like Etta, who puff when she walk, period.

I find Peter at home. I call him out on the porch, say I have something private to tell him.

"What do you suppose Old Etta want with me? I hardly know her," he say.

"Probably just wants a share of the bribe money you took," I say real casual. I never seen anybody sweat instantly before. His face bead up and his breath get short, all at the same time.

"Nobody was supposed to know," he whisper.

"Everybody *always* knows about something like that," I say. "Don't worry though, Etta probably only wants a cut. Etta is kind of like the church: If you pay her off she'll leave you alone; if you don't pay, she'll be on your back like a bobcat."

Peter is a real pain in the ass; by the time Etta talk to him for a few minutes he is in tears. She is real patient with him, though. If Frank was here he'd just say "If you can't do the time, don't do the crime."

"I don't want to go to jail," Peter sob. "I don't want to lose my job. I didn't want to do it in the first place, but Rickey made me," and he go to snuffling some more. "Why is he going to the police? He was the one real anxious to take the money. He can't do that.

Lucien Benoit and his friends will kill us both." He even go and stand beside Mad Etta, who perched way up on her tree-trunk chair at the back of her cabin, actually cry on her shoulder.

"You go and see Rickey tonight," she tell Peter. "Silas will go with you to make sure you say the right thing. You tell him you need a week to decide what to do. If he's going to confess you might want to be in Toronto, or someplace just as far away when he make his confession."

"I got a cousin in Washington State," sniff Peter.

"Go sit in the truck. Silas will come out in a minute," she say.

"What if Rickey won't give him time?" I say.

"He will," say Etta, "and if he'll give one week he just might give another, and by then he may come to his senses. There ain't nothing as sad as a guy who wants to clear his conscience and take everybody down with him."

Rickey do give the extension, but over the next few days both him and Peter hover around Mad Etta's like a couple of crows waiting for food. Etta try to talk turkey with Rickey Westwind, but he insist he have to confess so he can live with himself.

"Hmmmph," is all Etta says. But if you know Etta, you know it could take a politician six days of steady talking to say the same thing.

The morning of the fifth day, Etta say to me, "Go tell Rickey Westwind to come up here on his lunch hour. I used up all my speechmaking on him last night. Today I take action. After you tell him, you drive into town and bring his wife and kids out here. I want them to see what kind of a faker he really is."

Rickey's wife, who is a plain-looking white girl, name of Jennifer, ain't thrilled to ride to the reserve with a strange Indian in a truck held together by rust. But when I tell her it have to do with Rickey, and how the only person in the world likely to convince him not to confess is Etta, she put on a bright green jacket have her name on the sleeve and "Senior Women's Softball" on the back in gold letters, bundle the kids into the truck with me.

"He what!" is the words Rickey yell when Etta tell him her piece of news. Then he repeat it, "He what!"

"You heard me," say Etta. "You been saved a whole lot of trouble. Peter Cougar went to the RCMP this morning and confessed everything. You won't have to worry anymore; it may take a day or two, but the RCMP will be around to arrest you."

"You crazy old woman," Rickey shout. "You had him do this, didn't you?"

"The idea did cross my mind," say Etta. "Guess Peter Cougar must of read my thoughts." And she smile like that Mona Lisa picture.

"Don't you realize what you've done!" Rickey go right on yelling. "They'll make a hero out of him. He'll get his wrist slapped, maybe not even get fired. I'll get dragged in just like a cheap crook. It'll look like I was trying to keep the money instead of give it back."

His voice run down like a record player been unplugged. If Etta wasn't so much bigger than him, I'm sure he'd attack her.

"And," he carry on, "they . . . Lucien Benoit and his friends, may think I put Peter up to it. They know he's too stupid to think for himself."

Rickey is pacing around the cabin.

"What I'm going to have to do," he say, as if he talking to people who aren't there, 'cause right now he sure ain't interested in me, or his family, or Etta, "is deny, deny, deny. There was never anything written. If we all stick together we can make Peter look like an idiot, which he is."

"Come to think of it," say Etta. "I may have got my information wrong. You know how old women are. I think it tomorrow that Peter Cougar going to the police. You still got time to beat him to it."

I can see that pale white woman, who done nothing so far but sit at Etta's kitchen table and smoke a cigarette, kind of expanding. She glaring at Rickey Westwind, got a crease between her brows look like she been tomahawked.

This time he don't say "What!" to Etta's statement. He heard her clear enough.

When I was a kid one time, Ma bought from the Goodwill for ten cents, a plastic clown tall as me, that you blowed up full of air. There was sand in the bottom so us kids could punch it hard on the nose and it would rock backward and bounce upright again. I played with that clown for a week or more, until one day my friend Frank Fencepost borrowed a .22 rifle from Louis Coyote's cabin and shot that clown right through the nose. After it was shot it lost its air slowly, taking maybe a minute to sink down until it was just a puddle of airless plastic on the floor.

Rickey Westwind has had the air shot out of him, just like my toy clown. And gonna take years to plug up the bullet holes.

"Hmmmph," say Etta, don't need to be translated.

I got the feeling Bedelia Coyote's charity going to get two big donations later this week.

The Miss Hobbema Pageant

W e thought it was going to be a problem when my friend, Frank Fencepost, decide to enter the Miss Hobbema Beauty Pageant, but it wasn't until the pageant was over and Frank already lost, that things get sticky.

"Why in the world do you want to enter a beauty contest?" I ask Frank.

"Why not?" say Frank. "There's a $500 dollar cash prize. Winner get to compete in the Miss Indian America Contest going to be held in Edmonton end of the month, right up on the stage at the Circus there in West Edmonton Mall."

"But you're not a Miss!"

"A Fencepost never worry about trivial details. That's why I got you as a friend. You worry enough for both of us. Besides, you ever seen any ads for the Mr. Hobbema Beauty Pageant?"

I have to admit Frank is right about the contests being only for girls.

"I'm a equal-opportunity beauty pageant contestant," says Frank.

We just been to Robinson's Stores in Wetaskiwin, with our girlfriends, where Frank pick up an entry form along with a couple of five-finger bargains. On the entry form where it says, Name? he fill in: FRANKIE FENCEPOST. Then he lie about everything else on the form, especially his measurements.

"You're almost six feet tall; you got a mustache, and you ain't developed in the right places," we remind him.

"Half the girls in Hobbema got mustaches, and those are the good-looking ones," says Frank, dodge a slap from his girlfriend, Connie Bigcharles. "I'll just comb out my braids, put on a pair of pantyhose, strap my friend Cochise here to my leg, and I'm in business."

"You just want to use the same dressing room as the other contestants," I say.

"Hey, nobody should be shy," says Frank. "I been to bed with all but two of the contestants anyway. We got no secrets from each other."

I guess he forgot his girlfriend was there. He glance over at Connie, smile like a dog been caught sucking eggs.

"Just kidding," he say, smile pretty weak. "Not that a lot of these girls don't throw themselves at me. But a Fencepost is able to turn aside temptation . . . ."

"No problem," says Connie, reach over, grab the knife that Frank always wear on his belt. Frank dance backward down the street, just out of Connie's reach. "I just perform a little operation," says Connie, "make you fully eligible to be Miss Hobbema."

It take an hour or so before they make up. Connie has a good heart; she know Frank like her best or he wouldn't keep coming back. But nothing we say can stop Frank from entering the contest. And a few days later when the pageant people realize Frank ain't a girl, they are only able to make a lot of noise, because Frank, he read the rules careful and there ain't a thing say the contestants have to be female.

If there was a panel of judges, like in most beauty contests, Frank wouldn't stand a chance, but the Miss Hobbema Pageant is decided by the general public buying tickets at 50 cents each, the money go to provide sports and recreation, buy craft supplies, help run a daycare center at Blue Quills Hall. When it come to buying tickets people ain't shy, and surprisingly, I can only remember once when the prettiest girl didn't win the contest, and even then it was close.

One year Rider Stonechild come back from working up north on construction, buy $300 dollars worth of tickets for his ugly daughter Brenda. The reason she is ugly is she look just like her dad. But that make other people work harder and Cindy Claw, who is as pretty as any girl on the reserve, win Miss Hobbema that year.

The winner, though I guess she always been eligible, never gone on to the Miss Indian America Contest, 'cause there never been money to send her far away. And past pageants ain't always been well organized. Two years ago, the Hobbema Chapter of the Ermineskin Warrior Society print up three-color posters and distribute them as far away as Edmonton. But that was about all they did. A few hundred people show up for the celebration. But as Frank say, "Whole day was kind of run on Indian Time."

There was a big pow-wow in Saskatchewan that weekend so all our dancers were away; instead of Molly Thunder's Dancing Troupe which is called the Duck Lake Massacre, there is one hoop dancer, Gatien Fire, who is about 60 years old, and wasn't a good dancer even when he was young.

They advertise canoe races, but we haven't got either a lake or a river on the reserve. So the races have to be held on the slough down the hill from our cabins. The slough got about an inch of green stuff on top, look like muskeg moss, and when the racers dip paddles in what pass for water, they come up pretty muddy.

Also, the only dignitary they could get was Mr. J. William Oberholtzer, the ex-mayor of Wetaskiwin who, when he was mayor, wouldn't have come to the reserve if we held a gun to his nose. But being out of politics for a couple of years make him anxious for a crowd to bore.

There are six girls and Frank in the contest, including Melody Crying-for-a-vision, who got to be the prettiest girl, white or Indian, within 50 miles of Hobbema. What happens is that every contestant and their friends go around selling tickets to everybody else. Half the people in the Alice Hotel bar and the Gold Nugget Café have booklets of tickets sticking out of the pocket of their jean jackets.

Soon as they see Frank ain't going to change his mind, our girlfriends get right into the act. Connie Bigcharles get some Super Glue and with a big pair of scissors cut Frank some breasts from the inside of a sofa cushion. One turn out a lot larger than the other, but don't look too awful after the girls strapped him up in a brassiere.

All this happened a couple of months ago and I think Frank still picking bits and pieces of sofa stuffing off his chest. Whoever named Super Glue sure knew what they was doing.

Almost everybody, except the other contestants, like the idea of Frank. He get himself a couple of dresses from the Goodwill Store, a green cocktail dress with fuzzy green trim, and a peach-colored evening gown. People who know him buy lots of tickets because he give them a good laugh, but what turn things in his favor is we go door-to-door in Wetaskiwin selling tickets. White people ain't used to Indians coming to their door, but they sure surprised when six of us show up on their porch, the leader wearing a dress, a cowboy hat, lipstick and a mustache. They buy a couple of dollars of tickets just to be sure we go away.

There never been so big a crowd out to Blue Quills Hall as the night of the pageant. I feel a little sorry for the girls when everybody line up on stage, 'cause the audience all seem to be there to cheer Frank. Except for knobby knees and being a little thick in the waist Frank look pretty good in a bathing suit, and when it is his turn, he parade across the stage, high-stepping like a majorette. The rudest guys in the audience, the rodeo riders like Eathen Firstrider, and Simon Sixkiller, holler out, "Show your tits!" And Frank peel down the front of his bathing suit give them all a cheap thrill. And all the rodeo guys buy maybe $20 dollars each in votes from the Blue Quills Ladies Auxiliary, who stationed around the hall, wearing blue aprons and holding fistfuls of tickets.

There is sure a lot of strange Indians around Blue Quills Hall. I heard that some come from as far away as Great Slave Lake and even Manitoba for this here contest. I don't know what they feed them that they grow so big, but, boy, there is a couple of strange Indians about seven feet tall, lean near the stage, make dents in whatever they lean on. They eye the contestants.

One nod his head toward Frank. "Say, George, you ever seen anything so ugly this side of the stockyards?"

"I think I'm in love, eh?" say George. "I like ugly women. They're easy to catch. Once you got one they try harder. And they never get mad when you fool around on them; they just glad to have you come home at all."

The first guy point at Frank again. "*That one* you couldn't even drink pretty."

But George is in love.

"Hey, sweetheart, I got something to show you I bet you'd like," George say as Frank and the other contestants parade down off the stage.

Frank suggest that George do something to himself that ain't humanly possible.

"I like a woman plays hard to get," says George, blow Frank a big kiss.

"What are you going to do for talent?" I ask Frank, right after he paraded across the stage in his green fuzzy dress, shimmy his backside at the audience who howl like he did something funny. There's no explaining why people get all happy when they see a guy dress up like a girl.

"That is a problem," say Frank. "Guess this audience ain't ready for me to display my real talent," and he grin evil. Frank like to tell the story, though I'm not sure it's true, of how he went into Mr. Larry's Men's Wear in Wetaskiwin, the snottiest, most expensive store within 50 miles, and Mr. Larry, who got a voice that could lubricate cars, say to him, "What's your pleasure, sir?"

"Sex with pretty girls, and driving hot cars," say Frank. "But I'm just here to look for a ten-gallon hat."

Frank and me try to figure out how you display to an audience your ability to con people.

"Maybe I could show how I stuff five-finger bargains down the front of my jeans and boogie out of a store."

We puzzle over that for a while until Frank decide his talent will be storytelling. Two of the girl contestants do the chicken

dance, one twirl a fire-baton, would have done her costume a certain amount of damage if it hadn't been fireproof. Another one
sing a Loretta Lynn song, and the last one do gymnastic exercises,
look like she could tie herself in a bow if she set her mind to it.
When it's Frank's turn, this is the story he tell:

"Last year on the July first weekend in Edmonton, I meet this
really pretty girl. It is Friday afternoon and after I tell her I'm one
of these rich Indians got more oil-money than brains, we go down
to Edmonton Motors, where I pick out the hottest car on their
lot; I have them make out the registration form in her name, put
every extra except manned space flight on it. Then I write that
car dealer a check for the full amount.

" 'This is Friday,' the dealer say, 'no way to clear the check
until Tuesday.'

" 'No problem,' I say. 'We just come back Tuesday morning.
You make sure she's got a full tank of gas, eh.'

"Tuesday morning I drop by, just in case there's been a mistake,
but there hasn't. The check bounced all the way to Wetaskiwin
and back and is still quivering on the salesman's desk.

" 'If you knew you had no money why did you write the check?'
that salesman ask me.

" 'For one hell of a weekend,' I tell him."

When they tally up the votes, Frank brought in a record amount of
money, have almost double the runner-up, Melody Crying-for-a-vision.

Chief Tom Crow-eye, looking kind of sick, shake Frank's hand,
make a point of *not* kissing him, plop on his head the cardboard
crown been sprayed with silver paint and sparkles, that make
Frank Miss Hobbema.

Frank, who always been one for surprises, make a real nice speech, leave everybody happy.

"It's especially hard for a Fencepost to be humble," Frank begin, "but I want to thank everybody for voting for me. I'm glad we raised a lot of money for a good cause—my prize money. And that's all I'm gonna take is the money. I settle for being first runner-up in this here contest." And while people cheer louder than ever, Frank walk across the stage and put the crown on the head of Melody Crying-for-a-vision.

Miss Hobbema Pageant was one thing but Miss Indian America is another. That contest held over a two-day span at West Edmonton Mall, a place that got about a thousand stores, a carnival, a zoo, and an ice rink all under one roof. Frank describe West Edmonton Mall as "Ten acres of plastic Indian jewelry and french fries." We are there just like big dogs; it impossible to keep Frank away from a place where there's gonna be the 20 prettiest Indian girls in North America competing for a prize.

Soon as we get there this tall, beautiful Indian girl come toward us; she have hair down to her belt, wear a white blouse show off her coffee-colored skin.

"Excuse me," say Frank. "I'm just a poor but handsome Alberta Indian, and I realize we're from two different worlds . . ."

"At least," say the girl, swivel around and leave Frank talking to empty space.

The people who organizing Miss Indian America is from the United States and is professional Indians, in every sense. In charge are Joe Evening and Princess Paula Three Stars. Reason they chose Edmonton was the owners of the mall agree to pay all the expenses for the contest.

After we get a look at the organizers, Frank he say, "I bet Joe and Paula there wear buckskin pyjamas to bed."

Joe Evening probably have some Indian blood in him, but we'd all bet money that Princess Paula Three Stars come from New York City and used to be in advertising. She dress the way people in foreign countries think an Indian should: in plastic beads, imitation buckskin, and moccasins made in Korea.

All the time the Miss Hobbema Pageant going on, Bedelia Coyote and her friend Constable B.B. Bobowski have their noses turned way up in the air, as they always do. They each memorized a page from Ms. magazine about how beauty pageants exploit women, and they repeat that little speech every time they get a chance. What we forgot was that Melody Crying-for-a-vision was a friend of theirs. She was in the Miss Hobbema Pageant for the money, just like Frank. But when it come to other things she have a mind of her own.

And how her mind thinks start to show up the first day of Miss Indian America when all 20 contestants show up for a press conference. Everyone except Melody Crying-for-a-vision is decked out in what the contest call "Traditional Indian garb."

Miss Hobbema is wearing a canary-yellow dress, with a black belt and black shoes, and a big yellow bow in her hair. She stand out among all the artificial buckskin and plastic wampum, like a yellow flower on a brown hillside.

Princess Paula Three Stars is quick to point out that every contestant is to be judged on her "authenticity of traditional dress, knowledge of Indian culture, traditional craft, and modern talent."

"Where does it say I can't wear a pretty dress?" Melody want to know.

"You'll wear what we tell you to wear and nothing else," say Princess Paula.

"Hey," say Frank, who been eavesdropping, "we was at this trade show a few weeks ago, where they elected a Miss Relocatable Structure of America."

"So?" say Princess Paula, stare at Frank like she's spoilin' for a fight.

"So a relocatable structure is a portable outhouse, right. The point is this Miss Relocatable wasn't wrapped in toilet paper, and she sat on a regular chair not a two-holer Johnny-on-the-spot."

"Listen, if I want any advice from you, cowboy, I'll send up smoke signals."

Instead of going bare-knuckle with her as I would of expected, Frank he back off, while Princess Paula turn her attention back to Miss Hobbema, tell her in no uncertain terms that she better dress like everybody else or they disqualify her.

"See, I've learned to take criticism," say Frank, puff out his chest, "instead of assault, now I just think bad thoughts and plot revenge."

"Don't you threaten me," is what Melody Crying-for-a-vision say to Princess Paula. "I'll wear whatever I please whenever I please. And once Miss Hobbema, always Miss Hobbema, you can't do a damn thing to me." Behind her Bedelia Coyote and Constable Bobowski, who is on her day off and dressed like a regular human being in jeans and red sweater, nod their heads and smile.

Some of the reporters there heard most of the kerfuffle, and in the next morning's *Edmonton Sun* is a headline: INDIAN QUEEN BUCKS TRADITION, IRKS OFFICIALS.

Buckskin isn't for Melody Crying-for-a-vision, 19, who says she's been asked to step down as the Miss Hobbema entry in Miss Indian America because she prefers modern dresses to traditional Indian garb. Pageant officials were apparently angry because she wore a conventional dress to a press conference kicking off the two-day contest. Crying-for-a-vision, a member of the Dakota Band on the Ermineskin Reserve, south of Edmonton, said the organizers gave her 24 hours to conform or step down because she won't be a pow-wow princess. She vowed not to resign.

The three judges for Miss Indian America are Jacques Raute, a hockey player who might be one-quarter Indian, used to be third-string goalie for the Montreal Canadiens; a lady with her own afternoon TV show who wear a pound or so of make-up on her face and whose favorite word is *cute*, and a DJ name of J. Paul Bunyan, who over the air, sound 21 and handsome, but in person is at least 45 with a pot-belly and look like he scrunched about 400 years of hard living into his life so far.

There is a big breakfast for all the contestants and the first contest events scheduled for the afternoon. All the contestants except Melody wear their Indian get-ups to breakfast; Melody have on a red blouse the color of a cardinal and a white pleated skirt.

Frank only have to tell a couple of lies to get us in to the breakfast. The white people who work here are a little scared of Indians and tend to believe Frank when he say we are from the Indian TV Network.

"I am Fencepost, TV director to the stars," Frank say to the girl in the red jacket who collecting tickets for the breakfast. "I left our tickets in our room . . . ." Before the girl can say anything Frank stare into her face, step back so he can get a closer look. "You're exactly the type we're looking for," he say. "We need a white girl for that series we going to start filming next week." He turn to me.

"My assistant, Silas Standing-around-with-wet-clothes-on," is how Frank introduce me. "Silas, give this here future TV star our room key so's she can audition right after breakfast."

Guess Frank forgot we slept in the back of Louis Coyote's pickup truck in the parking lot last night.

"I left the key in the room, sir," I say.

"Well, never mind, Room 405, soon as breakfast's over," and we push past and find a seat across from Melody and Bedelia.

We hardly dug into the grapefruit when both Joe Evening and Princess Paula Three Stars bear down on our table.

"Either you dress according to the rules or you're out," snap Princess Paula. Behind her Joe Evening nod his head.

"We've checked the rules," says Bedelia, "there is nothing says she has to wear Indian clothes, in fact," Bedelia go on, smiling kind of sly, "there's nothing says she has to be a girl."

About this time the three judges appear, led by J. Paul Bunyan.

"We've talked this over and we can't see any reason why Miss Crying-for-a-vision can't dress as she pleases," says J. Paul.

Well, Princess Paula turn on the judges, and if her eyes was machine guns she'd mow down all three of them. Up close I can see that it is cherry-colored make-up make Princess Three Stars look like an Indian.

"Listen, you three can be replaced just by my snapping my fingers; there are lots of has-beens and freeloaders who'd kill for a

little publicity. You think there aren't a few dozen alcoholic ex-
athletes, over-the-hill TV hosts, and sex-maniac disc-jockeys
who like to pat a little ass back stage, just waiting for your jobs?"

The three of them shrug their shoulders and retreat, but their
eyes are hard.

Princess Paula give Melody one last chance which Melody
don't take.

"Alright, we've had enough of your defiant attitude. You're out
of the competition. The first runner-up will become Miss
Hobbema."

None of us do anything but smile secret smiles. We want to
wait until everything is official before we introduce Princess Paula
to the new Miss Hobbema.

And with the judges feeling as they do toward the organizers, it
not too hard for me to guess who they going to elect as the next
Miss Indian America.

Forgiveness Among Animals

On the night Freddy Powderface began circling his cabin, trotting round and round in a circle pure as if it been drawn for him, I'm sure I was the only person on the reserve who knew what he was up to. He started his run about five in the afternoon, jogging in an even, relaxed way, always staying the same distance from the house whether he passing the front, back, or sides.

I wasn't there for the first half hour or so of his circles. I was down at Hobbema Pool Hall shooting a game of eight-ball with Eathen Firstrider when my friend Frank Fencepost come running in.

"There's about twenty people up at Freddy Powderface's place," Frank puffed. "I always figured Freddy was eight cents short of a dollar, but now he's taken to running in circles around his cabin. Not only that but he's runnin' right through the briars and nettles and he's cutting himself all to rat shit. Looks like he's spent two hours in a bagful of bobcats, or," and here Frank smile his happiest smile, "he look like he spent a night with a girl I knew over to

313

Duffield Reserve, name of Marion Youngdancer. She raked my back with her nice long fingernails every time she come. And you know me, if a girl come less than twenty-five times I figure I'm losing my touch. But even after that night I didn't look as bad as Freddy does, and I had fun getting my scratches."

Frank, without knowing it, has hit on part of the reason Freddy is behaving like he do. A woman. Or, as it turn out, two women. One is Freddy's wife, Isobel. The other is named Cleo Fire.

Everybody from the pool hall troop up the hill to have a look, and sure enough, everything that Frank said was true. I been expecting Freddy to do *something*, but what he's chosen to do come as a surprise to me, though if I'd thought it through carefully it wouldn't have.

We ain't the only ones who is curious. For whatever reason, people like to watch when somebody doing something weird, so there must be 200 of us there to gape at Freddy.

Freddy's house sit all by itself in front of a poplar grove about a mile up the hill from Hobbema General Store. The house was built by Indian Affairs Department and at one time was painted white on top and kind of a fuchsia-pink on the bottom, but over the years the paint and even some of the siding peeled off. Freddy and Isobel Powderface been living there for maybe three years and got at least that many kids with another one on the way.

The dirt in front and to one side of the house is packed hard from where Freddy parks his car and from people walking and kids playing: nothing grow there but some two-inch-high pigweed and bits of creeping charlie. At one end of the house is a door with a woodpile outside and a path to an outhouse. Nobody been behind the house for years. Back there was waist-high raspberry canes and wild grasses, including some deep green sting nettles tall as a man.

I was sure surprised to see Freddy lope into that mess at his natural speed. He wear mud-colored track pants, running shoes, and no shirt. The raspberry spines rake his skin and the nettles scorch him every pass he make. But Freddy don't change speed or let on that those hurts bother him none.

There is bright blood on Freddy's chest and arms, and even his face have nettle burns on it. After the first hour his track pants is torn and covered with burrs and thorns. The cloth is bloodstained in a lot of spots too. But I can see by standing at one corner of the house, where I can get a good look at the briars he running through, that the worst is over. He gradually breaking a path through that thicket. In a few more hours the raspberry vines won't be clawing at him no more.

Freddy and me got to know each other because he took a course at the Tech School one winter. He was studying biology and have it in his head that he'd like to be a veterinarian some day. But he give up on the courses before long.

"They don't teach nothing practical," he say to me one noon-hour. "I know more animal medicine than the vets who teach these courses. I know more about animals, too."

I explain all the stuff counselors tell us, that if you want a good job you have to put up with the stupid bureaucracy, dumb courses and instructors, until you get that magic diploma. But Freddy wasn't interested and he drop out of school the next week. He do come around and visit me though, which is how I come to know about his troubles, and the reason he decide to run in circles around his cabin.

Freddy sat a broken-backed kitchen chair about 50 feet from his front door. The padded back been lost and the chrome posts look cold and rusty. The seat got a three-cornered tear in it, and when the wind blow, bits of stuffing float off like dandelion fluff.

He rest for about 15 minutes of every hour, have something to eat, a drink, a cigarette, head off to the outhouse. He pay the Coldwind twins to keep him supplied with food, coffee, and such. After the first couple of days he use most of his break-time for sleep. He just drop onto the chair, legs stretched out, shoulders against the chrome posts, put his chin down on his chest and sleep until his helpers wake him up. By taking breaks that way he get about five hours sleep a day, and I hear him tell Carolyn Coldwind, when she deliver him a six-pack of Coca-Cola, that he figure he can keep jogging for six months at least.

By the end of the first week everyone who interested been by to have a look at Freddy. His path is clear now, the scratches on his body is healing and his feet beat a noticeable path into the earth that get deeper with every circle he make. The crowds thin out to almost nothing: they find that watching a guy tromp in circles ain't very exciting. He ain't racing against anybody; there don't appear to be nothing at stake. People stand along the road for a while, or just sit in their cars and stare. Some come by at night after the bars close, shine their headlights on the cabin, pick up Freddy's shadow as he trot by. But it is a little like sitting by the airport to watch planes land and take off; people get bored real quick and go away.

The one person who appear totally uninterested in what Freddy is doing is his wife, Isobel. She ain't even curious enough to pull back the curtains and see what he's up to. They say that about every third day, in a time when Freddy is sleeping, she come out of the house, her arms full of babies, and take the car down to Hobbema to buy groceries. One afternoon when Frank and I was there, his oldest kid, a little girl whose hair hadn't been combed for a couple of days, come out the side door, bare-chested like her daddy, and run a couple of circles with him before her mother call her back inside.

Isobel is a big woman, taller than Freddy, who is skinny with hair wild as twitch grass. She is big-boned, wide of face and body. I've spoke to her a few times at Hobbema General Store or at the Gold Nugget Café in Wetaskiwin, and she seem a nice woman, slow spoken and patient with her babies.

Even after a couple of weeks I still seem to be the only one who know that the reason Freddy is running in circles is that he want his wife to forgive him. There is a long story as to why he believes his wife will forgive him if he run around their cabin long enough. It have to do with badgers.

Freddy Powderface always been full of stories about badgers. I never quite understand how he come to care so much about them ugly, bad-tempered little animals.

"They is just glorified groundhogs," I said to him once.

"Oh, no, no," he say back. "Badgers are special animals. They're smart. Let me tell you some of the stories my grandfather, Powder Horn, the old-time chief, told me before he died. He was a Worthy Man, the last President of the Badger Society."

Then he tell me a story about badgers. Actually he tell me about ten stories about badgers. Trouble is they all sort of blend together after a while. I've never been big on legends, either the white man's or Indian's. They have a sameness about them. First he tell about how a smart badger trick the otter into cutting its own throat. Then he tell how another smart badger lead some starving hunters to where the buffalo are. There are stories of how

Badger outsmart Crow and Raven and Coyote. There is even a story of a grateful chief give Badger his most beautiful daughter. The daughter and the badger produce Indians who is brave and smart and loyal. Freddy stop that last story before he get to the ending, I guess because he can see me yawning.

"Powder Horn predicted the exact hour of his own death," Freddy told a bunch of us at noon hour at Tech School one day, letting his voice rise and his chest stick out to show how proud he was.

"I had an uncle who was a medicine man; he did the same thing," said Frank. "Predicted the exact hour and date of his death . . . . The warden told him." Frank and the rest of us have a good laugh while Freddy go off and sulk 'cause we not as impressed as he think we should be.

But Freddy ain't one to be discouraged by disinterest. He come by my cabin on a sunny Saturday morning, convince me to go walking in the back country with him. He is looking for what he call badger mounds, which is places where badgers live or used to live. We was walking for an hour or so when he spot one.

"There! Right there!" shout Freddy, pointing. "A badger mound."

Looking across a bullrush-choked slough to a clearing in front of a poplar grove, I could see a mound maybe 12 feet across, breast-shaped, only three feet or so high at its top.

Freddy plunged right through the bullrushes instead of walking around; we both get our feet wet and some of that feathery cat-tail-down cling to our clothes.

"This mound's abandoned," he say, standing atop it, peering at the angled hole in the earth, where the dirt cut to look like the jutting eyebrow of a skull. "But not very long ago. A year maybe."

As he come down off the mound his foot seem to sink into the soft prairie grass. Freddy drop to his knees and pluck up handfuls of grass.

"Come here, Silas!" he yell, his voice high and excited. "Come see this. It's special. I've only found one other in all the years . . ." His voice fade away as he busy tearing grass out of what look like a deep rut maybe three inches deep and twice that in width.

"What is it?" I ask.

"It's a circle of forgiveness," he say. "This is a path I'm uncovering. When one badger did something to upset its mate, the one that had been bad would start circling the badger mound. It would circle and circle, creating a path, wearing the earth down. That badger would continue on for days, maybe weeks, just stopping occasionally to eat or sleep."

"How long did it keep that up?"

"Until its mate forgave it for whatever it done wrong."

"What if the mate wouldn't forgive?"

"Then the badger circled until it died. But none ever died. The offended mate always forgave."

Freddy was crawling along ripping grass out of the rut, which looked like the impression a tire makes when it been abandoned for a long time then lifted from where it settled into the earth.

I could see he was determined to explore the circle of forgiveness. When he got to where I was standing I had to step out of his way. As I moved aside I stepped on something in the deep grass, make me lose my balance and I almost fell. Freddy kept removing tufts of grass until the whole circle was visible, all the time repeating stories his grandfather Powder Horn had told him about badgers forgiving each other. Forgiveness among animals, he called it.

I could almost see the short-legged badger, his little claws digging into the ground at every step, his belly brushing the grass as he circled, waiting to be forgiven by his mate for whatever wrong he had done.

"You sure you could trust your grandfather?" I ask Freddy once, and he get real mad at me, run through that list of badger legends the old man taught him, as if they proved something.

What I heard about Powder Horn was that as a chief he was kind of like Chief Tom Crow-eye, the guy we is stuck with now. It said Powder Horn had a hankering to be white, and gave away Indian rights like a cowboy gives away his pay. I also heard Powder Horn have a strong liking for moonshine.

"There used to be a Badger Society," Mad Etta tell me, after I ask her about some of the stories Freddy told me. "The societies are pretty well gone now, disbanded, replaced by the Canadian Legion and the Hobbema Curling Club. Badger Society was one of the first to die out, long before I was born."

"How about the stories, are they true?"

"In those days women weren't allowed in the societies. Women weren't told the mysteries. Society members were sworn to secrecy for life. A lot of the secrets died with the last members of the societies."

"Freddy says his grandfather passed on the badger legends to him before he died. Freddy claims they're true."

"Then I guess Freddy is the only one who knows for sure," and Etta get up from her table, waddle to the stove where something evil smelling is simmering in a deep, black frying pan.

Ever since the day we found the badger mound with the circle around it, Freddy been aching to try out his theory on forgiveness. It wouldn't surprise me if Freddy, without really knowing why he was doing it, get involved with Cleo Fire just so he can do the test.

Cleo was in my class at school, was always the kind of girl who like to get a good time out of life. If you was to see Cleo sitting in a bar, she is the kind of woman you take one look at and know she be easy to take to bed.

"She have an odor about her," Frank say. He has taken her home on more than one night. "She smells like she's horny," is how Frank describe her.

I'm not sure that's true. She do like tight jeans, bright sweaters and lipstick, and she laugh and joke a lot. She is a nice friendly girl to talk to, one who, like our girlfriends Sadie and Connie, is smart enough to take her birth control pills regular, so she's got to be 22 without being tied down by a slew of kids.

"She looks like a slut," is how I heard Isobel Powderface describe her. I'm not sure if Isobel got her own tribe of kids because she is careless, or stupid, or religious.

Nobody pay much attention the first couple of times Freddy cozy up to Cleo at her table in the Alice Hotel bar. A few single guys like Gorman Carry-the-kettle and Victor Powder are a little pissed off that Freddy move in on their territory.

"Why don't that skinny little sucker go home to his wife?" Gorman say when he see Freddy and Cleo leave together at closing time for the second night in a row.

But Freddy don't go home. He stay for about ten days at the apartment in Wetaskiwin that Cleo share with Jenny Three White Loons, who work as a cashier at the Co-Op Grocery Store.

Word travel fast in a small community, plus there are always a dozen people ready to pass on bad news. Everybody is allowed a couple of mistakes, but the morning after the third night Freddy spend at Cleo's, a whole string of women come calling on Isobel Powderface, offer home-made cake and sympathy over the rotten way she being treated by her husband.

Different women have different ways of handling news like that, some figure it is their fault their husband run off so they try to do things that will make him come home, others just go wild and their friends have to keep them from going after the husband and his girlfriend with a gun. Isobel, they tell me, don't say much at all; she just get a dark look on her face, have one of her brothers change the locks on the house, pile all of Freddy's clothes, records, tools, and his guitar on the front porch of the house.

Freddy I guess figures if he going to get forgiven he might as well have a lot to be forgiven for. He gather up his stuff and go to move it into Cleo's apartment. But that's when Cleo put her foot down, say something like, "You're a nice guy to party with but I don't want an old man, especially one who just dumped his family. You better go back home while you still got the chance."

Freddy haul his stuff back home, but Isobel won't let him store it in the house even when he promise to stay outside himself. There ain't even a garage, only place he have to store his stuff is in a dog house used to belong to a real ugly German Shepherd name of Woofer who got run over by the mail truck last spring.

It is about this time that Freddy begin to circle his house.

One afternoon down at Hobbema General Store, when Freddy been jogging for close to a month, after Isobel cash her welfare check, somebody ask her how long Freddy plan to keep doing what he doing.

"I don't know or care," she say. "If the son-of-a-bitch runs around in circles long enough he'll wear the path so deep he'll be completely underground. Then I want him covered up, and I get to throw the first shovel full of dirt on his head."

I don't report that back to Freddy, but it sure don't sound to me as if Isobel is about to forgive him in the near future.

I also find out, by asking what I hope was subtle questions, that Isobel don't know the badger legends. She don't know why Freddy is running or what he expect her to do to stop him.

September first come last week along with the first frost of the season. Freddy got a month or so to get his problem solved or he going to be running in snow up to his belly button. The kids are back in school and there is nobody to watch him at all. Even the drunks don't come around after the bars close anymore.

"You believe in these stories about forgiveness among animals?" I ask Mad Etta one night when we having tea at her cabin.

"I've heard stranger things," she say. "Animals don't have wars, or booze, cars, or television, or fools who form governments. Maybe they do forgive. It wouldn't surprise me."

Yesterday I stop by to see Freddy. The circle of forgiveness is cut deep into the earth by now. There is a chill wind blowing down off the mountains. Freddy look thin, cold, and unhappy.

"Isobel don't know the badger legends," I say. "You've got to at least tell her," I add logically.

"Instinct," he reply. "Sooner or later she'll sense what it is I'm doing."

"Make it easy for yourself and help her out," I say.

"Instinct," he repeat. "She has to sense it herself. It's only a matter of time."

There is something I never told Freddy, and I don't suppose, since I've waited this long, that he'd believe me now anyway. But the day we were out at the badger mound, when I stepped out of his way and almost fell, what I stepped on was a skull, a little slant-browed skull of a badger.

Tricks

Someday, my friend Frank Fencepost is going to get murdered because of his practical jokes. Frank he thinks everything
is funny.

"That's your trouble," I tell him one night at Hobbema Pool
Hall. "You can't tell the difference between what's funny and
what's stupid."

What make me say that is Frank been telling for about the one
hundredth time how, a couple of years ago when we was in Card-
ston for a rodeo, he fixed me up with the Big Shield twins. Frank,
when he tell the story, get so excited that if he in the bar he bounce
on his chair, make the glasses on the table slop over their edges.

I have to admit it was a good joke even if it was on me. I was
pretty excited to have a date with twin sisters. Even if it turned
out they wasn't as good looking or as willing as Frank said they
was, a date with twins would still be pretty thrilling.

"Silas never even guessed that one of the twins was a guy. I
don't know who was more surprised, Archie Big Shield or Silas."

"And Archie was the cute one," chime in Robert Coyote, who will also tease me about that evening for the rest of my life.

"Even if it was a good joke, I don't like hearing about it over and over," I grumble. "You play too many tricks," and I miss a shot I'm taking at the green ball.

"There's never too many tricks," yell Frank, take off his black, ten-gallon hat, bow and smile as if there's 10,000 people out in front of him. "Tricks make the world go round. Tricks give people something to be happy about. Tricks keep people talking. When you ain't seen somebody for a long time, first thing you do is spend time remembering the silly things you done together. You don't talk about the time you was sick, you laugh about the time you tore the culvert out of the road and somebody important drove into the hole."

"Yeah, well I for one have had enough of games and tricks," I say.

"Don't be so grouchy, Silas," somebody say to me.

"You just don't like it when the joke's on you," somebody else say.

"I'll make everybody a deal," says Frank. "Let's call this National Trick Month, whatever month it is."

"June," says Frank's girl, Connie Bigcharles.

"I'll bet," says Frank, "the Great Fencepost will bet that he can play a trick on everybody in the room, within, say, ten days."

"What if you don't?" say Robert Coyote.

"How many people is here?" and Frank walk around the pool hall, count on his fingers. There are 11, not including Frank: there are Connie, me and Sadie, Robert Coyote, Eathen Firstrider and Julie Scar, Donald Bobtail, Bedelia Coyote, Rufus Firstrider and his white girlfriend Winnie Bear, and Mad Etta sitting against the back wall on her tree-trunk chair, look like something out of an old-time movie. "If I can play a trick on each of you by the end of the month, you each got to pay me ten dollars . . . ."

"And if you don't?" says Eathen.

"Well . . ." says Frank.

"We get to kill you," growl Robert Coyote, who is about the meanest dude within a hundred miles.

Frank swallow hard until he see that Robert is joking.

"Not me," I say. "I don't want nothin' to do with it." But I get shouted down.

"Don't be a spoilsport," say Bedelia Coyote, who ain't noted for her sense of humor, especially when the joke is on her.

"Come on, Silas," say my girl Sadie. "You taking yourself too seriously these days."

"Well . . . but Frank's got to have something at stake too."

"Hey, Fencepost is invincible," say Frank, "and sometimes invisible too. If I don't play a trick on everybody in the next ten days, nobody have to pay me, especially Wetblanket Ermineskin here. If I lose I pay for everybody's pool game for a whole evening, with Frito chips and Pepsis all around."

Everybody clap their hands. There is lots of laughing and backslapping. I wonder if maybe I am growing up or something, because even though I agree to the idea, it all seem pretty childish to me.

The next day when we on our way to the Tech School in Wetaskiwin, all the guys talk about is Frank's bet. Everybody pretend to peek over their shoulder in case Frank is in view, and they check under the seat of Louis Coyote's pickup truck looking for snakes.

I keep a close eye on Frank myself. I am pretty determined he is not going to make a fool of me. But Frank is his same happy-go-lucky self. I have to admit it is fun to see him so joyful and busy.

"Well, he got me already," say Donald Bobtail, when I come back from lunch at Goldie's Café. "I took off my boots in the lunchroom, and when I went to put them on, one was full to the top with water, and Frank was rolling on the floor, laughing like a maniac."

"I figured if they was waterproof from the outside, they'd be waterproof from the inside too," yell Frank, slapping Donald on the back. "And they was."

Donald Bobtail laugh along with the joke.

I think if it had been me, I'd of made Frank drink the water. And I say so.

"Come on, Silas," says Donald, "it's only a joke."

"Yeah, you're right, it's only a joke." But I sure watch Frank careful and try to keep one eye looking behind me at all times.

The next day Frank bang off three more tricks in a row, but I stopped him from getting me. As I was walking up the hill to my cabin from Blue Quills Hall, I seen something move in the willows at the foot of the hill, and when I stare real hard I can make out Frank's shape crouched there. I still can't figure what it was he had planned, even though I sneaked back later in the day and checked over the ground where he was hiding.

When I was sure it was Frank, I scooped up a handful of gravel from the road and hucked them into the willows until Frank yell and come out with his hands up saying, "Okay, okay, you was too smart for me this time."

That evening Robert tell how Frank strung wire across the path to Robert's cabin, tripped Robert right on his face in a puddle.

"We're gonna nickname him Muddy Coyote from now on," chortle Frank, and everybody laugh lots, even Robert, who I would of figured to be mad for a year.

"I'm just gonna enjoy what happens to everybody else," says Robert. "Especially Silas. I hear Fencepost has something special for you—so special you'll be able to write one of your stories about it."

Again, everybody laugh.

"You have to catch me first," I say. "An Ermineskin can be pretty slippery when he wants to."

"Nobody gets away from Fencepost, when Fencepost puts his mind to it," crows Frank.

I tell about how I drove Frank out of the willows, and everybody boo Frank while he try to make excuses.

It was that same night, while we was having supper at Goldie's Café in Wetaskiwin, that Frank trick my girl, Sadie One-wound, though I thought again the trick might have been aimed at me. While I was gone to the washroom, Miss Goldie deliver Sadie's order of chips and gravy, spill it right down Sadie's sweater and jeans. Then Miss Goldie apologize, say that Frank paid her to do it. Connie Bigcharles was carrying some extra clothes with her and by the time I got back they already gone to the washroom to clean-up and change.

"You picked the right time to leave," grin Frank. "Sadie was second choice."

Boy, now I am on guard every second while Frank is around, and I'm even more careful when he ain't.

I wasn't there, but it was right in the Alice Hotel beer parlor that he trick Julie Scar. She is Eathen's girl and ain't been too long with our group, so Frank take it easy on her. She tossed her jean jacket on her chair, and when she come back from the restroom and sit down she find Frank put a whoopee cushion under her jacket, which make a loud, rude noise for everybody in the bar to hear.

"Everyone turned around and looked at me and I thought I'd die," say Julie, who is quiet and shy most of the time.

"Four down and seven to go," grin Frank.

"Keep your ass covered, Silas, 'cause I'm gonna get you best," and he laugh and hop from a chair to the top of one pool table, then to the second table, skipping among the snooker balls, while Eathen wave a cue at him.

Mad Etta is the next one to suffer. The joke he played on her was a classic and I bet gonna get talked about for years and years to come. Since there is electricity down at Blue Quills Hall, the Band Council have installed there two washers and two dryers, so people can do their laundry.

When Frank done it nobody knows, but he somehow got Etta's box of soap powder. The next time Etta huff down to Blue Quills with her laundry and an orange-colored box of Tide in a pillow case, Frank was lurking close by.

What Frank done was to mix fine-ground white-pine sawdust in with Etta's detergent. When she finish washing and open the machine she find her clothes speckled with millions of white dots. It take the rest of the week with her clothes hanging between two poplars at the back of her cabin, to get them part of the way back to normal.

Before Frank would agree to the bet he got Mad Etta to promise in front of all of us, that she not do him any irreparable physical damage for whatever joke he play on her.

"It was a good joke," admit Etta, smile from way down deep in her face. Her eyes twinkle like she got pen lights buried there.

As the days pass I get so I sleep lighter than ever before. I always walk looking both in front and behind me. I jump at shadows, start at every loud sound. Once I wake in the middle of the night think I hear someone on the roof. I creep out of the cabin, silent as a ghost, but I don't find nothing. Guess it was just crows walking on the shingles. Even so, next day I pound a row of nails up from under the eaves, make a nasty surprise for anybody climb on top of the cabin.

I remember old Gladys Bigcharles, who, a few years ago, got to thinking everybody on the reserve was trying to kill her. She look over her shoulder all the time, finally get so she cover her head in Reynolds Wrap, to protect herself from all the bad thoughts everyone was thinking about her.

Now, I know how old Gladys felt. Each day I get more determined Frank ain't going to get me.

"Well, he sure pulled one on us," Rufus Firstrider say that night at the pool hall.

"Did he ever," say Winnie Bear. "You're all invited for dinner tomorrow, except Frank."

Frank pound his chest and grin, raise his hands in the air like he was this Rocky guy the boxer.

What Frank done was to somehow sneak up on the turkey Rufus and Winnie keep in a pen behind their cabin. He kill the turkey, pluck it, clean it, carve his initials on its chest. Then he sneaked into their cabin and put the turkey on a plate on the table for them to find when they get up in the morning.

The more people Frank trick the more determined I become. Just in case he is after me while I sleep, I trade beds with my littlest sister Delores, though I have to pay her a dollar a night to use her bed. I also won't ride in to the Tech School with Frank anymore, and I stay clear of him both in and after class. At night, in the pool hall, at the bar of the Alice Hotel, or in Goldie's Café, I sit with my back to a corner and stay watchful at all times.

My story-writing is suffering, because I even jump when a meadowlark burble outside my cabin window, and I can't read or write but two or three lines without stopping to peer all around, make sure Frank ain't set me up for something.

There is still three days left to the end of the month when Frank trick the last person except me.

"You bastard!" Bedelia Coyote yell at Frank, outside the Tech School one morning. "I had to wash for about an hour to get clean. And I'm gonna kill you for what you done to my new blouse." She shake her fist at Frank, call him many bad names, while Frank bow from the waist just as if she was praising him.

It been raining a lot lately and the road by Bedelia's cabin is three inches deep in water. Bedelia was picking her way across that wet road. Ordinarily she could hear a car coming from half a mile away and get off the road, but Frank he hid behind a willow stand in Louis' truck, gun out onto the road when Bedelia is right in the middle. All she could do was put up her hands to protect her face from the wall of mud and water coming at her.

Even Bedelia get in the spirit after a while, and everybody laugh for about an hour over what happened to her.

Frank he save a special trick for his girl, Connie Bigcharles. I'm not sure how he accomplish this, but he put a Merle Haggard tape into Connie's purse while the two of them was in Robinson's Store in Wetaskiwin. Connie sure is surprised when the store detective grab onto her arm as she leaving. They detain her for about an hour, tell her they called the RCMP to come get her, when Frank show up with the sales slip for the tape and they have to let her go.

"I was gonna be mad for a year," says Connie. "I knew Frank was behind it but I didn't know if he was gonna rescue me or not. It was the idea of getting pinched for something I didn't steal that really bugged me. I mean I've picked up my share of five-finger bargains from Robinson's over the years."

"Now you see me, now you don't," laugh Frank, step out from behind a tall spruce tree, as I walking up the hill later toward my cabin. I jump about a foot in the air, land with my fists up to defend myself. "Live in fear," Frank cackle, and run off through the woods. "Be sure and look above you as well as behind you. I'm gonna have an eagle shit on your head," he yell from deep inside the woods.

That night I tap little stakes into the ground, string brass-colored snare wire twice around our cabin.

The way he got Eathen Firstrider involved playing a trick on another person as well. What I hear is that Frank got Constable Greer, who is a nice old RCMP, to put on their computer a description of Eathen right down to his buckskin jacket with the beads on the back in the shape of a yellow sun rising out of a purple lake. Eathen be labeled *armed* and *dangerous*.

Then Constable Greer send Constable Bobowski, the lady RCMP who spend most of her life giving us Indians a bad time, down to the Alice Hotel. Soon as she arrive, Frank have Eathen paged to the telephone.

As Eathen saunter across the bar, Constable Bobowski see him, go into a crouch, draw her gun, tell Eathen to lie down on the floor with his hands and legs spread wide. She search him real careful, handcuff him and march him off to the patrol car, while about a hundred Indians stand around make rude remarks at her, then give Eathen a big round of applause as the police-car door close. But when she get Eathen to the police station, Constable Greer tell her the warrant been canceled and she have to let him go.

I am the only one left. I try to remember the kind of tricks Frank played on everybody else, stay on guard for each and every one, as well as anything else Frank's strange brain might come up with.

The final two days I stay right at home. I'm glad the cabin got only one door. I tack two gunnysacks over the big kitchen window, peer out careful, one eye at a time.

Ma sure get mad at me when she trip on the snare wire traps I laid, spill a bag of groceries in the yard. And she get even more madder when I won't go out to help her clean up.

"That's just the kind of thing he's waiting for," I say. "He's probably in one of the tall spruce behind the cabin waiting to drop something on me."

"What's *paranoid* mean?" Delores ask me that afternoon when she get home from school.

"Why?" I say.

"Because that's what my teacher said you were, after I told how you're hiding in the house scared to death."

"I'm not scared. And I'm not paranoid. I really have something to fear, Frank."

"Is he going to hurt you?"

"Not really. It's like we're playing a serious game of hide and seek. It's a contest, and I'm gonna win."

My girlfriend Sadie may never speak to me again. It wasn't really my fault; I mean I told her I'd rigged the cabin door. But Sadie forgot, and a quart of 10-30 motor oil poured on her head when she come to visit me without knocking. I haven't let her stay over for almost a week, 'cause I figure Frank will try to get me through her.

"For a guy who didn't want to do this, you sure take Frank's challenge serious," she said on a day when she was still speaking to me.

I try to explain to her that it wasn't all competition.

"It's kind of like when you know the doctor gonna prick your finger for a blood test. You don't want it to happen, even though you know the thoughts is worse than the pain."

"It's because you can't stand to have Frank get one up on you," she say. "The tricks you pull to keep from getting tricked is sillier than anything Frank does," and Sadie go home mad.

The tenth day roll around. That evening I hear Eathen Firstrider call to me from way out at the road.

"Everybody's meeting down at the pool hall," he yell.

He is careful not to get close to any of the boobytraps I laid around our cabin.

"I'll be down later," I call back to Eathen.

I know the bet don't expire until midnight, and I suspect Frank is laying for me, close by, maybe even on the roof of the cabin, or in the slough at the foot of the hill, or any of a hundred places along the trail.

About 11 o'clock I squeeze out the window at the back of the cabin. I make a long, careful circle, going at least a mile out of my way, and come into Hobbema from the highway, instead of through the reserve.

I case the back of the pool hall, peeking out of a stand of pig-weed and sting nettles, then I skulk along the side and slip in the front door. I stand with my back against the door until my eyes get used to the light. I stare around careful until I spot Frank shooting eight-ball with Eathen, Robert, and Connie.

I make a dash for a chair in the corner. I check it out careful, above, below, and behind, not even letting on that I hear all the people saying hello to me. I can't figure out what Frank got planned. He just look self-satisfied, fire a ball into a corner pocket.

I settle into that chair, lay a cue across my knees and wait. It only 15 minutes until midnight.

Frank continue to act like nothing unusual is happening; he laugh and joke with everybody. In fact lots of my friends are laughing over the tricks been played on them, tricks that sure wouldn't amuse me.

They are trying to recall the best joke ever been played on Hobbema Reserve. What always come up is Dolphus Frying Pan leading a moose to Father Alphonse's church and asking him to marry them. Everybody always been split about 50-50 as to whether it was a joke or not.

"It's been five years and Dolphus and the moose is still together," say Frank.

It is seven minutes to midnight.

My friends finally decide that the best joke ever been played was when Jean Paul Silversides and Noreen Snakeskin got married. They had a brand new Indian Affairs house to go to, and weren't planning no honeymoon, so they were about as careful as me, 'cause they expect their friends to try and play some kind of trick on them. After the wedding and reception party, they check their house over real careful and go to bed.

What they don't know is that Donald Bobtail, who study the electronics at Tech School with me, has wired their mattress so if there any moving around on the bed a big spotlight be attached to the chimney blink on and off. Well, Jean Paul and Noreen do the kind of moving around a couple supposed to do after their wedding, and by the time they finish up there is about 500 people standing outside their house in the glare of the spotlight, clapping hands in time to its blinking.

For all Frank seem to care I might as well not be here.

Midnight arrive.

"I won," I say, jumping up. "I'll just have me a Pepsi and some Frito chips now, get an early start on tomorrow night's party. We gonna cost you an arm and a leg," I say to Frank. I look around, feeling real good, expecting everybody else to be happy too.

"Hrrrmff, hrrrmff," go Frank, clear his throat. "I think there's something I forgot to tell you, Silas.

"Like what?" I say real sharp. "You mean it ain't midnight yet."

"Oh, no, it's midnight alright."

"Then what?" I sure don't like the way everybody is looking at me.

"There never was a contest," say Frank, smile like he just been freshly oiled. "It was just a few of us figured you was getting to take life too seriously."

"What do you mean there was no contest? You tricked everybody but me. I . . ."

"Did you see any of the tricks happen?" ask Frank.

I get a terrible sinking feeling in my stomach, because as I shoot every trick through my brain, playing them like a movie, I realize I only been *told* about every one. I never actually seen even one happen.

"But I ate your turkey," I say to Rufus and Winnie.

"You ate a Safeway turkey," say Rufus. "Blind Louis Coyote storing our turkey, Chief Tom, in his hen house."

"There was only one trick," say Robert Coyote, "and it was on you."

"Did you have a good time sneaking out your window and traveling two miles cross-country?" ask Sadie.

"You *were* watching me," I yell. "I knew it."

Boy, I am gonna have to live with this trick for the rest of my life. I want to be mad, but my friends are all smiling, waiting for me to smile too. They *are* my friends or they wouldn't go to this much trouble to set me straight.

I stretch my cheeks so they'll think I'm smiling, but I bet it will be a day or two before I actually do.

Graves

It was about six o'clock on a Saturday evening when we buried Phil Cardinal right in the middle of the long, green lawn that slope from the front of his house down the hill to Jump-off-joe Creek. There was quite a crowd of people including reporters from TV, radio, and newspapers; the TV people had their bright lights set up, even though it was a clear August evening and the sun wasn't even thinking about setting.

Originally Phil wanted only his family to be present: his little son, Wallace, who is three years old, and his wife, Valerie, plus Mad Etta our medicine lady, and me, 'cause he arranged to pay me to see that nothing went wrong. But his wife wouldn't have nothing to do with the burying; her and Wallace were inside the house but I don't think they even peeked from behind the living-room drapes. When reporters knocked on the door no one answered.

It wasn't as if Phil Cardinal was dead. He is as alive as me or my friend Frank Fencepost or our girlfriends. All of us was there to see the burying, along with lots of Indians from the Ermineskin

Reserve, which is close by, and every kid from the subdivision where Phil's house is located. The kids hang around outside the rail fence on Phil's property, sort of kicking at the ground and sneaking glances our way, as if they expect to be chased away.

It kind of hard to explain who Phil Cardinal is, because there are about 20 families with that name on the reserve. He is known as Restigouche Cardinal's son, so he won't be confused with Blackie Cardinal's tribe, or One-ear Felix Cardinal's family. They is all cousins or uncles anyway, but Restigouche Cardinal sent his kids to school, and they was one of the first families to get running water and indoor plumbing when that sort of thing come available.

Phil work in Wetaskiwin where he is manager of the Co-Op Livestock Yard and Feed Mill. He studied agriculture at the University of Alberta, where he met up with and married Valerie Redwing. Valerie is so beautiful she make men breathe in sharp, just by walking into a room. She was a city Indian, a model who got her picture in the Hudson Bay Department Store ads in the *Edmonton Journal*, and her face and body was actually in the Sears mail-order catalog, in color. She was modeling blue jeans. It never occurred to me until I recognized Valerie Redwing, that people in catalogs was real.

Valerie keep modeling after the marriage, and her and Phil buy a house just off the reserve, in a new subdivision that was developed by friends of Chief Tom Crow-eye. It is called Totem Pole Estates, *the ultimate in modern living*, and it consist of 35 split-level houses built on both sides of Jump-off-joe Creek. There is also a playground, a three-hole golf course, a community center with a hot tub, a pool table and an exercise room where somebody who come down from Edmonton twice a week teach aerobics to those who want to jump around like they been bee-stung.

As far as anybody can see Phil and Valerie got everything any couple either white or Indian could want, including a real cute little boy. Wallace look so much like his daddy he could of been made with a small size cookie cutter. He is long and rangy like Phil who, I bet, could of played basketball if he'd wanted to. Wallace got long arms and he swing one of his long legs way out to the side when he walk, just the way Phil does.

I was at Mad Etta's the night Phil come to see her. He wore a business suit and white cowboy hat, park his Chrysler outside the door to Etta's cabin. I answer the door because Etta don't like to move no more than she has to. She was sitting on her tree-trunk chair against the back wall of the cabin where, in the light from the ragged wick of the coal-oil lamp, her eyes glint a kind of red. Phil is real uneasy.

"I don't suppose you know who I am?" he say.

Etta's voice come from out of the shadows, sound mysterious and scary like something Pastor Orkin, the fundamentalist fanatic, would preach about. Etta not only name Phil, she recite his family back for five generations, more than I bet he knew about. Etta she know the history of every family on the reserve, which she learn from her father, Buffalo-who-walks-like-a-man.

"Well," Phil say, "Mrs. ah . . . Black Horses, I'd like to discuss something with you . . . in private."

"Silas here is my assistant. He can hear anything either of us has got to say."

"Well . . ." Phil say again.

"Take it or leave it," say Etta.

"I'm sorry, Mrs. Black Horses," Phil say, like a school boy talking to his teacher. It sure sound odd to me to hear Etta called by her "slave name," as Bedelia would say.

To boil down what became over two hours of back and forth talk between Etta and Phil Cardinal, his problem, as he describe it, "is an ethical one." He is happy to be successful in the white man's world but he worried about leaving behind his culture and his traditions. And he is particularly worried about his son.

"Wallace isn't even going to know he's Indian until someone points it out to him," Phil say.

"How does your wife feel about this?" Etta ask.

"She's unconcerned," say Phil. "She doesn't think it important for us to remain Indian. I had to fight to buy our house here close to the reserve and not in Edmonton. She even suggested we change our name to Card, and not mention we're Indian unless somebody asks."

"What exactly do you want me to do?" asks Etta.

"I want you to listen to me. I know you understand."

Etta nod her big head up and down.

"Come back anytime," she say at the end of the evening.

Soon as his car pull away from the door, she say to me, "What do you think about him?"

"I think he's sincere," I say. "I didn't know at first—I thought he was just wanting to play Indian . . . ."

"Enjoy a little reservation chic," say Etta.

"Yeah, like Indians who wear plastic feathers when they go downtown, and buy a tape of real Indian pow-wow dancing. But I like him. What do you figure to do with him?"

"We'll wait and see. He feels real lost inside. I'll talk with him and see what he decides to do."

But Phil deciding to get buried alive sure wasn't Etta's idea. In fact he didn't tell her what he was going to do, just said he was going to do something serious.

At Etta's suggestion, Phil he hired me to watch over him once he was down under the earth, just to see that local kids or curious people didn't break off, plug up, or pour things down that vent pipe.

My friend Frank Fencepost hang around with me, spell me off when I need to go somewhere. Phil said he didn't have any idea how long he would stay buried, but he have provisions enough to last the whole six weeks of holiday what he saved up from the Co-Op Feed Mill.

His grave was a pre-cast concrete tank about eight feet long and four feet high. He stock the place with a chemical toilet, bottled water, dried food, and a sleeping bag. From the house he run an extension cord with a 100-watt bulb on the end, and thread it down the air pipe.

"Sure you don't want to take a TV, tape deck, electric blanket, maybe some Willie Nelson records?" ask Frank. But all Phil do is give him a look that could hard-boil an egg in two seconds flat.

Phil had to hire a backhoe to dig the grave, and it make a certain amount of mess steelwheeling across the big, moist lawn, before it even start with the digging. I understand Valerie was a little bent out of shape because Phil used their savings to buy the concrete tank, pay for the backhoe, and hire me for up to six weeks to keep an eye on him. Apparently they had a screaming argument in the lobby of the Toronto-Dominion Bank in Wetaskiwin the day before Phil went underground.

"We going to call you Potato Phil from now on," joke Frank. But Phil don't see anything funny about being compared to a potato.

"You know, Silas," Frank say to me, "if this guy had a sense of humor, he wouldn't have to go burying himself." I wasn't sure about that at the time, but over the weeks I think I've come to agree.

At first, all the people in the district who don't have nothing better to do, and a few who do, spend some part of every day hanging out along the southern edge of Phil's property, leaning on the white painted fence and speculating on the what, why, and wherefore of Phil burying himself in his front yard.

It get so Phil Cardinal's fence replace the sidewalk in front of Hobbema General Store as the place to hang out of a summer evening. Both kids and adults stock up on soft drinks, potato chips, chocolate bars and cigarettes, then walk down the gravel road to Totem Pole Estates, lean on Phil's fence and stare for an hour or two.

Trouble is there ain't anything quite as unexciting as staring at a four-foot length of galvanized pipe sticking up out of the earth in the middle of a lawn. The media people lose interest first, though on the third day, a lady reporter from CFCW, the country music station in Camrose, name of Elaine Crutchfield, come by and do an interview with Phil by yelling her questions down the top of the air vent, then holding her microphone over the pipe to pick up his answers.

After she set the scene for her audience she said: "The obvious question, Mr. Cardinal, is why are you doing this?"

"That would be very difficult to explain in a short time," say Phil's voice, which sound hollow and reflected back on itself, like when me and Frank were kids and played telephone by using two pork-and-bean cans tied together with string.

"Well, you'll have to admit it's unusual for someone to have themselves buried alive?"

"Yes, it is. To answer your first question, I am trying to come to terms with my fears. I felt trapped in the life I was leading. I felt as if I was already in a grave. In Indian history, if a warrior was afraid of something, say a bear or a wolf, he deliberately sought out what he was afraid of and confronted it. In my own way I'm trying to do the same thing."

"I see," say Miss Crutchfield, but it plain by the tone of her voice that she don't. "I must say you're very articulate for an . . . for a . . ."

"For an Indian," Phil cut in to say. "I have a university degree, Miss Crutchfield, do you?"

"I'm sorry," say Miss Crutchfield, who Frank when he talk to her always call Miss Crotch and then add the *field* as an afterthought. "This interview isn't live, so I'll edit all that out. But let's get back to your reasons for burying yourself. Is it death you fear, or the idea of being trapped?"

"Aren't they one and the same?"

At that point Frank whack the palm of his hand on his forehead and roll his eyes. Frank don't have any more use for people who waste their time thinking instead of doing, than I do. He lift up the front of his *Alabama* tee-shirt to show his bare belly and say: "Excuse me, Silas, but I'm gonna stare at my belly button until it start popping out gold coins." Then he spit onto the grass under his chair.

Phil and the radio lady talk a while longer.

"Does your doing this have anything to do with your being an Indian?"

"It does."

"Would you care to elaborate?"

"I suppose it's that I feel I've missed out on something. The experience of the young warrior going out and isolating himself in the wilderness, camping in one solitary spot, waiting to dream, to catch a glimpse of his future, the animal that will be his totem, dreaming a new name for himself."

"Do you plan on taking a new name after you've spent your time underground?"

"I hope so. I want to dream like my ancestors dreamed. I want to learn the secrets of nature and humanity. Mostly I want to dream."

That interview never get broadcast. After she finish talking to Phil we walked the radio lady to her station-wagon. All the time she was packing away her recording equipment she was shaking her head.

"I was hoping this guy was a real goof," she says to me and Frank. "A fruitcake, twelve cents short of a dollar. People like to hear real weirdos rant and prattle. It makes them feel sane. But this guy's just trying to find himself and doesn't know how to go about it. Nobody cares about something like that."

"Your listeners should be interested in an Indian burying himself," say Frank. "You could pass it off as progress—white people been burying us for years—now we learn how to do it ourselves."

The radio lady smile at Frank but she don't look as if he convinced her.

Phil been buried three full days before Valerie come out of the house. All that time the drapes never been opened once, and little Wallace ain't been outside to play. A couple of Valerie's relatives drove down from Edmonton to see her, and two of Phil's brothers, one with his wife and kids along, come by. They park their cars in the driveway and try to walk to the front door without looking out over the lawn to see the grave. A few feet east of the grave is a 15-foot growth of white poplars and wild grasses separate Phil's property from the one next door. Me and Frank set up our sleeping bags there, where we have a radio and tape deck, a campfire to cook hot dogs, and our girlfriends who spend the evenings with us, even spend the night a time or two when it was warm enough and there was a breeze to keep the mosquitoes away.

For the first few days, every eight hours or so me or Frank would go to the graveyard pipe and holler down, ask if there was anything Phil needed, or wanted us to do. He always said no.

Then on the day Valerie come out of the house for the first time, he say for us not to bother him again. "I'll let you know if I need anything. I want time to dream," he say.

Valerie, when she come out of the house, do the same as her visitors, try not to look toward Phil's grave. She drag Wallace, who is dancing around and pointing out over the lawn, straight to the car. As they drive away he have his face up close to the back window staring. Valerie look drawn and tired; she wearing blue jeans and a red turtleneck sweater, both show off how beautiful she is.

She have a way of swinging her long hair, show off her neck and profile, that make my mouth water. Guess I'm not the only one.

"Oh," groan Frank, "can you imagine leaving a woman like that alone for six weeks while you bury yourself in the ground to think?"

"I can't," I have to admit.

Valerie's father, who is some kind of department manager for the post office in Edmonton, drive down on the fifth or sixth day. He is a short man in an expensive suit. I was watching over the grave alone, and he wave me away as he walk up to the pipe, in his black, city shoes, clear his throat to have a conversation with Phil.

The second week, Phil's youngest brother, Milton, come by. He is a professional cowboy, ride the rodeo circuit most of the year. He was in Phoenix, USA, when he heard about what Phil done and he fly home quick.

"Jeez, man, if you want to get away for a while, I'll take you on the circuit with me for a few weeks. It's a lot more fun than being buried. We can fly out this afternoon from Edmonton if you like. How about it?"

Phil just thank Milton for his trouble, say he'll stay put.

One of the things Phil didn't take with him, that I think he should have, was a watch.

"I don't want to be bothered by time," was the reason he gave. "My ancestors lived by the seasons, didn't have to worry about hours, or days, or even weeks."

But he *was* bothered by time.

I read in a magazine about how people who are locked up in small places, deprived of time, was what they called it, lose all track of hours and days.

On the sixth morning, which was the seventh of August, Phil called up to me: "I figure it's about the eighteenth," he said. "How close am I?"

I had to tell him it was only the seventh. He sounded real confused after I told him that. But he wouldn't let me drop my wrist-watch down to him, one that by coincidence is called a Cardinal watch, tell the date, the month, and the time down to a fifth of a second.

I sure wonder if he's used up 18 days' worth of food and drink, but I figure that's his business so I don't ask.

By the end of the second week almost everyone gone back

about their own business. Phil don't have anyone to talk to but me and whoever of my friends is keeping me company. Still he go for days without saying a word, though sometimes I think I can hear him talking to himself down there, whispering, humming, mumbling.

It was August 12th when Pastor Orkin, the fundamentalist preacher from The Three Seeds of the Spirit, Predestinarian, Bittern Lake Baptist Church show up driving a yellow school bus with the church's name hand-painted on the side, the letters all pushed together because whoever painted the sign didn't figure in advance how much room was available. There is six little kids in the bus with him, each one got a musical instrument of some kind.

The pastor come hotfooting it across the lawn, look disapproving at everything he see, strut to the air pipe and shout into it: "Woe to him that buildeth his home by unrighteousness and his chambers by wrong."

Pastor Orkin's booming voice must have scared Phil half to death.

I know both Frank and Pastor Orkin would deny that they are anything alike, but they both have a lot of nerve, venture into places nobody in his right mind would go. A couple of priests in brown dresses come by one of the first evenings Phil was underground, but they just skulked in the underbrush, fingering their beads, the setting sun flashing off the crosses at their waists.

I remember once when Phil talked about taking courses in philosophy and religion at the university, and how he wished he could have taken a lot more of those because he found them more interesting than crop rotation and animal husbandry.

"I'm glad you came by, Pastor Orkin," Phil's voice would say.

"There are a lot of things I'd like to discuss with you."

"Shalt thou reign, because thou closest thyself in cedar? Jeremiah 22:15," Pastor Orkin holler.

I want to point out that Phil has *closest* himself in concrete, but I guess that's the best Pastor Orkin can do, since they didn't have precast concrete in biblical times. It's too bad that Pastor Orkin ain't one for discussions. In his religion only the pastor talks and everyone else listen.

I am surprised though when Phil quote right back at the pastor, something about someone *which rejoice exceedingly, and are glad when they can find the grave.*

"He shall be buried with the burial of an ass," shout Pastor Orkin.

"Job said: 'O that thou wouldst hide me in the grave,'" Phil call back. "Tell me, Pastor, what comes after the grave?"

Pastor Orkin used to be a parts clerk at John Deere Tractor in Camrose before he started his own religion. He only knows things he memorized from a mail-order course on how to save souls. He look at a card he made a lot of notes on, and quote again: "But thou art cast out of thy grave like an abominable branch. Isaiah 14:19."

"'Marvel not at this,'" Phil call back, "'for the hour is coming, in the which all that are in the graves shall hear his voice': John 5:28. Don't you want to talk seriously, Pastor?"

They quote scripture back and forth but Pastor Orkin ain't smart enough to answer any of Phil's questions. The little kids get out of the bus, circle the air pipe, Pastor Orkin blow a pitch whistle and the kids play recorders and tambourines, sing "Let the Sunshine In," two or three keys away from how it supposed to be done.

The eighteenth of August do finally come around. It was along about dawn on that morning, when everything dripping with dew, that I heard the door of the house click. I had stayed alone overnight. I peek out of the poplar thicket, see Valerie on the front steps, close the door careful behind her. I crawl out of my sleeping bag and slip deep into the poplars. Valerie walk careful, as if she afraid the ground will squeak, leave black footprints behind her on the silvered lawn. She look over to where my sleeping bag is, even step one foot in the long grass, crane her neck until she sees no one is in it. She walk over to the vent pipe, put her mouth right against it, call to her husband in a whisper. I don't hear his answer, but the second thing she says is in a harsh voice, the S's sizzling.

"Asshole! How could you do this to me?" she hiss. There is a pause. "You what? You what? Well, so do I, and so does Wallace, but we don't make fools of ourselves and our family . . ."

She have a lot more to say, and I guess Phil does too, but I move off through the woods to give them privacy. Eventually I circle around and get to the truck. Valerie look my way when I start it up, but only for a second—guess she figure I got cold and went there to sleep.

It was the middle of the third week when Valerie moved out for good. Her papa and a couple of other relatives arrive first, then the Mayflower Van Lines truck, painted that same too-bright yellow as traffic signs. I'm surprised that Phil don't yell up to me to find out what going on, for the truck grunt and rumble and the storm door flap back against the house every time the movers carry out another piece of furniture.

By the end of the day the house is vacant, even the drapes is gone, and the place sure look cold. A piece of cord droop down in a sad loop, lay cockeyed across the front window pane. Valerie's papa change the locks on the doors.

Over the next few days, me and Frank and our girlfriends joke about what we'd want to take into the grave if we was planning a six-week stay.

"One thing for sure," say Frank, "Phil is proving you can't take it with you, and Valerie just proved you can."

"I'd want a TV for sure," says Connie. "And a mirror and lots of make-up to try out."

"I'd rather have a six-pack of Lethbridge Pale Ale for each day," says Frank. "A six-pack is an Indian television."

"I'd want a big stack of paper and about fifty colored pens," I say.

"I'd be afraid to be alone for that long," says Sadie.

"I'd want somebody to drop Kentucky Fried Chicken down the vent every evening," Connie add. But I agree with Sadie, what I'd really want with me is Frank, so I wouldn't be alone.

Frank grin like he just won a lottery. But what it come down to, when we get serious, is that even though it is easy for us to make fun of him, none of us would want to do what Phil is doing.

Phil's been in the dark for quite a few days now. When Valerie left forever she must have shut off the electricity at the fuse box, and the house have so many locks on it, even Frank, who claim he can melt locks by staring hard at them, ain't been able to get in. Besides, somebody who work in Wetaskiwin say Valerie arranged with Calgary Power to have the electricity cut off the same day she left.

Today, Phil's voice in the first air of daylight wake me and

Frank. The sky is low and black and I can smell the wheat ripening in the fields across Jump-off-joe Creek.

"I want to dream," Phil shout. "I want to dream!" His voice rise out of the pipe and drift off into the cold, dewy-smelling dawn.

"He ain't never gonna dream if he don't shut up and go to sleep," whisper Frank.

Coming Home
to Roost

S omewhere along the way my sister Minnie has grown up without my really noticing. I find this out when, real late of a Saturday night, while I'm sittin' at the kitchen table, writing on a story, drinking coffee and thinking hard, Minnie come through the door. When I look at her I get a real shock. Instead of being a little girl with a tooth or two missing and her braids unravelled, she is all of a sudden a woman, and a pretty one at that. Her hair is blue black as a crow's wing, hang loose on her shoulders, and she filled out in all the right places. She got on bright lipstick and blue eye-shadow.

I stare at her a second and third time. I can tell by the smell of her she been drinking beer; she might even be a little unsteady on her feet.

"Hi, big brother," she say to me, flashing a big smile.

"What the hell are you doing coming home at this time of night?" I say, both louder and meaner than I intend to.

"You rather I'd stay out until morning?"

"Don't be smart. It's after two o'clock."

"Ducky Cardinal wanted to take me home with him. I could of gone."

I realize what I'm feeling is fear. As if Minnie is about to walk in front of a speeding truck. Only I don't have any idea how to pull her back.

"Ducky Cardinal's a bad dude," I say. "You don't want nothing to do with him. He's been in jail."

"Hey, lighten up, Silas. You're not my old man, and you're not a school principal, even if you act like one."

She stands with her hands on her hips, stare at me with a real surly eye, her lower lip turn out in a pout, the same one each of my sisters have. My inclination is to light into her like I was a fox and she was a chicken. I can already see the air of the room full of floating feathers. But I hold my tongue. I've seen the mistakes everyone else makes raising their kids and I've always thought I'd never be that way with my own. Minnie may be my sister and not my daughter but I still feel responsible for her.

"Sorry, sis," I finally say. "Sometimes I forget you're not nine years old anymore," and I smile over the rim of my white coffee mug.

She take her hands off her hips. I guess she was all set for a fight too. She carrying a string shoulder bag and from it she dig out a pack of cigarettes and light one up. I've seen her smoking when she walking down the hill from school with a group of her friends, but I think this is the first time she ever light up at home. She is looking at me out of the corner of her eye, daring me to say something. I consider for a while but decide not to.

"You want some coffee?" I say.

"Sure," and she get a mug off a cup-hook by the stove and I pour some for her.

"So, who are you embarrassing with your stories this time?" and she wrinkle her nose at me the way she done as a little girl. To see her do that make me remember how much I love her.

"I'm telling about the time Peter Lougheed Crow-eye was a snitch for the RCMP."

"Oh, long as you're not writing about me. I'd die if you ever wrote about me."

I take a close look at Minnie while she sitting there across the table. People you're with every day change so slowly, like a tree growing, that you never notice the small changes, only the total result.

What I see scare me a lot. To start with Minnie is pretty, even beautiful. She's wearing tight jeans with a wide, black belt, a purple blouse with all kinds of ruffles on it, and some real nice cowboy boots I bought her for her 16th birthday. As we talk about small things I realize I ain't that much older than her. I don't know how to be a father, or even if I should try to act like one to her. It's just that so many Indian girls her age go bad; the unluckiest go to the cities alone, end up drinking too much and selling themselves on the street. Others manage to get in lots of trouble at home; they get pregnant, sometimes two or three times in a row, end up living with some guy who is too young to have a family, and, when he get tired of being poor, seeing all his money go just to survive, he up and go away, and the girl and kids are left alone.

A couple of years ago I talked to Minnie about birth control. I was real embarrassed to do that and so was she. To cover her unease she make jokes while I'm talking to her. But at least she know how *not* to get pregnant. "I know I sound like a teacher or something," I told her, while I explained as best I could that a guy who'd get it on with her and not use protection is a bum, and she should run away from him like he got dollar-sized sores on his body.

But I also know that you take a healthy girl, a few beers, a car with reclining seats, a guy like Frank Fencepost, Robert Coyote, or Phil Carry-the-kettle, guys who can talk a bird out of a cat's mouth, and a girl don't stand a chance. And every time I go out to a bar with my friends, them, and sometimes me, is on the other side of the fence, hoping to score with a willing girl.

I remember Frank saying about one of his sisters, "Girls shouldn't be allowed to be teenagers until they're about twenty-five years old at least."

I try to talk to Minnie about what she going to do after she's through school. I figure if I keep talking that way it never occur to her to drop out like so many of her friends is doing right now. She's in her second half of Grade 11, and her grades are so low I don't figure she'll ever see Grade 12.

"You never went through high school," she say to me, "and you've done okay."

I have to admit she's right. "I stopped school when I was fourteen because I didn't know no better. There was nobody to tell me different. But I went back to the Tech School. I wish I had Grade 12, and I wish I'd gone to university. I was lucky to have Mr. Nichols take an interest in me. Otherwise I'd be just drifting along like most of the guys I went to school with."

"Driftin' ain't so bad, Silas. I got to party now, or life get away from me pretty soon."

I bite my tongue to keep from giving her a half-hour lecture. My stomach hurt when I think of Ducky Cardinal having his hands all over Minnie. Ducky is the kind of guy nobody want their sister to go with; he is short and squat, wear about a three-inch square belt buckle with a picture of a marijuana leaf on it. He work the rodeo circuit, and I guess is actually a pretty fair bronc rider. Good thing is that in about six weeks he'll hit the road, and if we're lucky he won't be back on the reserve until November.

I understand how Minnie thinks. I thought exactly the same way when I was 16. I'm lucky to be alive today. I just hope Minnie is as lucky.

The next day I go tell my troubles to Mad Etta. We talk for maybe an hour, drink tea from her huge blue-and-white tea pot.

"Is your mom worried about Minnie?" she begin.

"You know Ma; she's an old-time lady. She let us grow natural. She figures if half of us turn out okay she done a good job."

"But you don't agree with her."

"Etta, teenagers now got so many choices, choices that even me and Frank and my friends didn't have a few years ago."

"By the way," Etta say, making like it just an afterthought, "how did Sadie's old man, Collins One-wound, treat you after you took up with his daughter?"

"He's always been nice to me," I say. "But he's an old-time Indian. 'I got enough of my own troubles,' he said one time. 'Sadie will have to work out her own life.'"

"You figure you deserve to be treated nice?"

"I always knew I was nice," I say. And we both laugh. "But when I was sixteen I was a crime just waiting to be committed."

"Why don't you have a beer with Ducky Cardinal one night?" say Etta, "all the time remembering what you were like six or seven years ago."

"I might," I say, after a long pause.

"Ummmm," say Etta, nod her head up and down. "You found a good girlfriend to keep you in line, and you turned out better than some, and no worse than most."

If I was saying it, I would of thought I turned out a little better than *that*.

Though I am sometimes a worrier, what happened to me the next week was something totally new. I think that for three or four hours I went a little bit crazy. It was a week night and I was writing as usual. After supper Minnie said she was going down to the Hobbema Pool Hall to hang out with her friends.

"Be home by eleven," I said as she was going out. "You got school tomorrow."

Minnie didn't say a word, but she give me a look let me know how old and stupid I am. I recognize it as one I've thrown out more than a few times.

About midnight I start getting worried. By one o'clock I'm pacing around the kitchen and peering out the window every time a car turns off the highway, a dog barks, or somebody walks past the cabin on the gravel road.

My girl, Sadie, who hardly ever get mad at me, gather up her jacket and purse and head to her folks' cabin. "What's the matter with you?" she ask me. "You're acting like a worried father straight out of a movie."

Even though I know she's right, I say, "I'm worried about my sister, okay? I'm worried about who she's out with and what she's doing."

"Give her some credit, Silas. Minnie's no worse than her friends. She's got her own life. You can't look over her shoulder." Sadie bang the cabin door as she leave. Ma and the other kids are asleep.

I just don't want to see Minnie go wrong, I tell myself. If a girl can get to 18 without getting pregnant or running off to the city, or moving in with someone useless . . . .

It seem me and Minnie are almost enemies. I know that for the last few days I been coming down on her like a mean cop, and that all I have is questions, no answers.

A couple of nights before I was lecturing her about going out with a dangerous guy like Ducky Cardinal, when she look me right in the eye and say, "How old was Sadie the first time you took her to bed?"

That is what Mr. Nichols might call a rhetorical question. It don't need no answer. I can't say a word, because all I could say is, "That's different." And I guess it ain't different at all. I was 16 and Sadie was 14. Ducky is 18 and Minnie 16. It's just that when I look at Minnie she's so pretty, and *so* young.

By two o'clock, if there was anybody I could have phoned I would have, if we had a phone. I walk past Ducky Cardinal's place but the cabin is dark and his truck ain't there. I'm boiling inside. I get a feeling of panic as I imagine all the terrible things could of happened to Minnie. Then I get mad when I think that maybe she's off partying, getting drunk and having sex with some guy in the back seat of a car.

By three o'clock I know I ain't entirely rational. I hear a car turn off the highway, but I recognize its backfire as it strain up the hill; it is Louis Coyote's pickup truck. Frank Fencepost and Eustace Sixkiller went off to Camrose on business that afternoon.

But instead of stopping over by Fencepost's, the truck stop by my place. I'm already outside by the time the dust drifting past the doors. Minnie get out of the passenger side, holding a bottle of Labatt's Blue in her hand.

Frank come strutting around the truck grinning like he is happy about something.

"Where the fuck have you been?" I yell at Minnie. She is at least half-drunk, her eye-shadow smudged. She is wearing her same jeans and boots, one of my old white shirts, the tails tied in a knot on her belly. She ain't wearin' any bra and I can see her dark nipples under the thin white cloth.

"Hey, Silas, glad to see you're still up. I could sure use a coffee," say Frank, walk right past me into the cabin.

"And you look like a hooker," I yell at Minnie before she can answer my first question.

Minnie put her hands on her hips and stare mean at me.

"I'm not your kid. And it's none of your fucking business where I been, or how I look, or who I've been with." She toss her bottle into the weeds alongside the house and start to walk past me too.

I grab her arm.

"Leave go of me," and she lurch against the door jamb. "Who the fuck do you think you are, King Shit of Turd Island?"

I am so mad I can feel tears rising behind my eyes. There are so many things I want to yell, but none of them can get out of my mouth. At the same time I feel a little like laughing because Minnie's last sentence was so childish. I haven't heard anyone say that since grade school.

"Tell me where you've been," I finally yell; I've got her blocked off between the table and the stove so she can't get to the bedroom.

Frank has sat himself on a backless chair by the stove. He grin and raise his coffee cup to me.

"Hey, you know what they say, if you got the name you may as well have the game," Minnie yell back.

"If your argument's personal, just say the word," says Frank.

"You think the worst of me," yell Minnie. "So I been off turnin' tricks tonight. I fucked Frank and Ducky and Eustace, and a couple of guys I don't even remember their names. And what are you gonna do about it?" She throws the jean jacket she been carrying, into my face, and duck past me. I swing at her but just graze her shoulder. She gone behind the blanket that's the door to her and Delores' room. If you can slam a blanket behind her she does.

"Don't look at me," says Frank, still grinning. "I didn't . . . ."

"Don't talk down to me, you bastard," I scream at Frank. "I know all your filthy tricks. You screw anything that twitches . . . ."

Right then I do one of the things I am least proud of in my life. I hit my friend Frank Fencepost. Me and Frank been friends since we was babies together. Never since we growed up have we fought serious. We've always horsed around a lot, and Frank always win. Even though I'm bigger, Frank is stronger and tougher.

What was so bad about what I done was Frank wasn't expecting to get hit. I whacked him on the side of the head and knocked him off his chair. He sit on the floor next to the woodbox for a few seconds, rub his head, then it take him two tries to get to his feet, even then he have to grab onto the warming oven of our old cookstove to steady himself.

Oh, boy, I think, I am gonna get pounded good now. I get my fists ready at waist level. I ain't mad anymore. I'm not gonna try to hit Frank again. But I'm gonna defend myself.

Frank don't say a word. He just sweep his black cowboy hat off the table, cram it on his head as he goin' out the door. He don't look back as he disappear into the darkness. I think I'd of hurt less if he'd pounded me a couple of good ones.

I wait around for an hour or so in case Frank decide to come back. The sun come up but he don't. Eventually I wander over to Mad Etta's.

"Usually it people forty years old come askin' how to handle their teenagers," say Etta, after she gived me a strong cup of coffee.

"I didn't ask to be the *man* in our house. It just worked out that way."

"Has Minnie ever been in trouble?"

"No. Minnie's not a bad girl. It's just that she's so young to have to make choices."

"So you'd like her to be safe, and sober, and smart, and for her friends to be the same way."

"No," I say, but I drag the word out for three or four seconds 'cause I'm thinking about it.

"You'd be happier if she stayed home and read books, and if she went to a craft class at Blue Quills Hall on Saturday night."

I don't even answer that because I know it's silly. But it's also true.

"You ain't one bit different from other parents," Etta go on. "Seem to me I remember you pulled a deal to help Julie Dodging-horse run off with her boyfriend a couple of years ago."

I nod that I did. I wonder how Etta come to know about that?

"How'd you feel if some guy helped Minnie run off with Ducky Cardinal?"

"I'd kill him," I say. "Ducky Cardinal's a bum."

"Ummmm," say Etta.

There is a saying about your chickens coming home to roost. I don't like that feeling at all.

"Silas, I'm gonna tell you what you don't want to hear. First of all you got to give Minnie credit for being the bright young woman you've helped make her. When Illianna was her age she'd already gone off to Calgary and was on her own. She didn't have anybody behind her pushing her along, or anybody watching over her . . . ."

"But everything's more dangerous now. There are more guys like Ducky Cardinal. There are more drugs. The streets in the city are meaner."

"Silas," say Etta, and she come and put her big arm around my shoulder. "You'd never admit it even to yourself, but you're a little jealous of Minnie and her friends."

"Never."

"Whatever. But the thing you got to remember is, if you don't let her go you'll lose her altogether." Etta guide me toward the door. I think she doled out all the advice I going to get, at least today. But she surprise me by following me outside.

"Silas, I want to walk you down to the bush behind my cabin here, show you something."

It is April and the trees are still bare, but covered in swollen-up buds. We kick last year's soggy leaves as we walk maybe a hundred yards into the poplars behind Etta's cabin.

"You probably don't remember, Silas, but there was a well down here. Stopped using it over twenty years ago. My old man was still living then; he built a fence around the well so's kids or animals wouldn't fall in. The casing rotted and the well caved in years ago, so the place is safe, but some of the fence is still standing. It's the fence I want you to look at."

What I see in front of me is a strange sight: a fencepost wired to a tree. The bottom of the fencepost is about four feet off the ground. What I guess happen is when Etta's husband build the fence, he wire a little sapling to the fencepost. Over 20 or more years that tree growed way up, got bigger around, and pulled the fencepost out of the earth, carry it up in the air until it hanging useless.

"Well," says Etta, "what do you see?"

"A tree pulled a fencepost out of the ground," I say. "Does it have something to do with Frank?" I ask.

"No," she say, real cross. "It don't have a damn thing in the world to do with Frank. I didn't think you were so stupid, Silas."

"Sorry," I say.

"That fencepost was part of a gate. Only my husband, Lawrence, closed up the gate. The circle of wire was part of the gate. That little sapling grew up through the wire circle, over the years it got bigger and bigger, until it pulled the post up and out. But you don't pay close enough attention. See what the wire's done to the tree."

Sure enough, the wire has cut almost clean through the tree; the tree is going to be cut in half in maybe just one more year.

"The young tree and the post stayed too close together," Etta go on. "Now neither of them is good for anything. Do I have to take a picture of this scene and have you carry it around in your pocket before you catch on to what I'm saying?"

"No," I say, after a long pause. "I catch on. But it ain't gonna be easy. I don't want to cut those wires."

"Silas, you're usually smarter than this. Look, I've seen you take your little brothers and sisters out sliding on the long hill by your place. You bundle the kids up good, put them on the sleigh, push them down the hill—once you let them go, ain't a damn thing in the world you can do but hope the sleigh goes straight, don't tip over or hit no trees."

"You make a good point," I say. I don't tell Etta, but what I always wanted was to sit on the front of that sled and steer.

I don't sleep at all. Come morning, instead of ride to Wetaskiwin to Tech School with Frank, Rufus Firstrider and Donald Bobtail the way I usually do, I get out on the highway at seven o'clock hitch a ride with a school teacher driving up from Ponoka. I sit in a different part of the classroom from my friends, don't even look at the spot where I guess Frank is sitting.

I would of felt a lot better if at least part of what I accused Minnie of was true. But it wasn't. Turn out her and Ducky was visiting some married friends of theirs in Wetaskiwin, have a couple of beers and play cards until midnight. On the way home Ducky's truck broke down, and a while later Frank and Eustace come along in Louis' pickup. They work on the truck for a while, then Eustace, who is a pretty good mechanic, say he'll stay and finish up with Ducky, while Frank drive Minnie home.

Boy, do I have some apologies to do.

It is easier to make up with Sadie. I spend the next two nights at her place so I don't have to face Minnie. I hate to feel this way, tense as if my ribs was taped; it mean I can't concentrate on my writing or much of anything.

I figure the worst thing Frank can do is punch me out good. If we're even, he won't have reason to be mad at me anymore.

On the third day at lunch at Tech School I walk up to Frank where he leaning on the sunny side of the building having a cigarette.

"I was wrong," I say. "I'm sorry I hit you. I haven't got enough friends I can afford to lose one."

Frank he grin out of his missing-toothed mouth.

"Hey, you got a left almost as good as Connie's. If I'd seen it coming I'd of flexed my ear and broke your hand."

I apologize for a while more and Frank joke some more. I am sure happy to be his friend again.

I feel so good I cut class that afternoon and head back to the reserve in Louis' truck. I'm parked outside the Reserve School when it let out for the day. Minnie and about five of her friends come laughing down the road. I beep the horn a couple of times, lean across and open the passenger door.

Minnie scowl at me.

"What do you want?"

"I come to apologize. Get in."

"So let's hear it." She sit on the outside edge of the seat.

"It's not near as hard to say you're sorry when you know you were wrong. I *am* sorry, Minnie. I know you're not a bad person. I was way out of line the other night."

"Everybody's entitled to get crazy once in a while," she say, close up the truck door.

"I'll try not to be so hard on you." I let the truck coast down the hill, turn it onto the side road to our cabin.

"You expect too much from me. I'm not smart like you and Illianna, or even Delores. I don't like disappointing you all the time. But I'm not a baby."

"I know that. But life was a lot easier when you were a little girl." We get out of the truck and go inside. I put on the kettle to make coffee.

"Do you remember when Pa left us for good?" Minnie nod her head. "You said you wanted me to be your father. And I said I'd always be around if you needed me . . . ."

"And you have been."

"I guess I just don't want to let you go yet."

I pour hot water into the coffee mugs. Minnie get the Carnation milk off the counter.

"We can be close, Silas. Just don't hold on so tight. You want to make my decisions for me, clothes, school, friends . . . ."

"I feel responsible for you."

"Silas, I don't need a father, or a brother," and she pause for almost too long. "What I need is a friend. One that don't give orders or make judgments. One who accept me for what I am . . . . You do that with all *your* friends, why can't you do it for me?"

"But I see all the mistakes you could make."

"Let me make my own, Silas."

"Minnie, I've been down the road ahead of you; I just want to show you where the potholes are."

"It's okay to show me; just don't try to carry me."

I smile at that. I'm just about to step around the table to hug her. But before I can everything come crashing down.

"That's why you got to understand about me and Ducky," she go on. "I'm goin' on the rodeo circuit with him. He bought a camper to fit on his pickup. We take off for the States end of next week."

"No," I shout.

"I thought you agreed to loosen up your grip."

"You're not going on the rodeo circuit. Ducky Cardinal's nothing but a . . ." And even though I know it is about the worst thing I can do, I yell on and on, until Minnie stand up to my face and say some awful things back to me. She slam out of the cabin, promise as she leave that she gone for good.

"So go!" I yell. But there is only the thud of the shut door to hear me. I am as much mad at myself as I am at Minnie.

I pick up my heavy, white coffee mug and throw it against the far wall. It don't even got the decency to break; it just bounce off the wall, lay in the corner next to the stove, staring at me like an all-knowing eye.

The Sundog
Society

"I don't have to defend myself to no one," William Two Young Men shout into my face. He got a hold of the front of my shirt and his nose is about two inches from mine. "I'm only gonna tell you this once, so you never make a mistake like you just did again." He got me pushed up against the door of Blue Quills Hall. All I done was say to my girlfriend, Sadie One-wound, that I heard the story many times of how William Two Young Men cheated Moab David, but I said it too loud and William overhear me.

"You come here and listen too," he say to Ruth Two Young Men, who until about five minutes ago was Ruth David. He loosen some the grip that he got on me. Ruth wearing her bride dress and she hang on to the arm of her new man, William's son, Grafton Two Young Men.

"Forty years ago," William say to us, "Moab David and me start up a lumber business with nothing but two axes and a pony to skid out the logs. We work hard and make a pretty good start. I deposit my share of the money in the bank to use for more equipment and to hire men to work for us. Moab David, he deposit his money too, in the Alberta Government Liquor Store and the Alice Hotel beer parlor. I try to talk to him, but he just don't give a care about the business. All the equipment was bought with my money," and he wave his big brown finger right under my nose when he say that. William Two Young Men have a square jaw and a head full of hair the color of melting snow. His brown eyes is clear and he hold his shoulders straight.

"Finally, I suggest to him that we split up. Your papa," he say staring straight at Ruth, "come out of it with his ax and his wages; that was all he had owing to him." William stop and take a deep breath of the cold air. "That is the truth of what happen and I don't want to hear about it no more." He turn away from me and the wedding party, head down the steps of the hall.

That sure ain't the way the story been told when I heard it, but then I always heard it from Moab David.

That business at the wedding happen to me about a year ago now. Tonight, as usual, old Moab David is drunk. I spot him weaving across the Alice Hotel beer parlor toward the table where I'm sitting with my friend Frank Fencepost.

"Your ears good and empty, Silas?" Frank say to me. "If they ain't, you better clean them out 'cause Moab sure to fill them full."

Frank is right. Moab David is one of them old men who got only one story to tell, but he spend the whole rest of his life telling it over and over.

I always wonder where guys like Moab David get money. He ain't worked in years yet he always seem to have change to buy a

beer. He sleep most nights at the Salvation Army what occupy
the basement of a dark brick building over behind the Saan
Department Stores. The door to the shelter painted a boxcar red,
and as soon as you open it you get hit in the face by a Lysol smell.
The basement floor painted a slippery gray and there is a dozen or
so roll-away cots scattered about the big room. Me and Frank
slept there one night when Louis Coyote's truck wouldn't start on
account of the cold.

Salvation Army in Wetaskiwin is run by a Brigadier Birkland, a
man about 35, who wear a blue uniform and a wine-and-blue cap
that too big for his head. His skin is a pale yellow color. He got
warts on his face and flat orange eyes like a chicken. But he got a
good heart and I've heard that on nights when Moab David stay
too long at the bar, Brigadier Birkland open up the door to the
shelter and bring Moab in from where he sleep like a dog curled
up in the doorway.

I'm not sure if Moab David know Frank and me by name or
not, but he settle in to our table as if he do. He smile a lot and
pass the time of day real friendly, but he have a kind of authority
about him, and it seem, at least to a couple of young guys like us,
that it wouldn't be polite to tell him to get lost.

We know we going to hear the story of how him and William
Two Young Men start off in business together a long time ago, get
timber leases from the Government, cut, saw, and sell lumber. But
then something happen and they don't be partners no more.
Moab be back on the reserve not do much of anything, while Two
Man Lumber Ltd. grow into a real big company.

When Moab get started on the beer I buy him, he don't disap-
point us. I've heard the story so many times I can almost move my
lips along with him. When I was a kid he used to come by our

cabin and tell the same story to Ma and Papa. He would talk to me and my sister Illianna too, tell us not only his sad story, but others about when he was young and used to belong to the Sun-dog Society.

The young men of Indian tribes used to form kind of exclusive clubs that they called societies. In real old days, they compete with each other to see who could act the bravest, take the most scalps, steal the most horses and women from enemy tribes.

"We'd go out on raiding parties," Moab would tell me and my sister, "usually just against other bands from this reserve. Us Ermineskin Indians we'd go raid the horses of the Louis Bull Band, or the Dakotas. One time we went as far west as Duffield, stole from the Stony Indians I bet fifty horses," and Moab would chuckle and tell how they'd crawl on their bellies through the grass, sometimes sneak right into the other Indians' camp to steal furs and supplies.

"I was what was called a Worthy Man," Moab go on, " 'cause one time I creep all alone right into the *tipi* of a Stony Chief, take his blanket and medicine bundle. In the real old days I would have had to take his scalp too, but when I was young we don't kill like that no more.

"Our society would do dances at the pow-wows too," say Moab, "we'd dress up in feathers and beads, put mean warpaint on our faces, sometimes dance for a whole day 'at a time."

Moab David's society pick the name Sundog, he say, because of the magic reflections that sit in the sky on one or the other side of the sun when the weather is terrific cold. I read in the dictionary up at the Tech School that there have to be ice crystals in the air for a sundog to take shape. It sure strange that something so fiery depend for its life on ice.

Moab tell us kids stories for hours and hours at a time, and boy, I sure do figure Moab David was at one time an important Indian. I bet that if he'd lived a hundred years ago he would of been a chief. Moab don't say so outright, but it pretty plain he think so too.

"It is Indians who learn and take on white-man ways that break up our lives more than white men," he say. "White people ain't interested in us. Give them the chance and they'll mostly leave us alone. It's Indians who want to be white that hurt all of us," and that start him off on the story of how he was cheated by William Two Young Men. My folks would nod their heads in all the right places, and I remember thinking how sad it was that a brave man like Moab David have his life turn out so awful.

"And he take my woman too," Moab David would yell, bang his fist on the kitchen table in our cabin, make the teacups bounce. Moab claim he and Bertha Monoose was promised to each other, but after he lose his business she leave him for William Two Young Men.

"All them horses I stole from the Stonys, I give them to Bertha's father like a brave supposed to in those days, and her father promise Bertha would be my woman when I was ready for her."

Back at the Alice Hotel bar Moab is repeating his story. "One day William and his lawyer got me to sign a paper. I don't read so I put my X where they tell me, like I done lots of times before. But that time was the last. They tell me I signed away my share of our business. William say I can stay around if I want, work for him for wages. Can you imagine me doing that after I owned the company?"

He slam his fist on the table, make the change and beer glasses jump in the air.

I'd guess Moab to be 60 years old. He must have been pretty good looking as a young man, but now he got a bad strawberry for a nose and a face like red cabbage. He is short and stocky, stooped some in the shoulders, but his eyes bright as a weasel's in a trap, and they look out of his face with about as much hate.

I watch him close and finally figure out how he always manage to have beer money. When he come to sit with us he put down in front of him 40 cents for a beer. Then he drink one of ours. We order another round and while the waiter is putting down the beer and picking up money Moab drag his 40 cents over the edge of the table into his hand. After the waiter is gone he drop the money back on the table, nod his head to indicate it pay for his next beer.

"After I had the business stole from me I went on a good drunk for two weeks," he say. "Bet you'd of done the same thing if you was cheated. I should have took my gun and evened things up right then," and he bang his fist on the table again.

Then he retell the story of how Bertha Monoose go off and marry William Two Young Men. He actually get tears in his eyes and hit his hand on the table so hard a glass of beer tip over on the green towel tablecloth.

I remember how Ma say she never remember Moab having anything to do with Bertha Monoose. But if Moab say it, it must have been so.

I don't call him on the business about the money. Me and Frank just got our unemployment checks, and, no matter how you look at it, Moab ain't had a good life. So I guess we can afford to buy him a beer or two. He must have been 40 years old before he

married to a lady who died and left him with a baby girl named
Ruth just a couple of years older than me, who been raised up
mainly by a couple of Moab's sisters.

Mr. Nichols, my English teacher and principal down to the
Tech School in Wetaskiwin, when I told him that Grafton Two
Young Men and Ruth David was getting married, said, "That
reminds me of the story of Romeo and Juliet."

I read about Romeo and Juliet because Mr. Nichols say I
should, but it got too many *thous* and *thees* in it; it difficult for me
as if it been wrote by a white lawyer. I seen the show though,
directed by a man from Italy whose name start with Z. The movie
was sad enough to make me cry, and I guess if you stretch things a
little, William and Moab could be the fathers in that story.

"But, by God, I get some of my own back," Moab say to me and
Frank. "You know last year when my Ruth marry with Grafton
Two Young Men?" I nod to show that I know. "I wasn't even
invited to the wedding, did you know that?" I nod again.

"Well, sir, I went out there anyway. Walked right up to them as
they was coming out of the ceremony. I speak to William in Cree
'cause I know he don't like to talk in the old language no more. I
say to William Two Young Men, 'I want some of what's coming to
me.' And that bastard, you know what he say to me? He say, 'You
coming to sell your daughter, Moab?' But I stand right there and
stare him down.

"'How much do you want?' he finally ask.

"'A thousand dollars,' I tell him. 'I give my word I never ask for
more, 'cause a thousand dollars is a lot of money to a poor old
man like me,' I say. 'And about all I got left to give in this world is
my word. You took everything else that belong to me.'

"I just keep staring him down. Well, you should of seen his

face. He get all excited because I'm making him look bad in front of his rich friends.

"'I think you deserve that much, Moab,' he say to me, and he reach into the pocket of his fancy white suit, bring out his check book and lean it up against the door of Blue Quills Hall while everybody stand around in the cold. Then he write to me, Moab David, a check not for a thousand dollars, but for five thousand."

Both me and Frank make faces to show we is really impressed.

"What did . . . ?" Frank start to ask, but Moab interrupt him.

"You know what I done with the money?" Moab smile and slap his hand, palm open, on the table again. "I got it all in the bank. I go over to the Bank of Nova Scotia in Wetaskiwin and I tell them, 'Hey, I got a lot of money here and I want to sign it up in an account, one that I can't touch, to go to the first grand-child of Moab David,' and boy, for a few minutes those bankers treat this old Indian like he was really somebody.

"I been to see Ruth a few times since she married," he go on, "and she cry some when I tell her what I done with that money she seen William give to me, and she don't think so many bad thoughts about her old papa no more."

Moab smile at us with his sharp brown eyes, take a drink from his beer, reach across the table take a cigarette from my package. Then he stand up and wander off toward the toilets, weaving a little like he walk into a strong wind.

"Boy, it must hurt him to tell a story like that," say Frank.

"I think it really do," I say, but I am already remembering the day of the wedding.

What Moab don't have no way of knowing is that his daughter Ruth and my girl, Sadie One-wound, is friends. Sadie was one of the bridesmaids that day, and because she was there I got invited too. There was six bridesmaids and Sadie was the one walk at the far end of the line, so I guess her and Ruth wasn't that good a friends. Sadie wear a salmon-colored dress of slippery material, and have some yellow roses pinned to her chest. Moab don't have any idea that I was there when him and William face each other down.

It was cold on the day of the wedding. There was a single sundog off to the north side of the sun, pale yellow as an orange in a bowl of milk. Everything covered in white frost, thick as whiskers. Most of the sky was white too, and come down real close and wrap everything up; it seem even to come right into the Blue Quills Hall, which today being used like a church. Off in the distance there is cloud on top of cloud, black on top of white, look like thunderheads boiling around, except we all know there ain't thunderstorms in February.

A preacher come all the way from Calgary to do the marriage service, some say it is because William Two Young Men donate so much money to his church, one called Alliance Pentecostal. The reverend have a face like a bowlful of apples and say lots of "Praise the Lord," and "Praise Jesus," before he get around to the actual wedding.

Ruth David wearing a long white bride dress and Grafton is in a white jacket they say cost over $50 to rent from a store in Edmonton. When the reverend ask "Who gives this woman?" Chief Tom Crow-eye say, "I do," in a voice loud enough to wake up anyone who might have dozed off. He too have on a white jacket and got his hair combed up to a peak in the front.

Chief Tom's girlfriend, Samantha Yellowknees, was with him. The Chief stare all around with his beady little eyes, trying I bet to figure how he can get invited to "say a few words" to the congregation. I hear he been asked to give a toast to the bride at the reception party later. "I bet it be more like a whole loaf than just one toast," is what Frank have to say about that. Chief Tom can talk for an hour without stopping, and he don't even have to be asked a question to get him started.

It was as we coming out the doors of Blue Quills Hall after the ceremony that I spot, in the distance, Moab David walking up the hill toward us. He taking long steps and kick a leg out to one side as he walk. He must of mooched a ride down from Wetaskiwin, as I sure don't figure him to walk the whole 11 miles. He wearing a red-and-white checkered mackinaw, old khaki pants and work boots. His head was bare.

The married couple was in a hurry to get in the wedding car which warmed up and waiting by the side of the hall. It was a new Chrysler New Yorker, their wedding present from William Two Young Men.

As Moab David get closer, he staggered to one side as if somebody put a hand on his shoulder and give him a good push. Everybody just stand and stare at everybody else until he reach the bottom of the stairs.

"Hello, Papa," Ruth said to him, but he hardly look at her. He stare up at William and Bertha.

"I want some of what is coming to me," Moab David say in a voice a lot louder than he need to use. His voice thick with drink and the white part of his eyes look red as a dog's.

"You come to sell your daughter, Moab?" William Two Young Men say as he walk forward to the head of the stairs. "How much do you want?"

"A thousand dollars," say Moab David, stick out his chin and chest like he is looking for a fight.

William Two Young Men reach into the inside pocket of his suit and take out a shiny brown wallet. He open it and look inside. I'm near to him and see that there are lots of red 50's, but he take out a $20 bill and put the wallet back. He fold the bill three times and toss it so it lands on the packed snow a couple of feet in front of the bottom step.

"That's all you'll get, and it's more than you're worth," say William Two Young Men.

I whisper to Sadie that I hear the story many times of how William cheated Moab out of his interest in the lumber business they started when they was young. Soon as I say it I can tell my voice carried, and I see by the mean look on William's face that I'm in trouble. But at that moment he still staring down at Ruth's father.

Moab David glared all around, like maybe he wish he had some friends to help him out. The $20 bill was unfolding itself on the snow, twisting slow, like maybe it was a worm don't like being on the cold ground.

The weather seem to have got warmer as the black clouds move closer and darken the white sky. The sun still glowed through a white haze, but the sundog was gone. Moab's boots chirped on the packed snow as he move forward. He slip a little as he bend and grab the bill up into his hand. Then he turned and walked away as fast as he was able, kind of sideways at first, like a dog afraid he gonna get kicked.

The Election

"Chief Tom been elected by acclamation for the last four terms," say Bedelia Coyote. "I, for one, think it's time we did something about it."

"Who is this guy Acclamation who cast all the votes for Chief Tom?" ask my friend Frank Fencepost. "I bet he's just like Chief Tom and don't even live on the reserve. At least I never met him if he does."

"Be serious," say Bedelia.

Being serious is what Bedelia is best at. Frank describe her as a feminist, conservationist, anti-nuclear trouble-maker. And that's on a day when he ain't mad at her. But we have to admit Bedelia been a permanent thorn in Chief Tom's side for quite a few years.

"If we run a strong candidate, we stand a chance of beating Chief Tom. He's forgot how to fight an election."

"Baptiste Sixkiller is the strongest guy on the reserve," say Frank. "I seen him lift the back wheels of a Fargo pickup truck two feet off the ground, and there was ten guys in the truck box."

"Baptiste also has an I.Q. the same size as his hard hat," snap Bedelia.

Chief Tom Crow-eye ain't done nothing but line his own pockets, and the pockets of a few friends, all at reserve expense. And the pockets he's lined with mink belong to his girlfriend, Samantha Yellowknees. Chief Tom left his wife a few years ago, and him and Samantha live in a highrise apartment in Wetaskiwin. Samantha is an Eastern Indian, a Huron somebody say, come out here from Ontario to be the brains behind Chief Tom, who would still be cutting brush for the CNR if Samantha hadn't showed up.

"Alright, alright, my friends," says Frank. "Hold the applause, please. I agree to be your candidate. After all who would make a better chief than me?"

"Don't make us answer that," we say, frowning. When we feeling happy, we joke that Frank would make a great politician because we know right from the start that he is lazy, incompetent, and dishonest.

"I've got one indispensable quality," Frank grin.

"And what could that be?" we ask.

"I been to bed with over half the women under thirty on this here reserve, and a few over thirty too. That the best preparation for political office I know of, if you're a politician you spend *all* your time screwing people."

We have to agree that's true, but we still don't want Frank for our chief. What we do is try to talk Bedelia into running. But she won't.

"We want to be certain to win," she say. "I don't think the people of Hobbema are ready for a radical leader just yet."

Nothing we can do will change her mind. So we have to search out a candidate.

"Be serious," say Bedelia. "Last guy to run against Chief Tom was Rider Stonechild. For every vote he got, Chief Tom got five."

"If you ain't gonna do the obvious and nominate me," says Frank, "then how about Mad Etta?"

"I agree," I chime in. "There ain't nobody wiser, or kinder, or . . ."

"Larger!" yell Frank.

". . . and she can be tough when she has to be," I go on.

"People wouldn't go for it," argue Bedelia. "We know Etta is best but she wouldn't fit the image of a chief. Plus, much as we hate to admit it, Etta is old. We need somebody who is smart, young, and look good too. Somebody tough but not greedy, who can't be bought off by white men or crooked Indians."

"Father Lacombe is dead," I say.

"And Wayne Gretzky is too busy," says Frank.

After arguing among ourselves for about three hours we finally decide to approach Victor Ear. Victor look too much like a used-car salesman to suit me, but he do have the qualifications we is looking for. He live on the reserve, is engaged to a pretty girl name of Philomena Bluewater who is training to be a nurse. He been to a community college in Edmonton, have a diploma in business management, earn his living keeping books for a big construction company in Ponoka. Vic is not quite 30, but he can speak real good in public, belong to the Ponoka Lions Club, work for the United Way campaign and belong to something called Toastmasters, sound like an advanced cooking class for bachelors which Victor is.

"Chief Tom *can* be beaten," we tell Vic, when we call on him at his house. "People are sick and tired of Chief Tom, they just don't know it yet. Name one thing he's ever done for us?"

Vic and the rest of us are silent.

"Tom Crow-eye don't even live on the reserve. Him and Samantha travel all over the world at our expense. All they've ever done was find cushy jobs for a few of their friends."

"*We're* all gonna expect cushy jobs if *you* get elected," Frank say.

"No we're not," shout Bedelia. "We want an honest chief."

"Okay," say Frank. "Just one cushy job, for me."

Victor take a day to think over our proposition, talk about it with his fiancée, before he say yes.

Right after Victor submit his papers, we ask the Hobbema Chapter of the Ermineskin Warrior Society to throw a dance at Blue Quills Hall raise money for the campaign.

It is by the turnout at that dance we know how many people agree with us that Chief Tom need replacing.

"Everybody and their tomcat is here," Frank yell above the music. We charged everybody five dollars to get in. Ben Stonebreaker donated a couple of cases of soft drinks and Frank liberated another couple of cases from a Dominion Bottling truck in Wetaskiwin. An Indian musical band called Wounded Knee pound out country rock and everybody have a happy time.

With the money we made, Bedelia arrange to have posters printed; they have black letters on fluorescent pink paper, say VOTE VICTOR EAR FOR CHIEF. Me and Frank and about two dozen other people paper abandoned buildings in town with posters, tack them to trees and telephone poles, tape them to abandoned car bodies, and anything else that ain't liable to walk off.

By the time Samantha arrange to get posters done for Chief Tom, almost every space in Hobbema been plastered. Besides his posters is covered in big paragraphs of fine print, tell in too many words, just like Chief Tom himself, all that he accomplished for us Hobbema Indians in the last few years.

People on the reserve ain't noted for going to political meetings, but at the very first candidates meeting at Blue Quills Hall about a hundred people turn out and they all come to hear Victor. Each candidate get ten minutes to talk. Victor finish in seven. But by the end of ten minutes Chief Tom ain't even warmed up yet, and Rider Stonechild, who chair the meeting, have to ding a bell about ten times to get the chief to shut up. Victor got cheered long and loud. When Chief Tom try to keep on talking, people boo until he sit down.

As everyone filing out we can hear Samantha Yellowknees yelling at Chief Tom.

"I wrote you a ten-minute speech and you never got past the introduction. You rambled like an idiot. This isn't the legislature, you have to be brief and pretend to be intelligent." Samantha stomp her foot hard and walk away from the chief, scribbling notes on the clipboard she always carry. We all thankful that Samantha ain't an Ermineskin Indian or she'd run for office herself and we'd have a really hard time beating her.

"Trouble in paradise," say Bedelia, laughing behind her hand.

Victor Ear set up his campaign office in what used to be a hotdog stand next to Fred Crier's Texaco Garage. When she can get time off from the hospital, Philomena Bluewater help out at that office. We have so many people interested it hard to find something for everybody to do.

"Hey, this easier than I ever expected," say Victor. "Everybody I meet tell me they going to vote me in," and he smile his nice, friendly smile.

The campaign couldn't be going better. That is until one Saturday morning we walk into the office right after breakfast and find Samantha Yellowknees sitting across the desk from Victor Ear.

"What are you doing here?" demand Bedelia.

"Just visiting," say Samantha, who is wearing a raspberry colored dress with white trimming, have her hair pulled into a tight bun. "Just because Victor and Tom differ on political matters doesn't mean we can't all be friends."

"Maybe after Victor is elected we'll be friends with Tom again," say Bedelia, "but until then you're not welcome here."

"Don't be so unfriendly," say Samantha. "Victor doesn't mind conspiring with the enemy, do you Victor?"

"Samantha doesn't mean any harm," Victor say, but he have kind of a guilty look about him when he say it.

"Samantha always mean harm," snaps Bedelia. Then to Samantha she say, "You know we don't have anything against Tom Crow-eye personally. Most of us can remember back to when he was a nice guy. It's you we're after, Samantha, and it's you we're gonna get."

"Have it your way," say Samantha, smile nice at everybody and walk out.

"What did she want?" Bedelia ask Victor.

"Like she said, she was just visiting," Victor say back. "Weren't you pretty hard on her?"

"You don't know her like we do," say Bedelia.

By this time, it look like Chief Tom pretty well given up. He ain't campaigning much at all. Unless something bad happens, Victor Ear going to be our next chief.

That's why it surprise me a lot when a couple of days later

Victor suggest me and him go for a walk 'cause he have something serious to talk about.

"I think you're the one who's likely to understand what I have to say, Silas. You're a smart fellow." Victor put an arm around my shoulder when he say that, have to reach up to do it. "I've spent the last two evenings discussing the political situation here on the reserve and in the Alberta Indian Community in general with Samantha Yellowknees. She's made some very telling points, mainly that none of us, especially me, has any political experience. What Samantha says we need, not only in the campaign, but after the election, is somebody with real political know-how."

"Somebody like Samantha?" I say.

"Right. And I think she would be an asset to my campaign team. The problem is I don't know how to tell Bedelia and the others."

"And you think I can help."

"You're not as radical as Bedelia. I mean she does get pretty pushy at times. And you seem to be able to keep your boisterous friend Frank Picketfence under control."

"Posthole," I correct him.

"Yeah, him. Listen, Samantha promise she can bring all her and Tom Crow-eye's friends over to our side too. That way we won't have to be enemies, and Samantha can teach me the ins and outs of political fighting. Her experience will be invaluable."

"But if you work with Samantha nothing will have changed. She'll just have a new puppet to pull the strings on."

"Believe me, Silas, I'm my own man."

"Then why not prove it by going it alone? Without Samantha and her friends you could really do some good for our people."

"Silas, in politics things never change." Victor spread his hands wide, palms open to show he going to explain something important. "If you were a hockey player who would you rather play for, the Edmonton Oilers or the Hobbema Wagonburners?"

"That's easy," I say. "The Oilers are champions and get paid a bundle; Hobbema Wagonburners are just a pickup team."

"Case closed," say Vic.

It sure didn't take Victor Ear long to become a politician. Or for Samantha Yellowknees to abandon a sinking ship. But Samantha she just take a short swim from one ship to another. We now see Samantha and Victor and Chief Tom's sneaky friends having dinner at the Travelodge Restaurant in Wetaskiwin, and I bet, putting the bills on an Ermineskin Band credit card.

Then one evening Samantha's little red sports car spend the night in Victor Ear's driveway. Philomena Bluewater go around with a permanent scowl on her face, and when somebody (Frank Fencepost) have the bad taste to ask, she say her engagement to Victor is off.

We can only imagine how bad Chief Tom is feeling. To add to his troubles Premier Lougheed went and retired, and some other guy who used to play football for the Edmonton Eskimos is now Premier of Alberta. The rumor is that the new premier going to sweep out the deadwood among his MLAs and there ain't no deader wood than Chief Tom. A big rancher name of Harvey Niedenfuhr already claim to have the nomination in his pocket.

Some of us is disappointed by what's happened, but Bedelia Coyote is MAD. She is madder than all of us put together.

"It's really ironic," say Bedelia. "Here we been working to get Vic elected because we thought he had our interests at heart. Now he's gone and hooked up with Samantha and all of Chief

Tom's old cronies. After the election what we gonna have is a new chief, whose strings is still pulled by Samantha Yellowknees, except Vic is about three times smarter than Chief Tom, which make him three times as dangerous."

"And just as crooked."

"So what are we gonna do? The people are wild about Victor. Half the people who vote don't know or care who Samantha is."

"We're not gonna give up," shout Bedelia. "We're gonna have to do something I never thought I'd hear myself say. We're gonna have to side with Chief Tom."

We all groan. Then there is a silence go on for about four minutes. Nobody disagree with Bedelia, mainly the ten or so of us is just trying to figure out how we got in this position.

"I don't know," Frank finally say, "Chief Tom couldn't pour piss out of a boot, even if he had an instruction booklet in both official languages and Cree."

"Nobody ever said he was smart. But if we manage his campaign, we could keep him honest after he's elected. It's really Samantha we're fighting. But we have to contact every Indian on the reserve and explain why we've had to change our mind. I mean people believed us when we told them to vote for Victor."

We all travel off to Wetaskiwin and visit Chief Tom in his highrise apartment.

"Hey, Chief Tom," we say as we troop in, "we got some good news and some bad news for you."

"I only want to hear the good news," say the Chief. It plain to see he ain't shaved today and the apartment is a mess, dirty dishes and newspapers everywhere.

"I didn't know he shaved," say Connie Bigcharles.

"Well," say Frank, puff up his chest, smile like a TV anchorman.

"The good news is Constable Bobowski arrested Victor Ear for pissing in the snow."

Chief Tom smirk with one side of his face.

"That's hardly a serious crime," say the chief. "How did it happen?"

"He was outside the Blue Quills Hall after the dance last night, and he was spelling out VOTE VIC in the snow, when the Constable come along."

"Serves him right," say the chief.

"That brings us to the bad news," says Frank.

"What can be bad about Vic getting arrested?"

"Well, he wasn't alone."

"So?"

"The bad news is everybody recognize Samantha's handwriting in the snow."

We all laugh like maniacs. But Chief Tom, who look as pale and peaked as an Indian likely to get, actually let a tear trickle out of one of his eyes.

"I never suspected Chief Tom had feelings," whisper Connie.

"Even weasels have feelings," say Bedelia.

"Oh, young people," say Chief Tom, "I don't know what I'm going to do. I'm about to lose the election, and I've lost Samantha, and . . ." he snuffle up his face and actually go to crying.

"I'm sure you'll all be very happy to see me go. You won't have your old friend Chief Tom to kick around anymore."

"That's where you're wrong," say Frank. "We just formed the Chief Tom Crow-eye Admiration Society. We want you to keep on being chief. In fact I make up a slogan for you, The Chief of the Past is the Chief of the Future."

The Chief perk up visibly; he wipe his eyes and nose on his shirt-sleeve.

"But, young people, why do you all of a sudden want to help me? You've been opposed to me for years."

"We've been opposed to Samantha. We know you're not smart enough to dream up all the schemes you've been involved in."

"Thank you," say Chief Tom.

"So, since Samantha has deserted you for Victor Ear, we've decided you're the only person who can beat Samantha and Victor."

"Well, my friends," he say in a voice a little more like his own, "your gesture is supremely appreciated." He puff out his chest and go back to being his old self. "We will strike while the iron is hot. We will hunt down that elusive buffalo called Victory. When the going gets tough, the tough . . ."

"Where do we start?" ask Frank.

"Oh dear," say the chief. "I don't know. I've never run a campaign. If only Samantha were here. She'd know what to do," and his eyes get all watery again.

"You got to fight hard, Chief," we say. "How long you figure Samantha to stay with Victor Ear if he's the second place candidate?"

"We've got to think devious," say Bedelia. "We've got to think like Samantha. What would she do if she was on the Chief's side and he was behind in the election?"

"Desert him and go over to his opponent," say Frank.

"Maybe we could capitalize on his arrest," say the Chief.

"That was a joke," say Frank. "We was teasing you."

"Oh," say the Chief. "I'm afraid I never know what to take seriously."

"Well, you better take Victor Ear seriously. If you don't want to be on the list to work part-time cutting brush on railroad right-of-ways, you better dream up something," say Bedelia.

We talk for quite a while and decide that the answer is personal contact.

"We're gonna have to work harder than we've ever done before," say Bedelia. "We'll have to personally call on every eligible voter and make sure they know we've not only switched candidates, but that they understand why we've switched. We've got to beat Samantha and Victor. If they ever get into office we won't be able to blast them out with dynamite."

"I don't know," the Chief say, "the last thing Samantha told me was to keep a low profile."

"Is Vic keeping a low profile now that Samantha is managing him?"

"Well, no . . ."

"I'm still willing to be a candidate," say Frank. "I'll run as the Me First Party. My emblem will be a pig sitting on top of the world . . ."

"Listen!" Bedelia say to Chief Tom. "If we get you re-elected, you're gonna have to change your tune. No more fancy trips all over the world. You're going to have to work for the good of all us Indians."

"Young people, you have my word on it," say the chief.

"Yeah, that and a quarter will get you a telephone call."

"I won't make a move without your approval," Chief Tom go on. "Ms. Coyote, you just tell me what you want done. You and your friends will be my advisory board. And you'll be my personal assistant." He reach across the table and pat Bedelia's hand. "At a substantial salary, I may add."

Bedelia glare at him and pull her hand away.

"At a reasonable salary," say the chief.

Bedelia nod.

For the next three weeks we all work night and day. We contact every Indian eligible to vote, even track down ones who work away from the reserve. One afternoon me and Frank drive to a farm somewhere near Lacombe where a guy named Paul La Croix, who we hardly know, have a job as a hired hand. Turn out Paul drove a load of grain to the elevator, but the farmer invite us in to wait.

"You boys are Crees, are you?" he say to us.

"Not Crees anymore," say Frank. "We're the Fecawi Indians. Small independent tribe, short on numbers but long on courage."

"I didn't know the name," say the farmer, "but I remember how that chief took his little tribe back into the hills. Five or six years ago, wasn't it?"

"We're older than that," Frank continue. "About a hundred years ago we broke away from the Crees. Our leader was a warrior named Bulging Belly. Actually Bulging Belly was the first woman chief in Alberta. Though it come as a surprise to him that he was a woman. Bulging Belly's parents wanted a son, so they just kept her covered up and told her she was a boy. Originally she had another name, but it was by her bulging belly that she got found out.

"But her followers didn't mind. 'Go off to the hills and have a dream vision,' they said to Bulging Belly. 'Then you'll know what direction to lead us so we can find our promised land.'

"Bulging Belly went off to the hills to dream. She came back in eight days and said, 'I know what direction to lead you in so we'll have good hunting, warm weather, and much happiness.'

"'What will we call ourselves?' someone asked.

"'I'll tell you in good time,' said Bulging Belly. Then she gave the signal and led her little group of warriors on pinto ponies, off at a mad gallop across the prairie.

"They galloped for a few miles until Bulging Belly led them right over a high buffalo jump. They all landed in a cloud of dust, a heap of Indians, ponies, bones and buffalo chips.

"Bulging Belly pulled herself to her feet, looked around and gasped, 'Where the fuck are we?' And we been the Fecawi Indians ever since."

"You should be a comedian," the farmer say to Frank. "No," say Frank. "Comedians make up stories. I only speak the truth."

Bedelia write and rehearse some speeches for Chief Tom, so he don't sound totally ignorant at the next campaign meeting. Samantha and Victor want to have a public debate, but we shy away from that. Things still don't look good for us when election day come around. What we did do was tie a red bandanna around Chief Tom's head, get him to wear a buckskin jacket, though he insist on wearing the pants to his Conservative-blue suit and shiny shoes.

We spend all day hauling people down to the Blue Quills Hall so they can vote for Chief Tom. We have Louis Coyote's pickup truck, and Rufus Firstrider's 1957 Dodge with big green tail-fins and one back door missing.

Victor Ear and Samantha Yellowknees have rented for the day, a long white limousine, come from the Hertz stall at the Edmonton International Airport. They can haul about 20 bodies at a time, and people who have never voted in their life turn out just to get a ride in that fancy car, even some people we *know* is on our side. That is about all we have to feel good about.

We all hang around Blue Quills to see the counting is done honestly. It don't take long for us to start to feel better. Chief Tom build up about a ten-vote lead right away and hold that and even increase it as the evening wear on. The counting is all over, checked and rechecked, in about two hours and Chief Tom declared the winner by 27 votes.

After the announcement, the crowd, led by Frank and Connie, start chanting, "Crow-eye, Crow-eye, Crow-eye . . ."

Chief Tom shake Bedelia's hand, then mine, stand up and head to the platform. Lots of people cheer him. He smiles fit to bust his face.

Victor and Samantha been sitting at a table near the stage. Victor look kind of shocked, but he have an arm around Samantha's shoulder and whisper a lot into her ear. Samantha is busy writing on her clipboard, look as if her mind is on something else.

"My friends," Chief Tom begin. "I want to thank you all for re-electing me. You won't be sorry. My opponent fought a good fight and I congratulate him."

"We've got him, Silas," Bedelia say from across the table. "We're gonna be able to do things our way for a while."

"Most important of all," Chief Tom go on, "I want to thank my political advisor, who pulled victory from the jaws of defeat, and without whose brilliant planning I never could have triumphed. I owe her a great debt, for her keen political sense is solely responsible for my victory. I want her to come up here and share this auspicious moment with me."

Bedelia has been getting happier with each line Chief Tom speak. She is halfway out of her chair when the rest of what the Chief saying get through to her.

"Not only is she my political advisor, but she is the love of my life. Samantha, come up here, please."

Homer

One of my first memories is of *Uncle* Homer Hardy, though he sure wasn't my uncle, he being about as white as I'm Indian. Still I remember him being at our cabin, sitting sideways at the oilcloth covered kitchen table, his chewed-up-looking brown hat on his knee, him banging his coffee mug on the table to make a point, never once noticing the black coffee slopping over the top.

Homer was short, with fierce brown eyes buried in gray whiskers. A few strands of gray hair hung down the back of his neck, but he was mostly bald; his head was freckled, and what could be seen of his face was sun and windburned to the color of red willow.

"Homer's a prospector," my pa would say to us kids after Homer had left. I didn't understand about mining or gold, and it was a lot of years before I come to know what it was Homer did.

Usually he came by to try and get something from us, which, looking back, was not a smart idea, for there wasn't many people as poor as us.

"Paul," Homer would say to my dad, "I just need a grubstake. A few pounds of flour, some coffee, sugar if you can spare it. I'll shoot me rabbits for meat," and he'd nod toward the window, where, outside, his tall, buckskin horse munched grass, a .22-rifle in a leather scabbard just behind the saddle.

"I know where there's gold," Homer would say, and his eyes would blaze. "Back on the Nordegg River. Sittin' right there for the taking. You grubstake me, Paul, and we'll go ridin' into Wetaskiwin in a Cadillac automobile, lightin' our cigars with leftover ten-dollar bills," and Homer would smile, showing that his teeth was mostly missing, and his gums was the dark pink of ink erasers.

Pa would give Homer a few supplies. Ma would grumble, but she admit to me in recent years that she didn't mind too much. "It was like buying a ticket on the lottery nowadays. You know you ain't gonna win, but it give you somethin' to live for until next week or next month."

Homer would pack the groceries up in a canvas sack, and he'd smile and jig around just like a kid been given a new toy. He'd dig in the pockets of his overalls and come out with a few hard dimpled raspberry drops, or some triangular Vicks Cough Drops. They was used-looking and covered in lint and specks of tobacco dust, but boy, I remember how my mouth water while I'm seeing him search his pockets.

We wouldn't see Homer again for three or maybe six months. And when we did nothing would have changed. He wouldn't be rich, and if anybody asked, he'd just grin kind of sheepish and say, "That one didn't pan out like I figured. But I *know* where there's gold now. Right there for the takin' . . . ."

It was strange but no one I know ever felt cheated by Uncle

Homer. He would sweep in and out of the reserve, kind of like a one-man carnival—what he promised always being 100% more than he delivered.

One of the reasons everybody liked Homer Hardy was because he was a storyteller. In his saddlebag, in the front of a floppy black Bible, he carried a picture of his parents. In the middle-distance, in front of a sod house, a huge, barrel-chested, bald-headed man stood in knee-deep prairie grass, a slight, long-skirted woman with knitted eyebrows beside him.

"That's my papa, long before I was born. He walked to Utah with the Mormons. My mama was his fourth wife, a shirt-tail cousin of Brigham Young. Papa could play the fiddle and was the best jig-dancer in the Plains States. Why one time in Wyoming, Buffalo Bill heard about my papa and sent for him to come to his camp outside of Cheyenne somewheres. And papa went, played the fiddle and jig-danced like the devil himself. Buffalo Bill gave him a gold coin—a month's wages, my papa said it was.

"Another time papa was out herdin' sheep in Oregon, or maybe Utah, he was never too plentiful with details. He took his rifle out of the scabbard, dropped it accidental like, and it hit a rock and discharged. Shot him right here in the chest," and Homer'd grab the left side of his chest, while us kids, and my folks too, sat watching him, our mouths hanging open.

"Bullet went through his lung, and through to his back where he could feel the point of it pushing against his skin. Well, sir, he lay down in his little line-cabin and figured he was a goner. He took a pencil and wrote on his soft, brown cowboy hat, 'I shot myself accidental,' so's his wife, the one before my mama, wouldn't think he committed suicide.

"He lay there for over a week until a rancher happened by and found him. Nearest doctor was over forty miles away and they rode papa there in a buckboard. There weren't no roads, just went cross-country over the open range. He should of been dead six times but he wasn't. Doctor looked him over and said, 'This bullet's got to come out. You reckon you can stand it without anaesthetic?' "

Homer was like his daddy when it come to wives. He had at least four, maybe more.

"I never been ashamed of the fact that women find me attractive," he'd say, and smile, his eyes glinting like maybe some of the gold he spend his life lookin' for was in there.

Even Mad Etta like Homer Hardy. I was at her place one day maybe ten years ago when Homer Hardy turn up, driving an old, square-fendered truck, what used to be some color once, but was now just a sun-faded metallic.

"Etta," he say after she's fed him a meal and give him a cigarette. "Etta, if I just had enough money for a tire for my truck I could get that load of ore to Edmonton to the assay office, and none of us would ever have to work again."

Etta, she heard every hardluck story ever been told, and they roll off her broad back like a duck shed water. But next day Fred Crier down at Hobbema Texaco Garage put a new tire on Homer's truck, and I hear tell Etta, she rode down in the truck box, sitting on top of the ore, just so's she could pay for the tire. Also, Homer stayed overnight at Etta's cabin and some say she had a certain contented look about her, perched up there like a queen on that hill of chipped rock.

Homer's women was part of his stories. He never laugh at any of them, always at himself.

"First one should of knowed better," he say one time, "she

worked right in the assay office in Edmonton; she got to see the results from my samples. Her name was Bernice, a maiden lady, as we called them in the old days, and she was quite a bit older'n me. Come to think of it, all my wives have been a good bit older'n me," and he grin from behind his scratchy gray whiskers, what circle his face like a big vegetable brush.

People have been known to say that Homer married his wives for their money. Each one of them *had* money, at least when they married Homer Hardy. But Homer spend it on old trucks, and supplies, and mining equipment, pumps and generators, and lawyer fees for filing claims. Homer never deny that he gone through a lot of other people's money in his life.

"I could have settled in with any one of my wives and never worked again. I could have sat in Bernice's rooms there in the Kensington Apartments in Edmonton, but I'd of felt just like a gopher never come out of his hole, and besides, one of the reasons she married me was because I was dangerous. Women like to take risks, but they need somebody to push them along a little. Her eyes used to shine when I'd tell her about the gold we was going to wallow in. I'm real sorry I disappointed her. When her money was gone—she'd inherited a trunkful from her daddy who was one of the first managers of the Bank of Commerce in Edmonton—why she didn't have no choice but to throw me out. We stayed friends though. I was always welcome at her home, and she'd sometimes toss me a dollar or two to file a new claim. I hitchhiked all the way up from Montana when I heard she passed away. Was a day late for the funeral. But I went out there to Pleasantview Cemetery and stood by the flower-banked grave and said my goodbye. I think it was a good idea I was a day late. Her relatives would have been mortified. They never could figure what she saw in a bandy-legged prospector who only changes his underwear twice a year."

Homer he had stories about his other wives too, though he never did have a bad word to say about any of them.

Maybe five years ago he married for a fifth time, this time to an Indian lady, Martha Powderface. Martha was a widow lady, at least as old as Homer. Her family was wanting to put her in the Sundance Retirement Home in Wetaskiwin, but she married Homer and went with him to dig gold up on the Pembina River, and live in a tent on the riverbank.

"You know, Silas," Homer said to me the next year, "it's too bad Martha doesn't have money. Oh, now I don't mean that as a criticism. I just mean that if, fifty years ago, I'd had a woman *with money* who'd go out to the camp with me, I'd a been successful. I'd a made the earth give up the gold it keeps hiding from me. Martha's a good woman, Silas."

Uncle Homer was a musician of sorts himself; he could play the spoons. Spoon players, like prospectors, are few and far between these days. In fact, when I think about it, I don't know a single person able to take two teaspoons, and by holding them in one hand in some mysterious way, clack the undersides together to make music. A good spoon player can sound pretty close to a banjo, and a harmonica and spoon player can sound like a whole Western band.

Homer would no sooner be in the door of our cabin than we'd be beggin' him to play and sing for us. And I can remember seeing my sister run for the spoon drawer, where all the knives and forks and other cutlery was kept, when we heard the wheels of Homer's wagon creaking up the hill from Hobbema.

"Sing about the fly," we'd yell, and Homer Hardy would smile from under his chewed up hat, clack the spoons and sing:

The early fly's the one to swat,
He comes before the weather's hot,
And sits around and files his legs,
And lays about 10,000 eggs.

And every egg will hatch a fly,
To drive us crazy by and by,
Yet every fly that skips our swatters,
Will have 10,000,000 sons and daughters,
And countless first and second cousins,
And aunts and uncles scores and dozens.

That song went on for about 20 minutes, or at least it seemed like it to us kids—there was verses and verses, and we'd laugh and giggle, and Illianna would sit on Homer's knee, and pretend she was looking for insects in his beard, and finding them. And my brother Thomas, who was the baby then, lay on the floor in blue rompers, grinning from his toothless little mouth.

Other songs were about people his father grew up with; the names and places didn't mean anything to us, but the tune was always snappy:

When I was working on the ditch,
Near Shell, for Isaac Jones,
I got acquainted with a boy,
Who runs the gramophone,
He was a charming little lad,
And his mama called him Sweet,
But I had no idea that,
His Waterloo he'd meet,
His Waterloo he'd meet.

There was about 50 verses to that song too. And sometimes we'd all join in, even my pa, who was never very sociable, and like me had a voice flat as a prairie.

One time I was telling Old Miss Waits, my teacher from the Reserve School, about Homer, and what a wonderful storyteller he was.

"He claims he never been to school," I said. "Taught himself to read by having a friend print the alphabet, then matching up letters with those he found in the Bible."

"I suppose that's *possible*," said Miss Waits. "You know, Silas, one negative aspect of education is that it destroys the natural storyteller in us, for education makes us aware of our own insignificance. Our own life story, unless it is particularly bizarre or magical, becomes uninteresting beside what we have learned. The uneducated person, however, is still at the center of his limited universe, and not only considers his life experience worth repeating, but will do so without invitation."

At the time I just stared at Miss Waits and tried to remember how she strung together them big words. But now that I've had a few years to think about it, I agree with her. When I was a kid nobody on the reserve had TV and only a few had radios. We make our own jokes. I remember the time Collins One-wound was sitting on his corral fence smoking a cigarette, just gazing at the cattle and mud, when one of his kids, might have been David, or maybe even my girl, Sadie, though I doubt it was Sadie 'cause she always been real shy, sneaked up behind Collins walking soft as if they wearing moss moccasins, and go "Boo!" real loud.

Collins, whose mind I guess be a thousand miles away, fall forward like he been shot, and when he stand up he is covered in corral muck from head to foot. That story go around the reserve for days, and everybody who hear it laugh and laugh, slap their hands on their thighs, have to wipe tears out of their eyes. Even today, must be 15 years later, Collins One-wound is still called "Muddy" by some people.

Since television and movies and cars with stereo players come along, falling in the mud in a corral ain't near as funny as it used to be.

Homer Hardy thinks his life has been interesting and he tell about it every chance he get, and because *he* thinks it is interesting, it *is*.

One time Homer he took me with him on a mining trip. He had a piece of tattered paper in his saddlebag he claim to show the location of the Lost Lemon Mine, a story everybody in the West know about.

"Back almost a hundred years ago two miners named Lemon and Blackjack went into the mountains down near the Montana border, and they struck gold," is the way Homer Hardy told the story. "The biggest strike you could imagine," and Homer would ball up his fists to show how big the nuggets was that Lemon and Blackjack found.

"At their camp Lemon went crazy and he killed his partner, and he rode away with just a few nuggets. He was raving when he reached civilization, though his pockets was full of gold to back up his story. But try as he might, he never could lead folks back to the spot where him and Blackjack found the gold. Men is still lookin' for that lode." Homer paused as dramatically as if he was an actor on stage. "But I know the *real* story," he go on. "Two young Indians was hiding in the bush and watched the murder. They rode off and told their chief what they'd seen. One was named Crow Mountain, and the other took the name Kills Him Alone, because of what he'd seen, and nobody ever spoke his former name again. The old chief, Red Ears, was a wise man; he looked into the future and seen thousands of us palefaces ruining his hunting and tearing down his mountains piece by piece, so he swore the two braves to silence for the rest of their days. Then he had them ride out and move the campsite, Blackjack's body, and generally change the terrain so no one would ever be able to find that gold mine.

"But I'm gonna find it. And you're gonna help me, Silas. I got this here map from Red Ears' grandson; had to trade my truck and a case of whiskey for it, but it's the real thing. What are you gonna do with your million dollars, Silas?"

There is something about the word *gold* that makes the blood run faster, and makes your eyes kind of glaze over with hope. I don't know when I ever been so excited as in the days we making the trip from Hobbema to the Montana mountains. Where we going was off in the bush beyond a coal mining town called Blairmore. I remember looking at the mountain and feeling all tingly, seeing the trees angling up the ridge in single file, hitched together by shadows like a packtrain.

But once we got there it was sure different—it rained and the sun, when it did shine, was hot; the air was alive with mosquitoes and black flies, and it ain't no fun to eat half-raw fish over a sickly fire. That land was a lot tougher than we was. After two weeks we limped home—and ever since I been content to buy a lottery ticket when I get the urge to be wealthy. But it didn't faze Homer one bit, he just rest up until his rheumatism was better and his insect bites healed and off he go again.

Two years ago about now Homer had his accident. Him and Martha Powderface was prospecting a little river somewhere in the Rocky Mountain House country, when Homer slip as he scrambling over river rocks and break his leg, not just in one, but in two places.

"I'd a been a goner if it wasn't for Martha," he tell us afterward. "She rigged up a travois out of saplings and tent canvas, and she drug me over fifteen miles of rough country to where we'd parked the truck. And you know what? Martha had never drove in her life. But she's a quick learner," and he smiled across the little studio apartment in the Sundance Retirement Home, where they was living now, to where Martha was cooking oatmeal on the tiny white stove.

"Lucky that truck could be driven in Cree," Homer go on, and he laugh, showing where his teeth used to be, and Martha smile too, from under the flowered babushka she's taken to wearing over her white hair lately.

Homer is pretty well tied to his chair in front of the 12" TV. Between his broke leg and his rheumatism he need two crutches just to move the five steps to the bathroom. But his troubles don't stop him from dreaming.

"The streets of Edmonton are paved with gold. That ain't no lie. They gravelled them with rock right out of the North Saskatchewan River, and you could see the glint of gold in the first pavement of Jasper Avenue, and Whyte Avenue. One time I took my jackknife and dug a nugget the size of the moon on my thumbnail out of Whyte Avenue right at the corner of 104th Street."

One of Martha's sons, Eagle Powderface, listen to enough of Homer's stories that he get fired up to try his hand at prospecting.

But his enthusiasm run dry, just like mine, when he actually have to live in the rain, wind, and cold of the mountains for weeks at a stretch. Besides that, he never find any gold.

I guess prospecting is a little like storytelling, it ain't as much fun since life got easier and information more plentiful.

About two weeks ago I heard Uncle Homer was in the hospital. But before I could even get up to see him he was back at Sundance Retirement.

"Doctors just opened him up, took a look, and sewed him closed again," says Mad Etta. "I went over and took a gander at him, but there ain't no cure for old age."

The next night, though there is a wicked blizzard blowing, me and Sadie stop by Homer and Martha's place. Mad Etta travel with us, wrapped in a buffalo coat and covered in a tarp, she covered in about an inch of snow by the time we get from the reserve to Wetaskiwin. Homer has sure failed bad since I seen him last. He is propped up on pillows in the convertible sofa-bed, look shorter than I ever remember, his toes poking the bedclothes only halfway down the sheet, his whiskers ermine-white now, and his scalp pale, freckles like wheat grains scattered on his skull.

But he's still tellin' stories. Even has one I haven't heard.

"When I was just a boy in Wyoming, only twelve about, soon as the trees started budding, papa sent me and my brother up into the hills with our ponies, a packhorse drooping with grub, and about five hundred head of stock. Ben, he was a year older'n me; we rode herd on them cattle until round-up time. Never saw another soul all summer. There was a small buckaroo cabin, not much more than a log shelter, but someplace for us to put our bedrolls down out of the rain.

"The spring I was sixteen, when we came to that cabin, it was one terrible scene. Sometime in the winter, a wild mustang had pushed the door open in order to take shelter. Wind probably blew the door closed behind him. He'd died maybe a month before. Ain't no words to describe the smell. And you ever tried to get a dead, falling-apart horse out of a tiny cabin door? 'He must of had to kneel down to get in,' is what my brother said.

"Well, we lassoed his legs and tried to pull him out piece by piece, but we wasn't too successful, and as luck would have it, it rained a lot and we sure needed some shelter. Worst job of my life gettin' that carcass out of there. And the smell of death stayed with that cabin all summer. We finally covered the floor with cow chips," and when he see Sadie wrinkle up her nose at that idea, he go on, "You never figured cow chips would smell sweet, would you? Well they did. And they soaked up the odor of death." He pause for a few seconds. "I reckon Martha may have to do the same with this place in a week or two," and he kind of wink across the crowded room at Martha Powderface.

Homer rest for a while, but the wind that was blowing snow hard against the small window by his head wake him again. He must have been dreaming about someplace else, because he have a surprised look on his tired face.

"It's out there, Silas," he say. "Eagle, it's out there right now, even in the winter, in the snow. Little flecks of sunshine trapped in rock, lighting up the night. With gold in your poke you'll never be cold. All you need to get is a blowtorch. It's there. And I know right where it is."

Homer lay his head back on the pillow. Martha Powderface pull the cover up under his chin.

A Hundred Dollars' Worth of Roses

My mother, before she married Paul Ermineskin, was Suzie Buffalo. Her family all moved away from the reserve long before I was born. My grandparents have been dead a long time too. I guess Ma mentioned once or twice that we got an Uncle Wilf, but it don't sink in very deep.

I'm sitting in the sun in front of our cabin when this strange dude come hoofin' it up the hill. He's maybe 50, healthy-looking and muscular; he's packing an expensive saddle, and a black suitcase covered in a layer of red and yellow stickers. That suitcase got the names of more cities on it than most maps.

"Which is Suzie Ermineskin's place?" he ask me, squint one eye against the sunshine.

"You found it. But she's off to Wetaskiwin for the day. I'm her son, Silas."

"Silas, eh? You named after the guy in the Bible who spent a lot of time in jail?"

"No. My mom had a brother, died as a baby. They thought they'd give his name another chance."

"I knew him," the stranger say. "Only lived for ten days. Me and Max Buffalo built the coffin. Big Etta lived for the whole ten days at our cabin; tried every trick she knew to save that baby. Say, is Etta still around?"

"Sure is," I say, and point up the hill where Etta's cabin sit back in the poplars.

"I'm sort of your uncle," he say, set down the saddle and stick out a thick-fingered hand for me to shake. "My folks died when I was a baby; Max Buffalo and his wife, your grandparents, raised me as one of their own. Wilf Cuthand is how your mom would know me, though I've never been a guy to keep with one name for long," and he smile a big, open smile, show a lot of happy lines around his eyes and mouth.

Before Ma gets home, Wilf Cuthand has made a friend out of me. He is really interested to hear I write books, and when I go and get one he look it over real careful.

"By god," he say, "you know this is one thing I ain't done that I should have. I'm going to have to write a book about my life."

I can see that he means what he says. Then he tell me a story about something that happened to him at the Cheyenne Rodeo 20 years or so ago. A gambler want him to throw the calf-roping event, an event Wilf is the heavy favorite to win; that gambler offer more cash than first prize money for Wilf to lose, 'cause he got a bet on somebody else to win.

"I took his cash, then I went out and won the event anyway," Wilf says. "That guy was so mad I thought he was gonna kill me right behind the chutes. 'Let's go in the tack room and talk,' I said to him. He agree, grinning kind of sly 'cause he's dying to get me alone. Soon as we're inside that storeroom he pull a blue gun from inside his coat. 'I'm gonna shoot your knees off, cowboy,' he says to me. 'You're gonna be sorry for the rest of your life that you double-crossed me.'

"Just as he's aiming the gun at me about fifteen cowboys stand up from behind the packing boxes. 'They're all unarmed,' I told him. 'But the way we figure it, you got at most six bullets in your gun. Killing cowboys is like shooting tumbleweeds—so there'll be about a dozen of us left when you're out of bullets. You must have seen a car stripped down slow and smooth by experts. That's how we're gonna take you apart unless you start running in the direction of Phoenix, and promise never to attend another rodeo in your life.'

"We meant what we said about him travelin' on foot. We'd boxed his car in. You know nobody ever claimed it. At least not while the rodeo was in Cheyenne. And no one ever heard of that gambler again."

Wilf laugh a deep, hearty laugh as he finish up the story.

I'm kind of surprised that, when Ma gets home, she ain't near as excited to see Wilf as I would have expected.

"Oh, it's you," is what she said after she come in the cabin door and seen Wilf sitting across the kitchen table from me, a mug of coffee in his hand.

"I know it's only been thirty years, but I thought you might at least be surprised," said Wilf. "Boy, talk about your stoic Indian."

Ma get a smile around the edges of her face.

"I always knew you'd turn up. Why should I be surprised?" she say. But when Wilf Cuthand stand up from the table, tip his beat-up kitchen chair over backward and hug Ma to him, picking her right off her feet and swinging her around, she don't put up a struggle; she even laugh. Something I realize Ma ain't done a lot in her life. But all that evening Ma keep a wary eye on Wilf like she afraid he going to steal something from us.

"I was down in Newfoundland a couple of years ago," he say at the supper table. "I was supposed to be on that *Ocean Ranger*, you know, the oil rig that sunk. I lost a lot of good friends. I had some time off and I went to the mainland, met this girl in Halifax. Somehow I was a day late reporting back for work. Hey, I phoned up this flower shop and I sent that girl a hundred dollars' worth of roses."

"Did you marry her?" ask Delores, my littlest sister.

"No. I didn't even plan to see her again. I just wanted her to know I appreciated her saving my life."

"Hmmmmfff," say Ma, get up from the table, take her plate to the kitchen counter.

I bet there's hardly a place Wilf Cuthand ain't been at one time or another.

"I'm curious," he says, cutting into a slice of saskatoon pie. "There ain't nothin' worse than a person who ain't curious. You know what a cat's like when you place him in a strange house; he explores everything real careful. I been that way with the world. I've been like a cat exploring all the strange rooms of the world."

And he tell us a story about how he was a paratrooper during the Korean War, and how he float down behind enemy lines on a cold, clear winter night.

"I'm gonna see the world," say Delores. "I'm gonna do Indian dances all over the world."

"She's real good," I say. "Dances in a group called the Duck Lake Massacre."

"You've got the right idea," says Wilf. "You dance for me one of these days. I might be able to show you a trick or two. I was a pretty fair thunder-dancer when I was young. And Delores, you plan now to have your own dancing troupe when you're grown up: the Delores Ermineskin Dancers. You can do it if you set your mind to it."

By the time I've known him for a few days I've decided Wilf really has had enough experiences to write a book. He is as full of stories as I am, except his are truer than mine. He claim to have fought oil-well fires with Red Adair, the most famous oil-well fire-fighter in the world. He tell of once walking right into the center of a fire, all dressed up in an asbestos suit. Nobody who hadn't been there could describe it so believably. He knows too, how to pilot a helicopter. He been to Africa and drove a jeep alongside a herd of 10,000 wildebeests and zebras.

"Weren't you scared?" Connie Bigcharles ask him one afternoon at the pool hall. "How did you know where to start?" Connie is Frank's girlfriend and she ain't one to admit being afraid.

"You have to keep asking yourself questions," Wilf say. "Is it better to stay where I am or better to go to strange places?"

"You must have always chose the strange place," says Connie.

"Connie, what do you want to do more than anything else in the world?"

"I want to be an actress and see myself on the TV. I want to wear pretty clothes like actresses do."

"Why can't you do that?"

"I don't know how."

"Do you know where there's a TV station?"

"Yes. There are two or three in Edmonton. More in Calgary."

"Why don't you go to one of them and ask for a job?"

"Oh, I'd be too shy. They wouldn't have any work for me. I'm an Indian. I'd be too scared."

"Scared! Let's have a little ceremony. Everybody speak the word *scared* into their hand, then we toss it on the floor and stomp on it." Wilf do just that. Delores follow him quick, and in a minute so do Connie and Frank, Rufus and Winnie Bear, even me. "How do you think I got a job with Red Adair?" Wilf go on. "How do you think I got into the movies and TV? I walked right up, scared as I was, pretended I knew what I was doing, and *asked* for work."

"You did?"

"Sure. When I felt my knees shaking I just thought, Hey, I got rid of that word scared. It don't exist no more. 'What experience have you had?' Mr. Adair said to me. 'I was a firefighter for seven years in Bismarck, North Dakota,' I said. 'It's a tradition among the Sioux, just as the Mohawks are steelworkers, the Sioux are firefighters.' Red Adair squinted at me and half smiled. I don't know whether he believed me or admired my ability as a liar. 'You got yourself a job,' he said. 'Thank you, Mr. Adair,' I said. 'My name's Joe Dynamite.'"

The conversation continued back at our cabin at suppertime.

"That was all there was to it? You just walked up and asked for every job you ever got?" said Connie.

"Well, I got turned down ten times for every job I landed. But you got to have stamina too, and thick skin. Every time somebody said something mean to me I just pretended to grow another layer of skin so next time it wouldn't hurt so much. By now I got almost fifty layers of skin. Nothin' affects me anymore. Hell, there ain't anything mysterious about what I've got to say. You can do whatever you set your mind on doing," and he shift Delores from one knee to another where he been bouncing her like she riding a bucking horse.

"You believe I could be an actress like the girls I see on TV?" says Connie.

"If you want it bad enough. Most people are all talk and wishes. Listen, there's an old Navajo saying, 'If you want something and you don't know how to get it, then you don't want it bad enough.' We've all got to dream, and we got to have heroes or we ain't anything at all. Dreaming of heroes is what life is all about. Anyone can be like their heroes if they really set their mind to it."

"J.R. Ewing is my hero," says Frank. "Could I be like him? Rich and mean with beautiful women standing in line to shine my Mercedes."

"No, you couldn't," says Wilf.

"But you said . . . ."

"You could be rich if you set your mind to it. Seems to me you already got more women than your fair share. But you couldn't be mean. You've got a soft center, just like my girl Delores here," and he tickle her ribs to make her giggle. "Almost everybody here got a soft center—Silas, Winnie Bear, Rufus—seem like Suzie is the only one got a flint arrowhead where her heart ought to be." We all stare over at Ma, who been doing dishes in the blue enamel dishpan. Ma bang a couple of plates together, real hard, and keep on with her work.

"Tell us another story," Delores say to Wilf at supper a couple of days later. "I like your stories better than Silas'," she go on with that painful honesty little kids have.

"Let me tell you a little bit about my movie days," Wilf say. "By the way, I agree with Delores," and he wink at me. "Silas, you're okay as a storyteller, but you better hope I never decide to go into competition with you. You guys must have seen me in the movies or on TV, without even knowing me. Back in the fifties, when there were lots of westerns on TV, why I was in about two shows a week. Every time they wanted an Indian I'd be there. I'd wrap a blanket around myself and be eighty years old, or I'd whip off my jeans and shirt and run across the set in only a loincloth. I'd wear braids, or long hair with a headband and lots of eagle feathers. My name would appear way at the bottom of the credits:

Sixth Indian: Thomas Many Guns

"I made a good living doing that. I liked TV 'cause you only had to do things once, or twice at the most. Some of the shows we did were live. In movies you had to do a scene maybe forty times, until it didn't feel natural anymore. At the end of one movie we were making, I was supposed to walk off into the sunset with people waving goodbye to me. I walked down a path and turned left about twenty-five times, but the director kept having me repeat the scene. 'I want you to turn right next time,' he told me. I could see having to do twenty-five takes turning right. I walked down the path and turned left again. 'You were supposed to turn the other way,' the director hollered. 'I'm an Indian and it's Sunday,' I called back. 'Indians can't turn right on Sunday.' The director thought that over for a minute, then said, 'Okay, let's print it.'"

We all laugh and pound our thighs at that story.

"Seems like Suzie's the only one here don't like me," Wilf says.

Ma been sitting back in the darkness by the cookstove. Seem to me she got her babushka tied tighter around her head these days.

"If you're such a big wheel," she say harshly, "how come you got nothin' to show for it? For fifty-some years all you got to show is the clothes on your back and a bagful of stories sounds more like Silas' lies than truth to me."

Wilf stay silent for a minute. It the first time I seen him taken aback by anything since he got here.

"Suzie, you know what I've got to show for fifty-five years? I'm happy. I don't know how many people in the world can say that. My guess is not very many. You know how tough we had things when we were kids—well I didn't let that bother me. I just said to myself, I'm not going to wait around to see what life will bring me; I'm gonna go out and meet life. I done it. And I'm not sorry. Most people my age have lived one year fifty-five times. I've lived fifty-five separate years, and I'm gonna live every one that's left to me the same way. And I'm trying to teach your kids and their friends to follow my example. I don't apologize for it."

"Hmmmfff," go Ma, from her dark corner, but I'm not sure if the sound is scornful or if she's sniffing back tears.

A few days later, Wilf, who living in with Dolphus Fryingpan, because Dolphus have an extra bed in his cabin, show us an example of not taking no for an answer.

"You and me are goin' to the dance Saturday night at Blue Quills Hall," he tell Ma.

"I'm not," says Ma.

"I'm taking you," Wilf say. "Whether you get dressed up or not is up to you. I'll be by to get you at eight o'clock. You know, Silas," he say to me, "when your mom was young she was the best polka dancer in a hundred miles. An old man name of Conrad Raven used to fiddle and we used to dance until we pounded dust out of the floorboards of the community hall."

I've never thought of Ma as ever being young, though it reasonable that she was. She's never even had a boyfriend in all the years since Pa left us. I guess children don't like to think of their parents as being real people.

I am surprised as anything at the way Ma look that night. She chucked her head scarf, and her hair, that I only ever seen untied when she washed it, is combed out and fanned over the shoulders of a white blouse she borrow from Sadie.

That is something else that surprise me: Ma being able to wear Sadie's clothes. I've always thought of Ma as big, huge even. I know she only stand to my shoulder, but parents always seem big to kids.

Ma's blue-black hair got a few silver threads in it. I mean, I just never knew she was pretty. She wear a bright green skirt and green shoes she got from Connie Bigcharles. Ma usually wear a shapeless, colorless dress and brown stockings.

Wilf wear a pearl-colored western shirt and a silver buckle the size of a small book that engraved "Grand Forks Rodeo, All Round Cowboy, 1960." He polished that buckle until it shine like chrome on a new car.

"You're twice as pretty as the woman I took to the Academy Awards Dinner back in '62. I was in a picture that was nominated that year. I paid a guy a thousand bucks for his tickets, figured it was something everybody should do once in their life."

It is the first time I ever seen Ma do more than one dance with anybody. She never get to sit down from one end of the evening to the other. When there is a Virginia Reel, me and Sadie get in the same group and I dance with Ma for the first time in my life, even if it is just joining elbows and swinging in a circle.

Wilf and Ma stomped up a storm all that night at Blue Quills, and Ma is just as good a dancer as he said. Ma was really shy at first and Wilf about had to carry her onto the floor for the first waltz of the evening.

It is also the first night since I can remember that Ma gets in later than me. Day is pushing pink light in the windows when Ma come in. I hear Wilf say something about breakfast, but Ma shush him and send him on his way. I know Dolphus Fryingpan is off on the rodeo circuit, so it ain't too hard to figure where Ma and Wilf been for the past four hours or so.

"It's about time Suzie got herself a man," Mad Etta said that evening at Blue Quills, from where she sat high up on her tree-trunk chair, alongside the Coke machine.

And over the next couple of weeks it does look like Suzie Ermineskin has got herself a man. Her and Wilf spend almost every night together, though she never bring him to her bed. It seem funny, but I've brought Sadie home for years and years, but Ma don't feel right to bring her boyfriend home. They even go to Edmonton for a weekend where they stay at the Chateau Lacombe Hotel, go to the movies and to fancy restaurants for steak and Chinese food.

"It's like old times," say Wilf at Hobbema Pool Hall one afternoon. "Except in the old days, when your Ma and me was young, we didn't have two pennies to rub together. Though we were raised in the same house Suzie and me weren't related. Way back in those days I liked her a whole lot. I wanted her to go with me when I hit the road. I asked her to go with me." I guess Wilf can see my eyes get wide. "She was the prettiest and smartest girl on the reserve. I was afraid for both of us if we stayed, her more than me . . ." and his voice trail off.

The pool hall is completely silent. We is all standing like we was in a photograph, waiting for him to go on.

"She turned me down. It was simple as that. I even offered to get married if she'd come with me. Only time in my life I ever proposed to a woman. She was afraid of what was out there. I was afraid too, but the difference was I couldn't wait to find out what it was I was afraid of."

Wilf has by now got us all dreaming. Rufus admit he always wanted to be a bartender.

"Well, you can be," say Wilf. "A mixologist is what it's called. All it takes is a little nerve. You look up *Bartending Schools* in the Yellow Pages, call and find out how much it costs. Save your money. Enroll. Nothing's stopping you but yourself. After you graduate you go to hotels and big restaurants and sell yourself. Don't go whispering 'I'm an Indian,' or trying to pretend you're not. Say 'I'm the first Indian bartender in Alberta. Let me make you a drink called a Chicken Dancer . . .'"

"But I wouldn't . . .," say Rufus.

"You'd make it up. Play it by ear. Take a chance."

Wilf do the same thing to each of us. I'm thinking of trying to get an agent to really sell my books to big publishers and to the movies and TV. And Frank admit he want to own an auto-wrecking and second-hand business. Wilf got good answers to all our questions and objections.

"But we're Indians," somebody say.

This is the only time since he been here Wilf lose his patience.

"You can be a success and still be an Indian," he say real sharp. "Don't any of you ever use being an Indian as an excuse for failure. People are people wherever you go. Indian, Black, White, Yellow, doesn't make a damn bit of difference what color you are outside. It's what you've got inside that counts. The failures all excuse themselves by saying 'I'm just a poor Indian, what do you expect,' a whiner's a whiner, a loser's a loser, white or Indian," and he look around fierce at us, his eyes flashing.

"What do you figure's gonna happen with Ma and Wilf?" I ask Mad Etta.

Etta look at me for a long time. I feel like her old eyes are drilling holes in my chest.

"You know," she says.

"I do?"

"If I thought you were dumb I wouldn't of made you my assistant."

"What do I know?"

Etta smile deep in her face. "That Wilf is like the first soft weather of March; weather that turn the snowbanks soft as putty, put the smell of life in the air, set us to dreaming of summer."

"But what you're describing is called a false spring."

"Good," says Etta. "I told you you knew."

A few nights later Ma come home about midnight. Everyone else is in bed; the rooms in our cabin been made by hanging blankets on clothesline cord. Sadie is snuggled down deep in the quilts beside me. Ma make herself coffee and sit at the table a long time. I doze off, but wake as the cabin door close. I recognize Wilf's boots on the kitchen floor. Wilf has been carrying his suitcase. I can hear the metal edges clack as he sit it down on the linoleum.

"What do you want now?" says Ma. Her voice is tired.

"I came to say goodbye. And I come to apologize if I made you unhappy. I know you don't like what I been selling to the young people. Are you sorry I came back, Suzie?"

"No. I guess not," Ma say after a long pause.

"Are you afraid of me?"

After an even longer pause Ma says, "No. I'm afraid of me."

"I know. If I don't leave now I might never leave. I'm too old to put down roots. Yours are too deep in the ground to be pulled up . . . ."

I've never really thought of what Ma has missed out on. She's been like a windbreak for us kids. She's done whatever she could to help us, mainly she just kept us together, when over half the families on the reserve fell apart. She never let white social workers get their hooks into our family.

"What if . . . what if I was to come back in a few years, when Delores is on her own and you're as free as you were thirty-five years ago? Think you might travel a little with me?"

"I don't know," say Ma.

"It'll be something for both of us to dream about. Something to keep us going. Even if it don't work out it's better to wake up than not to dream at all. All the time I been here I been telling the young folks to find someone to look up to. Dreaming of heroes ain't such a bad occupation.

"Suzie, you don't think I know what you've done here. But I do. You chose a harder life than me, and you stuck it out in a way I might not have been able to. You've lived your life for your kids. I've lived my life mostly for me. The wisest thing you ever did was turn me down all those years ago. I think maybe you saved my life."

"You gonna send me a hundred dollars' worth of roses?" say Ma, and her voice is younger than I think I ever heard it. It is a girl's husky voice, no older than Connie's or Sadie's.

"Would you like that?"

"I don't know." But Ma's voice catches as she says it. There is a long silence and it would be my guess that they are holding onto each other.

"Keep lookin' out the window there, Suzie. Keep lookin' down the hill to the highway. One day a panel truck from Boxmiller Flower Shop in Wetaskiwin will come driving slow up the hill.

Painted on the side of that panel truck is a picture of a guy with a funny helmet on his head and wings on his heels. The driver will have a hundred dollars' worth of roses for you."

"No," says Ma, and I can tell she is crying. "There's other things we need. Delores . . . ."

"They'll be for Suzie Ermineskin and nobody else. You've spent all your life giving. There won't be any card. You just think of this old man with wings on his feet . . . ."

I hear Wilf walk across the floor, stop and pick up his suitcase and saddle, then head out the door.

Ma pull up a chair and sit at the kitchen table. She blow out the lamp. I can see tines of moonlight strung across the floor. I cuddle down in my bed. It gonna be nice, seeing Ma staring down the road, dreaming.

The
Medicine Man's
Daughter

M y friend Frank Fencepost insists that the most feared words in either English or Cree are not *"You're under arrest,"* or, *"Guilty as charged,"* but, *"I'm pregnant."* Frank also claim that since he started making it with girls, which he says was when he was ten, that the most popular names on the reserve is Frank for boys and Frankie for girls. Frank is the kind of guy who, when both of Elias Stonechild's twin daughters come around claiming they is pregnant and that Frank is the father, say, "Hey, I was only joking. You guys took something seriously that was poked at you in fun."

Frank figure it is his duty to get as many girls pregnant as possible.

"If my kids are all as smart as me, Fenceposts will rule the world in a couple of generations," he say, and laugh hearty.

It is a good thing that Frank's more-or-less steady girlfriend, Connie Bigcharles, was already on the birth control pills when they met.

"If you want babies, *you* have them," is what Connie says. "I'll consider getting pregnant, right after you bought us a four-bed-room house and a Cadillac."

Frank grumble and mumble and talk about wasting his valu-able assets, and that having sex with a girl who ain't liable to get pregnant is like building a dog-house when you ain't got a dog.

"Anytime you want to change dog-houses, you just let me know," says Connie. "You ain't the only fish swimmin' under the bridge."

Connie is the only person who can treat Frank like that and get away with it. If she cried or got sulky when Frank fools around with someone else, he'd dump her in a minute. But Connie is just as happy go lucky as Frank. She goes off with somebody she likes once in a while too. And don't Frank get mad. But it don't do him no good.

"What would you rather I do," Connie ask him, "go off and have a good time when I'm mad at you, or sit home waiting with a shotgun and blow your peter all the way to Saskatchewan the next time you show up?"

Frank cross his legs, grin, and say, "Have a good time."

With me and Sadie things are different. It was me who got Sadie to go on the birth-control pills. I seen a poster at the Tech School in Wetaskiwin, tell about the Free Clinic that held there once a week. I'd just started at Tech School, I was 16 and Sadie 14, and the last thing we needed in our life was babies. The school on the reserve is run by the Catholic Church, and they do their best to keep everyone ignorant about sex. Sadie is so shy I had to practically drag her to that clinic, go inside and sit with her, answer most of the questions the nurse ask, and do every-thing but go into the examining room with her.

That was almost five years ago, and everything's run smooth since then. The clinic sell birth control pills at cost—sometimes me and Sadie had to collect pop bottles and sell them to make the buy, but we always managed.

That is why it was such a shock to me, when, one night in the coldest part of March, right after we come out of the Alice Hotel from having a few beers, Sadie slide over beside me on the seat of Louis Coyote's pickup truck and, the cold air coming out her mouth like smoke, say, "I been to the clinic twice this week and the doctor says I'm pregnant."

I didn't say anything for quite a while.

"Do you think we'll get married?" Sadie say, as I easing the truck out onto the highway.

"I'm trying to figure how it could have happened," I say. "Did they give us some bad pills, or did you forget to take them proper?"

"I didn't forget," Sadie say in a small voice.

"Then they must have sold us bad stock. I think they sell samples, stuff they're given, some of it's probably pretty old."

"I guess," said Sadie.

"Sure we'll get married," I said. There was a bitter wind, and snow was blowing in sheets across the highway, cutting my visibility to almost nothing.

"I'm glad," said Sadie, and she laid her head against my shoulder.

"It's about time you two joined the population explosion," Frank say when I tell him. I don't quite understand why, but it has taken me three days to get around to telling him. "Hey, you can read to it right through Sadie's belly, and it'll be born writing books like its old man. Don't laugh, you ever seen how many books there are in the children's section of the library? There must be a lot of kids who write."

I give a polite laugh.

"You sure don't look very happy," Frank go right on. "Don't worry about the wedding. Fencepost, your best man, will take care of all the details. Nothing is too good for my best friend. You'll name the baby Frank Fencepost Ermineskin, of course. Venison. We'll have venison steaks at the reception. Your sister Delores and her dancing troupe can perform. I'll look after the bar. At cost. Well, almost at cost. And as a grand finale, Robert Coyote and Gaston Sixkiller will blow up a bridge on Highway 2A. Memorable, huh?"

"Yeah, memorable," I say.

"Hey, if you don't want to get married I can help too. Fencepost is a master of disguise. I can change your appearance so *you* won't even know you, let alone anybody else. You'll be able to live right here on the reserve. First thing you have to do is take that row of pens out of your shirt pocket . . . ."

"Frank, this is serious," I say.

"What's the matter? You figure it's not yours? I read where they can run tests. I'll take a lie-detector test; it wasn't me. I wouldn't do that to you. I got morals. Besides Sadie hates my guts."

"I just don't understand how it could have happened."

"I read about that too, there's these here eggs and sperms . . ."

"I know you're trying to cheer me up, but just can it, alright? If I thought it was really an accident we'd be married by now," I said.

"You better hash this out with Sadie. Maybe talk to a doctor."

"I already been to that clinic in Wetaskiwin. 'It can happen,' the nurse at the clinic told me. But she look at me out of the corner of her eye when she say that. Either it can't happen, or she just thinks Sadie was too stupid to take her pills regular, and don't want to say that to me."

"We got to have a serious talk," I say to Sadie that evening. We are sitting in the kitchen of One-wounds' cabin.

"I guess we do," she say, looking at the floor.

"I want to clear something up once and for all. You been around Etta and me long enough to know there is more than one way of telling the truth. When I asked if you forgot to take your pills, you said no. But that could also mean that you didn't forget, that you on purpose didn't take them. Is that what happened?"

Sadie raise her face from where she been studying the green-and-black tiles on the kitchen floor. And I don't need any more of an answer than the look in her eyes. She has never been able to lie.

She try real hard not to cry, but tears come anyway, roll silent out of her eyes and track down her cheeks.

"Why?" I say.

Sadie make a long sniffle. "If you really wanted a baby," I say, "you could of asked. We could have talked about it. "

"I was afraid I'd lose you," Sadie say real soft. "Lots of people read your books these days. You get to travel around. You been on the radio and the TV. I'm afraid you're gonna want a smart and pretty wife, maybe even a white one. I thought if we had a baby . . ."

Late that evening after I spent about four hours walking down the dirt roads of the reserve, thinking, I stop by Mad Etta's cabin and let her in on my troubles.

"If it was an accident I'd marry her in a minute, but I hate to feel I been trapped. I love Sadie a lot, but if I get married just to please her, I know I'm going to resent her for it."

"Two things," say Etta, "first, lots of couples live together and have babies without being married; and, second, it also possible to get rid of the baby. Sadie was dead wrong to do what she done, and I told her that when she was here a few days ago. My advice is to take a month to sort out the possibilities; you might come to like the idea of having a wife and baby."

I wonder how Etta knew?

Sadie and me always got along real good and her being pregnant don't change that a bit.

On a day when I get in the mail a small check for one of the stories I had printed up, me and Sadie drive up to Edmonton in Louis Coyote's pickup truck. Sadie sit close beside me, and though she is only four months along, I'm sure her belly is already pushing out the waist of her jeans.

"I can feel my breasts changing," she say to me, and smile. "I can feel them growing. Maybe they'll stay big after the baby comes." Sadie always been pretty small that way, not like Frank's girl Connie who burst out of her blouses.

"I got bigger boobs than Sadie," Frank has been known to say, and Sadie laugh along with us, but not very happily.

Being pregnant do agree with Sadie. "She is rounding off some of her corners," is the way Mad Etta put it. Sadie always been sharp-featured with no meat on her bones.

We have decided we will get married come the end of the summer. We will look for a small apartment in Wetaskiwin where the three of us can live while I finish up my terms at the Tech School. We also agree to let Frank plan the wedding, all but the bridge burning.

That afternoon we go shopping at the West Edmonton Mall, which is about a quarter-section of stores, also got a carnival and a skating rink all under one roof. We buy Sadie a red-and-white candy-striped maternity top, and she so pleased with it she wear it away from the store. She also pull me into a store for babies, and we pick out a dress of pink silky stuff, got about nine little petticoats under it. Sadie is positive she going to have a girl, and that would make me happy. Frank is the only one who really wants a boy.

"Anybody can make a girl," he says, "but it takes a real man to put a handle on the finished product."

That is one of the happiest days we ever spent together. I am getting excited about the baby too. We go to a movie and out for hamburgers, where we talk about naming our daughter. Sadie think it would be nice to name her Sigourney, after the movie star. I would rather give her an Indian name, something like Wolverine Woman. We decide maybe we will do both. We driving on the outskirts of the city, Sadie half asleep with her head on my shoulder, when she take sick.

The University Hospital in Edmonton was closest to where we were. By the time I get Sadie into emergency there already blood stains between the legs of her jeans.

They only keep her for one day, give her some shots to make sure any infection don't start.

"She'll be good as new in a week," the doctor say when I pick her up to take her home.

Maybe physically. But it been two months since that happened and Sadie still walk around like a dead person.

We'd made so many plans, and to have them snatched away from us was pretty hard to take. I know I feel, for most of a month, like I'm carrying a hundred pounds of lead inside me.

I do everything I can think of to make Sadie feel like her old self. I even suggest it would be alright if she wanted to get pregnant again. I say we'll get married just like we planned. But nothing help. The doctors say Sadie is healthy, give her some pills to make her feel better but they don't seem to help. We even make love, but only a couple times. There is nothing in the world worse than making love with someone who don't share your enthusiasm. Sadie just sit and stare at the little pink dress we bought that day; her hair get dull and matted, sometimes she don't even look up when someone calls her name. One night after she was asleep I took the little dress away and stuffed it in the Goodwill box at Wheatlands Shopping Center parking lot. But Sadie don't even ask what happened to it.

"*Depression?*" say Etta. "*Post natal depression?*"

I nod. "That's what the doctors say is wrong with Sadie."

"Doctors are too smart for their own good these days," say Etta. "They give people excuses. Your friend, Frank, have the right idea when he says, 'Life is hard and then you die.' We live. We die. There ain't much else. Best anybody can do is try to make living tolerable and dying painless."

"I came here hoping you might cheer me up," I say.

"Get me a beer from the bucket inside the door there," say Etta. She, as usual, sits way up on her tree trunk chair at the back of the cabin, where the light from the coal-oil lamp make her look like a copper colored goddess of some kind.

"Let me tell you a story, Silas. This happen to somebody I know well, oh, I bet, forty years ago. She was a young woman, married to a good man who loved her a lot. She was pregnant with their first baby. That husband was the happiest man on the reserve; he already made that baby a tiny drum, built him a medicine bag of his own, made a *tikenagan* (a carrying pouch) out of elk hide, tanned until it was soft as moss. The woman was seven months along when she took sick. The baby died inside her. The medicine man, Buffalo-who-walks-like-a-man, came to the *tipi*, used all the magic he had in his power, just to save the woman's life.

"That woman wasn't glad to be alive anymore. She grieved over that dead baby; she said over and over how she wished she'd died and the baby had lived, or that they both had died. Her husband was a gentle, patient man; but everyone, no matter how good a person, have a limit to their patience. He was a wise man and a believer in the old ways of the tribe. He went to the medicine man, Buffalo-who-walks like a-man; they spent a few hours in the sweat lodge together; they smoked a pipe, and sat silent across from each other in the medicine man's tent for most of a night.

"In the morning the husband said 'I think we should place my wife in the *tipi* of sorrow.'

"Buffalo-who-walks-like a-man nodded his head. 'I hoped that is what you would say. You have decided wisely.'

"In the real old days, grieving was a bitter process. Women cut off a finger joint when a relative died; both men and women scarred their arms in mourning; it was a custom for a grieving family to give away or to burn every one of their possessions.

"The husband, with the help of the medicine man, turned his own *tipi* into what was called a house of sorrow. He hauled out everything except the large bed, which was made by stuffing tanned hides with sweet clover. He gave away all his and his wife's possessions. She lay on the bed and stared at the smoke-hole, not caring what went on around her.

" 'This week is yours to grieve as you see fit,' the husband said. 'but it is to be the last week of your grief. Life goes on for us all.'

"The first morning the women of the tribe brought small gifts for the wife, a venison steak, a smoked quail breast, a dish of fresh-picked saskatoon berries. Most of them didn't speak, just pushed open the tent flap, smiled, and set the offering on the packed dirt floor.

"All week long the procession continued, children picked her bright bouquets of dandelions, fireweed, cowslips, or left her pretty stones they had found on the river bottom, left them shyly outside the tent. The woman all but ignored their efforts.

"Over the course of the week almost everyone in the tribe made a small gift to the woman. Many were pieces of clothing, a bowl, a household item; all things she would need to start her life over. One evening the women of the tribe gathered in front of the tent and sang a song encouraging her to join them in celebrating life.

"At the end of the week a celebration was planned. All week long when the women or children had been gathering firewood, they brought home an extra branch, or piece of deadfall. Now they all came slowly toward the tent of sorrow, moving stealthily, almost in slow motion, as if they were parting thick fog with each step, each carrying their burden of dry wood. The wood was stacked at the side of the tent.

"Buffalo-who-walks-like-a-man beat on his sacred drum. The men of the tribe, dressed in their finest beaded leather, their faces smeared with paint, drummed the day away. They, too, called for the woman to join them, to begin her life again.

"But the woman didn't come out. Inside the tent she lay like a log, her face buried in her bed. She knew what would happen if she didn't rejoin the tribe. She'd seen it once when she was a child.

"As darkness approached, the stack of firewood near the tent was lit. The drumming continued. The light from the fire reflected off the night sky and down through the smoke hole of the tent. It made patterns on the bed, like moonlight on water.

"The drumming got louder and the fire got brighter and higher. The old medicine man, Buffalo-who-walks-like-a-man, sit himself down cross-legged in front of the tent and sing to the woman, telling her how everybody is waiting for her come out and start her new life.

"When he don't get an answer he nod to the men who stoking the fire, one of them was the woman's husband, and they pile the new brush on the side of the fire run it right to the edge of the tent. Another minute and the fire will take the tent and the woman.

"The woman, who for all the weeks since she lost her baby felt she had nothing to live for, decide to take one last look at the sky before she die. She open her eyes and see the fire flickering off the sky and onto her own body and the shiny hair of the bear hide she was laying on. The inside of the tent get really hot; the fire started up the side of the tent, she could see it climbing the outside, like the sun do when it first rise in the morning.

"And with that she started thinking of the sun, and the striped tiger lilies that grew around the edges of the camp, and her husband who had been so gentle and patient with her these past months.

"Just as the fire burst through the wall of the tent, the flaps parted and the woman emerged. The rhythm of the drums changed from solemn to happy and the people began to dance. The woman's husband came to her and led her in among the dancers. Everyone came and hugged her and said how much they loved her and how glad they were she had chosen to live. They all celebrated far into the night, and the woman and her husband were given more bedding, clothing, utensils—all the things they needed to start a new life."

Etta stare down at me from her deep-set eyes, exhale to show the story finished, sound like a tractor tire deflating. I'm not sure what I'm supposed to have learned. That was then, this is now. Customs like that died out years ago.

"That woman was the medicine man's daughter," Etta say.

"You're a medicine man's daughter," I said.

"Yes, I am," said Etta with none of the sarcasm in her voice that I expected after my stupid statement.

Etta don't give me any advice or tell me any more stories. She just yawn and head over to her bed, make it plain it's time for me to go home.

I walk down to the Hobbema Pool Hall and tell Frank what just happen to me.

"No problem," says Frank. "A Fencepost understands these mysterious stories."

"What do *you* think I should do?"

"Improvise," says Frank. "We going to have to improvise. But that's something I'm good at. Remember how, when we were kids, I used to ride all the girls on the crossbar of my bicycle? Not one of them ever noticed it was a girl's bike . . . ."

"I think Sadie will get better by herself," I say.

But she don't. In fact she get worse. A lot worse. A couple of weeks later I take her to the doctor in Wetaskiwin and he put her in the hospital, where they don't do nothing for her but put her on a lot of medication make her move in slow motion.

After a week a doctor stop me in the hall as I leaving, "Mr. One-wound?" he say, assuming I am Sadie's husband. "We have a form at the desk for you to sign. We're going to try a different approach in treatment. It is a simple permission form for us to use electric shock therapy."

I tell him I got to check with the tribal medicine man before I can sign something like that.

"Bring it back tomorrow afternoon," he say, staring at me like I was a lot stranger than he expected me to be.

For one more time Etta surprise me.

"I'm glad to see they finally getting down to serious business," she say when I tell her of the shock treatments they want to do on Sadie.

"You're glad?"

"I suggested the same thing a month ago," she say, and look more smug than she usually do when people talk about medicine. "You wouldn't do anything then. How about now?"

"Native shock treatments?" I say.

"We had our treatment when doctors were still slitting wrists to let out bad blood. Like anything from primitive times, if it works it's a 100% cure, if it don't the loss is total."

"But Sadie doesn't know the story you told me. She won't understand what's happening."

"You'll tell her the basics. We'll get her off all the white man's medication, so her head will be clear. She's an Indian. She'll catch on."

"One of the Indian Affairs houses up on the ridge has been abandoned," I say. "We could use it; it going to be torn down anyway."

"You have to give away everything you *both* own. You'll have to part with your typewriter," Etta is saying. But I'm only half-listening. Visiting Sadie these past weeks, I seen the poor, stumbling, empty-eyed people who the doctors haven't been able to help, even with shock treatments. If I'm going to lose Sadie I'd rather lose her in a flash of fire, than see her exist in one of the dark wards of that brown-smelling hospital. I'm thinking too of Etta and maybe Rufus Firstrider sitting in front of the abandoned cabin drumming, and a whole lot of people standing around while the fire whooshes up into the night sky inching closer and closer to the cabin.

Brother Frank's
Gospel Hour

ACKNOWLEDGMENT
"The Elevator" first appeared in *Canadian Fiction Magazine* in a slightly different form.

For my grandsons
Jason Kirk Kinsella
Kurtis William Kinsella
and
Max Knight Kinsella

Contents

Bull 467

Miracle on Manitoba Street 485

The Elevator 503

Ice Man 517

Turbulence 535

Saskatoon Search 547

The Rain Birds 563

George the Cat 577

Conflicting Statements 595

Dream Catcher 613

Brother Frank's Gospel Hour 627

Brother Frank's
Gospel Hour

Bull

I t ain't very often that my friend Frank Fencepost gets real mail. He sometimes refer to himself as the King of Junkmail though, because he put himself on every trash mailing list in North America, get bulletins and advertisements from every church, cuckoo-clock maker, stamp dealer, and political party there is. But only about twice a year do anything arrive in a *white* envelope, one that don't have either a plastic window in it or Frank's name typed on by a computer.

This white envelope is covered with about three dollars' worth of stamps, have the word *Registered* in big red letters in two or three places. In order to claim it Frank have to sign his name in a book that Ben Stonebreaker keep behind the counter at the general store.

"First time I got a registered letter wasn't from a collection agency," say Frank, hold it up to the sunshine, try to guess what's in it.

The last time Frank got a registered letter from a collection agency, he read it real quick, smile big, crumple up the letter what got red writing all over it and the word *URGENT* in inch-high capitals, throw it away. He heave a big sigh and say, "Sure happy that outfit ain't gonna bother me no more. They say this here is their final notice."

Today's envelope is thick and have the Alberta Provincial Seal on the outside.

"You can open it," we say. "It addressed to you. It not like you sneaking a look at somebody else's mail."

"Right!" says Frank, look a little sheepish. "I knew that."

"Hey, I got to go to court," Frank yell. "First time I get to be the witness instead of the criminal."

"Why do you have to go to court?" we all want to know.

Turn out the place Frank have to go to is the Alberta Supreme Court, while the reason is on account of he got fired from a job last summer. It was a job he never should of had.

Frank is really good at getting himself hired on at jobs he ain't qualified for.

"I create qualifications," Frank argue. "Qualifications are a state of mind. Besides, I don't see the newspaper full of ads for what I do best. I keep looking for ads that say 'Handsome Indian Wanted,' or 'Great Lover Wanted,' but all I see are jobs for burger flippers and telephone solicitors. You know the kind, 'Make $100,000 a week in your spare time.'"

Like me, Frank been studying at the Tech School in Wetaski-win for the last few years on how to repair tractors. But there never seem to be any jobs in that line.

On the other hand, women, whether they is old or young, white or Indian, is usually charmed by Frank. But what really surprises me is that he can con men almost as easy as women. I was there the day he got hired for that job he shouldn't have had — foreman for Mr. Manley Carstairs at the C Bar C Ranch.

The day before, Frank seen the ad in the *Wetaskiwin Times* advertise for a ranch foreman.

"Let's drive out there," Frank say. "The job's as good as mine."

"You never even lived on a farm," I say.

"Hey, a foreman tells other people what to do. I can do that. 'Haul that hay! Fix that fence! Spread that manure! Brand those cattle! Get me a beer!' Silas, to get any job, all I got to do is look the part, act confident, and lie like a snake."

We drive out to the C Bar C Ranch, which south of Camrose. It must be worth a million dollars; the house is a mansion, and there are two Cadillacs and a Lincoln parked in the driveway.

Mr. Manley Carstairs is about fifty, short with a big belly; wear a white cowboy hat, a sky-blue western suit, and $500 boots. The three of us walk around the farmyard while Mr. Carstairs explain the job.

Inside of two minutes, Frank walking with the same gait as Mr. Carstairs, got a timothy straw at the same angle in his mouth. In another two minutes Frank even talk a little like Mr. Carstairs. And even though Frank don't have much of a belly he walk with it pushed out in front of him the same way as the boss of the C Bar C.

"Just call me Foreman Frank," he say, make a polite little laugh, and reel off the names of several ranches where he claim to have worked. He got the ranch names from a clerk at the Wetaskiwin Seed and Feed Store.

"I guess I'm what you'd call a progressive Indian," Frank say. "I work for you as foreman, but I'm sure you won't mind that three nights a week I go to Edmonton, study at the University of Alberta to get my degree in social work. My ultimate goal is to help my people."

Mr. Manley Carstairs eat this up just like Frank feeding him candy.

"Which," Frank go on, "is the reason I brought this unfortunate fellow here." And Frank point at me. "This young man is one of those Indians who live off government handouts, never done an honest day's work in his life. But I aim to change all that. With a menial position for him here on the ranch, and what with me supervising, why I'll see that he works. You know how most of these Indians are if you don't watch them all the time."

Frank is talking Mr. Manley Carstairs' language. They are buddies now. Mr. Carstairs forget all about references and experience. He can't hire Frank fast enough.

"My friend's Indian name is Standing-neck-deep-in-slough-water, but we just call him Stan. You won't give him no job where he has to read or write, or anything that might embarrass him. He has some pride, even if he don't look like it. First pay check I'll see that he buys some decent clothes. He don't have any idea how to handle money either, so it'll be okay for you to give me his pay for safekeeping. I'll see that it don't all get spent in one place." Frank kind of leer at Mr. Carstairs when he say that.

"Does he speak English?" Mr. Carstairs ask.

"Only enough to be dangerous. Ain't that right, Stan?"

"Right, Foreman Frank," I say, raise my hand up in front of me the way Indians do on television.

"Say, does your range go on for a long ways?" Frank ask.

"Over six hundred thousand acres. I guess you could say that's a good ways. Why do you ask?"

"It's just that my specialty is long-range planning," say Frank.

Mr. Carstairs slap Frank on the back and laugh and laugh.

"What do you figure to do, now you've got the job?" I ask Frank on the drive home.

"I figure I'll just ask the cowboys what needs to be done, and then I'll tell them to do it."

There was another registered letter arrive at Hobbema General Store, addressed to Standing-neck-deep-in-slough-water, but that letter never get claimed.

Both Frank and me are a little surprised to find there aren't any criminals in this trial. It's what is called a civil case: Carstairs vs. Ace Artificial Insemination Inc. I have to look up *civil* in the dictionary. There are about a dozen definitions, but some of the words mean the same as civil are *polite*, *courteous*, and *gallant*. It take a long time to figure out what is going on, but after a day or so, I understand that Mr. Carstairs, who raise purebred Charolais cattle, so white they look like snowbanks scattered about the fields, is mad. The Ace Artificial Insemination Inc. made his purebred cows pregnant, but what come out wasn't purebred Charolais calves, but plug-ugly little mavericks.

Mr. Carstairs want his money back from AAII, plus a lot of damages for the purebred calves he didn't get. The AAII say they did everything right. The cows must have already been pregnant. Mr. Carstairs say there was no way the cows could have been pregnant.

"What going on here is like fighting in slow motion," I say to Frank.

"How so?"

"Well, it's a little like walking up to a guy in a bar, one who's been staring you down all evening, and saying friendly, as if you talking to a school teacher, 'Excuse me, motherfucker, but you've been giving me the evil eye, and if you don't stop I'm gonna kick the piss out of you.'

"Then the other guy says, polite as you please, 'Fuck off, asshole. I wasn't looking at you.' Even when the fight start, it done in slow motion. Maybe that dude punch me in the face, knock me over a couple of tables, then I get up and kick him in the crotch. He pull a razor out of his boot and come for me. I take a gun from inside my jacket, we stare at each other and circle, all the time calling each other names, but polite as you please. Then the RCMP come along tell us both to behave or they'll do us a certain amount of damage.

"The fighters is like the lawyers, and the RCMP is like the judge."

The lawyers talk lawyer talk, but I'm able to translate enough to explain it mainly about how Ace Artificial Insemination Inc. collect samples of bull semen, and how they got foolproof ways to see the samples stay pure until they reach the cow.

Frank get all excited.

"I can do that," he says. "I'll collect my own samples, then I'll stop pretty ladies on the street and say, 'Pardon me, Ma'am, but for only $500 you can have a baby look just like me. I'll make a million dollars in no time."

"I'm not sure the world is ready for that idea," I say.

When it is Frank's turn to testify, the bailiff try to swear him in.

"Do you swear to tell the truth, the whole truth, and nothing but the truth?"

"I'll take the first one," say Frank.

Even the judge have to smile at that.

"'I do' will suffice," say the bailiff.

"Why would you give me a choice if I got to choose all three?" ask Frank.

"The appropriate reply is 'I do,'" the bailiff say.

"If I say 'I do,' I'm liable to wind up married to somebody. How about 'Okay'?"

"Whatever."

"Let me hear those choices again?"

The bailiff look cross, but place Frank's hand on the Bible and mumble, "Do you swear to tell the truth, the whole truth, and nothing but the truth? So help you God."

"Hey, I don't believe in none of this stuff," Frank say, pushing the Bible to one side. "But I take an Indian oath to tell the truth."

The bailiff and Frank look up at the judge.

"I believe that will be in order," he say, and sigh.

Frank, he leap down off the witness chair. He wearing Eathen Firstrider's beaded buckskin jacket, moccasins, a ten-gallon black hat on top of his braids, which his girl, Connie Bigcharles, tie for him with bright red ribbon. He shuffle along for a few feet then he crouch over, slap his palms on his legs just above the knees, and start to chant "Hoo-hoo, Hoo-hoo, Hoo-hoo," just like a train trying to pick up speed. He dance like that all around the lawyers' tables, stop to stare down the blouse of the woman who taking everything down on a tiny typewriter. Then he work his way back to the witness stand and sit down again.

He wipe his brow. "This here witnessing is hard work," he say. "I made my peace with the Great Spirit. I burst into flame before your very eyes if I was to tell a lie."

"His great spirits come from the Alberta Government Liquor Store," Mad Etta, our medicine lady, whisper to me.

Last night, me, Frank, Mad Etta, and a few friends closed up the Travelodge bar in Wetaskiwin. Frank got in a certain amount of trouble in the parking lot, and the skin under his eye is the red-black color of a ripe apple.

"Now, Mr. Fencepost," say the lawyer for Ace Artificial Insemination Inc., "you are employed as a foreman at the C Bar C Ranch?"

"Just call me Foreman Frank. And I used to be employed by the C Bar C. I'm practicing my unemployment right now."

"How long were you employed by the C Bar C?"

"Two or three months."

"I see." The lawyer take a deep breath.

"Could we assume, Mr. Fencepost, that, as the information before me indicates, you were employed by the C Bar C Ranch from May to July of the year in question?"

"I guess so," says Frank. "Is the *year in question* like the station to which you are listening?"

"Now, Mr. Fencepost, could you tell us the exact day you were fired?"

"The day Mr. Carstairs got mad at me."

"Could you be more specific?"

"Well, see, Mr. Carstairs and his missus was supposed to have gone into Red Deer for the day. So soon as their car pulled onto the highway why I headed up to the house. See, the Carstairs got this pretty daughter name of Virginia Jean . . ."

"You misunderstand, Mr. Fencepost, I meant more specific about the date."

"It wasn't a date. We just got together whenever her folks went out."

"The date of the month."

"Virginia Jean was okay, but I'd never name her *date of the month.*"

"Mr. Fencepost, you're being very exasperating."

"Thank you. I always try to co-operate."

At this point the lawyer reserve the right to recall Frank sometime later. Guess he figure to get along better with Mr. Carstairs as a witness.

"Can you tell us," he say to Mr. Carstairs, who look like a bull-dog in a dark-pink western suit and string tie, "the circumstances that led you to discharge your ranch foreman, Mr. Fencepost?"

"I can't see that that has anything to do with those swindlers," and he point a short stubby arm at the man from Ace Artificial Insemination Inc., "impregnating my purebred stock with bad quality . . ."

"Answer the question, please," say the judge.

"I caught the sneaky son of a bitch in bed with my daughter. I walked into her bedroom, and there they were. He wasn't wearing anything except his hat. He looked at me cool as you please, and he said, 'Well, Boss, are you gonna believe Foreman Frank, or are you gonna believe what you see?' Lucky for him my hand gun was in the study and my rifle was in the pick-up truck. Last I seen of him until today, was him running north, pulling on his pants and carrying his boots."

"I see. Now, was this before or after Ace Artificial Insemination Inc. made their visit to your ranch?"

Mr. Carstairs take a notebook out of his inside pocket, study the calendar part.

"It was two days before."

About an hour before, during an intermission in the trial, something happen that I was afraid was going to. Mr. Carstairs stare at me as we pass each other in the hall, then say to his lawyer, "That's the other Indian we tried to subpoena. That's Stan Standing-neck-deep-in-slough-water."

"I'm afraid you're mistaken," I say, real calm. "My name is Silas Ermineskin, and I write books. I don't associate with common riffraff like Frank Fencepost. Apparently, to you white men, all us Indians look alike."

Mr. Carstairs stare at me for quite a while, then decide that I'm telling the truth. "Stan couldn't read or write," he say to the lawyer.

After all this time he still believe some of the lies Frank told him.

At another intermission in the trial, Frank smile friendly at that lawyer for AAII.

"I bet this case really gonna do a lot for your career, eh? When you talk about the big cases you've handled you can say you was defence lawyer for some bull cum. Must make all them years of law school worthwhile."

"I see you have a sense of humor, if a somewhat primitive one," say the lawyer. "We'll talk again tomorrow, in court, Mr. Fencepost, and you may just find out what it feels like to have your hide nailed to a wall."

But before he get to Frank he take another shot at Mr. Carstairs.

"Mr. Carstairs, is it true that on your ranch there are several animals that could have impregnated your purebred cows?"

"I run a large spread and I have two other bulls, one a Hereford, and one a mixed breed. But there is no way either bull could have had access to the Charolais cows."

Then he go on to explain how the purebred cows kept in a special corral separate from all the other animals, and how they have their temperatures taken every day so the people from AAII don't arrive at a time when the cows ain't fertile.

"That's all very interesting. Still, the possibility exists, does it not, that some other animal on your farm impregnated your cows?"

Mr. Carstairs glower at the lawyer, but he grunt that the possibility exist.

"And, do you not have on your ranch a male buffalo?"

Mr. Carstairs laugh loud. Kind of an inbreathing noise like a pig might make. "That old rat's nest? My eldest daughter rescued it from a zoo when she was a little girl. People didn't want to stare at a mangy buffalo, so they were going to have it put down. It's been standing like a willow clump in the south pasture for close to fifteen years," and he laugh like a pig again.

"Irrespective of its background, this is an unemasculated male buffalo which makes its home on your ranch?"

"It is."

On the second afternoon Mr. Angstrom, the lawyer who is defending the bull semen, with the help of a lady scientist in a white smock, put on a demonstration for the court. It seem to me it must be hard for them to keep a straight face while he doing it, because one of the things they have to show the court is a plastic cow's vagina. Truth is it don't seem hard at all for Mr. Angstrom and the lady to keep their faces straight. The lady especially have a face I'd guess been straight all her life. She have the plastic model as well as charts and pictures and tubes and wires.

Mr. Angstrom hand all these things to her one at a time while she demonstrate how the bull semen is deposited in the precise spot it meant to go, and how there could never be a mix-up of any kind.

I bet people can hear Frank chuckling and slapping his thigh all the way out to the street.

"I never thought about the exact placement," Frank snicker. "I always take the old shot-gun approach until right now. But if anyone can accomplish exact placement it is a Fencepost. I wonder how much money there is in this?"

The way the scientist end the hour-long demonstration is to say, "The only way the cows on Mr. Carstairs' ranch could produce calves that weren't purebred Charolais is if they were already pregnant."

As Mr. Angstrom promise, he call Frank to the witness chair to have another conversation.

"Now, Mr. Fencepost, would you care to refute any of the testimony you heard Mr. Carstairs give about the day you were fired from your job as ranch foreman?"

"Isn't *refute* the same as garbage?"

"*Refuse* is the same as garbage. *Refute* is . . ."

"Wait a minute. Doesn't r-e-f-u-s-e mean to say you won't do something?"

"In another context r-e-f-u-s-e does mean to turn down an offer . . . to decline . . . Mr. Fencepost, you're good at playing games, are you not?"

"You could say that."

"And could we say that your arranging to get Mr. Carstairs' daughter into bed was a game?"

"It was the one thing Mr. Carstairs warned me to be sure not to do. When you challenge a Fencepost you're asking for a certain amount of trouble."

"But you lost that contest, didn't you?"

"Well, yes and no."

"Meaning?"

"Mr. Carstairs caught us the day he fired me, but that was about the fifty-fifth time in two months that I'd been in her bed. So it looks to me like I'm ahead about fifty-four to one."

"And you were upset about having to run out of the house half dressed, and losing your job, and losing your lover. Is it safe to say that?"

"Pretty safe."

"Now, Mr. Fencepost, since you knew that the cows were in a special pen waiting for Ace Artificial Insemination Inc. to pay their visit, and since the only thing you were forbidden to do, other than callously seduce the boss' daughter, was to let a bull in with the purebred cows, isn't it safe to say that before you left the C Bar C Ranch that day you did the *second* thing you were forbidden to do?"

"You talk a good game," Frank say to Mr. Angstrom. "What if I was to say yes to your last question?"

"It would get my client off the hook, so to speak."

"And it would make Mr. Carstairs even madder at me than he is now?"

"Certainly a possibility."

"And would I be a criminal?"

"You would have played a nasty trick, but as to criminal charges, I am a lawyer, not a judge. I therefore have no opinion on the matter."

Frank consider the situation for a while. "Well, since a Fencepost cannot tell a lie, especially after taking an Indian oath where I'd be struck by lightning before your very eyes . . . yes, I did it."

After the courtroom quiet down Frank continue.

"As I was leaving I seen this here poor old buffalo standing out in the pasture looking sorrowful, and there was eight excited cows in that pen. I said to myself, why shouldn't everybody be happy? And I just let the old buffalo into the cow pen for a couple of hours. As they say, there may be snow on the roof, but there sure was fire in the furnace. By the time I take the buffalo back to pasture, everybody is smiling and . . ."

The judge interrupt Frank to say he's heard enough, and he dismiss the case right there. Ace Artificial Insemination Inc. is off the hook, and Mr. Carstairs is yelling that he going to have buffalo burgers as soon as he gets home to the C Bar C.

Interesting thing is that almost everything Frank said was a lie.

Out on the street, Frank jump in the air like a Russian dancer or a Toyota salesman, try to click his heels together. After he land he give me a high five.

"Confession is good for the soul. Or is it the liver? Anyway, I feel like a great weight been lifted off my shoulders. Honesty is the best policy. Always remember that, Silas."

"Everything you said in there was a lie," I remind him.

"How would you know that?"

"Because I worked on the ranch, too, remember. That afternoon you got chased out of the house, you kept right on going, walk the twelve miles into Camrose on your own. It was after Mr. Carstairs come down to the bunkhouse and fire me for being your friend that I let the buffalo in with the purebred cows."

"Oh. I was wondering how that happened. But I told a good story, didn't I?"

"And after you took an oath."

"Hey, you weren't listening. That was no oath. I was only translating the weather forecast off Channel 2 into Cree. 'Partly cloudy skies and light winds over most of central Alberta, lows tonight in the mid-twenties, highs tomorrow . . .'"

Miracle on
Manitoba Street

The second day after we moved into Gorman Tailfeathers' house in The Pit, Frank Fencepost began to work his magic. The Pit is a row of nine old frame houses on a gravel street in an industrial district near the Seattle waterfront. Gorman Tailfeathers is a stocky man of about sixty, with long, gray hair, who work for a bottling plant within walking distance of The Pit — Manitoba Street, as it was officially known.

When I first step out into the yard behind the gaunt, weathered house, where untended lilacs expand over the path to the end of the lot, there are new people moving into the house next door. There is a mother, young daughter, and a red-headed guy about my age. I watch them move in, help the red-headed guy drag a chest of drawers up the back steps, and then up the really narrow stairs to the second floor. The house is laid out exactly the same as the one where me and Frank is visiting.

Back in the yard, as I get used to the sunlight and the overpowering odor of lilac, I see a half-dozen children, all from our house I think; children, grandchildren, nieces, nephews, cousins; running carelessly through the tall grasses, dodging abandoned appliances, stacks of weathered lumber, two skeletal car bodies, one so old it has settled deeply into the earth. A couple of young guys, one with a red bandanna tied across his forehead, lounge on broke-legged lawn chairs, smoking and drinking from unlabeled brown bottles.

A very pretty girl about eighteen, named Ramona, is sitting on the paintless back porch, flicking the ashes from her cigarette into the grasses. She say something that cause the boy with the bandanna to emit a bark-like laugh, and cause the red-headed boy, who told me his name was Tipton, to glance in her direction.

I walk to the end of the lot. Behind a chain-link fence is a graveled acre, soupy from Seattle's continual rain. In the distance I see the fiery interior of a concrete manufacturing plant through twenty-foot-tall open doors. Cement trucks, their cone-shaped hoppers turning ominously, rumble in and out from before dawn until late at night.

There is rhubarb growing along the back fence, a few dead chrome chairs, a soggy mass that once was a mattress, broken bottles, cans, a refrigerator face down like a sleeping drunk.

"Just like home," say Frank as he come into the yard.

Frank is wearing a plaid shirt and faded jeans. His hair brush his shoulders, and he carry in one hand a black felt hat with a row of turquoise and silver conchos around the crown and in his other hand what appear to be a magazine. His face is wide open like a door.

The houses of Manitoba Street are crowded close together like large people in an elevator. Frank make eye contact with the red-headed fellow next door.

Tipton nods hello.

"You new here, hey?" Frank says.

"Yesterday."

"Don't mind these guys," Frank say, nodding toward the fellows on the lawn chairs. "They don't associate with white men. As you can see, they're so successful they already retired to enjoy the fruits of their labors. That one's Fred Horse." He point to the bandanna wearer.

"And Bob Iron Legs." He is a husky fellow in jeans and a denim jacket. "And the guy hiding under the lilacs is my friend, Silas. I'm Frank Fencepost."

Bob Iron Legs snicker loudly. He don't like Frank or me. I think he recognize that Frank is a bigger free-loader than him.

"Tipton Barnes," the red-headed guy says. He ducks around the lilac, steps across a jumble of chicken wire and weeds, and shake Frank's hand.

When he get close he see what Frank holding is actually a small sketch pad. Frank's shirt pocket is crammed with pens and pencils.

"You draw?" Tipton asks.

"Bet your life. One of my many talents. I'm so good at so many things I scare myself."

There is another loud snicker from Bob Iron Legs.

"Want me to show you?" Frank ask. Without waiting for a reply he flip open the sketch pad and, leaning against the splintered doorjamb, begin to sketch the bandanna-wearing Fred Horse.

His hands fly over the page like a hummingbird above a flower.

Suddenly, Frank push the sketch toward Tipton. I wander over to look at it. There is Fred Horse sitting in the broke-backed lawn chair with its twisted aluminum arms. Fred is grinning a cynical grin, the smoke from his cigarette spiraling perfectly. Frank ain't a great artist, but he have ten times my talent, which is limited to stick men.

"That's wonderful," Tipton says.

"If he's so wonderful, why ain't he rich?" says Fred Horse. Bob Iron Legs snickers.

"I got plans," says Frank. It sound almost ominous.

"Me too," says Fred Horse. "Next week, me an' Bob are gonna walk over to Swedish Hospital, perform a little brain surgery."

Both men laugh.

Frank turn to Tipton. "Okay if I draw you?"

"Why not?"

His hand flutter above the paper again. He take longer this time, to impress Tipton.

When he finish he tear off the sheet and hand it to Tipton. It bear him a good but not great resemblance.

"Note," say Frank, "how, though it's drawn in pencil, it capture an eerie quality that leaves no doubt your eyes are blue and your hair red. It's the same with this drawing of Fred, you can tell his bandanna is red."

I sense no such thing. What he capture was that Tipton's front teeth were long and slightly overlapped.

"You can keep it," Frank say.

"Thank you. It's really very good."

"You got a cigarette?"

The pack was bulging in the front pocket of Tipton's shirt. He take out the pack and shake a cigarette in Frank's direction. Frank pull one loose, but eye the half-full pack as if it was raw meat and he was a hungry dog. Tipton push the rest of the pack toward him.

"Even trade," he says, clutching his portrait.

Frank smile. Bob Iron Legs snicker.

Next morning I am sitting on the back steps with Tipton, drinking instant coffee, when Frank slip out the back door clutching his sketch pad.

"Bet you'd like this one," he says to Tipton.

"What is it?" Tipton ask.

Frank sit beside us on the sunny steps. The sketch is of Ramona Blackeye leaning against the splintered doorjamb of the Tailfeathers' house. He capture her shape perfectly, the high cheekbones, her blue jeans, the big-buckled black belt she wear, her blouse tied in a knot across her bare belly.

"Ramona says she likes you," Frank say to Tipton. "She don't understand why you don't make a move on her. She thinks maybe you don't like Indian girls."

"I thought she probably had a boyfriend. I don't want that Bob Iron Legs or one of those other guys on my case."

"You want this?" He push the paper toward Tipton, keeping a tight grip on it while eyeing his shirt pocket.

"This is an almost full pack."

"You think Ramona's sexy, right?"

"Right."

"Okay. I'll give you the sketch free. You give me the cigarettes for the info that she likes you and that's she's unattached."

"Deal."

A little later all three of us is strolling around in Tailfeathers' back yard. Frank is smoking, Tipton is not. Frank stop in front of a dead refrigerator. It is old and stoop-shouldered, weathered a seagull color. The stained enamel is eroding bit by bit, leaving tiny scars that from a distance look like black bugs.

"I've got an idea," says Frank, staring at the refrigerator door.

"Like what?"

"Art. You got to make art where you find it. You got a screwdriver?" he says to Tipton.

"There's one in our house."

"Borrow it to me, and a hammer too. I'll only use them for ten minutes," he go on, noting the skeptical look on Tipton's face.

Tipton walk back to his house and return with a yellow-handled screwdriver and a small hammer. While he's gone Frank sketch something on the refrigerator door in pencil. As soon as Tipton hand him the tools he begin chipping flecks of paint off the door by holding the screwdriver at an angle and tapping the flat end with the hammer.

Flecks of enamel fly. Frank has his eyes squinted almost shut.

"Not bad," he say, as he step back to admire his work.

"What is it?" Tipton asks.

"Step back a little further," Frank says. "You'll see."

We did. And we did. When the distance was right, I could see clear as a photograph what Frank had produced was the face of a woman: not any woman, but what would pass to religious peoples as the Virgin Mary.

"That's pretty good," Tipton says.

"Good enough," says Frank. "Now all we need is have it discovered."

"By who?"

"Somebody who believes in miracles?"

"You planning to pass this off . . . ?"

"Let's let it age for a few days. Help me push this sucker down on its face. The picture need to look as if it's been created by the weather."

"Those guys," I hear Ramona Blackeye telling Tipton, "ain't even cousins of ours. They followed Bob Iron Legs home from a bar down on Pioneer Square. They're Cree from Canada. Traveled down to Montana for a pow-wow and taking the long way home."

What she says is true. Of course, it was Frank's idea to follow Bob Iron Legs home. We sure do thank Gorman Tailfeathers for letting us sleep on his floor.

In the last week Tipton convince Ramona that he *do* like Indian girls. They've spent a couple of interesting afternoons in Ramona's room. Sound really travel in these old houses.

"Silas is okay," Ramona went on, "I sort of rubbed up against him when he first got here, but he has a girlfriend back in Alberta. Frank, on the other hand, thinks he's like one of these holy roller preachers, all he's gotta do is touch a woman on the forehead and she'll flop down on her back."

Ramona's got him pegged perfectly. There are two or maybe three teenage girls that are some relation to the Tailfeathers clan, and Frank share a bed with two of them, maybe all three. I sure get tired of sleeping on the back porch because Frank want his privacy.

Frank spend his early evenings downtown, do some sketch work on the street. He's okay, but not good enough to make more than four or five dollars of an evening. Bob Iron Legs, when he condescend to speak to me, say with what I take to be admiration that Frank know his way around locks. Which I guess is why he came home one night with about twenty cartons of cigarettes and a couple of boxes of melted Popsicles. Frank don't mooch cigarettes from Tipton or me any more, and he help Tipton indirectly by giving Ramona a carton of Winstons, which she shares with him.

"I think Grandma Tailfeathers is the one," Frank say to me about a week later. "She's the head of the house, and she been converted to a Christian when she was girl. She's gonna recognize a picture of the Virgin when she sees one. Trouble is her vision ain't that good."

Grandma Tailfeathers is about four feet nothing, always wears a black dress with a black shawl over her head. She scuffs around in the yard, looking for roots or berries, talks to herself in whatever language she speaks, and whenever she sees Tipton, points his direction with an accusing arthritic finger and says things that I'm certain are not complimentary.

"She's a neat old lady," Ramona says to Tipton one afternoon. "She says I shouldn't be fucking a white man, then asks if you're any good."

Ramona is full-lipped, salmon-colored, and as far as I can tell, totally uninhibited.

"So what did you tell her?"

"I told her the truth," says Ramona obliquely. "Granny says she'd probably fuck a white man, if she could find one as good looking as you."

"I guess that's a compliment," Tipton said.

"Better believe it. So what's Frank up to? He's been sucking up to Granny all week. Keeps crossing himself like a good Catholic, and says he feels the Spirit in the air, something momentous going to happen. He's drawn pictures of Granny Tailfeathers three or four times, always with a halo above her head. I don't like it."

"Today's the day, Brother Tipton," says Frank, when Tipton answer the knock on his door. "If things go according to schedule,

Granny Tailfeathers will be out in the yard in a few minutes, picking rose hips for that brew she keeps stewing on the back of the stove. While she's out there we're gonna upend the fridge and let Granny go nose to nose with the Virgin."

Which is what we do.

"Granny, come here and look at this," Frank say, after I've helped him set the fridge upright. There is mud and little clods of dirt stuck to the fridge door, and there is a small snail about where the Virgin's nose should be.

I'm surprised that Granny comes.

"I don't speak her lingo," says Frank, "but she understands a lot more English than she lets on."

Granny sticks her nose up against the fridge door, but she's so short she's practically looking up the Virgin's nose. She brushes the snail aside, flicks off a couple of clods of dirt.

"Are you thinkin' what I'm thinkin'?" asks Frank.

Granny Tailfeathers studies the image. Ramona ambles sexily down the back steps, and takes Tipton's arm. She gives the Virgin a baleful glance.

"So that's what Frank Shit for Brains has been up to," she says in a stage whisper.

Granny Tailfeathers finally nods her head, turns to Frank, and gives a long, for her, speech in whatever dialect is hers. Then she scuttles off toward the house, her black skirt skimming the grass.

"What did she say?" Frank asks Ramona.

"She says it's a fucking miracle. She's gonna go get a priest."

Frank smiles, showing the large gap in his teeth.

"You could be in serious trouble, asshole," Ramona says.

"This trouble is gonna make us all rich," says Frank. "Especially me."

An hour later Granny come squawking around the corner of the house, pulling a reluctant priest behind her. He looks about sixteen. I didn't know they took them that young.

"What's she want to show me?" the priest say in the direction of Ramona and Tipton. "I can't understand her."

"Take a peek at that fridge," Ramona say, drawing on her Winston.

Frank is lurking like a thief behind the lilac bushes. He take long, loping steps across the yard, arrive at the fridge same time as Granny and the priest.

Once he start to organize things, Frank is as officious as a Banana Republic General. He have us all running errands, spending our own money, which Frank promise faithfully will get replaced when the first visitors start arriving.

We buy some plastic surveyor's tape, flamingo pink. Frank pace off ten feet in each direction and create a circle around the fridge, then he cordon off a pathway from the front of our house, along the really narrow sidewalk down between Tailfeathers' and Tipton's, and up to the circle. I go down to an Army Surplus Store, buy a dozen of those cheap khaki pillows like they rent at ballparks, and he place them in two semicircles in front of the fridge.

"Tipton, my son, my son," Frank says, "I want you to go down to one of those discount stationery stores and buy a roll of brown paper. We going to cover up the inside of the chain link fence, keep people from getting a free view."

Then Frank grin even bigger than usual.

"I'm gonna send three of the little boys out there, give each one a stick and let him poke a hole in the paper. They each charge a dollar to look through the hole. I already checked it out, people won't be able to see nothing but the back of the fridge and the people who paid getting a good look. It will encourage them to come in around the front."

Of course it is Frank who man the entrance. He borrow a card table and a chair from Tipton, set them up close to the sidewalk. Between the table and the path to the back yard he have Bob Iron Legs and Fred Horse standing with their arms folded across their chests, looking mean, just in case somebody think they entitled to sneak a free look at the Virgin.

"First of all," Frank say to everyone come to buy entrance, "I don't think you should go in there. These kinds of thing are always frauds. Hell, anybody could scratch a likeness of the Virgin on a fridge door. All it take is a hammer and a screwdriver and a little bit of talent."

The people all act as if they ain't heard a word Frank said. They just push money at him and ask, "How much?"

"Don't say I didn't warn you. Here's the deal. For two dollars you get a general admission, that takes you within ten feet of the Virgin. You can stay as long as you like, but if you try to get closer, one of my buddies will break your knees. There are about a dozen pillows up closer to the fridge where you kneel and pray. Cost you a dollar a minute."

"I want ten minutes' worth," say a big woman in jeans and yellow sweater, must be at least sixty years old.

Frank take a piece of sticky note paper, look at his watch. "It's 6:15 now," he say. He write 6:25 on the paper, stick it on the back pocket of the woman's jeans.

"One of our attendants will tap you on the shoulder when your time is up. Have a good prayer." And he send the woman on her way. "You want to buy more time, you got to come back here," he yells after her. "The attendants ain't allowed to take your money."

Turns out most people want to go inside the circle. Next day we up the number of cushions to twenty and often still have a little line-up. One time two ladies get into a real hair-puller over who was to get the next available prayer cushion.

Then word come down that a delegation from the Catholic church, including a couple of four-star-general types, are on their way to take a look at the Virgin.

"I was a virgin once," Ramona says to Tipton. "I should have got this kind of attention."

"I wonder if we should let them in?" says Frank to no one in particular.

"If they approve, the crowds will increase," I say.

"If they approve, guess who'll be out on the street like garbage, and who'll be raking in the dough?"

The newspapers and television people refer to what's happening as The Miracle on Manitoba Street, snooping around asking questions or filming the line-up of people waiting to kneel in front of the refrigerator.

Frank have this theory that you don't have to know what you doing, that you only have to look the part. That seem to apply to the Virgin of the Refrigerator. Me and Frank and our friends know the whole operation is phony. The people who come must suspect it is phony, but they want really badly to believe, so they pay their money, pray their prayers, and come away believing their arthritis or back pain or blurred vision has been cured by the Virgin. Scary.

Frank suggest early on that we pay one of the Tailfeathers clan, preferably Gorman, to enjoy a miraculous cure and witness to the TV and newspapers, but we don't have to. Big women in cheap clothes and out-of-style hair-dos babble in tongues and come away from the refrigerator claiming their epilepsy has been cured, or their insides untangled, and one lady claim she reduced thirty pounds right on the spot. The crowd is about 90 percent women and children, and what few men there are appear to have been dragged along by a wife or mother.

"I wonder why women are more eager for miracles than men?" says Frank. "And what kind of miracle would appeal to men? Silas, I'm gonna have to look into that."

The TV confirm that some Catholic cardinal flying all the way from New York to Seattle next week, and they speculate that he going to view the Virgin on the Refrigerator.

That night Granny call a big meeting in Tailfeathers' living room. There are more people living in the house than I imagined. Ramona does the translating for Granny Tailfeathers, who gets right to the point by saying she wants her cut of the profits.

"One for all, and all for one, is the way I see things," says Frank.

Granny say it is the all for one aspect she don't like, especially since she suspect the *one* is Frank.

"Whoa! You must think I'm made of money here," says Frank. "I got expenses. I been paying Bob and Fred as guards, Ramona and Tipton enforce the praying time, Silas here run errands. There ain't much profit."

Granny let loose a long mouthful of Indian words.

"Granny says you're full of shit," says Ramona. "She seen you make the picture on the fridge. She wants to rent a Winnebago and visit her sisters in Montana before she dies."

Ramona pause, listen to Granny again. "She also wants one of them twenty-eight-inch TVs for the living room, a washer and dryer set, an electric can opener, and a deepfreezer full of buffalo meat."

Frank is in the middle of the room, and there ain't very many friendly eyes looking at him. He been using for a pillow an Albertson's grocery store shopping bag, stuffed fat with ten- and twenty-dollar bills. He have the bag under his jean jacket right now.

"How could you even think I wasn't gonna share with my brothers and sisters, and Granny," he say, smiling at the old woman who is all angles like she's made out of coat hangers. "If you was to make me divide up the money right now, why we could do that. But, I'd be forced to confess to the TV people that I drawed the face on the fridge. As I see it we got maybe another week before (a) that cardinal put the kibosh on our little gold mine, and (b) people just generally get tired of the whole idea."

Frank go on for about fifteen minutes, and by the time he's fin- ished he convinced everybody that he is really doing them a favor by acting as banker, and as soon as the incoming money slow down to a trickle, why it will all get divided up properly.

Even Granny seem to be sucked in.

In another week the rush is over. Hardly any new people com- ing to see the Virgin, but there is a group of faithful come every day with ten or twenty dollars, like people who go to an arcade or a bingo hall every chance they get. The story about the cardinal coming to see our Virgin turn out not to be true. He did come to Seattle, but not to see us.

Frank send me downtown to buy us first-class seats to Edmon- ton. "Tell them we want pretty flight attendants and lots of them After Eight chocolates," he say, as I heading off.

"Night after next we going to divide things up," Frank promise.

"I think that same night the fridge get destroyed by vandals. Who wants to be a vandal?" Frank ask, and quite a few hands go up.

"Sleep light," Frank say to me. "We'll sneak out about dawn."

The racket happen quite a bit sooner. At 4:00 a.m. the lights is all on, and the room fill up with half-dressed Indians and men in brown uniforms.

"Immigration and Naturalization," says one of the men, holding up identification with one hand, a nasty-looking gun in the other. "We have reason to believe there are illegal aliens here."

Who would have done this to us?

"We are citizens of the world," Frank explain, but it don't seem to do no good.

Me and Frank turn out to be the only illegal aliens at Tailfeathers' house.

"Hey, we got tickets to go home in just a few hours," Frank say.

"Okay, we'll just give you a ride to the airport and see that you use them," the Immigration guy says.

Now Frank is in a spot. He can't very well take along an Albertson shopping bag full of cash.

As we being marched out the back door, I see Granny Tailfeathers, grinning where her teeth used to be, imagining, I bet, that she zooming across the prairie in her rented Winnebago.

The Elevator

A beat-up red Fargo truck with a flatdeck and one green fender pull into Fred Crier's Hobbema Texaco garage one evening early in July. It is easy to see that the driver, a man about thirty, is the type who is happy when covered in grease. His gray railroad coveralls are oily, he have black smears on his face and arms, and even though he is white his hands is darker than mine, the nails chipped and black.

"You lookin' for a job?" he says, when he sees me leaning against the building taking in a little sun.

"What kind?" I say.

"Got a demolition job up in the Peace River country. I'm drivin' straight through."

He names the wages.

"A month or so's work and a bus ticket back. How about it?"

"Why not?" I say. "I ain't been off the reserve for a while."

The trucker's name is Gil, and all night we take turns driving. About dawn we pull in at a truck stop somewhere past Whitecourt, and in the café there, Gil talk another young Indian into coming with us.

The new guy's name is Leonard and he is skinny and shy. After I ask him quite a few times, he tell me he is Dog Rib come from someplace forever north of us.

About mid-morning we turn off the highway, drive on gravel for a couple of hours, then on a dirt road run parallel to the railway tracks. Gil finally stop at what look like a town. But when I get out of the truck I can see that nobody lives at this place any more.

"My boss got himself the contract to tear this down," Gil says, as we walk toward a tall, spooky-looking grain elevator.

I don't know what I expected; rows and rows of big sheet-metal pipes or some kind of compartments where grain could be stored. But whatever I thought, the whole inside had been gutted. It is cool and hollow, smell of musty grain and mice.

Our voices echo like we was talking into an oil drum. A pigeon flutters off a ledge up high, scared by our talking, and escapes through a hole only it can see. A single feather floats down, taking a long time in the heavy air.

There are ladders nailed against each wall, and it is so far up that they narrower at the top than at the bottom. Gil give us each a hammer and a small crowbar.

Leonard, he hook his crowbar in his belt and give the wall a thump with his hammer. When he do that a cloud of dust leap out of the wall like it was waiting to be released. I had taken off my shirt outside, and that dust settle into my hair and stick to my damp back and shoulders. The sound the hammer make is muffled, as if Leonard held a blanket against the wall and hit into it.

"You start at the top," Gil says.

Me and Leonard both bend back our necks and look way up to the hollow made by the peaked roof.

"You climb up the ladders," Gil go on. "First thing to do is hammer a hole in the roof. You toss the loose boards and shingles to the ground. When you get a good pile, you come down and make a neat stack. I'll be around every second day or so for a new load."

While we worked, Gil drove to wherever the closest town was and bought us each a thin green bedroll and a sheet of mosquito netting. That night we spread out the bedrolls in the long grass next to the elevator and hope it don't rain. Guess that is why they hire Indians to do this work. White men gonna want to be put up in a hotel or at least a bunkhouse.

This is about the quietest place I've ever been. Across the street is three houses and a tall building with a false front, have "General Store" painted on it in black letters that is pretty much faded. The buildings have all their glass busted away. No matter how far from civilization a place is, there is always somebody around to bust out the windows.

Grass and weeds peek in the lowest windows of the houses, so when the wind blows I can hear them ticking and swishing against the siding even when I am way up the elevator. The street, which never been anything but dirt, is now growed over by pigweed and creeping charlie. Thousands of dandelions bloom yellow as lemon candies.

In one of the houses Gil store a big box of canned food, a can opener, and a case or three of pop. There is an old well with a rusty pump out behind the elevator.

Every second day, regular as a clock, Gil show up with a new box of supplies. All three of us load the flatdeck truck with lumber, chain it on, and away Gil goes, the truck grumbling off in compound low gear.

The roof of the elevator is gone by now, and we worked down about three feet all the way around. Only the ladders stick over the top, look like a picture I seen once of how someone tried to build a tower all the way to heaven.

I bet we been there ten days already when I notice that even though the elevator stand right beside the railroad tracks, there has never been even one train go by.

I wonder, did the elevator die first or did the train stop running and kill off the elevator?

During the daytime the sky is a glaring blue, and the poplars along the right-of-way look black when the afternoon sun is behind them. Now that we worked the elevator down a few more feet, we are right out in the open and our hammering sound like gun shots, and the crowbar pulling nails make noises like something in pain, frightening the songbirds into silence.

The way I meet old Standing-in-the-bush, is because I got a good nose, and because I am hungry for coffee.

Leonard and me kind of enjoy sleeping out in the tall grass. The air is fresh and sweet and cool, but I sure miss not being able to cook up coffee.

"It is cruelty to poor Indians not to give us coffee in the mornings," I say to Leonard.

He just smile shy and crack open a bottle of 7-Up.

I make myself a cheese sandwich and crank up some water with the old iron pump. It is while I'm drinking down the water that I smell pine smoke.

"I didn't know there was anybody living close by," I say.

I figure where there's pine smoke on a July morning there must be a stove cooking coffee. I just follow the smell and sure enough about a half mile down the railroad grade and about a hundred yards back in a clearing sit a little log cabin. The cabin have pig-weed growing tall off the flat roof. The cracks between logs have been plastered with mud, just like we do at home. There are two small sheds in the yard and a corral hold a few cattle.

I knock on the screen door and try to see into the cabin, but I can't because of the way sunlight shine on the screen. There is a leather and sour milk smell in the air around the door.

From inside, a very old voice say to me in Cree, "Are you one of my grandchildren?"

A yellow dog come around the corner of the cabin, crawl on its belly, whine in a friendly way.

"No. I work up the road aways. I hoped you might have a cup of coffee to spare."

I been able to smell that coffee cooking for a long ways, the odor so spicy it make my mouth water.

"You speak Cree like a white man," say the voice, "and you smell of the city. I can smell beer and store food."

"I ain't had a beer for over a week or more."

"The odor stays on your skin," the voice say, and the screen door push open.

The doorstep is made out of two hewed logs, and big blue flies buzz around in the sunshine.

An old man in soft moccasins shuffle out, his knees stiff as if they been glued in straight.

"I am Standing-in-the-bush," he say. "How do you call yourself?"

"Silas Ermineskin."

"You are one of the ones tearing down the white man's big colored box," and he laugh, a soft, throaty sound. "They collect food up to the sky, but deep in the winter, when my cattle were hungry, they would not share."

He shake his head and motion for me to come inside the cabin, which smell of closed air and medicines. As my eyes become accustomed to the dark I see roots and leaves hanging on strings criss-crossed from wall to wall.

Standing-in-the-bush won't take no money for his coffee, which he pour for me from a tall gray-enameled pot that live on the back of his cookstove like a pet. While we drink, I find out that the town was called Frog Pond, but was never big enough to really be a town, get a post office, a gas pump, or even its name on the side of the elevator.

"Even the frog pond is gone," says Standing-in-the-bush. And he tell me how the place where me and Leonard sleep at night used to have thousands and thousands of frogs sing so loud they could be heard for miles on a summer night.

"When I was young and rode out at night to steal horses, we always hoped our enemies were camped by a frog swamp. Frogs have evil spirits, their noise clogs the ears. Once, I crawled right into an enemy camp and untied three ponies, and led them away." Standing-in-the-bush laugh softly again, showing a couple of bent, yellow teeth.

After I tell Leonard what Standing-in-the-bush has told me, he say, "So even the evil spirits have moved away from this place."

That is the most words Leonard has spoke since we been here.

Standing-in-the-bush invite me back the next morning. When I go, I take with me from our supplies a tin of peaches and a package of Export A cigarettes to leave in payment for my coffee.

It is three more days before I meet Simon. I am at the top of the elevator, banging loose first a board from the outside, then a board from the inside, when from far down the dusty road that run parallel to the rusted railroad tracks where saplings and thistles grow up between the rotting ties, I see a tall, stoop-shouldered man walking toward me. He is walking with his hands up like someone was pointing a gun at him, each hand closed on the end of a pole, the middle of which rests on the back of his neck. He wears baggy overalls so dirty and greasy look as if they might stand on their own if the man was to step out of them.

When he gets even with the elevator, he swing the pole down off his shoulder, look up at me and wave his hand.

"Mighty hot," he says. "Can you spare a drink?"

"Got a choice of cold water or warm pop," I holler down.

He take off his cap, pump some water over his head, then cup his hands and take a good big drink. His face is long, his eyes deep set, his forehead high and iron-colored. He got hollow cheeks and his gray hair is brushcut. His nose look cut from rock, just brown skin glued tight to bone.

He wave thank you and go on his way. I notice that the pole was not a pole, but a piece of metal pipe with some kind of holder on the top end. If I didn't know better I would think it was a speaker post from a drive-in theater.

Next morning when I go for coffee I find that same man sitting at Standing-in-the-bush's table. First thing I notice is his hands would make two of mine, the veins on the back make them look rough as spruce bark.

"This is Simon," says Standing-in-the-bush. "He already forgot his Indian name and take one like yours from the white man's book."

He don't say that with meanness, just repeating a fact he can't do nothing about.

A while later Standing-in-the-bush say, "The white man want to give me a name." He is smiling a crook-toothed smile from under a red cap have big earflaps on it. "When I won't pick one, they give me one. 'I am Standing-in-the-bush,' I say, when I go to collect my treaty money, and when I sign up to homestead my land.

"'Which one?' they want to know.

"'The only one,' I tell them.

"But they hand on me George. When white men live in the houses up the road, they call me George. For forty years they wonder why I don't answer them."

Simon mainly stay quiet, drink black coffee, smoke cigarettes, suck his lower lip in against his teeth.

"Simon lives up the road," Standing-in-the-bush says, waving his hand back in the direction of the elevator. He work thirty years for the drive-in theater. Paint their fence, repair the talking boxes that stand on sticks in their big yard."

"Drive-in?" I say, surprised. It seems to me I am somewhere in the middle of the wilderness.

"Um-hm," says Simon.

"There's a good sized town eight miles up the road, other small towns, lots of farmers and Indians. Now everybody got the talking pictures in their houses, don't have to go out no more."

"Um-hm," says Simon again, almost smile, but not quite.

"Three years ago, about the time the drive-in theatre closed up forever, a car come driving into my yard, filled with men in suits and a priest. I figured they was planning to take me away like they did to some other old people.

"So I point my gun at them and make them go away.

"After that the mounties come around banging at my door, so I ease myself into the bush and live in the hills for a summer. The winter mounties don't come looking for me. White men have poor memories and no patience.

"I was here when they built the first railroad," Standing-in-the-bush go on. "I don't know how much I remember and how much my mama told me. The men from the railroad used to come to our camps along the river. They make our men go with them to work on the railroad.

"'They work them like horses, from sun to sun,' my mother told me. The white men were given money, but our men were paid cheap wine in wooden barrels. They would roar like beasts, crash through the bush, do harm to their families and each other. Then the white men would come back with their guns, and take them away, dirty, reeking, trembling, to work again laying down the iron river."

Behind Standing-in-the-bush's cabin, Simon keep a stock of those metal posts from the drive-in theater. Some of them have the big, square-headed speakers attached, some don't. Simon have cans of paint, silver and black, for painting the posts and speakers. The air is sharp with their scent.

"He lives up there now in the building where they used to sell food," the old man says.

"Um-hm," agree Simon.

It is about this time I begin to catch on that Simon is working for Simon these days, not for the drive-in theater.

The elevator is now only about thirty feet tall. Gil truck away the lumber fast as we pile it up.

"Everything is changing for the worse," says Standing-in-the-bush. "Only Simon tries to make things better."

"The white man's colored pictures get in the blood like whiskey," says Simon, pulling in his lower lip real hard.

Another time he talk a little. We all three sit on the log steps, smoking, watch the sun set into the muskeg.

"I had an old lady one time," says Simon. "Name was Gladys. She was pretty. Grew her hair down to where I could tuck the ends in the back pockets of her jeans.

"Not much to keep a pretty woman here. At first she liked to watch the colored movies every summer night, but then she wanted to live like in the movies. Whenever my pay checks come, she go to town, sit in the bar, drink beer, smoke tailor-made cigarettes. 'Get drunk and be somebody,' is what she used to say.

"Guess one time she really got to be somebody. She disappeared. There was oil drillers around. I sort of expected her to come back when times got tough. But I guess they never did. I guess she's still somebody.

"The boys, Alex and Rufus, was little then, no place to leave them while I was at work so I sent them to live with Gladys' sister down in Peace River. I always meant to go see them . . .

"Maybe they got kids of their own, now . . . "

Next morning a short man with a round belly hid under a vest and a forehead like pink washboard come around give us our pay in cash. Near as I can figure he don't cheat us, pay us the money we earn without none of those deductions the government ordinarily steal from us. That probably mean that whoever is paying him or his company to tear down the elevator is paying cash too, so they can't ask about where the lumber end up. On our first day here Gil tell us, "If anybody come around asking questions about what you're doing or who you work for, you don't know nothing."

"About what?" I say, and we both smile big.

The pink-faced man stare up at the elevator, which is now only about fifteen feet high, with ladders peeking over all four sides, like snakes trying to escape.

"Be ready to roll in the morning," he says. "You can ride to Whitecourt with Gil. He'll give you bus money from there."

He take a roll of bills from his back pocket and pay us our last day's wages.

"How come you keep repairing things at the drive-in theater?" I ask Simon the next morning, as the three of us drinking our last coffee together. It is blinding hot already, and the sky is hazy as if there was a forest fire close around.

"I don't want it to change," says Simon. "I don't want it to go back to bush like the railroad."

"He carries sacks of gravel down there, he grades the little hills where the cars used to line up beside the talking boxes. He had to move in 'cause kids used to drive out at night roar their cars around that big lot. Sometimes when the clouds were right I could see the colored pictures reflected off them. I used to peek through the fence sometimes. I seen cowboys fighting Indians, and people dancing."

Simon walks around behind the cabin and returns with a silver speaker pole resting across his shoulders and neck, then he hooks his arms up behind so the pole almost becomes part of him.

"You figure if you keep things up the white man going to bring his colored pictures back one day?" the old man say very slowly.

"Um-hm," says Simon, staring at his feet. "I can hope."

Standing-in-the-bush turns to stare across the clearing and corral to the scrub poplars standing all fluttery-leafed in the hot July wind.

"Don't do no harm to dream," the old man says.

"I'll dream those movies back," says Simon. "Everything's painted and in better shape than when they quit it. They'll be surprised when they come to open up again."

"You see your movies on that big white screen," says the old man, "sometimes when I look far away, I dream of the buffalo. I must be the only one who remembers them. I liked the train, but it went away. I liked the movies. Sometimes they made the earth tremble just like the buffalo."

They are standing almost back to back, Simon shaped like a cross staring off toward his immaculate theater, Standing-in-the-bush gazing across his corral where two skinny roan steers reach their necks through the poles for grass.

Ice Man

"**I**s that kid Jason Twelve Trees here again?" Ma says, as she look across the table to where he's sitting between me and my brother Joseph. "I'm gonna adopt him. Might as well make him an Ermineskin, he lives here most of the time anyway."

We can tell Ma is joking, but it is true that Jason Twelve Trees spend a lot of his time at our house. It is my littlest sister Delores who is the attraction. They ain't old enough to be sweethearts, though, if Delores ever gonna have a sweetheart, I guess I know who it's gonna be.

Jason Twelve Trees like being around Delores because she is about as independent as a sixth-grade girl ever gonna get. Delores' hair is long and blue-black. Ma says she always looks as if she just came in out of a wind storm. Delores got a three-cornered tear in her jeans and a toe poking out of one sneaker. She wear a green T-shirt that say "Kiss Me I'm an Indian," and has a dimple that twinkles when she smiles. Her eyes are brown as polished furniture and her nose wide, with a few freckles.

Delores collect empty bottles from all over the reserve and along the ditches of Highway 2. She earn her genuine chicken-dancer costume that way. Delores won many a blue ribbon at pow-wows in Alberta and Saskatchewan, and she dance regular at the Calgary Stampede and at Klondike Days in Edmonton with Molly Thunder's dance troupe, call themselves the Duck Lake Massacre.

Jason Twelve Trees like to hang around me, too. He sit at the kitchen table and talk while I'm trying to type my stories.

"You know, Silas, you and Delores get to do what you want to with your lives. My dad wants me to be something I don't want to be."

"And what's that?"

Jason's family live in a new housing project on the east side of the reserve. His dad is a mechanic who worked at the Texaco station in Wetaskiwin for about ten years, then take over the building where a Petro Canada station died and open up a three-bay auto repair shop that has done real well. The Twelve Trees got two telephones in their house, and their phones don't ever get cut off.

"My dad thinks I plot everything I do just to bug him," Jason say. "He thinks I could like mechanics if I wanted to. Life would sure be a lot simpler if I could."

Jason Twelve Trees is slim and coffee-colored, have his hair pretty long. His shirt is clean, even though this is probably the second day he's worn it.

"'Jay,' my dad's always saying, 'You ought to be in pig heaven. When I was your age I'd have killed to have a real garage to work in any time I wanted. We've got almost every tool known to the auto industry. When I was a kid I used to go to the auto wreckers in Wetaskiwin, beg for a busted carburetor I could tinker with.'

"Then Dad tells me how he saved the money he earned from pitching hay for some white farmer to buy a set of wrenches. 'Jay, I can't describe the feeling as I laid down my money and reached out to touch those beautiful silver tools. I wanted to cry I was so happy.'

"I try to argue, Silas, but it don't do me much good. 'What if Grandpa Twelve Trees had wanted you to be a rancher or a truck driver?' I ask.

"'I'd have become a mechanic,' Dad says. 'I was born to be a mechanic. And I'm waiting for the day I can change the sign to *Twelve Trees & Son Automotive.* If you'd just give it a try you'd get the feel for it, son.'

"But I ain't got a mechanical bone in my body."

"It's your life," I say absently, erasing another strikeover.

"But you know what probably bugs my dad worse than anything?"

I shake my head.

"My best friend being a girl."

Then he tell me, again, about how him and Delores stopped by his dad's shop, and how Delores dove right in and helped make some repairs and ended up covered in grease.

"When they finished the car repairs my dad said, 'Maybe Jason will make us lunch?'

"It didn't come out funny."

The idea Jason's dad can't seem to get a handle on is that he wants to be a chef.

"I can't seem to get across to my dad that I know *exactly* how he felt when he bought his first set of wrenches. It is kind of like we belong to different branches of the same religion, but won't listen to each other.

"When our kindergarten class visited the kitchen at the McDonald's restaurant in Wetaskiwin, I stared up at all that stainless steel. Everything was so white and bright. So clean. And the kitchen smelled so good. The cooks moved fast and sure seemed to be enjoying what they were doing. I decided right then and there that I was going to be a cook.

"Mom lets me help her in the kitchen, but Dad hates it, so Mom and I don't tell when I've helped with dinner, even if I cooked it myself with hardly any help."

Ma sympathize with Jason. She even asks questions that let him show off what he knows.

"You can do anything you've got the ambition to do," is what Ma's always told me and Illianna and all the rest of us kids.

Jason's face light up.

"Go out and meet life head-on," Ma tells us, "instead of hanging around waiting for life to come to you."

The first time Jason went to the kitchen of the restaurant in the new Wetaskiwin shopping mall, "I peeked in the back door," he said. "The cooks all looked like angels in their white jackets and tall white hats. There was so much bustle it remind me of Mad Etta's cabin that time you took me over to watch her boil up roots and leaves to make medicine.

"I must have stood there for an hour until the owner, Mr. Nick, came out to get some air. Nick is his first name. His last name is Greek and have about forty letters.

"'Mr. Nick,' I said, 'I want to work in your kitchen.'

"'What do you figure you could do in there?' he asked.

"I thought of the things I did to help my mother at home.

"'I . . . I could dry dishes,' I said. 'I could scrape plates. I could take out the garbage, peel carrots and potatoes, and I'm careful not to make the peelings too thick . . .'

"'Sounds like you'd be better than some of these guys. How old are you?'

"'Almost eleven,' I said.

"'You're Merton Twelve Trees' boy, aren't you?'

"'Yes.'

"'Well, you've got a few years before I can put you on the payroll, but come have a look around.'

"I bet I asked Mr. Nick a thousand questions. He invited me to come back any time."

And Jason did. I bet he could fill in for just about anybody but the head chef.

First ice sculpture Jason Twelve Trees saw was at Mr. Nick's restaurant. I was there with him. The restaurant was closed that day because Mr. Nick was catering a Greek wedding.

"Where's Mr. Nick?" Jason asked Stavros, the head chef, who was chopping squid, one eye on a cauldron of lemon-smelling soup.

"In the cooler," said Stavros.

When we opened the door to the cooler a flood of cold air rushed out like steam. Mr. Nick was standing with his back to us, a wooden packing case in front of him.

"What are you doing?" Jason asked.

Mr. Nick stepped to one side and there on the packing case was the biggest ice-fish I ever seen. It must have been four feet long and looked alive, curving as if he was leaping above the water of a lake.

Mr. Nick wore a white smock over his suit and held a glinting blue chisel in his hand. Other chisels and pointy silver tools lay on a piece of wine-colored velvet on the packing box.

"How do you like him?" Mr. Nick asked. "Caught him myself," he laughed.

"Did you make that?" Jason asked.

"How else," said Mr. Nick. "It's a table decoration for the buffet. You want to help me carry this one down to the freezer? Then you can help carry another block of ice up here. I'm going to carve a wedding cake with a bride and groom on top."

"Wow! Making things out of ice," Jason said.

I had never realized how beautiful ice could be.

As Mr. Nick worked on the new block of sparkling blue ice he explained the uses of each tool. Some of them were obvious, the tongs, the handsaw, the drill, a coarse-grained rasp, the calipers and dividers for measuring. But the flat, angle, and curved chisels, the six-point chippers, the one-point chipper — Mr. Nick said these were like an artist's brushes, everyone used them in a very personal way according to how they saw the world.

It was hard to find a store that sold ice-carving tools. Mr. Nick had brought his from the old country. Jason looked through restaurant supply catalogs until he found a place in Edmonton that stocked them.

"I'm going to make some ice sculptures," Jason said to Delores as we were driving up Highway 2.

"What?"

"It's something that a chef has to know. Some people carve things out of stone? I'm going to make them with ice."

"Etta say the form is there already," I say. "If you have the gift you'll be able to knock away whatever is covering it."

"I sure hope I have the gift," said Jason.

At the restaurant supply store there were aisles and aisles of shining dishes, glasses, and stainless steel kitchen equipment.

"I'd like some ice-carving tools," Jason said, swallowing hard.

The chisels and choppers were displayed on a background of midnight-blue velvet. They were a lot more expensive than I imagined.

"If you decide you don't want these any more," the salesman said, as he wrapped them up, "I'll buy them back at half price."

"Oh, no," said Delores. "He's going to be a chef. He'll always need these tools."

Friday afternoon we bought two blocks of ice from the machine at the Wetaskiwin shopping mall, wrapped them in gunnysack and stashed them in the freezer in the Twelve Trees' basement. When his mom and dad went shopping, Jason and Delores got one of the blocks from the freezer and set it on the workbench.

Jason's new tools glowed like surgical instruments under the bright light.

He blew on the clear, bluey ice and watched the little puff of frosty air bounce back toward him. He picked up a chisel, trying to decide where to start.

"We could go for a walk if we make you too nervous," I said.

"No, it's okay," Jason said. "See, I'm going to try and turn this block of ice into a hen sitting on a nest, like this little ornament of my mom's, and like the picture I've drawn here."

He took a felt pen and haltingly traced the outline of the template on the block of ice.

He placed the chisel against the ice and tapped it gently with a rubber-headed mallet.

An hour later we were all shivering. Jason's and Delores' clothes were soaked. The block of ice had shrunk. Jason's chiseling and chipping had revealed a form, but it didn't look much like a hen sitting on a nest.

"I wasn't expecting much first try," Jason said. "But I was expecting a little more than this."

We were still mopping up the basement floor when Jason's folks came home, so I explained about the ice sculpture.

Jason's dad looked amused. I guess he figured making art out of ice beat cooking. I don't think he ever connected the two, so Jason didn't make any secret about practicing ice sculpture in the basement.

After about twenty blocks of ice Jason started to turn out recognizable forms: a bird, a car, a big fish, and that hen sitting on a nest.

"Some evenings," he'd tell Delores, "my dad comes to look at what I'm doing. 'How come you want to make art out of something that turns to slush in a few hours?' he asks.

"I had to think about that for a minute.

"'All the cars you repair eventually end up in the junkyard,' I said.

"'That's different,' said my dad. But I couldn't see the difference.

"Another time he said, 'You know, I think you're getting better. Maybe we can get you art lessons. Then you could use *real* materials.'"

One day an announcement appeared on the bulletin board next to the principal's office at Jason's school.

CITY OF WETASKIWIN
RECREATION COMMISSION
COOKING
COMPETITION
For GIRLS 12-16
Soups • Salads
Appetizers
Entrees • Desserts

He read the notice over and over, then copied down how to get an entry form.

Jason told Delores about the poster, showed her what he'd copied down, and said, "That contest should be for boys, too. Don't they realize some boys like to cook?"

"So call them on it," said Delores. "The Baseball Association had to be hit over the head before they realized that some girls like to play baseball."

"How could I call them on it?"

"There're two ways," said Delores. "The first would be to get yourself an entry form, cook whatever you want and enter it. J. Twelve Trees could be either a boy or a girl. Or," and she looked at me kind of sideways, "you just call up that lady at City Hall, that Mrs. Duvall whose name is on the poster, and tell her you want to enter the contest. She might not give you any trouble."

"What if she does?"

"Then you go to somebody higher, and somebody higher after that. If it gets tough, tell them bias goes against the Constitution. That's the way I got to play baseball."

But everybody gave him trouble.

"As the poster clearly states," Mrs. Duvall said when Jason got her on the phone, "the contest is for girls only. The Commission also sponsors a dog show . . . maybe you could enter your dog."

"I want to enter the cooking contest," Jason said, stubbornly.

"I'm afraid that won't be possible."

Jason cleared his throat. "Mrs. Duvall, could I please speak to your supervisor?"

The supervisor's name was either Perkins or Parkins. He said the same thing as Mrs. Duvall, only he was firmer about it.

"If we made an exception for you, why just anybody could enter."

"I don't want you to make an exception for me," Jason said. "*Anybody* between twelve and sixteen *should* be able to enter."

"Quite impossible," said Mr. Perkins-Parkins. "I'm awfully busy, little boy." And he hung up.

"They sounded fairly polite," said Delores. "You should have been there when I tackled the Baseball Association."

That night there was a baseball game. The league is for ten-to fourteen-year-olds, and the teams are sponsored by local businesses.

Delores is better than the worst players, but nowhere near a star, but I like to watch her when she's at bat. She gets a fierce look in her eye, and her tongue peeks from the corner of her mouth. She's not very fast on the bases, but she runs with purpose. Instead of hitting the inside corner of the bag at first, the way the coach teaches, Delores plunks her foot right in the middle of the base, which takes a little extra time.

Delores used to hang around the baseball field, chase foul balls, until one night when the Little Buffaloes was short a player. Mr. Oldfield, the coach, said to Delores, "How would you like to play left field tonight?"

But as soon as she took the field the opposing coach went running out to the umpire.

"That's a girl," he said, pointing to left field. "Girls aren't allowed in this league." And he ruffled through a sheaf of papers until he found the rule that said the league was only for boys.

The umpire ruled that Delores couldn't play.

"Well, we'll see about that," said Ma.

Ended up there was a meeting of all the coaches and the team sponsors where Delores got to make a little speech about how much she enjoyed playing baseball, and how she didn't care whether she played with boys or girls, and why should anyone else? With only a couple of exceptions, everyone agree with her, and this year there's a dozen girls playing, at least one on every team.

Things weren't as simple when Jason decided to challenge the rules of the Recreation Commission.

"We should threaten to get a lawyer," I said. "The City don't want any trouble with lawyers. I bet they'll back down right away."

But I was wrong.

The local newspaper got hold of the story. They sent a photographer and a reporter around to Jason's house. The next day there was his photograph under a headline that said: WOULD-BE COOK CHALLENGES RECREATION COMMISSION.

"How could you embarrass me like this?" Jason's father come steaming up to our cabin looking for Jason.

"I have to face my friends," his father went on. "I'll have to admit I have a son who wants to enter a girls' cooking contest."

"But that's the whole point," Jason said. "*Anybody* should be able to enter that contest."

His father just glared at him.

The guys at his school were twice as bad.

"It's not worth it," Jason said that evening after supper.

"You can still quit, Jason," Ma said. "Though I took you for the kind of kid who might enjoy being a pioneer."

"I do like the idea," Jason said. "Me and Delores being first ones to . . ."

". . . fight off the Indians," said Delores.

"But I've got the Indians on my side, so I can't lose, right?" said Jason.

"Right," said Delores and Ma.

Thinking about the hearing at Wetaskiwin City Hall was one thing, being there was another. The three City Commissioners resent being there. They all have regular jobs; one is a bank manager, one runs the United Grain Growers elevator, and the other owns a car dealership. The City of Wetaskiwin is represented by their lawyer.

Jason have Mad Etta, our medicine lady.

"I'm kind of doctor, lawyer, Indian chief, all rolled into one," says Etta.

But when it come to sitting down all by himself at the hearing, Jason is glad to have any company, even Etta.

"Hmmph," say Etta, stare right through that lawyer fellow. Then she sort of puff herself up, like a prairie chicken, seem to get quite a bit bigger than she already is. She reach across and hold one of Jason's hands.

Jason makes his case by bringing up the Charter of Rights and Freedoms, and the Constitution. He reading from notes been given to him by our friend Bedelia Coyote. My guess is the lawyer for Wetaskiwin don't know if Jason is bluffing or not. I have a mixed-up feeling about what Jason is doing. I figure from reading the newspapers that only crooks and illegal immigrants use the Charter of Rights.

"The City Commissioners will make a decision later this afternoon or this evening," the lawyer for the City say to Jason. "Someone will call you at home."

"He'll be at my house, where there ain't no phone," Delores said. "With a lot of friends," and she dig Jason in the ribs with her elbow.

It was Jason's mother turn up at our door that evening.

"Did I win?"

"Well, let's say you won and you lost. Do you know what a compromise is?"

"When each side of an argument gives in a little, but not too much?"

"That's about right. The Recreation Commission decided that from now on their cooking contest will be open to both boys and girls. But, they said, this year's competition was too far along to change the rules. So you won't be able to enter the contest until next year."

"That's okay," he said.

"I got my idea playing second base," Jason told us later. "There was a runner on first and the batter hit a hard grounder to me. I fielded it on two bounces and tossed to the shortstop covering second. He leapt in the air to avoid the sliding runner and threw to first for the double play. What froze in my mind was the picture of the shortstop in mid air, his arm cocked to fire the ball, the runner sliding under his feet.

"As soon as school was over, I phoned Mrs. Duvall. She sniffed and said very coldly, 'What can I do for you now?'

"'I'd like to volunteer to do something else,' I said.

"'And what's that?'

"'There's no competition for ice carving, is there?'

"'What do you mean?'

"'Ice sculpture. I'd like to decorate the tables with ice carvings the day of the competition.'

"There was a long silence. I guess she was trying to figure out if it was a trick.

"'That's very nice of you, Jason,' Mrs. Duvall said, her voice softer, 'I think that would be a lovely idea. I'll have to run it by the board of directors, but I'm sure it will be fine.'"

"Alright!" Delores yelled.

Jason started practicing the next day in the cooler at the restaurant.

"I swear I can see that big eagle in there," he said to Delores as we stared at the diamond-like block of ice. "His eyes are fierce and his neck feathers are ruffled. All I have to do is chip away the leftover ice and he'll be there."

The night of the competition everyone was looking at Jason's ice sculptures instead of the food.

Jason's dad was standing by the crossed baseball bats that were surrounded by a baseball cap and three baseballs. "My son carved those."

"You must be very proud," a woman said.

"I am," Mr. Twelve Trees said.

And he hadn't even seen the centerpiece yet. Surrounded by roast turkeys, glazed hams, and jellied salads that looked like kaleidoscopes, was Jason's biggest ice carving, done especially for Delores. It was a baseball player, ball in hand, arm poised to throw, toe pointed like a ballet dancer, planted in the middle of an icy white base.

Jason understands the way Delores races around the bases, placing a foot solidly as she passes, staking out territory, making a statement, leaving her mark on each base.

Turbulence

I 'm what's known as a white-knuckle flyer, even though some whiney Indians would say I was downplaying my Indianness by claiming to have white knuckles. Those are the same Indians who think just because they're Indians they should get published, no matter how bad a storyteller they are.

Anyway, my belly growls in fright when the landing gear is lowered on an approach, and when the plane revs up to race down the runway my lungs seems to rise right up and fill my mouth.

My friend Frank Fencepost try not to show it, but he's as uncomfortable in an airplane as I am. The way Frank put it is: "I ain't afraid of flying, I'm afraid of crashing."

Until this past school year I ain't had all that much experience at flying: a trip to England on a really huge plane that have a walk-around cocktail lounge, where Frank Fencepost spend his time touching the girl flight attendants; a flight to Las Vegas on a charter plane full of praying Lutherans; and a plane to the Arctic, where I end up out on the tundra inside a dead cariboo.

But since September I been flying once a week, on Tuesday nights, from Wetaskiwin to Grande Prairie, way up north of Edmonton. I go with a writer named Thomas Hanging Crow, who is a college teacher here in Wetaskiwin. Because I had some of my stories published in books he arrange for me to team-teach fiction writing for Native peoples.

"Teaching is how most writers put food on the table," Thomas say to me as we filling out about a thousand forms so there will be government money to pay me.

I don't understand why Native peoples should have a writing class all their own, and with Native teachers, too. To me it imply that Native people either ain't good enough to mix in with the white students, or else they're too good to mix with them. Either way is a losing situation. Story writing is story writing no matter the color of your skin.

I sure don't mind getting my pay for teaching, more than I make from the books I had published. That big, red roll of fifties make up for getting my pants scared off at least twice every flight.

Late every Tuesday afternoon we take off from Wetaskiwin Airport, which consist of one runway with some poles holding red-and-white socks that show what direction the wind is blowing. The little plane, which have the Alberta government crest on the door, look like it been made of old salmon tins flattened out and glued together. It have only one engine, like a car, and a pilot named Malloy trussed up like a turkey in front of a boardfull of flashing lights.

To get in the plane we have to bend up almost double. The

plane wiggle and jiggle and rattle like it going to for sure fall apart, before it even take off.

I'm always busy imagining us way up in the air, then plunging straight down when the engine quits. I see Ma and Sadie and Delores and Joseph and Illianna, even my white brother-in-law Bob McVey, standing around my grave, while a priest, who I sure didn't invite, say something nice about me.

About that point, after every take-off, the plane level off, and Thomas Hanging Crow touch me on the arm. "You can relax now, Silas. We got well over an hour before we land."

I let go of the armrests and relax my legs, which are braced against the seat in front of me. Sometimes I can actually feel my bones pop because I been holding them so tense.

"How come you don't get scared?" I ask Thomas Hanging Crow. He is too big for a little airplane like this, six-foot-four, 260 pounds or so. He have shiny black hair above an oblong face, black eyes, white teeth. He wear jeans, a cowhide vest, and cowboy boots and carries his black cowboy hat.

"It's simple," Thomas say. "I don't have a fear of dying."

"I'm not just saying this to make myself look good," I say after I've thought for a while, "but I don't think dying would be so bad. What I don't want is leave all my friends and family. I have things to do yet."

Now it is Thomas' turn to be silent for a while.

Never one to let a good silence last, I keep explaining.

"I want to get married to Sadie. I want us to have kids. I want to watch my sister's kids grow up. I want to be there to take care of Joseph, my retarded brother, and to see Ma don't want for nothing. I want to learn everything that Etta got to teach me about medicine and live long enough to maybe

help a few people the way Etta done for the last sixty or
seventy years."

"You're lucky," says Thomas Hanging Crow. "I used to have
things to live for, too."

Thomas is fifty-five, though he don't have a single gray hair I
can see, and the only sign of age is nice crinkly lines at the corners of his eyes. There are men of fifty on the reserve who look
and act seventy. Thomas sure ain't one of those, so I'm surprised.

"I feel the same way about death you do," he says. "Death, in
most instances, is not fearsome. But on every plane ride whenever
we take off or land or run into turbulence, or on the road when
something dangerous happens, I just think, 'I've done pretty well
everything I wanted to do. If it's my time, I'm ready to go.' Saves a
lot of stress and worry."

The plane made a lurch like one wing about to fall off. I grab
the seat arms and stiffen my back, while Thomas act like he don't
even notice.

"Turbulence doesn't bother me," Thomas goes on. He reach
over and pry my hand off the chair arm. "When the plane goes
into a dance like that I just think, 'I'm ready.' And, hey, I'm still
here. And so are you. What good has your worrying done?"

Thomas been teaching at the community college in
Wetaskiwin for about five years. Before that he was at a college
in Manitoba.

His father was an Athabasca Indian from way up north somewhere. That was where Thomas was raised up, so far north the
Indians are mostly Eskimos. His father marry a white woman
come to teach at their reserve school; they have a couple of kids
before he take off. Thomas' mom is dead, his sister live in New
York City, married a Jewish man and Thomas ain't heard from her

in years. He was married himself, with a daughter raised by her mother and step-father in Manitoba. I seen him posting a birth-day parcel once, but I don't think he sees her.

He done awfully good at the university in Manitoba where he got his degrees; he published some stories early on, and a book I tried to read. It was about a writer named Thomas Wolfe, a white man in spite of his name, from North Carolina in the United States, who Thomas describe as a "garrulous bastard."

I had to look up *garrulous*.

As if he been reading my mind, Thomas say, "My daughter teaches Spanish in a Toronto high school. She lives with a boy I've never met. They want to have a hundred thousand dollars in the bank before they have children. I hope they get it saved up soon."

The plane lurch again and my stomach somersault. Turbulence ain't half as bad in a big plane, 'though it's scary, but I like the idea of four engines, 'cause I know one or even two can shut down without the plane crashing. But when there's only one engine . . . I mean, think how many times you stall your car at an intersection. In a small plane I imagine us dropping out of the sky like a shot duck. Splat!

We fly into Grande Prairie where a taxi meet us at the airport and drive us to the college, which is a bunch of concrete bunkers, where we hold a three-hour workshop for a group of Native writ-ers. We start with fifteen students, but are down to eight, and probably only three or four will finish. But that's not bad. Most people ain't supposed to be writers though everybody think they can write a book. Thomas tell a story about a doctor who come up to a writer at a book-signing and say, "You know, when I retire I'm going to write a novel." And the author say back, "That's interesting, because when I retire I'm planning to do some brain surgery."

A couple of months ago Thomas Hanging Crow met Juanita Thompson. She just show up one class with a folder full of handwritten pages and ask if somebody would have a look at it. I offer to do it but she say no, she would rather have "that guy." I can tell from the look on her face it ain't really writing she got on her mind.

"I seen her around the school last year, and she say hello a couple of times in the cafeteria, but that's it," Thomas say as we taxiing back to the airport.

"She's kind of pretty," I say.

I'm guessing she's thirty-five, managed not to go to fat. She just fill out her jeans in all the right places, wear a red cardigan sweater with long sleeves that she push up to her elbows. Her complexion is clear and her eyes wide-spaced and the color of oak. Her hair come down past the middle of her back, and is parted so the left side of her face and her left eye is covered at least part of the time.

Thomas ignore me.

"She's not that good a writer. That folder had some emotional poetry in it, and a couple of autobiographical pieces, just a recital of all the bad things that have happened to her. They aren't really stories, but I can't seem to make her understand that."

"She's kind of pretty," I say again.

"Everybody have bad experiences to catalog. Real writers are the ones who change them into a story. Juanita don't understand that alcoholic parents, a sad childhood, boozy boyfriends, and a mean husband or two don't necessarily make for interesting reading. Like you told the class last week, Silas, 'Stories are not about events, but the people that events happen to.'"

The next week Juanita show up just as the class break for inter-mission, go right up to Thomas and start talking, then lead him off down the hall toward the cafeteria. The intermission last about ten minutes longer than usual, and eventually I start the class without Thomas.

On the plane ride back I keep bringing up Juanita and Thomas keep stonewalling me, until Thomas finally say, "I'm gonna let her sit in on the class, okay? She's not registered or anything, so this is just between us, right?"

"Right," I say.

It is only a couple more weeks until I am doing most of the second half of the class by myself. Then Thomas and Juanita go to the cafeteria after class while I cool my heels by the Coke machine in the hall, and Malloy get paid overtime because we're an hour late to the airport. Bet they'd have coffee before class too, if Thomas could schedule the flight earlier.

Then I hear that Thomas Hanging Crow drove all the way to Grande Prairie of a Friday night and don't get back until noon on Monday.

The week after that I walk into the Gold Nugget Café in Wetaskiwin and there is Thomas and Juanita sit side by side in a booth study the *Wetaskiwin Times*, the apartments for rent section.

"Juanita is coming to live in Wetaskiwin," Thomas says, non-committally.

"We're looking for a bigger apartment," Juanita say, smile side-ways at Thomas so pretty it make my mouth water to see how much in love she is.

"There's an opening in the mail room at the college here,"

Thomas say. "I arranged for Juanita to get the job. Beats hell out of her waiting tables in Grande Prairie."

"Now instead of only being together Tuesday nights, we're only apart Tuesday nights," Juanita say.

The week before Juanita move to Wetaskiwin, the assignment we give our class is to write a poem pretending they are something other than human, like a biscuit, barn door, or a bird in a cage.

Thomas is real proud of what Juanita turn in.

TURBULENCE
My life's been an airplane flight
No smooth journey
All takeoffs and landings
Turbulence, crosswinds, air pockets
The cabin too hot
The food cool and greasy

I find out later that Juanita have a son just graduate high school and gone to work for the paper mill in Grande Prairie, and a daughter already married, gonna produce a grandbaby in a couple of months.

"You determined to be a granddad one way or another," I say to Thomas during our Tuesday flight. Before he can answer the plane hit some bad air and we tip up like we flying sideways.

"Damn this rough air," say Thomas. "Hey, Malloy!" he yell toward the pilot. "How long you figure we got left to live?"

"Don't tell me you care about whether you live or die?" I say.

"Not me. I'm ready to go any time. I just hate being uncomfortable."

This afternoon I sure wish we didn't have to fly to Grande Prairie. It's the last class before Christmas break. I'd like to stay right at home in front of the fire, with Delores and Joseph getting all excited about Christmas, watch the leaf-sized snowflakes cover everything, and the chickadees bounce in the mountain ash tree behind the cabin.

It seem the gray sky get lower every moment and there is an evil crosswind blowing so hard the snow ticks like sand against the door of Louis Coyote's pick-up truck. I park it as out of the wind as I can, so at least the truck won't get drifted in.

From inside the airport hangar I see our plane warming up on the tarmac, the wind actually make the wings vibrate, like the plane was a dead dragonfly. A guy in gray coveralls and a wool hat is spraying something on the wings to keep them from icing up.

Juanita drop off Thomas Hanging Crow, her old red Oldsmobile with the one black fender clunking up to the door of the hangar. She slide from under the steering wheel and kiss Thomas long and serious. As he is pulling his briefcase out of the back seat, Juanita run around the car, her feet skidding on the snow, throw her arms around Thomas' neck and press her belly up against his. He kiss her back and wrap his big arms around her, lift her right off her feet while snowflakes collect in her long black hair like it turning white with age.

Thomas shake himself like a bear as he walk into the hangar.

"You sure we ought to do this?" I ask. "Weather ain't supposed to get no better."

"It's up to Malloy," says Thomas. "If he say go, we go."

Unfortunately, Malloy say go.

"Piece of cake," he says. "I flew in the Arctic for years. This is a summer day in the Arctic." He slap me on the shoulder, which don't make me feel any better.

The three of us climb the little toy steps into the cold interior of the plane. Thomas and I strap ourselves in. If I stretch my neck I can see Malloy check his instruments, squint more than I figure a pilot should. Snow cover most of the windshield, each side being only the area of a good-sized book to start with.

Thomas got his face buried in a novel, the way he always does, both hands on his book to keep the vibration from knocking it out of his hands.

We slither down the runway, me gripping the chair arms like I'd hold on to a tree if I was being swept down a river. The wheels beneath us finally stop bucking as we lift into the air. The plane is like a cork bobbing in water, bounce first one way, then another, groaning at its seams. I can see my breath in front of my face. My insides got cold knots in them.

Thomas Hanging Crow has closed his book, stuffed it between him and the window. He's sitting forward, gripping the arms of his chair, and I think I hear him whisper, "Juanita."

Saskatoon Search

"H ey, if you think you got nerve," says our new friend Baptiste Johnny, "my cousin Lenny over there never even flinched when he got bit by a badger supposed to be rabid."

Baptiste Johnny point to a dude sit about four tables away, have a red handkerchief tied around his neck is the only way we can tell him apart from maybe forty other guys in this huge bar in Williams Lake, or as Baptiste Johnny calls it, Willie's Puddle; a bar so big that my friend Frank Fencepost joke they should hire a tractor trailer to deliver beer to the tables.

"Lenny's hand was all gashed and the doctor was sewing him up, telling him that unless we could find that badger quick and get it tested, Lenny he'd have to take shots with this needle look like a six-inch spike that get rammed right into the middle of his belly every day for two weeks."

Across the room Lenny, who have a wicked little mustache like black silk straggling down over his lips, smile across the table at a real pretty girl in a buckskin jacket. He look a lot like a Brahma bull, hefty, built close to the ground, and mean.

"'So I might be rabid, eh?' Lenny say to the doctor.

"'That's right,' says the doc.

"'Better get me a pencil and paper then.'

"'You want to make a will?' ask the doctor.

"'No,' say Lenny, never bat an eye. 'I'm gonna make me a list of people I want to bite.'"

From across the bar, Lenny nod to Baptiste, but give me and Frank at least half an evil eye.

The trouble start almost as soon as we pick up the hitchhiker. He was standing on the edge of the road in the spitting rain, looking like a muskrat just stick his head up out of a lake. Me and Frank Fencepost are driving Louis Coyote's pick-up truck up a highway in the middle of British Columbia. On our way back from Vancouver we take the long way home, drive north to Dawson Creek, then south to Edmonton.

It wasn't us who decide this. Mad Etta, our medicine lady, covered over with a tarpaulin, sitting up in her tree-trunk chair in the box of the pick-up truck, say she heard a rumor that there was a place up in the middle of British Columbia where they grow the largest saskatoon berries in the world.

A four-hundred-pound medicine lady who once turned an RCMP constable into a weasel, make him stay that way for over a month, she usually get her way.

"You guys look like Indians, but not much," the hitchhiker say, as soon as he get himself comfortable, light up a cigarette.

"Guess we could say the same about you," say Frank. The stranger is short and barrel-chested, got his long hair in braids. He is all covered in denim and wearing construction boots, except when he unsnap his jean jacket we can see he wears a pair of rainbow-colored Police suspenders.

"This here outfit's called a Chilcotin tuxedo, partner," the strange Indian say, and he make the point by poking a stubby finger at Frank's chest.

"Be careful," warn Frank. "Last guy who pointed a finger at me ended up limping through the Yellow Pages."

The stranger have a good laugh at Frank's joke, explain that he is called Baptiste Johnny and is heading for a place called Williams Lake.

"What is this here Chilcotin you been talkin' about?" ask Frank. "Two or three towns we pass through I seen signs, Chilcotin this and Chilcotin that."

"It's a state of mind," say Baptiste Johnny.

"I like your suspenders there, partner," says Frank. "You know what they call a guy from our home town who wears a three-piece suit?"

"The defendant," say Baptiste Johnny, sure spoil hell out of Frank's joke, but it good to see we got things in common with people who live in the state of mind called Chilcotin.

Just then the load in the back shift, almost cause us to go in the ditch.

"What kind of cargo you haulin' back there?" ask Baptiste Johnny. "I seen your rear end was almost dragging on the blacktop."

"Live cargo," says Frank.

"Yeah? You either got a black bear or fifteen people back there."

"Etta can be anything she makes up her mind to be," says Frank.

First thing Etta ask Baptiste Johnny, right after we thrown back the tarp and Baptiste Johnny got over his surprise at Etta's size, was, "You know whereabouts the big saskatoons are?"

"I heard of them," say Baptiste Johnny, "supposed to be out in the bush from Williams Lake aways. But only medicine men know exactly where. Maybe they don't exist at all, likely some medicine man just dreamed them up to make himself look important."

"Maybe you better introduce me to your medicine man," says Etta.

I was kind of surprised to find out that the reason Etta searching for the giant saskatoons is purely personal. Two years in a row, at the Red Pheasant Sun Dance and Pow-Wow in Saskatchewan, Etta come second in the bannock-making contest. Etta don't like to be second to nobody. Bannock is flour and lard and saskatoon berries all mixed together, pounded, and dried to the texture of an old cow chip. Etta figure if she finds the giant saskatoon berries, she'll finally beat out that Saskatchewan medicine man named Ewalt Kicking-down-the-door.

"Them saskatoons supposed to be as big as golf balls," says Etta. "You slice 'em up like tomatoes. And sweet as young love. With them in my bannock it will win the blue-ribbon prize just like I bewitched the judges."

"Here I thought you wanted them to cure rheumatism or stomach trouble or something," I said.

"First things first," says Etta. "A medicine woman who lose a bannock-making contest also lose face."

"She could stand to lose about fifty pounds off that face," whisper Baptiste Johnny.

Soon as we hit town, Etta make a few inquiries, send off a few messages, arrange for a meeting with a local medicine man.

Back at the hotel in Williams Lake, Frank ask Baptiste Johnny why don't he invite his cousin Lenny *and* that real pretty girl in the buckskin jacket to join us for a beer?

"Well, I don't know," say Baptiste. "Lenny only goes where he wants to go."

"Hey," says Frank. "My uncle Zeke Fencepost was like that, a real loner. The only people come to his funeral was three inflatable women in black veils."

"Now Cousin Lenny might like to hear about *him*." Baptiste Johnny stand up and beckon Lenny and his pretty friend to come to our table.

Lenny shake my hand, hardly glance twice at me, but soon as he look at Frank he recognize trouble.

"Up here in the Chilcotin they call me the Town Tamer, eh?" he say directly to Frank. "I'm so tough the Hell's Angels ask my permission to come to this part of the country."

Frank ain't about to be outdone. "I can't get a good fight in Alberta no more, so I come up here to the Chilcotin where I heard you flat-faced Indians really know how to get rowdy."

"I'm so tough," counters Lenny, "that I wear my clothes out from the inside out."

But Frank can top even that. "I'm so tough," he says, "that on Hallowe'en, instead of bobbing for apples, I go down to the Gold Nugget Café and bob for french fries."

"What is this, the Canadian Legion Liars' Contest?" says Baptiste.

Next morning, Lenny he say to us, "You guys want to go for a ride?"

"Where to?" we say.

"Don't matter. Nothin' like an after-breakfast drive in a big, new car to start the day right."

"We gonna steal one?" ask Frank.

"Hey, partner, we never steal. We borrow," says Lenny. "We'll just watch the door of this hotel for a few minutes. I'll let you know when the perfect one comes along."

"That's the one," he say, about ten minutes later, as a big, new Buick stop in the circular driveway and a well-dressed white lady get out. "Keys in the car," say Lenny, hopping up and down. "Probably a full tank of gas. Let's go."

"But there's kids in the car," says Frank. "No way we can steal kids."

"That's what that lady is counting on," says Lenny.

We walk around the car, peer in the windows, admire the deep velvet seats. There is a boy about five in the front, a baby in a car seat in the back.

Lenny tap on the side window, smile real nice at the kid who push a button and the power window whirr down.

"Your mom want you to bring the baby inside," Lenny say. "We'll give you a hand to get her out of the car seat, okay?"

The little kid open up the door. We release the kid's seat belt while Lenny untangle the baby from the car seat and fit her into the little boy's arms. He even shield the baby's face from the wind with the corner of the pink blanket.

"Wouldn't want her to catch cold, would we?" he say to the kid, who smile because he is real proud to be helping his mother. "Just wait by the front desk for your mama," Lenny say. He pat the kid on the head, send him up to the hotel door.

"Okay, let's roll," say Lenny, as at least ten of us climb over each other getting into the Buick.

Lenny get behind the wheel. He burn rubber for at least a block, and we doing eighty miles an hour by the edge of town.

A mile or so down the highway he turn onto a country road, which pretty soon deteriorate to a dirt road, then to a trail, then to nothing at all. But Lenny drive just as if we was still on blacktop.

"When Cousin Lenny there was in Boy Scouts," say a guy we ain't seen before, "only knot he learned was the noose."

We rip off the muffler and whatever ever else can get torn off the bottom of a car by rocks and logs, also do the passenger side a certain amount of damage get too close to a big tree.

I say, "When my friend Frank there was born, the doctor told his mother, 'Water it twice a week and keep it out of bright sunlight.'"

"That's enough from you, Standing-neck-deep-in-muddy-water," Frank say, after he come up from kissing on that girl in the buckskin jacket. Him and that girl get along like a couple of bandits.

"I think," the girl say to Frank, "I get you adopted into the Carrier Tribe. Once that's done you never be able to go away from the Chilcotin."

"Not necessary," say Frank. "One time I went to a doctor in Edmonton and he told me straight out I was a carrier."

After we arrive in Williams Lake, but before we went to the bar, Baptiste took Frank and me to his cousin's house where he arrange for all three of us to spend the night. It is kind of like at home in Hobbema, everybody with Indian blood is a cousin of some kind, and Janet Ghostkeeper at least trust Baptiste Johnny well enough to let him bring strangers into her house. The pretty girl Lenny was with just up and disappear late in the evening. I sleep on a blanket behind the sofa, but as far as I can tell, Frank never turn up at all. Last I seen of him he was going to meet a blonde girl who wait tables at the Last Chance Café, supposed to get off work at 4:00 a.m.

Me and Baptiste and Lenny head to the Last Chance for breakfast, meet Frank coming down the street, grin like a pumpkin.

"Were you tipi-crawling?" says Lenny.

"No tipis for me," says Frank. "Went home to a nice warm apartment with that girl from the Last Chance."

"Not the blonde?" says Lenny.

"The blonde," says Frank.

He look glum. "Me and Baptiste been hustling her for two years, all we ever got from her were dirty looks."

"What can I say?" says Frank. "She just never come up against a Fencepost before."

"Was she good?" ask Baptiste.

"That woman's so hot she could cook meat with her bare hands. Only trouble is, she was so white I kept losing her in the sheets."

Most of the day we riding all around the backwoods of the Chilcotin. Ain't a lot left of the Buick by the time Lenny abandon it, and we hitch a ride back to Willie's Puddle with a guy named Moses in a pick-up truck even more beat-up than Louis Coyote's.

"Ain't you afraid the RCMP gonna pounce on us soon as we hit town?" I ask.

"Hey," says Lenny. "What kind of description you figure the RCMP got of the car thieves, eh? Heavy-set Native males with long hair, some braided some not, some with mustaches, some not, all wearing jean jackets. Fit 90 percent of the men in the Chilcotin."

While we been getting rowdy, Etta been doing some detective work. She gone through a couple of medicine men who don't know nothing. But a third one tell her if she's a real medicine woman she be able to smell out the giant saskatoons all by herself, not need any help.

"I like his style," says Etta. "Fire up the truck."

It is dark by the time we get Etta loaded up, and it seem like we got every Indian in the Chilcotin traveling with us. Just as we pulling out of town, the truck and us making a certain amount of racket, an RCMP car pull in behind us, lights flashing.

Frank start to pull over.

"Make a run for it!" yell everybody. "It's Constable Mooseface."

"What the point?" says Frank. "He got our license number."

"Your license plates are under the seat. Me and Lenny took care of that," says Baptiste Johnny. "We're just another beat-to-ratshit pick-up truck full of Indians. Now boot it, partner."

Baptiste direct Frank onto a logging road crookeder than Chief Tom Crow-eye and Samantha Yellowknees put together.

"Fencepost will show you how to outrun a mountie," says Frank.

"In this truck?" say Lenny. "You couldn't drive out of sight in two days."

"One time," I say, "somebody with a speedometer timed this here truck on a straightaway in Alberta. Foot-to-the-floor Frank Fencepost there got it the all way up to forty-eight miles an hour."

"My skill at evasive driving make up for my lack of speed," say Frank.

On one of the sharp curves the truck tip about three-quarters of the way over, then right itself all of a sudden, spurt ahead like a kernel of corn just been popped. I think I hear some commotion in the back. Even though our lights are off and it pouring rain, the RCMP car stick to our tail just like we was towing him.

"About a mile further on there's a fork in the road," say Baptiste. "Keep left until the last second then take the right fork."

That fork is on us before we know it. Frank swing right at the last second, almost tip us over again. The RCMP keep left and disappear.

"You can slow down now," says Baptiste.

"We built that left fork with a borrowed bulldozer a few days ago," say Lenny, "just for a night like this. That fork only runs thirty yards then there's a nice deep slough. Constable Mooseface will be wet to the gonads by the time he wades out."

Another ten miles or so the road disappear altogether, and we drive cross-country for a while. Baptiste tell Frank to stop in front of a cabin appear in a clearing, have a coal oil lamp burn in its window.

"My cousin, Barbara Johnny," says Lenny.

"My cousin, too," says Baptiste. "And she make the best dandelion wine in all the Chilcotin."

"Anybody live around here ain't your cousin?" ask Frank.

"Constable Mooseface," says Baptiste.

"How come you call him Constable Mooseface?" we ask Baptiste Johnny.

"When that constable first come here," he answer, "somebody offer to teach him Indian. He think he's learning to say 'How can

I help you?' but he is actually saying 'I am Constable Mooseface. Let's get naked.'"

Frank tell Baptiste Johnny how, every summer, when the local priest, Father Alphonse, go on holidays, the church send in a replacement.

"First thing we do with that new priest is tell him the way to impress his congregation is to learn a few phrases of Cree. Then, so he won't be suspicious, we take him to Blind Louis Coyote. Louis is way over eighty, wear buckskins, have long white hair and milk-colored eyes. Louis speak soft and act gentle as rainwater. The visiting priest never suspect a thing.

"At Sunday mass, what show up is over a hundred people, cram the pews to bursting, to hear the priest give his welcome speech what Louis Coyote been rehearsing with him all week.

"The priest stand up real serious and recite the words Louis have him memorize. He begin by saying, 'Hide your daughters! I am Muskrat Breath.' Then he tell how naked he is under his black robe, and how he done things with his mother would land just about anybody in jail. Everybody smile and nod, clap their hands when he finish, just as if he on 'The Tonight Show.'

"After mass he shake our hands, repeat to each of us, 'Hide your daughters! I am Muskrat Breath,' which he think is some kind of greeting, while we smile and smile. Bet he wonders why there is only seven or eight old ladies in babushkas at church next week."

When we get out of the truck, the tarpaulin and the tree-trunk chair is still there, but Mad Etta ain't nowhere to be found.

"Remember when we went around that corner on a wheel and a half?" say Frank, "And how the truck suddenly went faster?"

"Four hundred pounds lighter," I say.

There are several scared-looking people in the truck box. "Yonder big lady topple off her chair, roll right over the tailgate," they say.

"Etta is sure gonna be cross," says Frank.

"And wet."

"And bruised."

"The longer we leave her out there the worse it gonna be," I say. "We better start back."

"What do you mean start back?" say Lenny. "Parties here in the Chilcotin usually go on for four or five days, and we ain't even got started yet."

We go inside Barbara Johnny's cabin, have us a quick glass of dandelion wine, listen to a few Merle Haggard records on her wind-up record player, spend only a hour, well, not more than two, anyway, then we head back to look for Etta.

On the way we catch up with Constable Mooseface hiking along the trail, a weak little flashlight glinting on the puddles.

Frank pull the truck over.

"Well, who have we got here?" says Constable Mooseface, peer in the window of the truck.

"We just a bunch of law-abiding citizens out for an evening drive. We don't usually pick up strangers," say Frank. "Never know what kind of riffraff you find on a dark road in the middle of the night. But you got an honest face, officer, so climb right in."

Etta is right where we left her, landed on her back in the muddy ditch, kind of like a beetle, not able to kick herself over on her stomach.

She is some upset with us, call us names I didn't even know she knew. But once we get her upright, instead of doing us all serious physical harm, even though Etta is wet as a drowned bear, mean-looking as a sasquatch, she is smiling.

Etta slam off through the undergrowth, travel about a mile, maybe more, with everyone, including Constable Mooseface, following along.

"Silas! Smell the air!" she say to me.

I smell the air. Smell like regular bush country to me.

"Stay put!" she tells everybody and crashes off again. The sounds of Etta in the underbrush seem to come from all directions at once.

"Bad medicine, bad medicine," Lenny the Town Tamer keep repeating. I wouldn't have thought of him as being a believer in the old ways. I thought he was just mad at Frank for messing with his girlfriend.

When Etta finally come back, from a different direction than she went away, she carrying her babushka like a pail, and inside, 'though at first I think they are wild plums, are about fifty giant saskatoons. In the truck box on the way back she let me eat one, and even though regular saskatoons are the best-tasting berries in the world, this giant saskatoon is so sweet and taste so *purple*, I know my mouth gonna water for years every time I think about it.

Next morning, when we ready to leave town, Frank he's sent both his white and Indian girlfriends on errands so he be a good twenty-five miles up the road toward Dawson Creek before they discover Frank spent half the night with each of them. "Hey," Frank explain, "I'm an equal opportunity stud," but Baptiste Johnny point out that Lenny hanging around down the block looking mean as a hail storm.

"You shouldn't have messed with Lenny's woman," somebody say. "Lenny didn't exactly turn you in to the RCMP, but he let them know when they questioning him about the borrowed Buick that you Alberta Indians are probably responsible for most of the crimes around here."

"A Fencepost knows no fear," says Frank. "Hey, a Fencepost has strands of steel wire for blood, an anvil in each fist . . . "

As me and Frank walk around the corner to where our truck parked, we see Etta and her giant saskatoons about to climb in the truck when Lenny come running down the sidewalk like he's being chased by something with sharp teeth carrying a shotgun.

He wrench the babushka from Etta's hand, say something about the secret of Chilcotin saskatoons not going back to Alberta, and race right on down the street.

When Lenny come by, Frank just stick out his foot and he take off through the air like a football player about to make a tackle, land hard, skid on his face for about twenty feet, and lay still. The giant saskatoons go bouncing like ping-pong balls, but not for all that far. Etta already waddling purposefully after them.

Frank smile and shake his head. "Real dangerous to run that fast. See what happens when a guy blows a moccasin at fifty miles an hour?"

When we're a good long ways down the road, Etta bang on the back window, and me and Frank both look at her, me pretty well keeping the truck on the road. Etta not only got her babushka of giant saskatoons, she's pulled from somewhere on her person, wrapped in wet newspapers, several slips from those saskatoon trees. Nice to know that next year when the Saskatchewan bannock-making contest come along we don't have to go on another saska-toon search in the Chilcotin.

"Look out!" yell Frank, as a semitrailer breathe past us, even though we were mostly in his lane.

The Rain Birds

"Lawyers," say my friend Frank Fencepost, "need a stack of paper high enough to burn a wet moose before they even take your case."

Me and Frank, Bedelia Coyote, and Mad Etta, our medicine lady, are sitting around the living room of Melvin Dodginghorse's big split-level farmhouse. Melvin been complaining that lawyers ain't been able to help with his problems.

At least until this summer, Melvin has been a real successful farmer.

"He have so much land, just looking at it make me tired," says Frank.

Among the many things that me and Frank Fencepost and my friends ain't is farmers.

Melvin and his family live like white people — two cars, a microwave oven, and a year ago he even set up his own computer.

"I'd sure like one of them computers," say Frank, who spend a lot of time since he learn to read and write messing with the computer at the Tech School in Wetaskiwin, where him and me take classes. "I'd get me a program called MacSperm, help me keep track of all the rug rats I've fathered. My motto is 'A Fence-post in every oven.'"

We haven't always been good friends of Melvin's, especially after we helped his daughter get together with a boyfriend Melvin didn't like. But things blow over, and Melvin even like his son-in-law now, and he especially like his granddaughter Buffalo Jump Woman (Buffy) who's just old enough to climb on his knee and hug his neck.

As we were driving over to Melvin's, Etta in the back of the pick-up on her tree-trunk chair, we joke that Melvin Dodging-horse musta used up all the options in the white world if he calling for superstition and Mad Etta.

Melvin's problem is his water supply is disappearing, being stole right from under his fields. Computer farmers have bought or leased all the land to the west and south of our reserve.

They put up expensive white-board fences where their land touch Highway 2A, and there is about five acres of lawn with flower beds full of sweet petunias, marigolds, and purple-and-white pansies that surround that computer building. There are two flagpoles at least fifty feet tall with Canadian and Alberta flags bigger than a bedsheet. There is a sign, low to the ground, four-foot-tall gold letters on a white background, spell out "Environment Farms of Canada."

"Even their name make it sound like they doing something good," say Mad Etta, but she frown when she say it.

That whole twenty-five thousand acres is managed by one cowboy in a plaid shirt and clean jeans, who don't even have a suntan. He sit all day in a concrete-block shack and stare at the bluey screen of a computer that tell him which acres need watering, fertilizing, weeding, or harvesting. When a job needs doing, he pick up a phone and, like magic, trucks full of workers appear to do the job the computer suggested.

"I bet you could be God if you wanted," Frank said, the time we visited that shack.

The pale cowboy didn't answer, but he smiled like he knew secrets we didn't.

The computer farmers grow crops that require more water than normal. Instead of wheat or oats or barley, they growing things like peas and cucumbers, plants that drink a lot.

To get enough water, they irrigate; "irritate," Frank call it. They drilled huge, deep wells and brought in wheel-line sprinklers, stand fifty feet tall, is built like the daddy-long-legs that dance over quiet slough water in summer.

Sometimes of a summer evening, when the weather is soft and the evening sky pink, me and my friends park on a country road far from the pale cowboy's concrete cabin, walk into the fields, and play like little kids in the cool water that drift down from the rain-birds.

Those wells suck up millions of gallons of water from underground streams, including streams under the reserve, particularly under Melvin's farm.

Not long after the computer farming corporation get established, a man wearing a western suit and a million-dollar smile come around the reserve and give a talk at Blue Quills Hall.

"We want to be good corporate neighbors," he say to us.

And we believe him.

"We will introduce several million dollars into the economy of central Alberta," the man went on. "Our studies show that we will put 30 percent more money into local hands than if each farm was individually owned and operated."

At first no one suspect what is happening. The computer farms was green and prosperous, load up the produce, and haul it off to Edmonton and Calgary.

Environment Farms been operating for almost three seasons when we first notice the bad taste. People who live along the south side of the reserve finding that their well water turn a pale yellow color, taste like a used car tire smell.

"Gopher piss," say Frank, spit a mouthful into Gus Cardinal's feed lot.

"The voice of an expert," I say to Gus.

"Cattle won't drink the stuff no more," Gus says. "I have to drive my herd two miles north, drink surface water from Jump-off-Joe Creek."

Melvin Dodginghorse take a water sample to the District Agriculturist in Wetaskiwin.

"Nitrates," is the answer he get back.

"Nitrates are seeping into the underground water supply," the District Agriculturist say. "They come from the computer farms. They use about five times as much commercial fertilizer as ordinary farmers, forcing the land to produce two crops in the short Alberta growing season."

Don't take Bedelia Coyote long to get her back up. She has friends who are greener than Kermit the Frog.

"Poison! Law suits! Birth defects!" cry Bedelia and her friends before they even have their first meeting.

"Speaking of birth defects," say Frank, "you hear about the 250 women on the reserve who was born without tits? The Indian-nippleless 500. Ha!"

If you ever been in the Parliament Building in Edmonton, first thing you notice is that every floor is circular. You can stand in the middle of the main floor, tip your head back and stare right up to the top of the dome.

"They do that so nobody can catch them on the corners," say Mad Etta, the time I drove her to see all the white marble and varnished wood in that stone building what smell of used paper and slow service.

The first thing Chief Tom Crow-eye, who is our MLA representative in Edmonton, say when we tell him what the problem is — "Environment Farms are our good corporate neighbors."

So we know how much help we'll get from the provincial government. And the only time the big government in Ottawa ever look at the west is if they figure they can steal something.

"Environment Farms may not know a lot about farming but they sure know their politics," say Bedelia Coyote. "They greased Chief Tom so good he don't have to drive to Edmonton; he just take a good run and slide the whole forty miles."

The pale cowboy say he will pass the complaint on to their Calgary office, and Calgary say it is something should be handled by the head office, in someplace that sound like *Mississippi*, Ontario. It is three months before they finally send a letter to us.

"Yes," they say, "your water does taste and smell bad, and you have our sympathy. However, after extensive investigation, there is no scientific evidence to show that your problem is related to our farming activities."

The problem, they tell us, is likely caused by natural sulfur deposits way below ground, the kind that make hot springs in some parts of the province.

"Dig deep wells," they say, and, as good corporate neighbors, offer us their well-drilling equipment at only half their normal rates.

The problems get worse. It is a dry summer. Environment farms irrigate more than ever. Some of the wells on the reserve stop producing altogether. Melvin Dodginghorse's crops lie brittle and dying in his fields.

"Environment Farms has pumped the water out from under your land," the District Agriculturist say sadly. "And coupled with the drought . . ." he shrug his shoulders.

Before we went to the meeting at Melvin's house we took a drive south of the reserve, stopped a couple of times on country roads where it was so silent the world might have already ended. At one spot I bet there wasn't a human being for twenty miles in any direction.

The computer farms have bulldozed farm houses and outbuildings, leveled the land, and planted it to crop. No matter how hard we try or how good our memories, we can't pick out a spot where a single set of buildings used to be.

"You're the medicine woman. Why don't you do something?" some of our people say to Mad Etta.

"A crooked stick will cast a crooked shadow," say Etta, look very pleased with herself.

"What's that got to do with anything?"

"Nature always win in the end," say Etta.

"Nature already been outfoxed, outnumbered, and outclassed."

Etta snort softly, like she do when someone from the government try to tell her they are there to help. Or like the time I suggest she should have the electricity installed so she could have a TV, and that maybe a microwave could cook up her medicines quicker than the woodstove.

Etta snort that snort and growl, "If I want the electricity, I'll make some myself."

Bet she could, too.

A couple of summers ago, Bedelia got stirring things up.

"That computer farm hires dozens, sometimes hundreds of part-time workers to harvest their crops," she say one afternoon at Hobbema Pool Hall, "and how many of them are Indian?"

"Six percent?" answer Frank, pick a number out of the air.

"Closer than you think," say Bedelia. "Do you know they truck people out from Wetaskiwin and even Edmonton? There are four thousand people on the reserve right here and 70 percent of them are unemployed."

"Indians ain't farmers," Frank answer, go on to quote Crow-child, Poundmaker, even Young Eagle — every famous Indian who had bad things to say about farming.

The argument go on all afternoon and evening, but Bedelia arrange that the next time Environment Farms put out a call for day workers, thirty or so of us be ready to answer.

Boy, if there's one thing I hate it is getting up early in the morning. The dew is thick on the grass and the sun just peeping over the horizon when that flatdeck truck pick us up at Hobbema General Store, carry us to the fields. They harvest the peas with a huge machine look like seven street sweepers joined together.

"Now that is what I call tearing up the pea patch," say Frank.

The foreman wear bib-overalls and a yellow straw hat, hand out baskets, assign us rows, and tell us what size of cucumbers to pick and what size to leave alone. Another couple of guys spend their time watching us. Guess they figure we might try to get even.

"Wait a minute," the foreman say when he spot Lawrence Canvas. Lawrence is over eighty years old, blind, have only one leg. "How can that guy pick cucumbers?"

"Lawrence is one of the few survivors of the battle of Little Big Mouth," say Frank.

"You mean Little Big Horn," correct the foreman.

"Little Big Mouth was my first wife," say Lawrence. "I outlived two more since her."

"Only one," say Mrs. Canvas. "Two dead altogether."

"I have known many cucumbers," say Lawrence. "I can harvest eggs from beneath a hen. Cucumbers do not run away, I simply find a vine and follow it along until there isn't any more vine."

"Well. . . "

"If you don't hire me I'll make it rain."

The foreman squint and stare at Lawrence for a few seconds before he thrust a basket into Lawrence's hands.

After people picked their cucumbers, the baskets was emptied into a wire-mesh cage big as a semitrailer and towed by a tractor. The cage full of cucumbers was then towed up to the Environment Farms warehouse where the cukes get put into real trucks and carried off to Edmonton.

The first time the cage was full of cucumbers the foreman ask for someone to drive the tractor over to the warehouse. I put up my hand to volunteer, but Frank was already firing up the engine without benefit of a key.

" 'King of the road,' they call me," Frank tell the foreman. "Eighteen-wheeler is my middle name. Ten-four. Roger, Good

Buddy. Hammer down, the bears are in hiding," and Frank take off with a screech.

You probably seen on TV what happened next. We was picking cucumbers on the east side of Highway 2A, and the warehouse was on the west side. Frank got himself and the tractor across the highway, but the wire cage and about half a million cucumbers met up with an eighteen-wheeler full of steel rods.

"Instant fresh cucumber relish," is the way Frank describe it.

The cucumbers make such a squishy mess that cars driving along Highway 2A skid into each other or into the ditch. It take the RCMP over twelve hours to get everything back to normal, with Constable Chrétien and Constable Bobowski covered in cucumber slime.

Frank, of course, get fired, and over the next three days the rest of us quit, all except old Lawrence Canvas, who turn out to be their best picker.

"You figure you worked long enough to apply for unemployment?" somebody ask.

"No need," say Frank. "We're already unemployed."

It was Bedelia Coyote who, through her connections with every protest group carry a poster or raise a clenched fist, got a civil-rights lawyer name of Mr. Elmore to take Melvin Dodginghorse's case.

The day that the case finally get a hearing, Mr. Elmore, Melvin, and Bedelia sit at one table, while six large, gray-suited lawyers, look like they had the same parents, stare at their reflections at another.

"The judge has taken the case under advisement," Mr. Elmore tell us at the end of the day. "Translated, that means he doesn't have any idea how or what he should decide, so he'll think about it for a year or two, hope like hell the problem goes away before he has to make a decision."

"Should put Melvin, Mad Etta, and them corporate lawyers all in a sweat lodge for a few hours," say Frank. "Decisions are a lot easier when you're naked."

"You just have to be patient," Mr. Elmore went on, smiling in a slow, friendly way. "In spite of what it looks like, Environment Farms Corporation is losing money."

That bit of information start Bedelia poking around in financial statements.

"They have millions of dollars invested in irrigation equipment, tractors, trucks, harvesting equipment. They're in a financial corner," Bedelia say.

"But how can they not make money?" I asked.

"What they forgot," says Bedelia, "was the human factor. None of the men who make up the color brochures, graphs, and charts has ever farmed. They never got up at four in the morning to milk cows; never had shit on their shoes.

"They figure that if a farmer and his wife can farm 640 acres with limited financing and inefficient equipment, they can make big money by farming that 640 acres and 25,000 more without the farmer or his wife, just with scientific methods."

"So why doesn't it work?"

"They forgot farmers work twenty-hour days, because they love the land. They don't even earn minimum wage. Environment Farms have to pay three shifts a day. When we worked there we went home after eight hours — and only worked as hard as we had to."

When we tell all this to Etta, she look like she's known it all along.

The last while I notice Etta's been rumbling around the reserve late at night. I hear her talking down in the slough, making conversation with someone who may not be there. Every day for the past week there's been a late afternoon gully washer of a thunderstorm dump oceans of water on the reserve.

I think I hear Mad Etta snorting softly, saying "Nature always win in the end."

There is the story about Etta and the Northern Lights.

George the Cat

Cats are all the time pretending —
Bobbie Ann Mason

A s I was hiking up the road toward her place, Rita Makes-room-for-them was ambling down the footpath from the door of her broken-down house, heading toward the gravel road and the lunch-bucket-shaped mail box. The black lettering that had long ago read "Rita & Sanderson Makes-room-for-them" was faded beyond recognition, and the pole that Sanderson had cut, hewn, and creosoted was wormy and pitched forward so that if the mail box had been human its chin would nearly have been touching the ground.

"I'm in about the same condition as that goddamn mail box," Rita said.

Rita is a big, thick woman a little over thirty, with wide-set brown eyes in a tobacco-colored face. Her hips are wide and her backside fills out her Levi's. She is wearing a blue work shirt and a wide black belt that I've seen Sanderson wear sometimes. My guess is Rita is an inch or two bigger around the waist.

"What you doin' here, Silas?"

"Sanderson was giving me a ride to Bluff Corners on his way home, but the truck hit a pothole, the front passenger tire blew, and we came out on the short end of a scuffle with a deep ditch full of water."

Rita shakes her head. She's spent her life receiving bad news.

"Sanderson okay?"

"Other than a bump on the head and being mad as a castrated goat."

"So how come you're here?"

"Well, Sanderson figured you'd worry if he was any later than he is already, so he sent me to tell you where he is."

"He was supposed to be home yesterday afternoon. If I didn't die of worry overnight another few hours wasn't going to hurt."

Rita bent way down and peeked into the mail box.

"What the hell?" she said, jumping back.

"What?"

"There's some animal in the goddamn mail box."

There was a piece of two-by-four lying in the ditch. "Hope it ain't a skunk," I said, reaching for it.

"I am certainly not a skunk," said a voice from the mail box. "Thanks for waking me up."

Rita scowled, placing her large right hand on her denim hip. I picked up the two-by-four and took a step toward the mail box. The door hung permanently open about three inches, but it was too dark to see exactly what was inside.

"Sanderson, is that you?" Rita asked. "You're playing a trick, right?"

"Tape recorder," I said.

Rita gingerly reached forward to pull open the door of the mail box. I stood to her left, the piece of two-by-four held like a baseball bat.

As Rita snapped the door fully open, a good-sized yellow cat poked his head slowly out of the mail box, looked both ways, and, as Rita jumped back and I flexed the two-by-four, leaped to the ground at our feet, landing awkwardly, front paws sort of collapsing.

"What the hell?" said Rita.

"Be careful with that stick. You could do me serious damage," the cat said to me.

"He talked," Rita said. "You talked," she said to the cat, who sat on his haunches, eyeing me balefully.

I reached carefully into the mail box. There was nothing but a couple of advertising flyers and some yellow cat hair. No tape recorder. No microphone.

"You talked," Rita said again, staring down. "But you're a . . ."

"Cat," said the cat. "George the Cat."

"Yeah, well every other goddamn thing is wrong in my life," said Rita. "No reason I shouldn't find a talking cat in my mail box."

The cat was as disreputable a cat as I'd ever seen. It was an average-sized, square-jawed yellow tom cat, but he looked as if he'd recently stuck a paw in a light socket and had probably slept for several nights in blackberry briars. He was scrawny, with uneven whiskers on each side of a scarred face. One eye watered and was half-closed in a permanent squint. His ears looked as if they'd been nibbled by hungry fish.

"I fell asleep while I was waiting for someone to show up," George the Cat said, speaking very clearly. In spite of looking like a cat wino, he spoke with an educated voice, sort of like my friend Mr. Nicholls down at the Tech School in Wetaskiwin.

"Sorry," he went on, "no personal mail, just a flyer from

K-Mart — no real bargains — and some advertising from Robinson's Stores — a good price on bicycle pumps, if you happen to need one."

"So, to what do I owe the pleasure of a talking cat?" asked Rita.

"You don't quite understand," said George the Cat, looking like something ejected from a garbage barrel, stretching to within a foot of Rita's scuffed black boots with the hand-tooled R on them. "I'm your power animal."

Rita guffawed. "You?"

"Why not?" George the Cat sounded vaguely offended.

"You're a cat."

"True."

"A mangy . . ." she kicked gravel and yellowish dust in George's direction, "goddamned barn cat who looks half dead. You've probably got ticks . . ."

"I admit to being down on my luck."

"Then don't even think about being my power animal. This is a joke, right? Gloria Lefthand set this up, right? Silas, you're in on it. That fucking Sanderson, there's been no accident. There's a tape recorder in the ditch . . ."

Rita stared out across the open prairie. There was nothing visible except the purplish hulk of Gloria Lefthand's house a mile cross country. She stared up the path toward her own house, a pitiful frame structure supplied by the Department of Indian Affairs about thirty years ago. It had once been painted a brilliant aquamarine. Somebody in Ottawa heard that Indians like bright colors, so the houses got painted rose and yellow, sky blue and crow-wing purple.

"No joke," said George the Cat.

"I should have known," said Rita. "Other people get a bear, a wolverine, an eagle. I get a barn cat looks as if it's got the distemper. I'm not a bad person, Silas. Why does this happen to me?"

"Never underestimate your generic barn cat," said George, moving out of range of Rita's boots, just in case.

"Yeah, well, all I need is another mouth to feed," said Rita. "And that's what you are, aren't you?"

George appeared to shrug.

"Sanderson's just out of jail, not that he didn't deserve to be there, and he's wrecked the truck. My car's sitting five miles down the pike with the tranny locked tighter than a banker's fist. It's been there for a week so kids have probably stripped it down until it looks like it's been X-rayed. I'm overdrawn at the Credit Union, and my kid needs an eye operation or she's gonna grow up to look like you.

"The welfare check's late. My twelve-year-old looks sixteen and is threatening to run off with a twenty-year-old named Billy Kills-his-own-horses, who has a record a mile long and whose only ability seems to be breaking his bones at rodeos and taking part in the closing-time riot at the Alice Hotel Bar. You want to hear about my big troubles?"

"One of my good qualities is that I'm an excellent listener," said George the Cat.

"I'm outa cigarettes," said Rita. "You wouldn't happen to have . . . ?" She stopped herself.

George's voice had a whiskey-soaked edge to it. He reminded me of an old, red-haired cowboy I met in a bar in Ponoka one time.

"Nobody ever said life was fair," said George the Cat.

"Thanks. You're a regular Phil Donahue. Instead of a screaming hawk I get a philosopher with fleas."

I took out my cigarettes and offered Rita one. She lit up and inhaled deeply.

"Things are getting better already," said George.

"So, what are you gonna do for me, power animal?"

"Perhaps if we strolled up to your house, you might have a saucer of milk to spare? I suppose a bit of cat food would be too much to hope for?"

"You'd be right. Catch yourself a field mouse, great hunter."

"Don't worry about me. I'm a cat, and cats suffer."

"A theologian, too?"

"I'm also a survivor. There was an emperor in Egypt who sent out an order to kill all the cats."

"So the Jews had Hitler, the Indians had the white man. You're not the only one who's been persecuted," said Rita.

"May I point out that Indians have reserves, the Jews have Israel. When you consult an atlas do you see any place called Catland?"

"What am I supposed to do, lead a hundred thousand cats to seize North Dakota?"

"I also have an excellent sense of humor. Those who are persecuted survive by making fun of their persecutors."

Rita laughed out loud.

"Jesus, Silas, do you believe this. I'm having a real conversation with a goddamn cat. So," Rita said to George, "What do you think of Morris?"

George's tail twitched.

"He has a certain panache," said George. "But he wouldn't last on the street for ten minutes. Now I don't have any proof of this, a rumor only, but it wouldn't surprise me if he was gay."

"Hey, one thing I've always wanted to know . . . how do you purr?"

"Can you explain the intricate operation of your digestive system?"

"No."

"Cats purr, that's all."

"Okay, so tell me something interesting about cats. Something that most people don't know."

"Let me see," said George.

We were walking, the three of us, up the path toward Rita's house. We both offered to carry George, but he declined.

"Do I look that bad?"

"You do," I said.

"Let me see," George repeated. "Are you aware that cats have twelve-hour orgasms?"

Rita laughed out loud.

"Did you know that a cat dressed as a baby survived the sinking of the *Titanic?*"

George's tail is straight up like a flagpole.

"Did you know that a cat rode to Little Big Horn in General Custer's saddlebag?"

"Do you know what Custer was wearing at his last stand?" I say. "An Arrow shirt. Ha!"

"Boo," says George the Cat.

"I mean, you gotta be kidding," says Rita, "you can't possibly be my power animal."

"I can talk. Doesn't that impress you? You do believe in power animals, don't you?"

"Good question," says Rita. "Silas, what do you think? Do we believe in power animals?"

Mad Etta, our medicine lady, has made some genuine magic a couple of times in my life. I know all the stories about power animals, but I've never had any experience.

"I guess it depends," I say.

"Great. Nothing like a definitive stand. If this thing we're talking to ain't a power animal, what do you suppose it is?"

"When you climbed out of the mail box, you said you were waiting for someone. Who were you waiting for?" I ask.

"I was waiting for someone to come walking down that road. I thought it might have been you, but I was wrong."

"So, who are you waiting for?" asks Rita.

"I guess I'll know when they get here."

"I think you're just a mooch. You're probably a reincarnation of my uncle."

In an hour or two, George the cat drank up two cups of milk, ate a cold cooked pork chop, a slice of mock chicken luncheon meat, and a plate of Kraft Dinner, which Rita made for her and me for lunch.

"You know what would solve a lot of the problems of the world?" asks George.

"If I was to win about fifteen million bucks in the lottery?" says Rita.

"If everyone learned to speak Cat, instead of having all these multiple dialects and languages."

"There's just one cat language?" says Rita.

"You can bring a cat off the boat from China or Sweden, one who's never heard a word of English, and we'll communicate like we've been buddies all our lives. By the way, did you know I have an IQ of 131? The Kuder Preference Tests show that I'm cut out to be a psychiatrist, a stockbroker, or a real-estate tycoon."

"Three kinds of swindlers," says Rita.

"Thank you," says George. "My Minnesota Multiphasic Personality Inventory shows that I am basically well adjusted, though mildly depressive. Which is understandable because, after all I'm a cat . . ."

"And cats suffer," said Rita and I.

"So what kind of cat are you?"

"I'm of the genus *catus archetypalis*, as opposed to *catus particularis*."

"Which means you're a plain old barn cat, a Heinz 57 of a cat?"

"Perceptive," sniffed George.

Rita is looking out the window across the prairie. I guess she's getting worried about Sanderson. He should have been back by now. When I left him he was jacking up the pick-up and letting it lurch forward a foot or two every time. I figured it would take a little over an hour to get clear of the water, then another twenty minutes to change the tire, and probably another hour or so for the spark plugs to dry out enough for the truck to start.

I think Rita and Sanderson, in spite of all their bad luck, really love each other. Sanderson has never been one to think very far ahead, and he does have a problem with latching onto things that don't belong to him. When he do win money on the rodeo circuit he's inclined to spend it foolishly, and he do drink too much, too often. But he is a happy drinker, and he never treat Rita or his daughter badly. There are a lot worse guys around than Sanderson Makes-room-for-them.

"So far all I've seen you do is talk smart and eat my food," says Rita to George. "Do something that a power animal's supposed to do. Do something that will make me strong, happy, famous, rich."

"It's not that simple."

"I'm sure," says Rita, giving George the baleful eye.

"I don't suppose you'd have some kitty litter?"

"I don't suppose," says Rita.

"You'll excuse me then, while I retire to the beautiful outdoors to relieve myself."

"You're excused."

Turning to me Rita says, "What do you think, Silas? Is this a bad hangover? Is your old buddy, Etta, sitting down in the slough cackling and shaking like four hundred pounds of Jell-o?"

Staring out the window, trying to come up with some kind of answer, I notice some movement about a quarter-mile down the road.

"That must be Sanderson."

"Thank goodness," says Rita. "You know, life may be pretty bad with Sanderson, but it'd be worse without him."

We watch the figure make its way up the road to the gate and then on toward the house. As he gets closer we can see that Sanderson is soaked from head to foot, his clothing and hair covered in thick mud. Even though he's been on a forty-minute walk, he's still wet.

"Jesus, what a mess," says Rita.

"He must have had some serious trouble with the truck," I say.

"I'm glad to see you," says Rita as we meet him at the door. "If you weren't covered in so much guck, I'd give you a hug. So what happened?"

"Son of a bitch of a truck tipped on me. Fucking near killed me. About half an hour after Silas left, the jack went over sideways, the fender pinned me right under the water."

Sanderson pulls his mud-caked work-shirt out of his pants, lifts it up and shows us a big, semicircular bruise and scrape along his left side. "It wouldn't surprise me if a couple of ribs was broken." He holds his left hand to the sore spot.

"Take your clothes off here on the doorstep," says Rita. "Take a shower and I'll see what I can do to put medicine on that scrape. Maybe I'll have to walk down to Gloria Lefthand's and phone somebody we know with a car so we can take you to the hospital in Wetaskiwin."

"Phone's cut off again, eh?"

"Day before yesterday. They got this thing about if you don't pay the bill they turn it off." Rita laughs her good-natured laugh and shrugs to show there is worse things than having your phone disconnected.

"Hey," Sanderson say, "I just want to give you a big hug and a kiss. That's all I was thinking about as I was walking all the way here."

Rita grin, and laugh happy.

"Take off that shirt, then I'll kiss you."

Sanderson Makes-room-for-them is just about to unbutton his shirt when George the Cat amble around the corner of the house.

"What are you doing here?" George says to Sanderson.

Sanderson doesn't appear to hear or see George.

"You ain't gonna believe this, Sanderson, but that scruffy excuse for a cat is supposed to be my power animal."

"What cat?" says Sanderson, staring right at George.

George stiffens his back, his ratty hair doing its best to stand on end. His rat-chewed ears stand straight out from his head. George hisses and screeches like he just found three strange cats in his own private dumpster.

"What are you guys talkin' about?" says Sanderson.

Before we can do anything, George coils and springs, landing with his back feet on Sanderson's chest, a paw hooked on each ear, his burr-infested belly blocking off Sanderson's face.

It is now Sanderson's turn to scream.

He turn and run a few steps down the path, swatting at George every step.

"What the fuck is he doing?" yells Rita. "Do something, Silas."

Sanderson is running toward the road, wildly, like a person on fire. He is screeching, cursing, swatting, but George is now fastened on the back of Sanderson's neck.

"I'll shoot the son of a bitch," yells Rita.

She pushes me out of the way and runs into the house. She comes back in about thirty seconds with a single-shot .22 rifle and a handful of cartridges which spill as she tries to stuff them in the front pocket of her jeans.

Sanderson is all the way to the gate and on his way down the road, running full out, still yelling and swatting.

Rita aims.

"Better not," I say. "Unless you got the eye of an eagle. What do you suppose got into George?"

"He must of mistook Sanderson for somebody else."

"Could it have been Sanderson he was waiting for?"

"Not likely. He's just a goddamned barn cat."

"Should we go after them?"

"When Sanderson gets to where the ditches are full of water he can leap in, that will get rid of the cat. Cats hate water."

Rita lays the gun on the top step. "I better find me the mercurochrome bottle. Sanderson is gonna look like he been picking blackberries from the inside of the briarpatch out."

Rita ain't much of a walker. We make our way slowly down the gravel road toward where Sanderson left his truck. It took me forty minutes to walk to the house, but it take us a lot longer going back, as Rita like to stop and rest and have one of my cigarettes every little while.

Finally we come over a little rise, where we can see Sanderson's truck in the deep ditch, but there is also an RCMP car there with its blue and red lights whirling, and what looks like an ambulance is just pulling away in the direction of Highway 2 and Wetaskiwin.

Though we try to hurry, it is most of a mile to the truck. When we get there we find my friend Constable Greer sitting in his RCMP cruiser, writing notes on a clipboard. Constable Greer is gentle and friendly as an old dog, which he kind of resembles, and he knows that rules is meant to be expanded, and most of the time broken.

"Rita," Constable Greer says when he sees us, "Sanderson is okay. He got his ribs banged up pretty badly, and he needs X-rays to be sure there's no internal damage."

"We know," says Rita, which draws a quizzical look from Constable Greer, who chooses to ignore it and go on with his explanation.

"Sanderson was trying to jack the truck into shallower water when the jack tipped and pinned him down. He said he figured himself for a goner. But some stranger came walking by and pulled his head above water. Sanderson says it was a big man with red hair and green eyes, called himself George. He says George wasn't strong enough to move the truck, but eventually he shifted Sanderson enough that he could get a grip on the bumper and keep his own head above water.

"Then, as near as we can figure, this George walked over to the highway and flagged down a car, told them about the accident and to call us and an ambulance as soon as they could."

Rita and I just stare at each other.

"Did you and Sanderson have a big fight or something?" Constable Greer ask Rita.

"No," says Rita.

"Sanderson's face was cut and scratched, like he'd been wrestling in a bag full of bobcats. A real mess. But he couldn't remember how it happened to him. I guess he was in shock," says Constable Greer. "I was holding him above the water while the ambulance people were getting the truck off him, and he said he had the strangest dream while he thought he was dying.

"He said he dreamed he got free from the truck and walked all the way up to your place, because he wanted to give you one last kiss before he died. But he said just as he was reaching for you, Rita, he felt like he walked into a buzz saw, and next thing he knew this fellow George was holding his head above water, and pushing at the truck with his legs.

Constable Greer eventually gave us a ride to Wetaskiwin Hospital.

"That is the weirdest story I ever heard," says Rita, as soon as we're out of the car.

"Do you think it could have really happened?" I say. "Do you think that wasn't really Sanderson came to your place, but his spirit? And George the Cat had to drive him back to the scene of the wreck in order to save his life?"

"I don't want to think about it," says Rita.

"You should," says a voice from the marigold bed.

George the Cat appears, tail straight up in greeting, looking like he just crawled out of a wet, muddy ditch.

"You really are my power animal?"

"Never underestimate your run-of-the-mill barn cat."

"Thank you," says Rita. She reach down and pet George's head.

"Just doing my job. To add to my other excellent qualities, I'm also modest."

"I see that. What can I do for you? Do you need a home? I'll buy cat food. I'll take you to the vet for a complete overhaul. You can sleep on the sofa. I won't bitch about cat hair."

"A can of salmon would be nice. Red salmon. Then I'll be on my way."

"That's all?"

"Well, if you ever need me, I'll be around. Just think hard on me. And a little fresh meat just outside the back door wouldn't be a bad incentive."

Rita feels in the pockets of her jeans.

"All I got is twenty cents and some cartridges."

"Don't look at me," I say. "I been broke for longer than I can remember."

"Not to worry," says George the Cat. "After all, I'm a cat . . ."

". . . and cats suffer," we all three say.

Conflicting Statements

Based loosely on a Japanese folktale

"What we have here, Silas, are conflicting statements," Constable Greer say to me, shuffle a bunch of white paper covered in black typewriting. Some of the sheets been stapled together at the corners. There look to be five or six sets, some only two sheets, some more.

I stopped by the RCMP office 'cause Constable Greer always gives free coffee, and because for an RCMP he is a nice man. Because he is nice, he's made it almost to retirement age without ever being promoted. His hair is gray, his shoulders a bit stooped, and he have sad pouches under his eyes like an old dog.

The conflicting statements that he have on his desk have to do with what everyone thinks was a murder here on the reserve a couple of weeks ago. Ain't nobody been arrested for it yet, and there is as many rumors going around as dandelions growing on hillsides.

"You know, Silas, I don't believe for a minute that you came by just because you like to drink this swill we call coffee," Constable

Greer say. "In fact, I'd bet," and he sort of smile at me over top of his blue-rimmed glasses, "that a bunch of your friends suggested you stop in to see what you could find out about 'The Matter of Charles Alphonse White Pheasant.' Might be that the old medicine woman insisted that you come and see me?"

"You could be right," I say. "This coffee ain't very good. I've tasted moonshine don't burn as much on its way down."

"And the old woman?"

"Mad Etta? She's out front, sitting on her tree-trunk chair in the back of Louis Coyote's pick-up truck. But really, we was just driving by when I remembered I'd like some coffee." I smile at him when I say that.

"Well, Silas," say Constable Greer, stare around to make sure we is alone, though it is obvious the RCMP office is empty at this time of night. "I can't see that it would do any harm for you to read the statements we have on file. Might even do some good if you and Etta were to quiet some of the speculation going on. This is a strange case, but the rumors I've been hearing are twice as strange as the facts."

"Ain't that always the way," I say as he hand the papers across the desk to me. The office smell of paper and floor wax, burned coffee and something sweet, maybe that liquid soap they have in the washrooms.

"If one of my young colleagues should come in, you hand it all back real quick, start drinking your coffee, and tell me about the next book you're going to write."

The first page is headed: "Statement of Fulton Firstrider." Fulton Firstrider is a cousin of my friends Rufus and Eathen. He is about eighteen, and don't go to school, work, or do much of nothing.

I was the one who found the body.

It was Tuesday morning and I woke up about six o'clock and decided to go berrying before the sun got too hot. Yeah, if you say it was August tenth, it was August tenth. I know it was Tuesday because I watched "Cagney and Lacey" on the TV the night before.

I got me a galvanized pail, put on my straw hat and headed for the blueberry muskeg. It's about two miles straight west of where I live. Of course that's the Hobbema Reserve, where do you think? One of my little brothers woke up and tagged along, even though I told him it would be too hot for him out there.

There was heavy dew on the grass and our cuffs and shoes was soaked by the time we got to the blueberry swamp. At the front edge of the muskeg, just to the right of the best berrying spot, there is a small grove of white birch trees. Maybe it was because there was a no-good smell in the air, maybe because there was a two-gallon Gainers lard pail on its side at the edge of the blueberry patch, but I decided to walk into that grove. I told my kid brother to watch my pail and pushed through the willows and into the little clearing.

That's where I found the body.

No, there was no weapon. No gun.

I recognize the guy laying there as Charlie White Pheasant. He's married to Leona Carbine, who's a cousin of mine. He might be my cousin too, everybody around here is somebody's cousin.

Charlie was laying on his side and it easy to see he been shot through the chest. His shirt was soaked with blood, dried. Didn't look as if he was still bleeding, though him and the grass around him was wet with dew. His mouth was hanging open, his lips pulled back from his teeth. His lips had dried blood on them, his teeth looked dry, and there was big green flies crawling on his mouth.

No. I didn't touch him at all. I was scared. I just stood and stared for a few seconds, then I heard my kid brother pushing his way through the willows. I didn't want him to see the body, so I ran to meet him and led him back to the berry patch.

"I want you to run back to town," I told him. "Go to where the phone is at Hobbema General Store. If Ben Stonebreaker ain't opened up yet, pound on the back door until you wake him. Tell him to call the RCMP. When they come, you lead them out here." He took off.

Yes, the grass in the clearing was bent and flattened, asters and tiger lilies was broke down. Looked to me like there might have been a good fight.

Right beside the body I seen a leather thong, a long thin one, the kind loggers use to lace their boots.

I suppose there might have been two, but I only seen one. Only other thing I seen was a bright red button in the grass, look like it come off my cousin Leona's red western shirt.

How do I know that? Cause I'd seen Leona walking around the last couple of days in a red shirt with red buttons.

The next statement was from Flora Snakeskin, who is about fifteen, live in a shack between Hobbema town and the blueberry muskeg.

> I seen them about noon the day before. That's right, Monday the ninth. I seen Charlie and Leona heading off to go berrying. No, I didn't talk to them. They were carrying a bucket, that's how I know.
>
> Clothes? She had on a silk western shirt, bright red, with a white fringe on the shoulders and across the back. I wish I had an old man who'd buy me a shirt like that. Leona was lucky to have a good husband.
>
> Charlie? He wore a creamy-colored shirt, short-sleeved, I think. They were both wearing jeans.
>
> A gun? Well, sure, Charlie always carried a gun, a sawed-off .22. He had it stuck in his belt. He shot crows and magpies for bounty and squirrels for food.
>
> Hey, if people didn't do nothin' illegal, you guys would be out of a job, right?
>
> Nah, Leona didn't do any shooting. At least I never seen her. But Charlie could pick a sparrow off a willow tree from clear across a slough.

Constable Chrétien's report was headed: "Statement of Constable Luc Pierre Chrétien."

> On the afternoon of Wednesday the eleventh, I brought the suspect, Edward Raymond Wolffinder, in for questioning. He is known as "Big Eddie" Wolffinder, first of all because he is big. I would estimate six-foot-

two and 220 pounds. He also has a young brother, age perhaps six, who is known as "Little Eddie," and a cousin called "Black Eddie" Wolffinder.

Big Eddie had only recently returned to the reserve after serving a term in Fort Saskatchewan jail. He accosted a young couple parked in an isolated spot on the reserve. He pulled the man from the car and assaulted him, then reportedly sexually assaulted the woman. At trial there was some question as to how much co-operation he received from the woman — she was an ex-girlfriend of his — so he was acquitted of the sexual assault charge and convicted of assault causing bodily harm.

Edward Raymond Wolffinder is known to law-enforcement personnel as a dangerous and volatile person.

That afternoon I found him drinking in the Alice Hotel beer parlor in Wetaskiwin, and asked him to accompany me to the RCMP headquarters to answer some questions. He was quite co-operative, even boastful, and gave a statement of his own free will. He freely admitted being in the company of Charles and Leona White Pheasant on the day in question.

Our foremost concern was to discover the where-abouts of Leona White Pheasant. At that time she had been missing for over forty-eight hours. By questioning Mr. Wolffinder, we hoped to establish if Mrs. White Pheasant was still alive or, if not, the location of her body.

He did not have a gun in his possession, though he carried a hunting knife in a sheath on his belt.

Statement of Nellie Carbine, taken Wednesday, August eleventh.

Yes, Leona White Pheasant is my daughter. Last time I seen her was three or four days ago. She's eighteen and been married to Charlie for about a year. He's five years older than her, but a nice guy. He's never raised up his hand to her that I know of, though it wouldn't surprise me if she give him cause sometimes. I was glad when they decided to get married, Leona been a big worry to me.

Well, Leona's young and pretty and, even if she is my daughter, a silly girl. She been awfully wild all her teens. If you ask me, she was real lucky not to have two or three babies by now. Charlie's a good guy, kind of serious, not very handsome. He had to take Leona on the rodeo circuit with him 'cause he couldn't trust her to behave herself at home on her own. I was sorry about Leona being like that.

I'm real sorry something happened to Charlie. I hate to think I might lose them both. I hope you catch whoever done it.

Statement of Big Eddie Wolffinder.

I killed Charlie, sort of, but not Leona. I don't know what's become of her. Honest. Hell, if I'd wasted them both I'd tell you. What have I got to lose?

I'd been staying with my cousin, Ignace Cardinal. I'd just got up, must have been about noon, and was gonna walk down to Hobbema Pool Hall and hang out until evening, when I met Charlie and Leona on the trail. They were off to go berrying. Leona hit me up for a cigarette and we got to talking and laughing. Pretty soon I was walking with them toward the berry patch. I'd seen Leona around a couple of times and kind of had my eye on her. I also knew she was trouble. She's one of those women who know how to be sexy, she could let a guy know with just one glance that she was available.

She was wearing a western shirt, silky-smooth, unbuttoned until almost all her tits showed. She not wearing a thing under that shirt. Her jeans are tight and sexy and there's a rip in one knee. Charlie wasn't very friendly, but I never let that bother me before. I knew after we all been together about two minutes that I was gonna have that sexy girl that day.

I'm a guy who always takes what he wants. I knew all I had to do was wait until some time when Charlie was away or when Leona was in town alone, but I had to have her right then.

When we got to the berry patch this grove of birch trees just past a willow-stand give me an idea.

"Hey, Charlie," I said. "Yesterday I left a bottle of moonshine stashed out under one of them birches. Let's go have ourselves a drink."

He looked like he didn't trust me, but finally he said okay. Guess he was glad to get me away from Leona. I think we both been making it pretty clear we was hot for each other.

"You start picking berries," I said to Leona, "and

when we get back we gonna check your mouth make sure it ain't blue, make sure you're picking more than you're eating." I winked at her, and she lick her lips and smile sexy.

Charlie walk ahead of me, push through the willows to the clearing. Soon as we got there, I reached around and grabbed the gun out of his belt. He was scared.

"I ain't gonna hurt you," I said. Couldn't find a thing, so I made him sit down while I unlaced one of my boots, then I tied his hands with the long leather lace. I made him put his legs one on each side of a birch sapling, and I used the second lace to tie his ankles so's he couldn't go no place.

Then I called out to Leona, "Come here! Have a shot of moonshine with us." I held the gun on Charlie to let him know I'd shoot him if he warned her. I dunno if I would of or not. Probably. I wanted her awful bad.

What she saw as she came into the clearing was Charlie tied up on the far side and me grinning at her and holding the gun. It was a dirty thing to do to both of them, but I wanted to show off. I wanted him to see how hot she was for me. I wanted her so hot for me she'd do it right in front of her husband.

I sure was surprised at what happened next.

"You son of a bitch," she said, and mean as you please kicked me in the shin. She had on pointed cowboy boots, the kind they make for women. It hurt like hell.

Here, let me show you the bruise. Look at that, still all swelled up. Looks like when we used to get drunk and have shin-kicking contests when I worked winters in the lumber camp.

I tossed the gun out of everybody's reach and grabbed onto Leona. The button holding her tits in popped off her shirt, almost hit me in the eye. I forced her down on the grass. She was fighting like a bitch, had to sit on her to pull her boots and jeans off. She was scratching at me like a bobcat. We did it then.

Yes, intercourse. What the hell you think, played checkers? I'm a good man, let me tell you. After a while she forgot she was mad at me. She moaned and cried and dug her nails into my back. She was enjoying herself.

When I was finished with her, I just figured I'd keep the gun and head on my way. I'd take my chances they wouldn't call in the Horsemen.

But while we was pulling on our clothes, she whisper to me, "What am I gonna do? He'll never live with me again. You shamed us both, you bastard. Why couldn't you wait?"

I didn't say anything.

"Fight him!" she hissed. "If he wins he'll take me back. If you win I'll be your old lady." She sure did look beautiful, tucking her red shirt in her jeans, her hair all wild and smeared across her face.

I know it's hard to understand but I believed what she said. And I wanted her more than I ever wanted anything. I'd have killed as many people as I had to to make that girl mine.

I walked across the clearing, untied Charlie's feet,

put the lace in my pocket. As I undid his hands, I said, "We'll fight. Whoever gets the gun uses it." He nodded. When I finished untying his hands I let the bootlace fall to the ground because he butted me in the belly and knocked the wind out of me. He kicked me in the face as I went down.

He sprang right over me and got to the gun. He could have shot me in the body, but he wanted to shoot me in the head, so he came in close. I hooked my right foot behind him and pulled him down, grabbing his arm as I did. We wrestled all across the clearing. I tell you, I'm a hell of a fistfighter but I never fought anybody as tough. I gradually bent his arm back until the gun was pointing at him. Then I gave his arm a real sharp pull and the gun shot him in the chest.

He slumped to the ground. There was blood in the corner of his mouth, and his breath come short and noisy like a dying animal. The gun fall out of his hand and lay on the ground. Then he gasped and his eyes rolled back in his head.

I turned toward Leona, but she was gone. I rushed to the berry patch, but she wasn't there either. I stood and listened but I couldn't hear a sound. I don't have any idea what became of her. I didn't kill her. I'd never kill her.

The next statement was on a different colored sheet of paper and was taken at RCMP Headquarters in a town called Rimbey, maybe forty miles west of Hobbema. An RCMP Constable Doerksen found Leona White Pheasant wandering, incoherent and suffering from exposure, not far from Rimbey, on the morning of Thursday, August 12, three days after she was last seen at Hobbema.

The first two pages of her statement don't tell anything that I ain't heard already, but the rest was new.

When Eddie was through with me and while we were both pulling on our clothes, I tried not to look at my husband, all tied up there and having to see what was happening to me. I sure hoped Eddie wasn't going to kill us now that he'd got what he wanted. But he hardly looked at either of us, just buckled up his belt and walked off toward the berry patch, never once looking back.

I stumbled over to Charlie, and, oh, the look on his face was something terrible to see. That look scared me half to death, told me he blamed me, wanted to kill me.

"It wasn't my fault," I whispered. He never spoke one word. His eyes were just dead full of hate for me.

I went over and picked up Charlie's gun from where Eddie had tossed it. I cocked it and put it up against my head, right in front of my ear.

"I'll kill myself if you tell me to," I said. "Just say it."

Charlie stared at me for quite a few seconds. Then he said, in a dull voice that didn't even sound like him, "Kill me first." I could tell that he meant it. There was so much pain in his eyes.

"I'll join you, I promise," I said.

I put the gun barrel against the center of his chest,

and, looking away, I pulled the trigger. He slumped over on his side. His breath made kind of a gargling sound in his throat.

A .22 holds only one bullet. I looked in all Charlie's pockets, he always carried bullets, but I couldn't find any. Maybe he forgot to bring some, maybe Eddie made him hand them over, I don't know.

I was screaming, I was so angry. I threw the gun on the ground. Then I saw that Charlie was still tied up. I couldn't leave him like that. I untied his hands and feet.

I guess I went crazy then. I wanted to kill myself, I'd promised Charlie. I was going to run until I dropped. Then I came to a creek. I tried to drown myself, but the water wasn't deep enough. I hit myself on the head with a rock. You can see the bruises, and there's a cut in my hair there. But I didn't die. I hoped maybe a bear would find me, but even that didn't happen. I was out for a couple of nights before this trapper found me and took me to the RCMP.

I don't know what's going to happen to me. I killed my husband, and I promised to follow.

What we know now was that, even though he looked like a corpse when Fulton Firstrider found him, Charlie White Pheasant wasn't dead. Constable Bobowski of the RCMP answered the call. It was her who felt Charlie's neck for a pulse, and when she found one radioed for an ambulance: the ambulance guys had to carry him on a stretcher for almost half a mile, 'cause that's as close as any trail come to the blueberry muskeg.

Charlie didn't regain consciousness until Thursday morning, about the time that trapper was finding Leona forty or fifty miles away. He was only awake for twenty minutes. Constable Greer recorded his statement at the Wetaskiwin Hospital. Charlie died that afternoon, without ever knowing what had become of Leona.

Again, the first few pages of Charlie's statement said the same things I already heard, but then he add some surprising stuff.

> When he grabbed my gun I figured he was going to kill me. But instead he tied me up and called for Leona to come into the clearing.
>
> Then he raped Leona. He went on with her for a long time. I couldn't make myself look but from the noises they made I think Leona got to liking it. I mean she's young and wild, and once she forgot that he started out by forcing her . . .
>
> When they were finished and putting on their clothes, he was talking away to her just like they were old friends. Even though I couldn't hear all that was said, I know I heard Leona laugh once, and that broke my heart open. I always been mad-jealous of her, but I loved her more than anything. I'd have always stuck by her. But I guess she didn't care.
>
> Big Eddie was saying, "Now that you been with a real man, you won't ever be satisfied with nobody but me."
>
> I could have been yelling all along, but I got my pride. Everything was my fault anyway, for letting Big Eddie trick me. I only said one thing. "Don't believe him!" That was all.

Then I heard Leona's answer, and my heart really broke open in my chest.

"Yeah," she said, and paused that way she has, and I knew she was giving him a sexy smile. "I think I might like being your old lady."

Just as her and Eddie was ready to leave, her hanging onto his hand like it was them that was married, she stopped dead still and glanced across at me, really looked at me for the first time since all this happened.

"Kill him!" she said to Big Eddie. "I don't want him telling around what I done, giving me a bad name. Shoot him!" And she yelled that three or four times, hanging like a spoiled kid on Eddie's arm, begging him to kill me.

I felt so empty. I wouldn't put up a fight. If Eddie wanted to kill me, okay.

Eddie stared at her, and he stared at me, and all of a sudden he slapped her hard, once on the forehead, once on the side of the head. She went down, rolled over, and sat up, stunned and crying, there was blood on her forehead.

"What do you want me to do with her?" Eddie asked me. "Just say the word." And stared down at her with a mean face.

"Leave her for me," I said.

When she heard that Leona sprang up and staggered through the willows toward the muskeg.

Soon as she was gone, Eddie walked over to me, his shoulders kind of slumped. He took his knife out of its sheath and cut the bootlace on my wrists. While I untied my feet he turned and walked slowly away.

When I was sure he was gone I picked up my gun, put the barrel against my chest and shot myself. A long time later, when everything was dark, I hear someone come back. I opened my eyes but it was still dark, like I was blindfolded. But I could feel someone pry my fingers off the gun.

"This is all?" I say to Constable Greer. "I mean who done what to who? Ain't you cops supposed to figure out the answer?"

"Sometimes there aren't any answers," says Constable Greer.

Dream Catcher

D elores won't talk about it with me, or my friend Frank
Fencepost, or even Joseph, our brother who's retarded. "Develop-
mentally delayed" they call Joseph now, like he's a bus that's not
on schedule.

Delores won't talk to us because we're male. She's talked some
to Ma, but not a lot. And when she wake up every night at two or
three in the morning, crying and screaming, she don't let no one
but Ma hold her.

What happened to Delores wasn't as bad as it could of been,
but Bedelia Coyote, who works down at the Rape Crisis Center in
Wetaskiwin, say it how bad Delores feels that is the important
thing. And Delores feel really bad.

She was attacked right here on the reserve, not two hundred yards from home. She'd been down at Blue Quills Hall
rehearsing with Molly Thunder's dance troupe, the Duck
Lake Massacre. Delores, when she perform, is all decked out
in blue and red feathers and beaded buckskins. She use finger

cymbals, clatter and stomp around the stage like a prairie chicken strut.

Delores was wearing jeans and a New Kids on the Block T-shirt; she carried her costume in a plastic Safeway grocery bag. She was heading up the hill from Blue Quills Hall toward home at about ten o'clock of a September Saturday night.

The guy who attacked her was somebody Delores knowed all her life, Ovide Lafrenierre, who live with his grandmother, Bertha Crossbow, in a purple-and-white Indian Affairs cabin just down the road from our place.

Ovide is about eighteen, but none of us know him very well. Dropped out of school when he was fourteen, been watching TV or playing video games from the Wetaskiwin library ever since.

He is a polite-looking boy with neat water-combed hair and hunched-up shoulders, a slight build, and brown eyes that look off over your shoulder if you talk to him. He usually wear a black corduroy jacket, black jeans, a black T-shirt, and he don't have any friends that I know of.

What Delores told Ma was that while she was walking home, she heard footsteps on the trail behind her. She figured it was me or Frank or some other neighbor. She didn't pay much attention, even when the footsteps got real close. Then somebody throw an arm around her neck, drag her down the hill into the tall grass and bullrushes of the slough, which in September is so dry the grass is crackly-brown, bullrushes ripe and soft as a horse's nose.

Delores say the person don't speak at all, but she recognize the feel of the black jacket because it is the only one like it on the reserve, plus Ovide Lafrenierre always got the warm odor of cinnamon gum about him. The moon so bright it almost like daylight, so she can tell it is Ovide soon as he turn her around and start pulling at her clothes. Delores may be only twelve but she is a lot stronger than she look. She been dancing since she was a little girl and the muscles of her legs is birch-hard. She also took karate lessons for a while and one time let go a spin kick that accidentally hit Frank in his private parts.

Frank had been teasing Delores and had hidden some of the beer bottles she collect from alongside the highway, which is why Delores is known as the Bottle Queen. All Delores intend to do was kick the cigarette out of Frank's hand, but Frank move right into the kick, squeal like a pig just had its throat cut, double up on the floor, and groan. Frank claim the world going to be deprived of any more little Fenceposts, say that he gonna have Delores charged with libel and slander, which are words he read in one of my book contracts, assault causing bodily harm, and illegal possession of lethal feet.

As Ovide Lafrenierre split her T-shirt all the way down the front, Delores kick him on the right kneecap and scream, "No! No!" loud as she can, just like she been taught at a class Bedelia Coyote and Constable B.B. Bobowski of the RCMP held in the school basement one winter.

In the clear fall air her voice carry all the way to Blue Quills Hall, and a few people there start up the hill toward her scream. Her kick to the knee knock Ovide down, but he pull Delores with him. She make her right hand stiff and poke Ovide three times in the neck, make him let out a howl, break free, and go limping off up the hill.

I been known to make a lot of fun of the RCMP, but they handle everything about Delores' case quick and efficient. Me and Ma and Delores ride in Constable Greer's patrol car all the way to Wetaskiwin, where he phone to get Constable Bobowski down to

RCMP headquarters. It being a Saturday night, she was in a frilly dress with a white shawl over her shoulders. I hardly recognize her without her RCMP hat, with her blonde hair hanging loose over her shoulders.

Constable Bobowski take Delores into her office and keep her there for over an hour. She come out a couple of times, whisper to Constable Greer. Constable Greer strap on his gun, which usually live like a weasel in the bottom drawer of his desk, say he driving back to the reserve to arrest the perpetrator.

"As long as he get Ovide Lafrenierre, I don't care who else he arrest," Ma say to me in Cree.

When Constable Greer bring him in, at four in the morning, Ovide don't look very dangerous, just a skinny, sleepy-eyed little wimp with a bad knee. He can't raise no bail so have to stay in jail for the three months until his trial.

When Delores get called to testify, they clear the courtroom even of me and Ma.

At home that night, Delores tell as much as she can remember. She say both the lawyers were nice to her. The prosecutor lawyer was a pale young fellow look like he should still be in high school. Ovide's lawyer, a good-looking Indian guy, come all the way from Calgary.

That defence lawyer ask if she knew Ovide before, and if they ever talked or visited, and if he ever tried to do anything to her before. Then he ask if Delores ever played with Ovide, and Delores say that a few times when she was younger Ovide been outside playing with her and her friends, and that they all kick a soccer ball around, and that they might have played tag or kick-the-can.

"Did you ever wrestle with Ovide Lafrenierre?" the lawyer ask.

"Well, sort of," Delores tell him. "One time Ovide chased us little kids around, pretending he was a bear and was going to eat us up."

"And did he wrestle you to the ground?"

"Yes."

"And was it all in fun? Or were you afraid of him?"

"It was all in fun."

"At that time did Ovide Lafrenierre hurt you in any way?"

"No."

"Isn't it possible that when on the night in question Ovide Lafrenierre put his arm around you and tried to wrestle you down, he was just continuing the game?"

"I don't think so," Delores answer.

"But you're not sure?"

"It was different."

"How?"

"It wasn't the same."

"Can you tell me how it was different?"

"He was going to hurt me."

"Did he say he was going to hurt you?"

"No."

Delores say the lawyer keep asking those same questions, in different words, for a long, long time.

That defence lawyer call up as a witness Ben Stonebreaker who run the general store on the reserve.

"How many packages of cinnamon gum do you sell in a week?" he ask Ben.

"Thirty or forty," Ben answer.

Then he call a person from the company that make the jacket Ovide was wearing.

"How many of these jackets did your company manufacture?"

The fellow look at a computer page he got in his hand.

"Three thousand."

"And during what period of time were they shipped to retail stores?"

The fellow explain they started to manufacture them three years before, ship the last of them six months ago.

"How many were shipped to stores in Alberta?"

The man consult his computer page. "One thousand, nine hundred, approximately."

"No further questions," say the lawyer.

Ovide's grandmother, Bertha Crossbow, need a Cree-speaking translator because she is an old-fashioned Indian lady, wear a long, dark skirt and matching babushka, and never spoke a word of English in her life. I guess, like most older Indian people, she figure any white-man oath don't mean a thing, so she only say things that be good for Ovide's side.

Mrs. Crossbow say Ovide been a good boy all his life, never in no trouble and so shy he don't want to leave home, even though he was one time offered a job as a clerk in a video store in Wetaskiwin.

Then she swear that Ovide was home with her the night he attacked Delores. She say she sat in the kitchen all night listen to the singing sounds of Ovide's video games, and that Ovide never left the house even for one minute.

"There ain't enough evidence to convict," the judge say.

Ovide is free to go home.

We decide to make a social call on Ovide Lafrenierre.

"We ain't gonna do him no physical harm," say Frank, after his girl Connie Bigcharles say she's afraid we gonna get ourselves in trouble. "Guy like Ovide ain't as valuable as roadkill."

Out of the darkness at the back of her cabin, Etta sit high up on her tree-trunk chair, sip from a bottle of Lethbridge Pale Ale. The light from the coal-oil lamp glint off the rim of the bottle, amber as a cat's eye.

"There are other ways of dealing with him," Etta say.

Delores was waking up only once a night instead of two or three times, but Ovide was back living right near us, and Delores say she don't want to go out of the house at all. Ma has to walk her to school and back. And instead of bouncing into the cabin all pink-faced from the cold weather, Delores stay in her room, don't even have friends over to play.

One day after Frank fire up his Poulan chainsaw he take a few whacks at a spruce stump behind his cabin. Then he take a few more, and before long that stump look like a face, and before long it isn't just any face, but Chief Tom Crow-eye, complete with the sullen smirk we all love to hate.

Frank could probably make some money from his talent. Some guys carve out animal shapes from big chunks of tree trunk at flea markets and the opening of auto dealerships. Trouble is, what Frank carve best is little men with penises big as their bodies. Self-portraits, Frank call them. Frank been chased off from a craft fair or two because his art embarrass the old white ladies who come to buy Depression glass or velvet pillows with the face of Jesus or Elvis in sequins.

About eight o'clock one night a dozen or so of us, including

Bedelia Coyote, gather in front of Old Lady Crossbow's cabin. Frank fire up the chainsaw which belch out blue smoke and make the air stink of oil and gas.

Eventually, she peek out a window then come to the door.

"Send Ovide out," we say.

"What you gonna do to him?"

We feel a little sorry for the old lady. One of her daughters gone off to the city, had Ovide, then died of drinking Lysol or huffing WD-40. The welfare brought Ovide to Mrs. Crossbow when he was about four, said he been abused something awful. Old Lady Crossbow didn't have to take him, but she did. Ain't her fault he grown up to be a pervert.

"We want him to watch a demonstration," says Bedelia. "We won't hurt him. But if he don't come out we'll come in and get him."

Mrs. Crossbow go away for a long time. If there was a back door Ovide would have been long gone, but there ain't. So after a long while she bring Ovide to the door, though he stand behind her and look as if he wish he was far away.

"You don't need to be scared of us *tonight*," Bedelia say.

Frank step forward, the belching chainsaw in one hand, a crooked piece of tamarack, with a foot and a leg from the knee down carved out in the other.

"Just in case you ever get the urge to attack another girl the way you did Delores Ermineskin," Frank say, "here's what gonna happen. We'll come round for a visit in the middle of the night, truss you up like a bundle of oats, and whittle little pieces off you like this."

Frank hold up the tamarack leg, touch the blade to the foot part, and the little toe go spinning down onto the ground.

One by one, Frank amputate the toes.

"When the toes are all gone we take off pieces of your foot about an inch at a time. When we get up to your knee, we start on the other leg."

Even though he ain't bleeding, Ovide Lafrenierre get paler by the minute.

"We'll take our time. Etta be there to stop the bleeding, make sure you stay awake to enjoy the show. We wouldn't want you to get off easy and die."

Etta wave a big hand at Ovide, let him know Frank ain't just making things up.

"You getting the picture?" Bedelia ask Ovide.

He nod.

"I seen healthier looking dead people," says Bedelia, as we walk away.

It is Etta who bring the dream catcher to our cabin.

"I got something for Delores," she say to me when I stop by her place on my way home from the Tech School. She suggest I drive her over to our place. When Etta suggest something it is good as law.

A dream catcher been hanging on the curtain of Etta's cabin for years and years but I figure it is mostly superstition.

The dream catcher Etta bring for Delores is fresh made from a red willow sapling, bent into a circle about four inches across. The ends are sewed together and heavy thread criss-cross the circle make a web kind of like a volleyball net. They says if you hang a dream catcher by your bedroom window it will catch the bad dreams and the good dreams will slip through the holes.

Almost ever since she was attacked, Delores go to see a

counselor in Wetaskiwin once a week, talk with this lady about how she feel, but those sessions don't seem to be doing much good. Delores is still depressed, frightened, wake every night crying, and don't leave our cabin unless she forced to.

"I figure we've given all this talk stuff enough of a chance," says Etta. She go into Delores' bedroom, stay a long time, talking softly to Delores.

It been two weeks now since Etta fastened the dream catcher on the curtain by Delores' bed. The first night I got up and checked on her a couple of times, the way I been doing every night. She was tossing and turning a lot, had the sheet all wound around two or three times, whimpered some, but she didn't once wake up crying and frightened the way she usually do.

By the end of a week I don't have to check on her no more. She sleeps calm on her back with her head on the pillow, the covers hardly disturbed at all, a little bump about halfway down the bed where her feet stick up.

During the daytime Delores is happier, too. She invite Tanya Little Circle over to play Barbie dolls, and she laugh and shriek with her friend the way she used to. She even getting to like me and Joseph again. The other morning she give me a hug around the neck like she always did, and I seen her cuddled up in Joseph's lap.

"It worked," I tell Etta.

Etta just stare at me, raise one of her old, gray eyebrows maybe half an inch, let me know there was never a doubt, and that she is a little annoyed I feel I have to report back to her.

What Etta do admit to me later on, while she boil us up some cocoa on her big cookstove, is that there is also a dream catcher can hold on to the good dreams only, let the bad ones slip through.

"Did you?" I ask.

Etta let me know by her expression this don't deserve an answer either.

I notice then, that even in the dull light of Etta's coal-oil lamp, with a wick that always burn crooked at one corner, there are scratches across Etta's cheeks and forehead, look like she been in a bag with a bobcat. And the backs of her hands are in even worse shape.

"There is a real nasty bank of blackberry vines behind Old Lady Crossbow's cabin," I say. "Grow right up to that skunk's bedroom window."

Etta look at me like she just push aside a rock and there I am.

Walking home, the moon is bright as a penny in a high, clear sky. Everything is night-silent except for the occasional yelp of a lonely dog and the crackle of the Northern Lights.

At Old Lady Crossbow's house, I step stealthily across her front yard, and down the side of the cabin to the bank of blackberry vines, take a scratch on the cheek staring along the back of the house toward Ovide's bedroom.

From the window come a wild eerie sound, a nightmare clawing its way out of a throat, the cry of an animal been hurt sudden and bad. I hear the flap of an owl taking off from one of the tamarack trees behind the cabin. It look to me like the dream catcher that hang from the corner of the sash is wiggling in the moonlight though there ain't even a hint of a breeze.

Brother Frank's
Gospel Hour

O ne of the weird things the government does for us Indians, not that everything the government does for us ain't weird in some way, is they provide money for us to have our own Indian radio station. The station is KUGH, known as K-UGH. The call letters were chosen a long time ago by Indians with a sense of humor. The white men are always a little embarrassed saying the name, so they call it K-U-G-H.

A year or so ago I read a letter in an Indian magazine, maybe it was the *Saskatchewan Indian*, where some woman was complaining, saying it was demeaning for it to be called K-UGH. One of the problems of Indians getting more involved in the everyday world is that they lose their sense of humor.

To tell the truth no one I know on the reserve pay much attention to the radio station. It originate in someplace like Yellowknife, which is about a million miles north of us, and instead of playing good solid country and loud rock 'n' roll, it is mainly talk, in a lot of dialects. It is a place for people to complain, which is the national pastime in Canada, the one thing whites and Indians, French and English, and everybody else got in common. And it seem like the smaller the minority the louder they whine.

It does have a news program called the "Moccasin Telegraph," where the title been stolen from a story I wrote quite a few years ago. People send messages to friends and relatives who are out on their traplines or who just live hundreds of miles from anywhere and they can't get to pick up their mail but once or twice a year.

"This here's to Joe and Daisy up around Mile 800. Cousin Franny's got a new baby on the eighteenth, a boy, Benjamin. Oscar wrecked his car, eh? We're doin' fine and see you in the spring. Sam and Darlene."

There would be an hour or more of messages like that run every night.

K-UGH would have gone on forever with only a few people noticing it, but somebody in the government get the idea that things got to be centralized. That way everybody get to share in the money the government waste.

First we know of it is when one morning a couple of flatdeck trucks arrive at the reserve loaded down with concrete blocks. They followed by another flatdeck with a bulldozer and three or four pick-up trucks painted dismal Ottawa government green, full of guys in hard hats who measure with tapes, look through little telescopes and tie red ribbons to willow bushes and to stakes they pound in the ground.

That first night it is like a pilgrimage from the village to the construction site, which is on the edge of a slough down near the highway. By morning almost everybody who need concrete blocks have a more than adequate supply.

People got their front porches propped up, and I bet twenty

families have concrete-block coffee tables. A couple of guys are building patios. I helped myself to a few pieces of lumber as well and my sister Delores and me made some bookshelves for the living room. Me and Delores each own about two hundred books at least, and until now they been living in boxes under our beds.

Nobody bother to tell the construction people that the place they planning to build on will disappear under about three feet of slough water when the snow melt in the spring or when we get a gully-washer of a thunderstorm, which happens about twice a week through the summer. But it is fall now and the grass is dry and crackly, and there is the smell of burning tamarack in the air, and the sun shines warm.

The construction men get awful mad about all the concrete blocks that disappear. They yell loud as school teachers, but we just stand around watching them, don't say nothing. A guy in an unscratched yellow hard hat say he going to send a truck through the village pick up every concrete block he sees.

Mad Etta, our medicine lady, stand up slowly from her tree-trunk chair, her joints cracking like kindling snapping. She waddle over to the foreman.

"You got a brand on your concrete blocks like the farmers over west of here have on their cattle?"

The foreman scratch his head. "No." And after he think a while he decide that collecting back concrete blocks ain't such a good idea. But that foreman have a long talk with someone on his cellular phone and the next load of concrete blocks have a big red R stamped on them that there is no scratching off.

"By the way," Etta say to the foreman, "what is it you're building?"

Rumors been going round that they gonna build public washrooms like they have at highway rest stops. Somebody else says the government going to build a Petro Canada service station, though the spot ain't within two miles of any kind of regular road.

"We're buildin' a twenty-by-twenty concrete-block building," says the foreman. "What they do with the building after we're finished ain't no concern of ours. Our department just build."

"I'm sure you do," says Etta, which the foreman take as positive.

The building seem too small to house anything important.

"I bet they gonna store nuclear waste, or a whole lot of these here PCBs," me and Frank say to Bedelia Coyote, knowing this will send Bedelia's blood pressure up about 100 percent. Bedelia belong to every protest group ever march with a clenched fist. She been out in British Columbia picketing the forest industry for cutting on Indian land, and down in southern Alberta trying to stop the dam on the Oldman River. Bedelia turn paranoid if you even hint somebody might be doing something not good for Indians or the environment.

"Her natural shade is green as I feel after partying all Saturday night," Frank say.

Bedelia kind of scoff but it's only a day or two until her and her friends is investigating like crazy, trying to find which government department is building the concrete-block building and for what.

"If you want something done all you got to do is delegate somebody to do it for you, even if they don't exactly understand that they been delegated," say Frank, smile his gap-toothed smile.

By the time Bedelia and her friends pin down what the building is for, a couple of flatdeck trucks is bringing in pieces of skeletal metal that eventually going to be a tall antenna with a red light on top to keep away airplanes.

"It's going to be a radio station," Bedelia shout as she crash through the door of the pool hall. "They're going to move the Indian radio station here to the reserve."

We didn't suspect it then, but those words were going to change the lives of me and my friends forever.

After the construction workers leave, a group of men in white coats arrive, unpack boxes full of electronic stuff. By peeking through the only window in the building we can see them with little soldering irons, hooking all this stuff together. There is a couple of snow-white satellite dishes set behind the building. The installers push some buttons, and the satellite dishes hum and turn, pointing their centers, which have a big stick like in the middle of a flower, at different parts of the sky.

There are boards full of flashing red, green, and blue lights that run the whole length of the building, which is divided into three cubicles, one big and two little, each one outlined by thick, clear-plastic walls.

One of Bedelia's "friends in high places," as she calls them, sends her a press release all about the Indian radio station K-UGH being moved to our reserve. It's part of a process of central-ization of federal government and Department of Indian Affairs affiliates, whatever that might mean.

Painters turn up and paint the building all white on the outside (not a good sign, Bedelia says) with the call letters K-U-G-H in big green letters with red feathers, like part of a head dress, trail-ing off from each end.

At night we are able to receive K-UGH on our radios, but it still broadcasting from Whitehorse or Yellowknife, or one of those places with an Indian name. And it's still mainly talk and go off the air at 11:00 p.m., just when real radio listeners are waking up.

Frank, who is able to open doors by not doing much more than looking at them, let us into the radio building. Frank push every button he can reach, but nothing appear to be hooked up. We all go into the room with the microphone and Frank sit himself down in front of that microphone and pretend he is on the air.

"Good evening, all you handsome people out in radio land. This here's Frank Fencepost, a combination of whiskey, money, and great sex, all things that make people feel good, just waiting to make you happy."

"Make-up," say Frank's girl, Connie Bigcharles. "I need lots of make-up to be happy."

"A CD player," add my girl, Sadie One-wound.

"A credit card," say Rufus Firstrider.

"With no credit limit, and they never send a bill," say Rufus' big brother, Eathen Firstrider.

"And one of them Lamborzucchini cars that go about a thousand miles an hour," says Robert Coyote.

"World peace," say his sister, Bedelia.

"Boo!" we all say.

Then Frank ask the question that in just a few months will make him a little bit famous, and maybe gonna make him real famous.

"What do you need to make you happy? Tell Brother Frank, my friends. Brother Frank can make your dreams come true."

He repeat the question.

"I want you to pick up the phone, brothers and sisters. I want you to pick up a pen and write to Brother Frank in care of the station to which you are listening. I want all you wonderful people to let me know what it would take to make you happy."

"You're crazier than usual," we say to Frank.

"Thank you," says Frank. "But I think I'm on to something here. I sure wish I could figure out how to turn this equipment on. I really want to talk to people."

"Get a life," somebody says.

A few days later the radio station go on the air. One afternoon two cars pull up and park in front of the concrete-block building. A thin Indian with a braid, dressed in jeans and a denim jacket, get out of one, and a hefty Indian, look like he could be a relative of Mad Etta, get out of the other car.

"We been expecting you," Frank say, sticking out his hand to the thin Indian. "I am Fencepost, aspiring broadcast journalist. Me and my friends are at your service."

Both guys look at us real strangely. The thin one is Vince Gauthier, the announcer. The fat guy is Harvey Many Children, the engineer.

That's it. Takes just two Indians to operate K-UGH. Vince open the mail, decide which letters get read on the air. He do all the talking. Harvey make sure what Vince says gets out over the air. Other people, maybe in Edmonton or somewhere, sell advertising, fax in the commercials and the times when Vince is supposed to read them.

The station only open from 3:00 p.m. to 11:00 p.m. Monday to Friday.

"If there's a holiday, the station ain't open," Vince tell us. They can only afford two employees. When Harvey go on holidays, I have to do both jobs. You think that ain't fun . . . . When I go on holidays the station shut down for three weeks."

Vince and Harvey ain't very friendly at first, but Frank just study them and, as he says, figure their angles.

"Everybody wants something. Harvey's easy. We just bring him food. McDonald's, Kentucky Fried, chicken fried steak from Miss Goldie's Café. That will get us in the door. But Vince is the important one. I can't figure his angle yet."

It sure ruffle Frank's feathers some that I am the one Vince invite to be on the air.

"I know your name from someplace," he say to me the second day we hanging around while they is working.

"'America's Most Wanted,'" say Frank.

Vince stare Frank into the concrete floor.

"I've written a few books," I say.

"Okay, you're *that* Silas Ermineskin. How about I have you on the show tomorrow? Bring your books in and we'll talk about them. I've always meant to read one of your books, but I never got around to it."

"That's what everybody say," I tell him.

"What about talking to me?" says Frank. "I'm the one inspired Silas to write. 'Sit down at your typewriter for three hours every day,' I tell him. Besides, I'm the one got him to learn to read and write. Also, I'm the handsomest Indian in at least three provinces . . ."

"This is radio," says Vince. "Girls think I sound handsome. And I never discourage them."

Now Vince is a scrawny little guy with a sunk-in chest and a complexion look like it been done with a waffle iron.

"I just figured me an angle," says Frank.

One thing that puzzles me is how many people actually listen to the radio. I mean *really* listen. We have the radio for background in the truck or on portable radios.

"Sometimes we have over twelve thousand listeners," Vince tell us. "For an area where trees outnumber people a hundred to one, that ain't bad."

We try to behave ourselves when we're at the radio station, and Frank coach Rufus Firstrider, who have a natural talent for electrical things, to see what it is Harvey do to make the station come on the air every afternoon and shut off at night.

One afternoon when I walk down to the station about an hour before opening time, I find Frank Fencepost sitting in the sun reading the Bible.

"Once you learn there's no telling what you'll end up reading," Frank say, smile kind of sickly. We've had lots of people who flog the Bible, from Father Alphonse, who come pretty close to being human, to Pastor Orkin of the Three Seeds of the Spirit, Predestinarian, Bittern Lake Baptist Church, who hate everybody who don't believe just like him.

"You know what I done?" Frank ask.

"Applied to have a sex change?"

Frank stare at me in surprise.

"A lucky guess," I say.

"I got out my Webster's dictionary and I looked up the word gospel. We think of it as all the 'you can't do that or you'll go to hell for sure' stuff. But it really mean 'good news.' I got me some really strong ideas. I just got to figure how I can get Vince to let me talk on the radio."

The day Frank got his Webster's dictionary, about a dozen of us go into the book store in Wetaskiwin. Everybody is looking at something different. I'm actually buying the new book by my favorite author, Tony Hillerman, who write about a kind old

Indian policeman, Lt. Joe Leaphorn, who remind me of Constable Greer, the one really good RCMP in our area. Frank stuff a big dictionary with a rainbow-colored cover under the raincoat he borrowed from Mad Etta without asking and boogie right out of the store.

"I'm the one who needs a good dictionary," I say to Frank in the parking lot.

"Steal your own," says Frank. But later on he get soft-hearted, like Frank usually do, and let me keep the dictionary near to my typewriter, though Frank spend a lot of time at my place reading in it. Frank try to learn a new word every day, and use it in a sentence, which get pretty tiresome when he try to use words like *gleet*, which mean sheep snot, or sutler, which mean a person who follows an army and sells them provisions. Not words for everyday conversation.

Every night at suppertime, Rufus Firstrider make a run into Wetaskiwin and come back with lots of fast food. Those forays sure cut into our spending money, but we're willing to help Frank as much as we can. Harvey, when he's full of fatty foods, take Rufus under his wing, and in a week Rufus knows how to turn on the radio station and get Frank's voice out on the airwaves.

We watch the station close up at 11:00 p.m., wait an hour, then Frank open the door like he never heard of the word *lock*.

Before we turn on the lights we hang a heavy blanket over the window.

Rufus fuss with some switches. Then, from his glassed-in cage he signal Frank that it is okay to talk. A big red light come on over the door, say "In Use."

"K-UGH is going to present a special program one hour from now," Frank say. " 'Brother Frank's Gospel Hour' will ask the question, 'What does it take to make you happy?' Be sure and tune in."

He make announcements like that every five minutes from midnight to 1:00 a.m. Then at one o'clock he cue up some music that he had me hunt up. The station have only about a hundred tapes. This one's some outfit with bagpipes playing "Amazing Grace."

"Welcome to 'Brother Frank's Gospel Hour.' Brother Frank wants everyone to feel as good as he feels, to be as happy as he is . . ."

And he's off and running.

"Silas," Frank has been telling me for weeks, "I'm gonna combine theology, mythology, history, ritual, and dream. Seems to me that covers everything. Got to have some Christian connection in order to get money, people will give to anything that they even suspect of being religious. And dreams is how we work in the Indian part."

Frank talk for a while about how everybody deserve to feel good, to be happy, to have enough to eat, a dry place to sleep, good friends, and happy dreams.

"Now, what I'm wondering, as I talk to this big, old microphone, is, is there anybody out there? If you're listening, call Brother Frank on the phone," and he give the area code 403, and K-UGH's telephone number. "We accept collect calls. Just let us know you're listening. Tell us what you need to make you happy. And if you got an idea, tell us how we could improve 'Brother Frank's Gospel Hour.' Remember, gospel means 'good news.' And Brother Frank is gonna make good news happen to you."

Frank sigh, and point to Rufus, who flip a switch and a trio start singing "Let the Sunshine In."

Frank has hardly lit up a cigarette when the phone rings.

"'Brother Frank's Gospel Hour,'" I say, in kind of a whisper. I'm betting it's either Vince or Harvey giving us five minutes to clear out of the station or they'll call the RCMP.

"Collect from Jasper, Alberta," say an operator's voice.

"Go ahead."

"Brother Frank is the biggest idiot I ever heard on the radio," say a man's booming voice. He apply a couple of unpleasant curse words to Frank, and a couple more to me, then he slam the receiver in my ear.

"Wrong number," I say. "They wanted a tow truck."

"Hey, I would of got them a tow truck," say Frank. "There is nothing Brother Frank and the power of prayer can't accomplish."

The record is about over before the phone ring again.

"Hello," say what sound like a young woman's voice.

"Go ahead," I say.

"If I tell you what I need to make me happy, what are you gonna do about it?"

"Maybe I should let you talk to Brother Frank," I say.

I nod to Frank. He nod to Rufus who got more music ready to go.

"What can Brother Frank do for you?" Frank ask.

"You really want to know what will make me happy?" say the girl.

"That is Brother Frank's purpose in life."

"I need a CD player and the latest Tanya Tucker CD."

"Don't we all," says Frank, with his hand over the receiver. "Why would that make you happy?"

"Because my parents belong to a religion that thinks music is sinful. I have to sneak my radio on under my covers after they're asleep."

"A day without music is like a day without sex," say Frank. "Give me your name and address and Brother Frank will mail you enough money to buy a CD player and Tanya Tucker." Frank write for a minute. "You start watching the mail. And when you get your own money, you make a contribution to 'Brother Frank's Gospel Hour,' so we can help somebody else."

The girl bubble with thank yous, and promise to send money when she is able.

"See, that wasn't so hard," says Frank.

"Only trouble is we don't have any money to send her," I point out. "All that's gonna happen is she'll watch an empty mailbox for a month or two."

"Never underestimate Fencepost Power," says Frank.

Frank launch right in. "Our motto is, 'Before my needs, the needs of others,'" Frank say, and he explain the girl who live in a house without music and ask listeners to send in a dollar or ten dollars to make other people happy.

Within an hour we got an old lady who need money to pay her heating bill. Another old lady need money to take her pet cat to the vet. And a woman who sound about thirty call to say her husband drunk up the welfare check and her kids is hungry, what will make her happy is a few groceries.

"Wow," says Frank. "I think we touched a nerve."

We get stupid calls, too. Smart-ass guys, sound like Frank just a few weeks ago, want money for beer, or a date with Madonna, or to touch the jockstrap of Mario Lemieux, the famous French hockey player.

Frank, without using any names, tell the stories of the people in need.

"Brother Frank going to see that those little kids don't go

hungry, and that lady don't have to be cold, and that cat gets to the hospital. If I have to steal to do it, I will. But you can help. Send what you can, a dollar, five dollars, ten thousand," and Frank chuckle, "to 'Brother Frank's Gospel Hour,' c/o K-UGH Radio," and he give the station's box number in Wetaskiwin.

Frank stay on the air until 3:00 a.m.

"Brother Frank will visit with you again tomorrow. And may *your* Great Spirit, whatever that may be, never rain on your parade."

Rufus shut off the equipment and give Frank the thumbs-up sign like we seen Harvey give Vince.

"From now on, Silas, you pick up Brother Frank's mail every day. Wouldn't want all this money fall into the wrong hands."

We kept expecting Vince or Harvey to discover what we been doing, but Frank keep up his late-night broadcasting.

I check the mail box every day, but there is nothing addressed to "Brother Frank's Gospel Hour."

People's requests all translate into money. The people who call in come mostly from a long way off. That girl without music live in a place called Blueberry Mountain, hundreds of miles up north.

Frank, doing some creative borrowing at a K-Mart in Edmonton, acquire the CD player, but among us all we couldn't raise the postage to mail it.

Connie stand in line at a post office, ask for seven dollars' worth of stamps, then just pick them up and walk out. The clerk yelling like crazy, but not running after her.

"They wouldn't feel so bad if they knew they were contributing to making someone happy," says Frank, as he stuff the parcel into a slot at the main post office.

One morning me and Frank head off to Calgary in Louis

Coyote's pick-up truck. Frank, he want to hear an evangelist on a Calgary radio station. This fellow he got a twang in his voice sound like the real Hank Williams used to.

"Entertainment, and touching the heart is what it's all about," says Frank. "I got to have the qualities of a good country singer, a striptease dancer, and . . ."

"A welder," I say.

"Damn right. A good entertainer melt solder with his bare hands. Look into that, Silas. See if there's a magic trick where I can pretend to melt metal."

We figure the place to listen to a radio in comfort would be at my sister's house up in the hills in northwest Calgary. It's been over a year since we visited.

I have to admit Brother Bob treat my sister pretty good, but he been insulting Frank and me ever since he first met us. He sic the police on us more than once, not that we are totally innocent. We one time wreck Brother Bob's new car, and another time we put live horses in his brand new house. Last time here, Frank did a certain amount of damage to the computer system at the finance company my brother-in-law manage. Brother Bob McVey make it clear we ain't welcome at either his home or his business. But we figure time dim the bad things, and we make sure to arrive in the middle of the afternoon.

Only trouble is, he at home.

"How come you ain't off repossessing trucks from poor Indians?" Frank ask when Brother Bob answer the door.

Brother Bob don't look very good. He is wearing a bathrobe and ain't shaved in, I bet, half a week. I always figure Brother Bob woke up already shaved.

He just wave us into the living room, where my sister Illianna patching some of little Bobby's jeans.

"You sick or something, Brother Bob?" I ask.

Brother Bob just stare at "The Price Is Right" on TV. Illianna answer for him. "Bob's been out of work — almost nine months now. He's feeling kind of depressed."

Illianna explain that the big finance company Brother Bob managed went out of business. They loaned millions of dollars to companies in the oil patch, and since the price of oil been going down forever, those companies couldn't pay their loans. The finance company close up after they used up all the company pension fund trying to stay in business. Brother Bob don't get a dime in layoff pay for all his years with the company, plus he lose all his pension money.

"Why don't you get another job?" Frank ask.

"There aren't any jobs in Bob's field. In case you haven't noticed," Illianna answer, "the economy is really bad."

"Sorry," says Frank. "Being unemployed all my life, it's hard to tell."

"I've been trying to get a job," says Illianna, "but it's years since I worked, and then I was just waiting tables. All I could earn as a waitress wouldn't pay the mortgage. Silas, I don't know what we're gonna do."

"I got maybe sixty dollars," I say.

"And you got my good wishes," says Frank. "But I got a scam going that gonna make us all rich. Six months from now Fencepost will offer you a job. Fencepost might even offer Brother Bob a job." Frank consider that possibility for a moment, then say, "Nah."

After that we are kind of uncomfortable. We wait long

enough to give little Bobby a hug when he get home from school, then we listen to the evangelist in the truck at a truck stop on Deerfoot Trail.

On the fifth day there are two letters addressed to "Brother Frank's Gospel Hour." I rush them back to the pool hall and Frank rip them open. One contain a two-dollar bill, the other a useless one-dollar loonie coin.

We is all pretty disappointed.

Frank is getting five to ten calls every night from people in need. It surprising how small people's wants are. A pair of eyeglasses, a toy, shoes, some dental work so someone can look passable when they go job hunting. Frank has written down everybody's requests along with their names and addresses in a notebook. There is close to forty and it don't look like we going to be able to fill none of them.

"If people could just see me in person," says Frank. "I could convince them to part with their money. We'd pay off the needy people and have a lot left over for us. Guess I'm gonna have to do like these real evangelists and beg hard."

Turn out the problem wasn't Frank, but our usual bad mail service. After about eight days, the mail box start to fill up. There is fourteen letters one day, total eighty dollars in cash and checks. The next day there is twenty-six letters, with over a hundred dollars. The lady from Drumheller get her grocery money. The lady from Obed get to pay her heating bill.

That night Frank thank people for their kindness, he get a tear in his voice as he say there is so much to do and so little time and money.

It take Bedelia and me and even Frank's girl, Connie Bigcharles, to talk him out of imitating that famous evangelist, I think it was Oral Robertson, who claim he going to be called to heaven if he don't get enough money donated from his followers.

"For one thing, we don't think you'd be called to heaven," we tell Frank. "For another, Oral Robertson didn't get all the money he craved, and he didn't die."

"All he got, I think, was a toothbrush named after him," says Connie Bigcharles.

"It would attract attention to me," says Frank. "That's what being a celebrity is all about. I read somewhere that unless you get caught in bed with little boys, all publicity is good publicity."

"Or unless, like that other evangelist, you get caught in the back seat of your car with a working girl."

"What's wrong with that?" says Frank. "I been in more back seats than a McDonald's wrapper."

Frank finally see things our way.

"Was that good, or what?" Frank say, after he is off the air. "I never knew I could get that catch in my voice. I figure I'm worth about a thousand dollars a tear from now on."

What Frank say is true.

In another week the requests are only twenty dollars or so ahead of the income. And the prospects are looking righteous. Unfortunately, whenever something is going good, something go wrong.

I only take the mail addressed to "Brother Frank's Gospel Hour." How am I supposed to know that people are writing to K-UGH to say how much they enjoy Frank's program?

One morning when I go to pick up the mail, Vince been there before me.

Vince and Harvey ain't mad. They just want a cut.

"Word will get back to the higher-ups eventually, but until

then, you got a great scam going. We checked in on your broadcast last night. You, Mr. Frank, have got charisma."

"I hear you can get antibiotics for that," says Frank.

For 10 percent off the top, Vince and Harvey agree to be deaf, dumb, and blind to "Brother Frank's Gospel Hour." There was nearly four hundred dollars in that day's mail.

We have to open up a bank account for "Brother Frank's Gospel Hour" at the Bank of Montreal in Wetaskiwin. Frank and me and Bedelia Coyote are the ones who can write checks. Frank cut Bedelia in because she got the stamina to deal with government.

"There is ways for every dollar we take in to be tax free, and I'm gonna research all those ways," Bedelia say.

Another month and Frank just keep getting better. Soon, there is actually money left over when the requests are filled.

"We put a definite five-hundred-dollar limit on what we pay out," Frank says. "I mean, no sex-change operations that ain't covered by medical insurance. No vans for the handicapped, no matter how worthy the cause. Three hundred dollars for bus tickets so Granny can see the daughter and new grandchild is what we're all about. That draw more tears than a $40,000 van for some guy who can only move two fingers and his pecker."

Things get complicated when the newspapers start coming around, wanting to interview Brother Frank. Soon as the stories run, the bigwigs at K-UGH start asking a lot of questions.

Since I am the worrier, I worry we been doing something illegal, and maybe all of us, or especially Frank, could go to jail.

But the bigwigs at K-UGH find that after only six weeks, "Brother Frank's Gospel Hour" draw more listeners at two in the morning than all their regular shows.

Frank get called in to K-UGH, and me and Bedelia go with

him. There is three guys in suits, one come all the way from Toronto, which, they tell us, is where everything really happen.

"Then how come I never been there?" Frank ask. He live life like he got nothing to lose. And I guess that's true. Until now.

The suit from Toronto chuckle politely, then offer Frank a contract and the 9:00 p.m. to 11:00 p.m. broadcast time.

"We'd like to offer you a five-year contract at $60,000 a year, rising $5,000 each year, so by the end of the contract you'll be making $80,000 a year," the Toronto suit say.

"I bet that's almost as much as the guys on 'Stampede Wrestling' make," says Frank.

At this point Bedelia Coyote break into the conversation. Bedelia has studied accounting by mail, and she has studied business management by mail, as well as how to organize a demonstration and how to get your organization's name in the newspaper without committing an indictable offence.

"Mr. Fencepost will be happy with your salary offer," she say, "but we only want a month-to-month contract."

Bedelia have to pull Frank off into a corner and have a pretty loud whispered conversation to get him to agree to that.

"Plus," Bedelia go on, "'Brother Frank's Gospel Hour' manage all the money that is donated. We pick which people get their requests filled, and Mr. Fencepost hire his own support staff and pay them out of the donated money."

The suits argue for quite a while because they had their eyes on the income donated to "Brother Frank's Gospel Hour."

"We can take our program over to CFCW, the country-music station in Camrose. Bet they'd be happy to have us. Or, we might contact one of the big radio stations in Edmonton," say Bedelia.

The suits give in.

I can't believe how fast things move after that. What Frank talk ain't exactly Christianity, but he mention the Bible often enough that Christians like him. He throw in enough fictional Indian mythology, some of which I make up, to what Frank call "make us politically correct."

"Everybody loves the idea of an Indian these days. So look me up a bannock recipe, and I'll include it on tomorrow night's program," he say to me. "And saskatoon pie. We'll tell them where to pick the best saskatoons. The country will be overrun with berry-pickers."

Frank also talk about fulfilling dreams and positive thinking enough that the people who believe in crystal power and having conversations with rocks and trees like him, too.

By the time Frank get settled in his new time slot, Bedelia is negotiating with the big radio stations in Edmonton and some outfit would do something called "syndicate" the show, putting Frank on over one hundred stations, many of them in the United States, where, Frank say, the real money is.

Frank make Bedelia his business manager and me his personal assistant, and he find jobs for Rufus and Winnie Bear, Robert Coyote and his girl Julie Scar, and about ten other of our friends. My salary in a month is as much as I ever made in a year writing books.

One night I try to phone Illianna, but all I get is a guy with a deep voice tell me my call cannot be completed as dialed. After I pretend I'm Frank and get real pushy with Information, they tell me the number I'm calling been disconnected for non-payment.

The day I cash my first check at the Bank of Montreal, I put a hundred-dollar bill in an envelope and address it to Illianna.

At supper one night a couple of weeks later, Ma say, "Illianna phoned Ben Stonebreaker's store and left a message that she coming for a visit."

"That's wonderful," says my sister, Delores. "I just love Bobby."

Bobby is only a year or so younger than Delores.

"That's what makes me worried," says Ma. "She's bringing Bobby, and What's-his-name, and she ask Mrs. Ben Stonebreaker if maybe the Quails' old cabin is available, 'cause they planning to stay for a while." After the Quails build themselves a new house, their old cabin sit vacant with half the windows knocked out and a few strips of what used to be bright green siding bulging loose under the front window.

Ma, over the years, has mellowed some toward Illianna's husband, Robert McGregor McVey. Now it's What's-his-name. She used to refer to him in Cree as He Who Has No Balls.

A few days later, Illianna and her family turn up on the reserve, and I can't help remembering the first time they visit after they been married. Brother Bob was driving a new car with racing stripes and silver hub caps, and we give him an Indian name, Fire Chief, just like the gasoline down at Crier's Texaco garage, and little Bobby was still a glint in Eathen Firstrider's eye.

Today they is driving what white people call an Indian car. It is a huge Pontiac, about a 1972, painted a pumpkin color, full of dents, sagging and clunking, with about a million miles on it, and a big U-Haul trailer with stuff tied all over the outside of it rattles along behind.

"They repossessed the house and the car and the boat and the snowmobile," Illianna say. Little Bobby start crying when he hear the word *snowmobile*. "Thanks for the money, Silas. I used it to put most of our furniture in storage, though I don't know how I'll pay the storage fees."

Brother Bob is, as they say, only a shadow of his former self. His suits hang on him like they was three sizes too big, and even his snap-brim hat seem to sink down over his ears. He hardly talk, and when he do he just sigh and whisper "yes" or "no."

The day we buy about a hundred yards of extension cord from Robinson's Store in Wetaskiwin ("Charge it to 'Brother Frank's Gospel Hour,'" Frank tell the clerk, and get a smile instead of a who-the-hell-are-you look) and run it across a slough and through a culvert from Blue Quills Hall so Brother Bob can hook up his TV to watch the soap operas and Illianna can plug in her microwave, Brother Bob mumble a couple of thanks yous and grip both my hands the way an old person do.

Brother Bob used to look right through us like we didn't exist. And when he did see us, he make bad jokes about our large families, how run down our cars are, and how clean we ain't.

Within weeks word come down that "Brother Frank's Gospel Hour" going international on 112 radio stations. At the same time Bedelia sell a syndicated newspaper column where I write up some of the letters Frank get, and how he send money to those people for the one thing that will make them happy. I tell five stories in every column. Four serious and one that we find funny, one where Frank usually say no. Like the kid who want karate lessons so he can beat up on his teacher. Or the woman who claim she getting messages from Elvis in her back teeth and wants a radio transmitter so she can share the messages.

The number of radio stations expand almost every day and soon television want to get in on the act. One hour, once a week, where they fly in some of the people we been helping.

"I'm gonna be bigger than Oprah," say Frank, when Bedelia

give him the news. "Let me rephrase that. I'm gonna have more listeners than Oprah."

"You wish," says Bedelia. "We're only starting in twelve stations. Besides, Oprah don't beg for money. But when you let that tear ooze out of your eye and run down your cheek, I can hear pens all over North America scratching signatures on checks."

Soon so much money come rolling in we rent Blue Quills Hall and hire Illianna to sort the cash and checks. When she need an assistant we hire my Ma, Suzie Ermineskin, full-time, and my sister, Delores, part-time.

Frank these days is dressing like Johnny Cash, frilly white shirt, black preacher's coat, western bow tie. He look a lot better than the time he wore a fuzzy green cocktail dress and won the Miss Hobbema Pageant.

The TV people want Frank to do a personal appearance tour.

"Forty cities," Bedelia tell Frank. "Starting in Calgary, working to Minneapolis and on to places I never heard of."

Bedelia arrange to buy a used bus, hire a lady sign painter with long red hair to paint tomahawks, eagles, and dream catchers all over the bus, and "'Brother Frank's Gospel Hour,' A Place Where Dreams Come True," down both sides.

The tour give me an idea. I argue loud and long with Frank, but I don't get anywhere until I take Frank for a walk around the reserve.

"What would make you happy?" I ask. "Pretend you could write a letter to 'Brother Frank's Gospel Hour.' What would you ask for?"

Frank stop and think.

"My biggest surprise is that some of the good things haven't made me as happy as I thought. Like renting that Lincoln

Continental, and having more groupies than a rock star. The car is nice, but it's just a car. And it was more fun when girls told me to get lost and I had to impress them."

"I know what would make you happy," I say.

"What's that, Silas?"

"Revenge," I say, "against He Who Has No Balls."

I let that sink in for a minute. I wonder if Frank is gonna buy my idea, and what I'm gonna do to help Illianna and little Bobby if he don't.

There is the beginning of a smile on Frank's face. "There is an old saying in the Fencepost clan," Frank say. "Always kick your enemy when he is down."

"This is your chance to really get back at Brother Bob," I say hopefully.

"By golly, Silas, you're right. I can make him suck up to me. I'll make him wear a sissy uniform like a theater usher, and a visored cap with BRO. FRANK in silver letters across the crown."

He grab my shoulder, turn me around, and our pace pick up as we walk in the dark, spruce-smelling air toward Brother Bob and Illianna's cabin.